PRIDE

A RAPUNZEL RETELLING

KRIS BUTLER

PRIDE

KRIS BUTLER

SINNERS FAIRYTALES

BOOK FIVE

Pride: A Dark Contemporary Reverse Harem Retelling of Rapunzel

Kris Butler

First Edition: July 2021

Published by Kris Butler

Cover design: © 2020 by Dazed Designs
Proofreading: © 2021 by Black Lotus Editing
Formatting: © 2021 by Bookish Duet Author Services

 Created with Vellum

To learning to have pride in yourself

There is no passion that steals into the heart
more imperceptibly and covers itself under
more disguises than pride.

— JOSEPH ADDISON

FOREWORD

This book deals with situations not suitable for readers under 18 years due to the sexually graphic material and language.

There are also triggers for sexual abuse, child pornography, drug addiction, and emotional and mental abuse from a parent.

This is a dark contemporary, meaning the subject matter may be dark. This is also a reverse harem romance, meaning the female character does not have to chose between her love interests.

Please do not read if any of those may cause distress.

Pride: A Reverse Harem retelling of Rapunzel

At night, I'm free.
Free from the restraints growing tighter each day.
Free from the pressures placed on me.
Free from the disappointment of never being enough.

At night I dance, and the movement sets me free, and I become whoever I want under the bright lights. My disguises offered me safety, providing me escape from the real me—Rapunzel. It started as a way to survive, but the thrill of the dance and the power I weaved soon became my addiction.

My life in shambles, my pride's the only thing keeping me alive, clothed, and moderately fed. Asking for help isn't in my nature, but I soon find a safe haven and place to belong at The Tower. Three men offer me something I desperately needed, and I find acceptance in their love.

When the safety I found in my disguises runs out, I must face the man who'd made me hide in the first place. Will I be able to find a happily ever after or am I doomed to always be trapped in a prison of my own making?

The root of all sin is pride, but what if it's the only thing that can save me?

This is the fifth book in the Sinners Fairytale Retellings series. Each installment can be read on its own, and each retelling is intended for mature audiences since it may contain triggers. Pride deals with themes regarding drug addiction and sexual abuse. Please read the forward for more information. Every author contributing to this series guarantees a HEA. This is a why choose novel.

CHAPTER ONE

ZEL

I was about to suffer from lockjaw syndrome if the dude I was blowing on my break didn't cum soon. Seriously, I'd been doing my best suck and blow for fifteen minutes already, and I only got a thirty-minute break.

Fuck my life.

It didn't help that this dude's cock was so small, even deep throating him, he barely hit the back of my mouth. I didn't judge a guy on size. Okay, that was a lie. *I totally judged.* But I'd been with guys who were shit in bed with a monster of a cock, and others who were rock stars with four inches. So yeah, this guy? I totally judged.

I began to wonder if he had a medical condition. Seriously, it was *that* bad. He seemed kind of young to have erectile dysfunction disorder. Maybe he was impotent? That was what it meant, right? They couldn't cum?

The fact I could debate in my head various medical diagnoses while on my knees in the crappy breakroom conveyed everything. This dude was the most lackluster blowy I'd ever given—and I'd given *a lot*. You could judge me all you wanted. But when you had to eat out of the garbage, you learned to use what you had to get what you needed. Yes, *needed*, not wanted. Believe me, there was a difference when it came to pride.

Finally, after what had felt like hours, the guy came. He tensed up and spewed down my throat without even a warning. Thanks a lot, *jerk*.

Wiping my mouth with the back of my hand, I wasn't shocked when the dude didn't offer me a hand off the floor. Instead, he tucked his flaccid cock into his pants and zipped them in a rush. *Now* he was in a hurry? Brushing off my knees as I stood, I checked to see if there were any marks from my long vigil on my knees. Thankfully, they were only red and would fade soon—I hoped.

Awkward shuffling from Bob or Jason, who the hell knew at this point, as he tried to figure out how to pay me. I made it a rule not to ask names; it was just easier that way. I wasn't going to remember it anyway.

Needing to speed this up, I offered up some help by pointing to the table, hoping to salvage the little time left of my break. Walking my ass to the staff bathroom, I left him to figure it out. Hopefully, he followed directions better than he orgasmed.

"Just leave it there. Laters."

Finger waving over my shoulder, I didn't even

glance back to check he'd paid. The brooding bouncer at the door would make sure of that. Quickly, I used the restroom and checked my outfit, ensuring it was still in place. Tonight, I'd dressed as Sailor Moon, well, a *sexy* Sailor Moon. The nerd boys loved it, and my tips would be astronomical tonight with them in town for a convention at The Tower.

Adjusting my long blonde wig, I swished some mouthwash before reapplying my lipstick. No one needed cum breath, that was just gross. I rubbed on some deodorant, sprayed some floral spritz, and checked my teeth for pubes—you didn't want to know.

Positioning the girls, I looked in the mirror one last time, assessing if I was stage-ready. The brown eyes staring back appeared so foreign, becoming more and more despondent as the days progressed. Sadly, I didn't think they would ever revert back to the happy orbs they'd been at one time. *I've seen too much now. Life was no longer magical. The fairy tale was truly dead.*

Walking out, I caught sight of the money on the table. Thank God! Grabbing it, I stuffed it in my locker after a quick count. Huh, at least lockjaw was a good tipper—small mercies.

Straightening my shoulders, it was time for the magic. As much as I hated this dumpy place, I loved the moments I was on stage. Because there… there, I was free. Free from everything. For five minutes at a time, I relished the feel of the movements as I pretended to be whoever I wanted. It was a needed distraction from the pressures piling on top of me.

Dance was my escape, and I indulged in it every night at The Pandemonium, or The Pan as we all referred to it. I hadn't known it back then, but the day I took the stage for the first time, I'd found freedom. Most people viewed stripping as degrading, saw it as *sinful*. To me, stripping was powerful. I'd taken control of my situation by holding a room oozing with desire and lust in the palm of my hand. To me, that wasn't demeaning, it was dignified. On this stage, I'd never left it feeling anything other than amazing by the end of the night, and to me, that was everything.

Sashaying past the broody bouncer, I nodded and faded to the background. Rapunzel was a desperate, meek, and ultimately, weak girl. Zel, on the other hand, was fierce, exciting, and brave. When I danced, I became her and left everything else in the break room. There was no room for weakness out here.

Emerging in a cloud of glitter and sex, I soaked in the music and energy of the club as it infiltrated my body. Vibrations ran up my legs as the bass thumped, and I felt the adrenaline coursing through me. The vixen in me purred at another chance to dominate, and I took the stage like I did every night. Like I fucking owned it.

Time to shine, motherfuckers.

NIXON

My irritation grew the longer this schmuck had Zel on her knees. He had no clue the treasure he had bestowing him pleasure. I loathed the fact she did this, but I had no right or voice in her choices. We weren't friends. We were barely coworkers. I didn't know if she even registered my presence most days. But I always knew. I could locate her anywhere— your heart didn't let you forget when it found its pair.

The first night I saw her dance, I'd become so captivated. I ran into a waitress, causing her to spill a tray of drinks all over me, her, and the customer. Not the first impression I'd wanted to make. Now, I made sure to be standing still when I watched her. The trance she pulled me in was inevitable.

Finally, the numbnuts came in her mouth, not even offering her a warning. Geez, this asshat was lame. No wonder he had to pay for blow jobs. I was two seconds away from slapping him when he didn't help her stand. Zel ignored him, sauntering into the bathroom without a care in the world, barely offering him any acknowledgment.

Her short skirt showcased her tight ass as it swished with each step she took, pulling my gaze to her. Breaking my love affair with her magnificent glutes, I returned back to glare at the loser just as the shitstain tried to stiff her.

"I wouldn't do that if I were you," growled out of me before I knew what I was saying. It was compulsory where she was concerned. Crossing my arms, I waited until the bastard pulled out his wallet and added money to the table. At my scowl, he quickly pulled out more—wise choice, dumbass.

For the most part, my job here was easy—protect the girls and keep the hooligans out. Of course, my physical stature helped with both. Over 6'4", covered in tattoos, bearded, and with half of my head shaved on one side, I painted a menacing picture I used to my advantage. Most days, all I had to do was glower, and people stopped.

Grunting at him as he passed, I was relieved when he was finally gone. My mixed feelings about her break room escapades always put me on edge. I didn't like it, but I preferred to be the one watching over her.

Some might say I was obsessed with Zel. I wasn't sure they were wrong anymore. My need to protect her had grown over the months I'd been here into something more. I refused to acknowledge it even if my heart already knew.

Zel strolled out of the bathroom, and I could always tell the moment she slipped into her dancer persona. Her shoulders squared back, her head lifted, and her walk more pronounced with each sway of her hips. Zel's confidence shone through when she danced, her sexiness was practically tactile with how it oozed from her. She nodded as she passed, offering me a small acknowledgment of thanks.

As sad as it was, those brief interactions made having to watch her with the sorry sacks of shit worth it. Doubtful she even knew my name, but I would be here protecting her in the shadows regardless. Yeah, even I could admit I was a bit pussywhipped without the pussy.

The music blared as I followed her out onto the main floor. It was Friday night with a convention in town, and she had most of the prime dance slots. Zel had danced here for a couple of years, amassing regulars and gaining preferential treatment. She always managed to draw a crowd with her outrageous costumes and dance numbers. Watching Zel dance was more than sexual, it was entertainment.

Say what you wanted about strippers, but Zel made it clear how talented a dancer she truly was. Captivating the audience with more than her body, she weaved a story of grace and sexuality flawlessly. Most of the customers didn't even come to see her naked; they just wanted to be charmed by her presence. When Zel danced, it was magic, and a lot of people in this part of the city could use a bit more of that.

Leaning back against the wall, I crossed my formidable arms as I scanned the crowd. It was already cramped in here, amping up my anxiety one of these fucktards would try something with her. Not on my watch, assholes. Roy spotted me through the crowd and made his way over to me.

"What's up, man? Your girl about to go on?"

Scowling, I ignored him. He was too damn chatty. He didn't take my hint, though, and continued to talk to me like we were buds.

"Wowee, she's looking hot tonight! Gonna have to fight them off after her set," he laughed.

Grunting was my only response as I kept scanning the room for signs of tension. Continuing to ignore my lack of response, he settled back on the wall next to me.

"Jason's bartending tonight. Better watch him after. He's been eyeing Zel all week. I think he's finally built up his nerve to ask her out after her set."

At this, I turned and acknowledged I'd heard him with a nod before focusing back toward the stage. It was about time for her to start, and I didn't want to miss it. Almost as if I cued it myself, the music switched to her intro and led into her dance number.

Striding out in her crazy-ass high shoes, Zel struck a pose in her fishnet stockings and short schoolgirl skirt. Paired with a cropped top, she painted every nerd boy's wet dream. Her wig had two long pigtails she used to wrap around her hands as she swayed to the music. I didn't know half the things she dressed up as, but each one was unique and sexy in its own right. Her extravagant wigs were always the main focus, and I never saw her without one.

What I wouldn't give to know what she truly looked like.

For five minutes at a time, when she danced, I failed at my job. Instead of observing the floor, I watched her. I didn't care. At this point, they couldn't stop me unless they scheduled me on different shifts. Not that it mattered because her grace on stage hypnotized everyone in the club. It was almost as if those five minutes, everything else ceased to exist but her on stage. We were all voyeurs to the love affair she had with it.

The music picked up-tempo, and she began to swing around the pole on stage. Dropping her top half backward as she flipped off in some backbend walk, she momentarily flashed her panties to us. The sound of groans rang out as the men held their breath for more peeks of her. Descending into a split, she slowly removed her top as she flipped backward from that position. When she stood, her top had magically vanished. She was so fluid, if you didn't watch her every move, you'd miss it. Zel was a fucking magician of stripping.

Her breasts stood at attention, spellbinding everyone, male and female, in the room as they swayed with her movements. Running, she grabbed high on the pole and spun around with one leg hooked over the bar, causing everyone to cheer at her acrobats. Zel performed more dance steps back on the stage, artfully capturing the crowd as her body bent and flowed with the music in a ballerina-type move.

Doing a half-waist flip through the air, Zel landed without her skirt to the uproarious applause of the men. Dipping low, she spread her knees wide, giving another peek of her red thong. Just as she was about to start her final move sequence, my phone buzzed in my pocket, distracting me.

Only one person called me at this number. *Fuck.* Peeling myself off the wall with herculaneum effort, I headed back to the break room so I could hear the caller.

"Sir."

"It's time. If you're going to approach the girl, it's now or never. The club will be shut down by morning."

"Understood."

The call ended, and I dropped my head as my heart rate started to increase. This following conversation would either go over well or be a complete disaster. I was beginning to lean toward the latter. Epic fucking disaster.

The door swung open a few minutes later, and Zel entered in her satin robe. She was back to being withdrawn, but there was a glow about her only present after dancing. It was only in these brief periods I saw her happy. Something about that broke my black heart.

She spotted me as she grew closer to her locker and looked at me quizzically. I wasn't usually so forward in approaching her and never spoke to her. Based on my position, it was clear I'd been waiting for her.

"Hey."

"Hey… Nixon, isn't it?"

Cocking her head, she waited for me to continue the conversation I'd started, but at the sound of my name from her lips, my brain stuttered. Shutting that down quickly, I focused back on the job at hand.

"Zel, I know you have no reason to believe me, and I would probably even think I was full of shit if I were you. But you deserve better than this dump. The owner of The Tower is interested in offering you a job. All you have to do is show up at this address tomorrow at 4 pm."

Handing her the black business card from my wallet, I started to head back out to the main floor. Stopping before I exited, I turned to see her staring at the card in earnest, almost as if she thought it might turn into a magic genie.

"Believe me or not, either way, this place will be shut down tomorrow. Just thought you should know you had other options."

I wasn't positive, but as the door shut behind me, I could've sworn I heard a very quiet, "*Thank you, Nix,*" firmly writing her name on my soul.

CHAPTER TWO

ZEL

I stared at the thick black business card in my hand, waiting for it to vanish into smoke. When after five minutes and it was still there, I had to accept it was real. Placing it delicately in my locker with my tips, I hurried back out onto the floor after redressing. I still had two hours before my shift was over. After my last dance, the hours tended to fly by faster with lap dances and private rooms.

Glancing around for Nixon, I wanted to ask him some more questions, but I couldn't find him anywhere. What had he meant about this place not being open tomorrow? Just *who* was he?

Another bouncer, baldy beer belly, waved me over to the line, and I slipped back into Zel. Confidently striding over, I moved my hips, flipping the skirt up with each step. A couple of my regular guys were in the line, and I gave them a little wave.

"Hello, boys," I purred.

Baldy beer belly, or Triple B for short as I liked to refer to him, opened the curtain as he handed me the card with what the customer had paid for. First up, a lap dance—no sweat.

"You know the rules. No touching unless I initiate it. Hands down beside you. Sit back and enjoy yourself."

The guy eagerly sat back, his cock already straining against his stonewashed jeans. Pulling the curtain closed, I nodded at the camera to start the music. Triple B was a decent bouncer, better than most, but there were still moments he gave me the heebie-jeebies.

When the music started playing, I began to sway to the beat, moving my skirt up over my legs, giving just a peek at what was underneath. I'd learned over the years that a tease went a long way. Too much too soon, and they lost interest, making my tips less.

Walking between his legs, I rubbed my front on his lap as I loosened my top. Undulating my middle, I rolled my body up and down in a rocking motion. Turning, I placed my ass on his front, sitting firmly on his crotch. I could feel his cock growing harder with each brush I made with my ass. Unfastening my shirt completely, I dropped it on the floor as I did more hip rolls.

"You're so pretty, Zel. When are you going to run away with me?"

This was a common occurrence. Middle-aged men wanted to rescue me from what they considered a 'poor life' choice. Yet, because of them, I had a job to begin with. Hypocrisy at its finest. Flipping back around, I distracted him from his grandiose ideas of saving me with my breasts as I shoved them in his face. *Worked every time.*

"But who would I have to dance for if I ran away with you? Besides, isn't this more fun?"

My boobs hypnotized him, doing their job as he nodded along with my nipples. Doing a few more body rolls, I leaned back on my hands, pressing my breasts even higher up as I rubbed my pussy against his now, very hard cock.

Had to give it to the dude; his cock felt *huge*, unlike my blowie from earlier. His wife had to be a very satisfied woman. Well, scratch that. If he was a regular at The Pan, probably not the case.

Sensing I only had about two minutes left from my music, I turned backward again, bracing my hands next to his legs, and bent forward, pushing my ass firmly against him. Getting some friction going, I rubbed up and down his cock through his jeans. His moan alerted me I had hit the spot, and just as time ended, so did my customer. At least he was easier to make cum than lockjaw had been earlier.

I found some clients wanted the fantasy of a girlfriend, others the illicit affair, and some the idea they could bag a stripper. If I figured out what they wanted and gave it to them, not only would they tip higher, they would become a repeat customer. A satisfied regular kept the bills paid.

Kissing him on the cheek, I patted his leg as I got up. Grabbing my shirt, I redressed in preparation for the next one. He sheepishly adjusted himself, trying to hide the massive wet spot, as he pulled out his wallet. Well-hung walked up to me and handed me a hundred on top of the twenty for the dance.

"Thanks, hun. I'll see you later this week. Don't forget my offer. One of these days, I'm going to convince you."

Smiling at him, I waved him off and prepared for the next one going into my zone. A stripper's job was more than being sexy, you had to engage with people too. I'd been acting for so long, it was easier for me than some of my fellow dancers. Unfortunately, being popular at a strip club bred jealousy, and I hadn't made many friends.

"Ready!" I shouted to Triple B, and that was how the next two hours went. Some of the guys were good tippers, and others were dismal. All in all, I ended the night with a grand after paying the house. Decent night work for four hours.

Grabbing my stuff out of my locker, the card on top reminded me I hadn't seen Nixon once he'd given it to me. Taking his words to heart, I gathered all of my belongings out of my locker and hoped he hadn't been an ass about the job offer.

If The Tower was calling, I wanted to answer.

Snoring and the midday sun woke me the next day. Shoving off the sweaty arm of my recent one-night stand, I glanced around at the room I was in. It wasn't the nicest room I've ended up in, but it definitely wasn't the worst.

Assuring my wig was still in place, I snatched up my clothes, purse, and boots as I tiptoed to the bathroom. Not really sure why I bothered since apparently, I'd fucked a bear based on the hibernating snores emanating from his chest. The door clicked with a soft snick, and I sighed a deep exhale. I'd made it through another night.

Dressing quickly, I gave myself a fast rinse off in the sink and swished some mouthwash around. It would suffice until I could shower somewhere—the where was yet to be determined. Finishing up in the bathroom, I slipped on my shoes and secured my purse strap. I'd stashed my bag and money in one of my safe spots my friend and I'd made years ago before I'd gone cruising. It was always a safer option, so I didn't have to stress about being robbed while I slept. I had enough to worry about as it was. Burn me once, and I learned quickly.

Carefully, I opened the door, still able to hear the logs being sawed in the bed. Thank fuck for an easy escape. Giving him my two-finger salute, I beelined for the front door. Leaving the morning after could be tricky. I never knew if I'd bump into roommates, or worse, parents as I made my escape.

Nothing said awkward like trying to dodge a mother in a tight hallway after fucking her son.

The apartment was quiet; the only sound was the ticking of a clock in the kitchen. Creeping down the hall, I had a sudden craving for some Pop Tarts and wondered if they had any. The odds were good, considering he was a college guy and it felt worth risking a few minutes to check.

My stomach rumbling appeared to agree, reminding me it'd been a while since I ate. Making a quick detour, I slipped into the kitchen to scour some food. Snorey McGee wouldn't mind. Opening cabinets, I, unfortunately, came up empty. Turning, I jumped when I found a hot guy with blonde hair sitting casually on the counter, eating a bowl of cereal. He smiled, lifting a spoon full of Oops All Berries in greeting.

"Fuck, you scared me," I gasped, clutching my chest.

"Shouldn't that be my line? You're the stranger in my apartment, after all."

His voice sounded familiar, a soft teasing tilt to it, but I couldn't place it. Blondie must've been at the club at some point. They all swirled together after a while, and why I never asked names. Mine were more useful to me.

"Oh yeah, um," pointing down the hall toward the snoring bear, "said I could grab some Pop Tarts."

"Did he now?" He grinned, and I didn't want to

like how it made his whole face shine. "That was an awful kind gesture of *Josh* considering he doesn't, in fact, have any Pop Tarts."

"Oh, well, fuck. It was worth a shot," I flirted, trying to throw him off. "Laters."

Spinning, I was desperate to escape this awkward encounter when the mystery sunshine guy jumped down, stepping in front of me. Peeking up his tall frame into his brown eyes, I found myself trapped before I could make it out of the galley-style kitchen.

"I said *he* didn't have any, not that there weren't *any*."

Furrowing my brow, I was no longer curious about the sunshine guy. What was this dude playing at? I didn't even want them at this point. I just needed to get out of here as my anxiety started to amp up at the feeling of being trapped.

"It's fine. I need to go. So, can you?"

His face fell at my comment, but he thankfully moved out of my way. I didn't ponder on the oddness or how I felt about it. Hurriedly, I made my way to the front door, my escape almost in reach. Unlocking it, the mystery blonde came up behind me, scaring me yet again.

"Here, take it."

Turning, I found the silver-wrapped package and a bottle of Gatorade in his outstretched hand. My mouth watered at the sight, already tasting the sugary goodness. But I couldn't accept it. I didn't do handouts.

"No, thanks. Bye."

Squeezing through the tiny slit in the door, I ran down the stairs as fast as possible, needing to get out of there. Something about the whole situation made me feel unsure, my body zinging all over. If I didn't trust my instincts, it was a death sentence for me.

Looking over my shoulder when I reached the ground, I located him standing in the doorway watching me. A look of confusion was plastered over his handsome boyish face, the silver wrapper and Gatorade still outstretched in his hand like he expected a ghost to come and take them.

You might wonder why I didn't take his offering, but it was never that simple with me. *Nothing* was ever free. So yes, while most nights I hooked up with random guys to have a warm place to crash or gave breakroom blowies for cash, I could accept those things because they were a reciprocal relationship and my choice. That was the thing about having nothing. You had to hold on to something to make it through the day.

For me, it was pride. It didn't always make sense, but no one said it had to. In fact, sometimes my pride was a right bitch, but no matter what, I could hold onto it. I might be homeless, I might be an outcast, and I might be a stripper, but I took care of myself.

I didn't do charity. Everything in my life had strings. Some were harder to see than others. Like I said, burn me once, and I learned. I had to. I wasn't going to be burned again. My pride would save me from that.

CHAPTER THREE

ZEL

Sorting through my costumes, I'd stopped by one of the storage units Max had fashioned for me. I basically had mini dressing rooms in several locations, showers included. Pulling the next garment rack over, I debated on what to wear to The Tower. Nixon hadn't said it was an interview, but in stripping, it was always better to be prepared to show the goods. I decided to go with a classic one —Marilyn Monroe.

White dress and blonde wig in tow, I put every-thing into a duffle/garment bag combo for travel-ing. I slipped on some clean clothes before securing the rest of my stuff in my secret hideout. I needed to stop by my mother's house on the way to The Tower, so I quickly finished dressing in a basic outfit of shorts, converse, and an old band t-shirt. Throwing on a hat, I shoved my hair up in it out of the way. It'd been a month since I'd last checked-in, and she tended to become self-destructive if I went too long.

"Mother?"

The screened door to the double-wide screeched open at my arrival. The TV blared info-commercials from the front room. The dingy couch sat lopsided against the far wall and was empty of any bodies. Wrappers, bottles, and other paraphernalia littered the coffee table in front of it. Pivoting, I headed toward the bedroom and prayed I wouldn't walk in on her naked, or worse, in the throes of passion with someone. I'd already been scarred enough. Knocking, I waited but entered the partially opened door when I didn't hear a response. Closing my eyes, I covered them with my hand as I braced the other in front of me to stop from stumbling.

"Mother? Are you back here?"

"Sweet girl, is that you?" a croaky voice asked. "Oh, thank Heavens. Put your hand down, child. I'm not naked."

Opening my eyes, I found her sprawled out on the bed, the fan blowing on her. She wasn't naked, but just barely, considering she was in a ratty tank top and panties.

"This isn't much better, Mother. Geez, dress yourself, why don't you!" Tossing a shirt I found on the dresser; I cleared off a spot on the bed to sit. "Here, I brought you some money. I paid the rent for the month, and the food delivery will arrive tomorrow."

At the mention of money, Gothel sat up, her

boobs almost spilling out of her stretched low cut tank at the motion, the shirt I'd tossed still lying next to her. Ugh, I didn't need this tonight. Dropping my head into my hands, I took in a deep inhale and reminded myself why I loved the woman. Giving her a quick kiss and hug, I stood to leave.

"I'll just leave it on the dresser. Maybe, I don't know, take a shower? You stink!"

Plugging my nose, I backed out the small doorway as she laughed at my comment, sticking her tongue out at me. She was already off the bed, counting the bills I'd left her, which would undoubtedly be used for drugs, booze, or gambling.

I'd learned long ago if I gave her everything, she would use it all and then be out on her hide in worse conditions. Now, I prepaid her rent and groceries so I knew she had a relatively safe place and wouldn't starve. Others might judge me for giving her spendable cash, knowing she'd use it for nefarious purposes, but I knew she'd do it regardless if she had the cash, and her means weren't always prudent. Making sure she didn't die was the least I could do for the woman who'd raised me.

"Bye, Mother. Try not to die."

"You're hilarious. Try not to fall off the stage or get pregnant."

Laughing, I stepped outside and began my trek to The Tower, hoping my luck had finally changed.

The Tower loomed ahead of me, but I still had a few hours to spare before my appointment. I didn't visit this area much, it was too close to Tiara Heights, and I avoided everything to do with the Heights. A modern rustic building was up ahead with wood paneling on the side, but it was the large open glass entryway that caught my eye. Glancing at the sign, it wasn't a place I'd heard of before—Hunter's Lodge. Better place than any to kill a few hours and freshen up.

Walking everywhere, I'd learned to be prepared for all types of weather and have plenty of time to spare. It was also wise to never walk in the outfit you planned to show up in, hence why I'd worn my basic outfit—easy to run in and washable.

Besides, I'd discovered an unassuming appearance helped me go unnoticed when I didn't want to be, well, noticed. My hat concealed my hair and helped me stay under the radar. Here in public, I didn't want to be recognized for my stage persona, or the real me. *Especially the real me.*

Walking through the glass entryway I noticed a restaurant on one side and a nice bar area on the other. Not in the mood to be bitched at for not ordering food, I headed to the bar instead. No one noticed as I walked in, the sounds of soft blues floating through the air. Taking a seat at the bar I scoped the place out.

"What can I get you?" the burly tattooed bartender asked, barely looking at me as he wiped down the long wooden bartop. He was covered in ink, his fingers not even escaping the artwork. Brown hair and tall, he'd be someone I'd hit up for extracurricular activities if I was on the hunt. I think his muscles had muscles.

"Whiskey sour."

My choice of drink always had them raising their eyebrows, but I didn't care. I liked it. They could think whatever they wanted.

"ID," he gruffed out, folding his impressively tattooed arms over his chest as he dared me to try and give a fake one.

Rolling my eyes because I was twenty-three and over this line of questioning. My baby face always belied my age, making most people believe I was barely legal. It helped with the pervs when dancing, not so much when I only wanted a damn drink.

Still, I handed him my ID, well, my fake ID. I was of age, but it didn't mean I wanted people to know my real name. Looking at me critically, he eventually handed it back, apparently satisfied with his inspection.

"One whiskey sour coming up, Tina."

Nodding, because what else did you say? *Thanks for believing me, fuck face?* Yeah, I didn't think that would go over well. Probably end up with spit in my drink or thrown out. Neither was how I wanted to spend the next few hours.

He sat the glass down with a thunk and walked away. I appreciated that about him, earning him some respect. I always hated when they stuck around asking questions. I didn't need a bar therapist, thank you very much. I already knew I was screwed up. I didn't need anyone to tell me otherwise.

The cool liquid hit my throat, soothing some of the frayed nerves I had. The sourness mixed with the burn of the whiskey made me feel like a fire-breathing dragon as I opened my mouth, allowing the whiskey to travel down. Other patrons entered as time went by, but I ignored them, enjoying my quiet for the first time all day. Here on this barstool, I didn't have to be anything. I could just be.

Finishing my drink, I threw bills down on the bar and made my way to the bathroom. I needed to change my appearance, so no one noticed me leaving here, but not enough to be recognized as standing out. It was a complicated balance I weaved.

The card house I lived in was stacked very precariously. Any sudden shift would create a complete collapse—I would really like to avoid that.

Freshening up, I took off my hat and put on a short brown wig. Taking the shirt around my waist, I put it on, rolling up the sleeves. Exiting the bathroom, I kept my head down to avoid making eye contact with anyone. Making it outside without any interactions, a sigh of relief left me. The Tower was my one chance to help change everything—or at least I hoped. I was kind of on my last one.

Spotting the back door entrance the dancers used, I headed there as The Tower came into view. It was lit up like some Vegas casino, calling attention to the debauchery occurring inside even if it was only four o'clock in the afternoon. But let's be honest, sin never slept. Despite being known as Sinhaven's newest den of iniquity, it didn't stop people from coming. If anything, it made it more ostentatious to be seen here. That was the allure of The Tower.

The place had four levels, and each level catered to a different sort of *clientele* from what I'd heard. There was a membership fee to enter most levels, meaning all the best-kept secrets were inside this club. Nothing bred interest like exclusivity. Rumors spoke of all kinds of sins inside from greed, lust, and gluttony; there was something inside for everyone. You just had to be willing to pay the price.

Nodding at the bouncer standing by the door, I started to head in when an arm reached out and blocked me. Following up the arm's path, I found a very annoyed face directed at me.

"No access."

"I have an appointment with the owner. Nix set it up." My response made him appear even more annoyed as I tried to move his sweaty arm from me.

"No access."

Fucking hell, this guy was starting to get on my nerves. I'd been around enough clubs to know the back entrance was always open to dancers, *current and seeking*. He was being an ass, to be an ass. Pulling from my inner Zel, I instantly felt the shift in me as my confidence soared.

"Listen, *sir*, I'm here to see the owner, and either you let me through so I can change, or—"

"Or what, *princess*?"

First, he had the nerve to cut me off, and then he used *that* word. My blood began to boil at this point. My index finger came out, and I started to poke him in the chest with it as I spoke.

"Let's get one thing straight, jackass—"

"I'll take it from here, Kevin."

The burly beast was wrenched away from me, stumbling as he was shoved aside. My hand was grabbed, and I was led through the door. I wasn't even aware of who had me as I kept my eyes locked with 'douchey Kevin' the whole time, promising retribution. I might've even done that whole 'my eyes will be watching you' thing with my fingers. I kind of blacked out from the anger; it was hard to be certain.

Once we were through the door and it shut, darkness encompassed the area. Blinking, I tried to adapt to the new level of light.

"Not a good first impression, princess," said a gravelly rich voice, promising all sorts of things.

What the fuck was wrong with everyone calling

me that today? And why did I like it when he said it? Realizing it was Nixon who had me, I relaxed into his hold, glancing up at him. His stare was penetrating, and I suddenly felt very naked in a very different way.

"Yeah, well, maybe jackasses shouldn't work here."

Dropping his hand, I crossed my arms in an attempt to cover myself from his all-knowing gaze. I probably made the perfect impression of a toddler throwing a tantrum at the moment, but I was still livid at the douche and unnerved by his ability to see me.

His dark chuckle sent shivers down my spine, and suddenly, I didn't care about the jerk outside. Assessing Nixon, I looked at him as a woman for the first time. He was older than me, probably in his late twenties. Tall, muscular, and had that whole dangerous air about him, making you want to throw your panties in his face. His head was shaved on the side, the top long, and flopped over it. His hair was a dark black mixed through with some early grey, but it worked for him. Nixon's eyes were dark blue pools of magnetism, and almost seemed to have scattered moonlight in them with how they sparkled. *I could drown in his eyes.* His trimmed beard looked rough, begging to be rubbed between my legs.

A sudden sense of arousal, accompanied by awareness, doused me as I realized I'd just lusted over him. *Shit.* This could be bad. I couldn't have feelings for people, not anymore. They always ended up biting me in the ass in the end, and I couldn't afford to be vulnerable. Hoping he hadn't noticed my sudden muteness, I pulled it together, allowing myself to escape to the place where I didn't have to worry.

"Are you going to show me to the dressing rooms, or do I strip down in the hallway?" I barked. Deflection at its finest, otherwise known as bitchiness.

"Humph," he grunted, disappointment on his features before turning and leading me down the hallway.

We were on the first floor, but it looked nothing like what I'd assumed the floor would appear as a restaurant. It was quiet and had that behind-the-stage feel to it, like in a large auditorium. Looking around, I saw no signs of anything to give away what this place was. Blank hallways and doors were all I could see.

Nixon stopped in front of a door, unlocked it, and opened it for me to enter. Once I was through, he shut it back behind me. Well, okay then, I guess he wasn't feeling chatty today. I didn't know what I was expecting. It wasn't like we were besties, but he'd always been nice to me, and then he'd offered me this job. I guess I assumed he liked me or at least respected me, but apparently, I'd read too much into things.

I ignored the thought that flickered up on how I'd somehow disappointed him. I couldn't deal with an attraction to someone, so I ignored all of my conflicting feelings, shoving them way down.

Slipping out of the clothes I'd worn, I began my show preparations, thankful for my shower earlier. Wiping down my body from sweat, I lathered myself in lotion from head to toe, applied deodorant everywhere, and even some hairspray in places. I began the process of pulling on all the bits of my outfit from the stockings and garters, underwear, and bra, to the slip, and then to the dress. Adding the heels, I checked my makeup and positioned the blonde wig securing it with pins.

I've gotten good at pinning wigs over the past few years. Needing to hide my identity, it was the easiest way to do it. Being upside down on the bar at times meant the wig had to be super secure. Shoving my old clothes and wig into my bag, I inspected the space to make sure nothing had fallen to the ground. Everything was too expensive to leave them. Lastly, I applied my lipstick, sealing the outfit's look.

Smacking my red lips, I pursed them together into a pucker. Kissing the mirror, I channeled Marilyn to give me the confidence I needed. When dressed up as other people all the time, it made it easier to pretend to be somebody you weren't, especially when you didn't want to be *you* in the first place.

"You can do this, Zel. This is your chance to make a difference for yourself. Don't take no for an answer."

Finishing my mantra, I opened the door and found Nixon standing across from me. His head was lowered, and he raised it at the sound of the door. When he looked up, he pierced me with his gaze, allowing me the first hint of emotion from him, or perhaps the first time I looked for it. He schooled it quickly, but it had been there.

Seemed quiet Nixon had a thing for Marilyn, or maybe it was me? The excitement caused by the feeling in my belly shouldn't have made me as happy as it did.

Fucking hell. Yep, I was in deep fucking trouble. Problem was, I wasn't so sure I cared at the moment, not when he looked at me like that.

CHAPTER FOUR

WESLEY

Tossing my cell phone onto my desk, I rubbed my hands over my face. Some days I wondered why I tried so damn hard when it felt everything I did was a failure—at least in my father's eyes. He'd sent me here, to Sinhaven, as a punishment of sorts to see if I could make a failing business worth something to him. *"If you can make something out of The Tower, perhaps not aborting you will be worth it. I won't hold my breath."*

Despite this being the tenth place I'd bought, redesigned, and sold for a profit, it still wasn't good enough. My father never let me forget how lucky I was to be alive. The most recent phone call only served as a spiteful reminder of how he blamed me for all the horrible things in his life.

Yet, here I was successfully turning around the previous failing strip joint he had into a thriving business, and he still couldn't utter the words he was proud of me. I was practically thirty. Why did I care so much about what my father thought of me?

My alarm on my phone beeped, reminding me my "wallow" time was officially up. Controlling every moment in my day was how I survived. Some might say I was obsessive, others anal-retentive, yet they would both be wrong because I was so much more than a diagnosis. I had my compulsions and obsessions, but I'd managed to make them work for me.

I'd learned many years ago that by order and control, I could decrease the level of uncertainty in my life, allowing me to feel more joy and freedom. With each thing I controlled, I gained power over it, and I could escape my mind. I prided myself on my success, and my attention to detail allowed me to focus on the thing currently in front of me until it was perfect, and The Tower was my best creation to date.

It had four floors, and three of them were open to the public. The first floor was named Consumption and boasted a restaurant, bar, and club area and the only floor not to require a membership. The restaurant hosted chefs on a rotation basis, and the competition to be selected was cutthroat. It was a glutton's dream come true with everything from gourmet desserts, Asian fusion, and Moroccan dishes. It was the pride of any chef to work there.

The bar had world-class mixologists with creative cocktails, and a club area rotated top recording DJs, singers, and dancers. They would routinely have theme nights during the week from line dancing, techno, and even tango. It was the place all the town locals went to let loose and meet their next bed partner. Just a cover charge and a wait in line, and you could bump and grind with the hottest singles in Sinhaven at Consumption.

The second floor was Wager and was greed and sloth personified depending on your poison. The slew of sins revolved around every type of gambling imaginable. From the fighting rings to the online gaming competitions and a casino, bets could be placed from dusk to dawn. They had open rooms for video gaming, tabletop gaming, and even had cosplay competitions. If it could be bet on, it was happening on the second floor. While certain parts were membership only, most of the guests bought day passes, staying all day or until they ran out of money.

The third floor was Desire and the most mysterious and the envy of all the upper class. The elites wanted in for the exclusivity of the membership, the process top secret. The main floor was included in the regular membership, where lust was weaved craftily through dancing. The entertainment entwined contemporary dance, pole dancing, burlesque, and stripping, creating flawless ensembles leaving the crowd breathless for multiple reasons. The pride in the dancers' expertise, the envy of the guests, and the lust felt by all were threaded throughout every aspect on this floor.

Though, perhaps, it was the private rooms on

Desire that garnered the most interest. You had to hold a specific key card to be allowed entry, and no one except members knew what the requirements were to obtain one. The women all dressed to impress one another, and the men showcased their wealth and stature. Whether hiding away a mistress, or private time with a dancer, it brought stripping to a level of elegance no one could ignore. Behind those doors, a range of things took place, enticing all kinds of sins, leaving it up to the people involved to decide their limits.

Sophisticated eroticism teetered on the edge, awakening the deepest desires in a place where it was okay to let go. Offering this safe oasis to the elite granted me both power and prestige in Sinhaven. Desire's boudoir nature made it explicit while keeping it acceptable to attend. Women and men alike filled the tables to watch our nightly numbers and shows.

Everyone entered The Tower full of life and promises, ready to taste all it had to offer, whether hoping to meet someone or have whatever need they sought filled, they all came with a purpose. If you weren't careful, The Tower would take more than you'd bargained. To escape for a moment was divine, but to linger allowed depravity to fester, sinking into your pores, activating destruction in its wake and leaving you with the pieces to collect. In the end, it was a business, and I tried to balance my own greed with the well-being of others in mind to not lose myself.

The fourth floor was the penthouse, my home, and off-limits to the public. My best friend and head of security lived there as well, and we'd remodeled it to fit our needs, allowing us to always be aware of what was going on while having privacy. Only a few of the staff knew we lived here, allowing separation when we needed it, but let's be fair. The Tower was my life, and I spent most of my time in my office housed on the third floor. I'd put everything into this project, hoping to finally make my father proud.

Despite it being a pointless mission, I was happy to do it with Nix. I didn't have friends, and since he worked here and lived here as well, we didn't find ourselves outside these four walls very often. Our meals came from the restaurant, and we had staff provide anything else we might need. These past few months with him undercover at The Pan had been different. I was glad he would be back. Even if we barely saw one another during our work hours, it was comforting knowing he was down the hall.

Nix and I met at a military school when we were assigned as roommates. He continued with the military while I attended the university. We both grew up outside of Sinhaven and were still gathering our bearings with this town. Whenever I thought I had it figured out, something new would occur, confusing me even more.

After Nix had been discharged a few years earlier from the military, he'd managed the security for my business. It was a natural fit for Nix, and he was gradually weeding out the rotten apples to hire people he trained. His stint undercover had been both a recruitment opportunity and evidence collection.

My father had sent me here to turn this club around, and I had. The difference was, while he thought The Tower and I were a failure, I operated and ran a separate successful business right under his nose—Hubris. It was a merger and acquisition corporation, and I was slowly taking out the competition right out from under him.

The irony wasn't lost on me since my father had wanted me to suss out information on his rivals, and yet it was his own hubris that had him failing to see it was me and the merit I had. Taking out the competition that treated their employees unjustly was always my first move. Nix would scout out the place and report any potential hidden gems before approaching the business for a takeover. Sometimes, I would redo the site as it was with new management, but most of the time, I scraped it and made it something new.

With The Pan, it was going to be a community center. Dante's Circle needed a place for kids and adults to learn new skills, provide after-school activities, and be a resource for them if they needed food, clothes, or shelter. Rejuvenating an area was vital to me, unlike my father, who only saw things through a profit margin.

Nix had only recommended two people from The Pan—a bouncer and a dancer. I was curious about the dancer since he'd been talking about her for a while. His fascination with her intrigued me since he didn't typically talk about women. In our friendship, I hadn't seen him ever fall for anyone, and he rarely even brought women home.

Nix had the exterior of a badass but the heart of a teddy bear. He didn't look it, not with his tattoos and scowl, but he cared deeply for people and very rarely let them in. He also had a good eye for talent, so if she was as good as he stated, I was looking forward to watching her dance. The third floor was my favorite, not because of the half-dressed women but because I got to surround myself in a world that was off-limits to me—dance.

Before my mother passed away, she'd taken me to ballet class several times a week, and even enrolled me in a school. I loved it, even if the other boys my age made fun of me for it. I didn't care because it was something I'd become passionate about. When she died, my father became a tyrant about everything, and when I didn't meet his expectations once again, he made sure I'd never step another foot into a studio. His actions sent me to military school, and once I was there, he'd successfully accomplished his goal of killing my dream.

Dancing had calmed my mind and allowed me

freedom from all the pain and guilt I carried. It allowed me a healthy way to control my obsessive thoughts and compulsions. Without it, I became even more obsessive in nature. My father had made it impossible for me to ever dance on stage again, but watching dancers and being surrounded by it gave me the next best thing. Each night, I lived vicariously through them, and I could infuse myself with their passion. I needed to remember, even if my father never saw value in this place, it had become a home and haven for Nix and me. That was something.

Finishing up the deposits from the night before, I was startled when the intercom buzzed. Checking the clock, it was earlier than I expected, so I wasn't sure who it could be.

"Yes?"

"Boss, your interview is here."

"Hmph. Well, she's early."

"Yep, do you want me to give her a tour and meet you on the main floor at 4 pm?"

"Yeah, actually. That would be perfect. I need to finish up the deposits."

"Noted. You're going to be in for a treat. See you then, boss."

Even more curious now, I wondered what I would be walking into. Focusing back, for the first time in a while, I found myself distracted by the anticipation. Pulling the rubber band, I snapped it a couple of times to focus myself back on the present.

Worrying would do nothing but get me off schedule, and I couldn't afford that.

Finishing up The Tower's deposits, I was pleased to see we were continuing to make a profit each night. Closing the laptop, I stretched my arms, snapping my neck to relieve some of the tension. My body was taut from the call with my father still. I would need to take better care of myself, so I could continue being successful. Fitzherbert Flynn could take dance, but I wouldn't allow him to take my pride any longer.

Grabbing my suit coat off my chair's back, I adjusted my tie in the mirror by the door. When my appearance met my required level of perfection, I exited out of my office and headed toward Desire. It was ten till four, so I had enough time to get into position. Nix and I had a system, and I liked to have an unbiased approach to hiring. Most people were only friendly to the people they assumed matter, but I wanted to make sure the people who worked in my establishments were good overall and not just their skill level.

Sitting back in the corner, I took a table out of sight and motioned for the waitress to bring me water. The decoy manager, my assistant, was in place up by the front of the stage, and a few other customers were scattered about. This time of day was slower and therefore worked best to audition new talent. There was enough clientele to have an audience, but not enough to hurt if the dancer was horrible. It filled the slow hours and gave me a realistic experience.

Nix walked in a few minutes later with a blonde beauty next to him. There was something about her that drew me instantly, and I understood Nix's obsession with her. Hopefully, she could dance, and it wasn't just his attraction speaking. He nodded as he passed, and I saw her glance over but kept walking with him toward the stage.

The dancer shook the hand of my decoy, and he explained to her what he wanted to see—mostly no nudity. I wanted to see if the dancer could sell it without being naked. I watched as she squished up her face at the news and turned and looked at Nix, almost like she felt he was pulling her leg. Finally, she glanced back at the decoy manager and nodded. Nix showed her to the back of the stage area and sorted her music with the DJ.

The waitress brought over my water and stood for a minute while we waited for her to start. Of course, everyone knew the deal once they passed their probation period; until then, I kept my identity hidden. I've heard others say it was my paranoia whispering, but I valued my privacy, and since I worked the closest with this floor, I took extra precautions.

The music started, and I was instantly transfixed as she began to dance. Nix's obsession with the women became clearer—she was *breathtaking*. Her movements were fluid and moved from one to the other effortlessly. She was dressed as Marilyn Monroe, yet, her dance was elegant and seductively graceful. She would fit here perfectly, just as Nix said.

After a few minutes, the waitress moved on, and I watched the Goddess by myself. For the first time, I wanted to be up there dancing with her, not satisfied to merely watch or live vicariously through her. No, I wanted to share it with her. Fear filled me at that realization, and I knew I would need to keep my distance, for the temptation was far too great.

I couldn't…

Swallowing my pride, I hoped it wouldn't consume me.

CHAPTER FIVE

ZEL

With each step I took, I felt my body relax and settle into the movement as I relaxed into it. Twirling, the dress slid against my skin in a seductive motion as I elongated my arm and leg into an arabesque. Giving in to the music, I flowed through the dance as I emoted the feelings the song instilled in me. *Surrender* was heartbreakingly beautiful and the rhythm powerful.

Removing a strap, I sashayed over to the left side of the stage when a pair of eyes seared into me. *He was beautiful.* The man was mostly hidden as he sat back in a booth, his pristine suit and perfect hair on display. His gaze was laser-focused on me, and I immediately felt drawn to him. This man was a mystery I wanted to unravel.

He tracked my movements methodically, and I could tell he enjoyed the dance for more than my sensuality. Lowering the other strap, I opened the wrap as I spun, leaving me clad only in my lingerie at the end of it. It was a move I'd perfected when I first started stripping, and had become a signature. Dancing was my first love and passion. There was even a time I thought it would be my future. Now, things were different. Dance was my escape, and incorporating stripping had become the way to survive on my terms.

I didn't regret it for one second.

Strutting forward, I balanced on my toes as I spun into a pirouette. The mystery man kept pulling my gaze, and I gave up pretending I wasn't looking at him. He was beautiful with his perfectly styled hair and chiseled bone structure, his eyes holding an intensity calling to me. It would be a shame not to indulge in what the club had to offer, right?

The manager sat with his eyes alight in wonder, and I felt confident I'd get the job. Something about him seemed off, though, like maybe he wasn't used to being in charge, and perhaps a little fake. Hopefully, for my sake, it meant he would be more hands-off. There was a limited amount of sincere niceness I could muster, and most days, it was spent before I got to work.

The music faded as my body rolled on the floor into a split. I was surprised there wasn't a pole on stage. It was one of my favorite things I'd learned. The number of bruises on my body I ended up with, however, was astounding. Falling to my stomach, I pushed up in a plank position to get up as gracefully as possible. Picking up my dress, I wrapped it back on as I exited the stage. Out of habit, I checked my wig as well to make sure it was in place.

Thankfully, It was secure, and I felt relieved as I walked out into the lobby. A few patrons applauded as I walked by, and I instantly felt the difference between this place and The Pan. No catcalls or dismissive remarks were thrown at me as I walked through. The guests were well dressed and sipped expensive scotch as they discussed million-dollar deals or something.

It was staggering, if I was honest.

Hope fluttered in my chest at the thought of working here, but I had it locked down by the time I reached the center table. Glancing to my left, I noticed the man with the hypnotizing eyes was gone. A lone tumbler left sitting in his place. *Damn.* I'd hoped to chat him up after and secure my place for the night. Focusing back on the man who held my future in his hands, I tried to keep my face blank as I awaited my fate.

"How did I do?"

"That was doable."

Well, okay then. I wasn't used to that type of response, halting me for a moment.

"So, does that mean I got the job?"

"Yes, I would like to offer you a position dancing. You can return tomorrow to work out the details with my assistant, and he'll get you on the schedule. Here is my card to call. Good day, miss."

After his dismissal, he stood and walked out of

the room, not turning around once. I'd never felt so confused in my life. His words didn't match with the way he'd greedily traveled my body or the lust simmering in his eyes. Not that I wanted to sleep with my boss for the job, but I was used to men wanting a peek. They would flirt and suggest, at the very least. This was odd, and I didn't know how to take it. A waitress approached with his departure, handing me an envelope and a drink.

"What's this?"

"The tips you earned and a drink from the owner."

Taking the offered items, I stared at them like they might bite me. Opening the envelope, I was even more confused now. There were about three hundred dollars here. That was more than I ever got for a five-minute song. Blinking, I looked up, and she smiled softly at me.

"Yeah, I know. This place, it's different. Mr. Flynn is different. If they offer you a job, which they will because you were phenomenal," she beamed, "take it."

Nodding, I tucked the money into my bra since I didn't have anything else with me. Pockets on dresses were a needed requirement. Tossing back the drink, I didn't even notice what it was as it slightly burned on its way down. I spotted Nix against a wall and decided to see if I could get more information out of him about this place. It was starting to feel too good to be true.

"Well, do you think I got the job?"

"Hmm," he grunted, keeping his eyes on the room.

Not letting it deter me, I tried a different approach. "So, do I have to leave, or am I, like, free to roam around?"

He looked at me finally, assessing my words before he answered, "Where do you want to go?"

Thinking about it, I contemplated the best place to score a bedmate for the evening. "Wherever I can go, I guess. Maybe check out the casino or the dance club?"

He studied me a bit longer before he walked off, leaving me standing there. Well, that hadn't gone as planned. Trying to figure out where I could meet someone, I was surprised when his voice called out my name.

"Zel."

Snapping my head to him, I found he had the elevator opened, waiting for me. Quickly, I made my way over to the open door.

"Sorry, I didn't realize your grunt and non-answer were, in fact, *an answer*."

His lips lifted a millimeter into a smile, but I received no other reaction from him. Oh well, settling back against the wall, I waited as the elevator went down one floor. The ding had it opening to a much louder area with casino machines pinging. Squinting at the lights and sound, I cautiously made my way out of the elevator.

Nix grabbed my hand as I passed, his callouses feeling rough against my skin, but not in a horrible way—no, not in a bad way at all. My breath caught as I tried to calm the erratic beating of my heart.

"Zel, tell any of the guards along the wall you need me when you're ready to leave, and I'll take you to your stuff." He paused before adding, "be careful."

"Okay," I mumbled, unsure how to take his concern.

I'd spent months barely talking to him, and yet, he was treating me nicer than most people I've known my whole life. I wasn't sure how to take it since he'd never hit on me either. He watched my face closely and then let my hand go. The elevator door closed, and I felt lonely suddenly with him gone, his assessing gaze no longer boring into me.

Dismissing that feeling, I turned back to the kaleidoscope of colors in the room and casually walked around, taking in my surroundings. It was still early, but the place had started to fill up. I meandered around, taking note of people as I familiarized myself with the layout.

This first room was the slots, but next to it were the dealers and tables. Roulette wheels spun around, calls of "hit me" and knocking on tables confronted me. The next room had several computers and video game consoles with couches and chairs. *Interesting.* Walking in, it was a little less crowded, which made me feel better for some reason. Seeing a group of guys, I walked over nonchalantly as I tried to snag their attention.

However, only one of them even seemed to notice me as the others focused on the TV screen. Sitting down, I watched them for a while as I tried to decide what to do. Typically, picking up a guy was a lot easier than this. I was starting to feel out of my comfort zone. I should've known by my friendship with Max the relationship between a guy and his controller.

"Do you want to play?"

The voice asked me from my left, surprising me. I hadn't realized he'd stopped and was now watching me, a small smile on his face.

"Oh, no. I don't know how. I'm just… I don't know what I'm doing." I shrugged.

He smiled in a friendly manner, instantly making me feel comfortable. Something in the back of my mind tugged at his appearance, but it was hard to make out exact details with the low lighting. He was handsome with what looked to be blonde hair, athletic build, and kind brown eyes. Suddenly, I realized where I knew him. He was the Pop Tart guy from this morning.

Thankfully, I'd been in a brown wig then and now in a blonde one, so there wasn't any reason he'd recognized me. The thought brought me comfort, but it meant I couldn't go home with him for fear of running into the snoring bear. I watched him curiously as he leaned over and placed the controller in my hand. I'd been too busy checking him out to realize what he was doing. Glancing down, I wasn't sure what to do with it now. I'd played games before, but they'd been more of the old-school ones. This controller had more buttons on it than a remote.

"Here, you press this to kick, this to move, and this to hit. Got it?"

"Oh yeah, sure."

He laughed at my sarcasm, causing heat to flare. I didn't like this. He was disarming me with his normalcy and charm, and I wasn't even seducing him. Guys didn't usually give me the time of day unless my boobs were in their face.

He nodded toward the screen, and I realized it had started. Using the controller like he'd shown me, I began to move my avatar forward. At first, I kept dying, but as I got the hang of it with his tutelage, I started making progress.

"So, mystery girl, can I get a name now that I've helped you take out all these zombies?"

Panic filled me when I realized I didn't know what to say, and before I could think about it, my actual name tumbled out.

"Zel."

"Zel, I like it. I'm Nolan, Nolan Ryder. It's been a pleasure to meet you and play tonight. I've got to head out, but maybe I'll see you around here again?"

Nodding, my brain was stuck on the fact he wasn't trying to get me to go home with him, again my mouth answered without thinking about it.

"Yeah, I work on the third floor, on Desire."

He looked shocked for a moment before he smiled wide. "Well, that makes it easy to find you, Zel. Have a good night."

Nolan blushed and walked off, his friends waiting for him at the door. I hadn't realized they'd gotten up either. Geez, I was losing it. Resigning myself to making the trek out to Max's since I didn't believe I'd find anywhere to sleep tonight at this point. I could go to my mother's if I had to, but her place wasn't much safer than the streets with the company she kept, especially after getting money. No, Max's would be the best bet, even if it was an hour's walk.

"Hey, Nix said to tell you when I was ready to leave."

The guard eyed me cautiously before speaking into his earpiece, "Boss, we have a Juliet requesting your assistance, over."

He nodded at me and then went back to scanning the area. Okay, chatty bunch these guards were. It was shocking to learn Nix was the boss and made me curious about what he was doing at The Pan.

After five minutes, I decided to find my way to

the room myself. I was tired and ready to be anywhere else. Walking around the room, I found a stairway and pushed it open, thankful when the alarm didn't sound. The stairs opened out into a dark hallway, and I wished I'd kept my phone on me, but again, no pockets.

Using my hand, I trailed it along the wall as I went right. After a few minutes of walking in the dark, I finally started to see some light as relief spread through me. I didn't want to admit to myself how dumb of a decision I'd made to leave on my own. I beat myself up enough as it was—no need to add new reasons.

Somehow, I managed to find the room my stuff was in and grabbed it. I thought about changing, but I was dead on my feet at this point. Walking to Max's sounded miserable, and I gave in and decided to tough it out at Mother's. Pushing open the door I'd been denied entry through earlier, I was happy when the asshole guard wasn't standing there anymore. A different guy eyed me but went back to his phone to what appeared to be an intense game of Candy Crush.

Hurrying, I booked it across the lot as fast as my high heels would take me. I regretted not changing, knowing they would be a nightmare to walk anywhere in. Sighing, I stopped and grabbed a hoodie out of my bag first and tugged it over before I started to unbuckle my shoe—stupid mistake number three on my part.

One—not waiting for Nix.

Two—not changing before I left.

Three—forgetting nowhere was safe.

Reaching for my other foot, I jumped when what felt like a barrel of a gun poked me in the back.

Well, fuck.

CHAPTER SIX

NIX

Anger laced through my body with a force I hadn't felt since my service. Taking a few deep breaths, I managed to center myself enough I wouldn't kill the guard who let her leave. I'd returned to the casino floor moments ago and was informed she left after waiting a few minutes. Of course, Zel wouldn't follow directions. Why would she? But the guards knew better.

Shoving him against the wall, I interrogated him as gently as possible. I couldn't let his insolence slide too much. "I'm sorry… I didn't know… she… went… down the… stairs," he finally croaked out. It could've been due to my forearm against his throat, but we wouldn't get technical. Pushing him back one more time for good measure, I turned and stalked toward the stairwell. I had half a mind to show her how angry I was—with my dick, of course.

I debated the merit of this decision as I stomped through the dark hallways looking for her. She couldn't have gone far. I was only a few minutes delayed getting to the casino after dealing with some drunken idiots on the dance floor. The door to the room her stuff was in was ajar, so I continued past it, not feeling it was worth the time to investigate it. If it was open, she wasn't in there. Deciding to take the first exit to get outside quicker, I pushed it open with excessive force knocking it into the brick wall. Jerry stood down by the other door staring at his phone, dropping it at the sound of me exiting.

Scowling, I'd deal with him later as I breathed in the night air. Striding across the lot when I didn't see her, I was momentarily taken aback at the scene when I'd come upon in the alley.

Some asshat had a gun to Zel's back. What the fuck?

Storming over, I picked up the first thing I saw and knocked the fucker out with it. The frying pan made a clanging sound as it reverberated off the bastard's head, and I grunted at his prone body laid at my feet. Kicking him for good measure, I gazed back at my princess. Zel hadn't moved, almost like she was frozen in shock or fear.

Dropping the pan, I instantly regretted it as the sound echoed off the enclosed walls of the alley. My mind raced with what-ifs as I came to terms with the fact I could've lost her. My anxiety spiked, the flashbacks of combat wanting to take over me. The whimper she made was the only thing that stopped me from going under. I focused on the positive of choosing the right door and my hellbent need to get outside.

Zel faced the other wall, one shoe in her hand, her bag precariously hanging off her shoulder in the crook of her elbow. Her body shook with assumed fear, and all the anger I'd felt a moment ago fled me at the sight.

"Princess," I soothed softly, hoping my voice would reassure her. When she made no move or acknowledgment, I tentatively placed a hand on her shoulder. Zel's body tensed, but no other response was noted. Shit, this wasn't good. Slipping her bag off her elbow, I tossed it over my head, securing the crossbody strap. Taking the one shoe she had in her hand, I zipped it up in the bag. She remained motionless through it all, and I wanted to gut the asshole who'd made her feel this way. Obviously, she had to be experiencing a flashback as well, her eyes not even tracking my movements.

Taking a chance, I wrapped her up in my arms and cradled her to my chest as I slowly made my way back into the club. I hoped my familiar smell would help, feeling relieved when she melted into my embrace, curling herself inward toward me. Zel felt so tiny in my hold, and I couldn't believe I finally had her.

Jerry swallowed when I neared, quickly opening the door to let me through. Taking the secret elevator up to the penthouse, I held my breath as it climbed. She seemed so numb, frozen in her fear. Zel, at least, appeared to know it was me as her body slowly stopped shivering, her breathing returning to normal pants when the elevator reached my home.

Carefully, I took her to my bedroom and walked into the attached bathroom, hoping a bath would help her. Taking off her remaining shoe, I tried to place her on the counter to get the water started. It became impossible when she clung to me like a spider monkey, wrapping her arms tight around my neck and burying her head into me. Easing the bag off, I kicked my shoes off, realizing I might have to get in with her at this point. Emptying my pockets, I placed my phone on the counter and started the water.

Zel wrapped herself entirely around me now, her legs clenched around my waist, and the proximity didn't go unnoticed by my dick as he started to wake up. Testing the water with my hand, I let it begin to fill the tub as I pondered how to get some of her clothes off without taking advantage. I'd seen her with less before, but it was a different environment now with very different rules. I couldn't assume I had consent here just because she stripped for a living.

Lifting her away from my torso, I was able to undo my pants and belt, dropping them to the floor with a clang. My shirt looked like it might have to stay, though, as I didn't think I could pry her arms off me at this point. Truth be told, I didn't want to try. I liked having her like this. Deciding to try asking her about her clothes, I gently rubbed her arms and legs to warm them with my body heat.

"Zel, I'm going to get in the bath. Do you want to take anything off?"

She didn't respond, so I decided to leave her clothes on. I could give her something to wear after if she didn't have a change of clothes. Slowly, I sank into the water as it began to cover most of my body.

Zel didn't seem aware, so I rubbed her back as she continued to burrow herself into me as tight as possible. When the water was high enough, I turned the faucet off, and the quiet of the room descended around us. I couldn't handle the loss of sound, and subconsciously I guess, began to hum an old song my mother had sung to me as a child.

Between the warm water, my palliative measures, and humming, Zel eventually began to return to herself. I sensed her body settle into me more, no longer tight with exertion to keep her legs braced around me. I felt her arms slacken as she loosened her death grip, and I detected the tears as she shed them against my neck. I continued to soothe my princess with comforting touches and humming different songs when I got tired of one. I couldn't tell how long we sat in the tub wrapped in one another's arms with her dress floating out around us in the water. The water temperature was the only indication as it began to turn cold, and I knew we'd need to get out soon.

"Zel, I'm going to stand now and dry us off, okay?"

"Mmhm."

Slowly, I stood, letting the water drip down our bodies as the saturated clothes fell heavily against our skin. Zel pulled back from my neck and stared at me, searching my eyes for something.

"You didn't wait for me," I admonished, knowing I shouldn't but feeling as if I had to. I was angry again, but this time at myself. I should've been there faster or never left her.

"I'm sorry. I thought you were too busy or had forgotten. I just wanted to leave."

"I could never forget you," tumbled out before I knew what I was saying.

Shock registered on her face, her guardedness slipping as she deciphered my words.

"Why?"

"Because I see you through every costume, despite your attempts to disguise yourself as someone else. I see who you are to your core, and she's someone I want to know. Someone I can't forget."

"You barely even know me." Her retort was bitter, a clear indication she didn't want to or know how to accept my answer, infuriating me even more.

"Don't tell me what I know." I couldn't contain

the growl, and the first sign of her fire sparked in her eyes at the sound.

"Fine. I won't. But you're wrong. *I'm just a fantasy*." Zel's tone was laced with bitterness, and I wanted to wash it out of her mouth with my tongue.

"Princess, allow me to show you just how *wrong* you are. The only fantasy here is the bed I will be fucking your brains out in."

Before she argued back, I smashed my mouth to hers, sealing our lips in a kiss I'd wanted for a while. Zel whimpered into me and returned my kiss with ferocity. I was momentarily dizzy as I tried to climb out of the tub while holding her. Somehow I managed, but our wet clothes impeded our journey from going any further. Propping her against the counter, I peeled off my shirt as I stared into her eyes. For the first time, I found desire there, need. Passion coursed through me as I flung my shirt onto the floor, not caring at the moment about the water.

Zel started to undress, but the wet material didn't cooperate with her, and all of the ties she had on it to make it easy to dance and strip in were tangled. Halting her hands, I ripped it at the seams, not caring as long as I managed to get her free. Her face held a look of shock as she took herself in, until she flung the rest of her wet clothes off, now she was free of her mummy suit.

Dragging her to me, I attacked her lips again as

we started to grind against one another, both of our bottoms still covering us. Opening the drawer, I reached in blindly as I searched for a condom. When my hands wrapped around one, my lips parted in a smug smile as I stepped back enough to shove down my wet boxers. Zel panted from our kiss as she regarded me. The ends of her wig were wet, but the rest had remained dry. Her breasts had never looked more delicious than they did right then on display only for me. She watched as I slowly rolled the condom on, licking her lips in anticipation.

"I thought you said bed?" she teased, her eyebrow-raising.

"Oh, *princess*, that will be round two. I need you now more than I need the next breath," I purred before pulling her panties down in one go.

Zel gasped at my statement, or perhaps my move, but it gave me the opening to plunder her mouth again with my tongue. Hooking her legs in my elbows, I positioned her closer to the edge and slammed into her as I found my target. Scooping her up, I lifted her into the air as I continued to impale her on my rock-hard cock.

Zel's moans echoed around the room as I plunged deep into her wet heat. She felt so good around me, and with each drag of my dick out, I rubbed her clit with my pelvic bone, causing her to gasp every few seconds. It was a brutal pace, but I'd been imagining being inside her for too long that I knew it wouldn't last long the first round.

Zel's moans joined my grunts as I pistoned myself in and out close to reaching my end. She held onto my neck as I lifted her off and on my dick over and over. My thighs and hamstrings screamed at me by this point, but I didn't care as I pushed onward in the pursuit of nirvana. Spreading her ass cheeks with my hands, I used her luscious globes to increase my speed and depth in her.

"Fuck, Nix, ah, oooh," Zel moaned seconds before climaxing.

Her walls tightened around me as her body began to convulse in a full-body shudder. The pressure had taken me off guard and sent my orgasm skyrocketing as I plunged one last time into her. Twitching inside her, we both panted as we came back to reality.

"If *that* wasn't the fantasy, I can't wait to find out what qualifies."

"Oh, *Princess*, that was just the beginning."

Her answering smile had my cock twitching again as I stalked into the bedroom, ready to make her mine.

CHAPTER SEVEN

NOLAN

The professor droned on about algebraic equations at the front of the class, making my head want to explode. Math was the bane of my existence. My father had only allowed me to enroll if I took the damn classes. He felt it would better prepare me for taking over the hardware store one day. The problem was, I didn't want to take over the store—I wanted to design video games.

These classes almost made it not worth it as I sat here and listened to a pudgy middle-aged man tell us how to divide and subtract or some shit. This professor was clueless about real life and had no indication of what we all went through. He was detached from the reality we all faced, still believing a college degree like my dad would save us. Everyone had been fooled by the glitz and glamor for too long in Tiara Heights that they forgot what it was like in Dante's Circle. Or more like they chose to ignore. The only math there that mattered was survival.

The class finally ended, and I sat up from the sprawled-out position I'd taken in an attempt to take notes. Looking at my notebook, though, I found only two lines of equations written down. Hell, homework would be difficult tonight. It looked like I'd be spending hours on YouTube tonight trying to teach myself quadratic equations.

My roommate, Josh, walked up to me, his book bag slung over his shoulder. His brown hair was carefully askew in that purposeful way he spent hours perfecting each morning. The smug look on his face didn't convey good things in store for me. Josh was all about the party life of college and not so much the studying part. He could afford to do that, though. He was, after all, from the Heights.

"Dude, I got us access for Desire at The Tower tonight. It's going to be insane. You have to come."

His enthusiasm already hinted at his belief of scoring with a chick he'd meet there. The girl he had brought home the other night flitted across my mind for a moment, reminding me how too good she was for him. How he managed to score with these girls constantly amazed me. At the mention of The Tower, Zel popped into my head, and I began to feel hopeful about meeting her again. She'd mentioned she worked at Desire a few nights ago.

Zel was the first girl I'd felt comfortable with since high school and even kind of reminded me of my crush from back then. That had been several years ago, though. It took me several years to convince my parents to allow me to attend college, and now, I found myself a college sophomore at the ripe age of twenty-three when my counterparts were barely twenty.

"Uh, yeah, sure. I need to knock out this assignment first. What time are you going?"

"Now, no time like the present! I'll leave your ticket at Will Call with your name. My dad is letting me use his passes for the night."

"Your *dad* has a membership to The Tower?" I asked incredulously.

"Dude, where have you been?"

Blinking, I realized how out of it I was sometimes. The other night out had been a rarity, and I spent most of it playing video games. My life revolved around shifts at the store, learning stupid math I didn't understand, and writing code in any spare time I had. Being an older student, I tried to stay out of the drama, effectively alienating myself from my peers at the same time.

"Ah, yeah, sorry."

"Nolan, you're one strange guy."

Shaking his head, he walked out of the classroom, leaving me staring after him, wondering what I was even doing. Maybe I should stay home and study in peace for once. Gathering my stuff from the empty room, I exited and made my way to our apartment. We only lived a few miles from the community college, so it was an easy walk to and from most days. The heat and rain made it difficult at times, but today was nice, so I enjoyed it. It was easier than trying to park my truck.

My phone buzzed as I walked, but I ignored it, knowing it would be my brother or father, and I didn't want to engage with either of them at the moment. Luck wasn't on my side, though, as I found my brother sitting on the stairs leading up to my apartment. Halting my steps, I hung my head as I prepared myself for this confrontation. Gavin Ryder was trouble manifested.

"Gav, what are you doing here?"

"Nolan, baby brother, why you gotta be like that? I stopped by to see how you were. Can't a brother check in on his family without getting the third degree?"

"Not when it's you, Gavin. You never bring good tidings."

"Now, now. None of that. This time, I bring good news."

"I highly doubt that, but can we get to the point? I have algebra to ruin."

"I'm getting married, little bro!"

"Uh-huh. How did you convince someone to marry you?"

"Ouch. You have such little faith in me."

"No, it's just you tend to make poor choices."

"Hitting me where it hurts, bro."

"That would mean you have feelings."

"Okay, that one did hurt. Listen, I get it. I haven't been the best brother to you, and I've made some bad choices over the years. But I promise, I've turned a new leaf, and I'm making a life for myself now. My girl, she's pregnant, and I'm going to do what is right by her. I've got a job with her family, and we've got a place. I'm becoming a family man. Can you believe it?"

His words hung in the air as I tried to fathom the insanity he was spouting. The thought of him bringing a spawn into the world sent chills through me. There was no telling what kind of job he would be doing for this family either. Everything he said was a disaster waiting to happen, and despite his bravado, I could hear his doubt. Gavin was scared, which meant he was in deeper than he'd ever been before.

How many times had I pulled him from the depths of despair only to find him back there a week later? I was tired of being his hero. I just wanted to be my own hero, but he kept casting me as his, inevitably making me the villain in my own story.

"Why are you telling me this?"

"Aren't you happy for me?"

"Yeah, thrilled."

"Wow, even when I have good news, you still treat me like scum. I wanted to ask you to stand up there with me, but maybe I was wrong."

He stood from his perch, pushing past my shoulder as he walked past. Exhaling, I counted to ten before I turned to address him, the ghost of my past prompting me to.

"*Wait.*"

Gavin stopped but didn't turn around as he waited for me to answer.

"I'm sorry. Congrats, Gav. I'm happy for you, and I can't wait to meet my niece or nephew. When can I meet my sister-in-law?"

He turned at the end, a broad grin on his face, and I realized how much I'd been played. Emotional manipulation was my kryptonite. I felt too much for others, and they always used it against me in the end. Every significant relationship in my life had been someone using me for their purpose, and I was tired of it.

"I'm glad to hear it. How about next week? I'll text you. Gotta go though, customers to attend to."

He practically skipped off after getting what he wanted. I had no idea why he needed me to meet this girl, but it couldn't be a good outcome for me. Exhaustion hung over my shoulders, and I realized I no longer had the desire to force myself to learn quadratic equations.

My motivation to do well and make my father proud despite my hatred for the subject had always been what drove me. Today, I didn't have it in me. My whole life, I'd prided myself on being the good kid, the one who stayed out of trouble and made my parents happy. The one they never had to worry about—especially after Nat. The burden was heavy, and I found myself questioning if that was how I wanted to live my life—making others happy.

When had I ever chosen myself first? Was there more to life than living it for others? It felt like there should be. Tossing my book bag onto my bed, I stripped out of my clothes and headed to shower.

Tonight, would be about escape and leaving all the shit that hung heavy on my shoulders here.

Tonight, I would join my roommate in the pursuit of something fleeting, but something that ultimately felt good.

Tonight, I would choose myself and be the college student I'd never been able to be.

"What can I get you, sir?" a waitress purred as I took a seat at the round table. Josh nodded but turned back to the dancer upfront. I was momentarily stunned as I caught a glimpse of the beautiful girl, but once I realized it wasn't Zel, I turned back to address the waitress.

"I'll just take whatever Pale Ale you have on tap."

The waitress nodded and walked away, allowing me to take in my surroundings more thoroughly. Desire was set up beautifully and different from any strip club I'd been to. Not that I'd been to many, but it was one of the few things to do in this town, so

I've visited them a time or two. I wasn't a frequent flyer like my roommate, Josh, was though.

There were some intimate booths on the sides that had what looked like curtains that could be pulled closed. The middle had tables scattered about, but they weren't close to the others providing room between them. A piano was set to the left of the stage, and the bar was in the back on the right. Hallways went off in opposite directions, and I assumed the restrooms and secret rooms were down there. Desire was exclusive and required a special key card for the elevator to even get to this floor. I never paid attention to Josh's family before, other than knowing they were from Tiara Heights. It shouldn't have surprised me when he mentioned his father having a membership, but it did.

The waitress returned with my beer as the dancer finished on the stage. I'd never been to a burlesque show, so it was intriguing to watch the dance movements tell a story that weaved sensuality and elegance of dance without being lewd. The next performer came out and began to dance, their back to us. A pole rose out of the stage, and "ah" rang out at the structure.

The dancer had one arm held over her head while the other clasped it, her hip timed with the music as she twirled her hand overhead. Her costume had instantly caught my eye with the long chain that hooked from the top to the bottom of her back, but the rest of her was bare. There was something sexy about seeing her back naked and not needing to see her intimate bits.

Her hair was red, but the color made me think it was dyed with how bright it was. It was braided and draped over her shoulder. The skirt she was wearing was iridescent and had many pieces that fluttered around her as she moved, catching the light. When she finally turned around, I was able to make out more of the iridescent patches as they trailed up her torso and, with a combo of the chain, covered her breasts. I could then tell that it was either glued on or painted, and she was bare-chested. The chain provided an illusion of a top there. She was an ethereal mermaid as she grace-fully moved across the stage, making you believe she was almost underwater.

I got lost watching her as she danced across the stage and spun around on the pole. She pulled you into the dance number with her, and you became part of the story. I was mesmerized, and it seemed I wasn't the only one as every person in the room watched her. Even the waitresses appeared to respect her dance and didn't interrupt customers while she was on.

When the number ended, it was like a trance broke as we came back down to reality. The wait-ress walked back over and took some orders from the others at my table, and I stopped her before she left, needing to know who the beauty was on stage.

"Excuse me-" before I could even get out my whole question, she cut me off, smiling.

"Her name's Zel. Talk to him if you want private time with her." She nodded to a man standing against the wall, his gruffness making me cautious about approaching. But with the knowledge it was my beautiful enchantress, I had to try. I watched as a few men approached the bouncer and he stared them down. It seemed to be a test of sorts to learn if you could get past the gatekeeper to make it to heaven. Out of the dozen or so guys to approach him, he'd only let two of the bunch into the hallway.

"You don't stand a chance, Ryder," chuckled my roommate.

"Oh, why do you say that?"

"She's the new star, and only guys who have, like, a password or something get through. I think it's more to do with Benjamins, and we know you don't fit that profile."

He had a point, but not only did I dislike him calling me by my last name like we were chums, I really hated being underestimated. Peers had notoriously done it my whole life and never believed I would amount to anything. It wasn't my fault I had a learning disability that made learning certain things harder, but my peers would never let me forget it when I had to take different classes. It didn't help the expectations I was held to were impossible to meet and made me feel small when I inevitably failed them. Nat had been the smart one and helped me figure out the best way to learn, proving all my peers, teachers, and even parents wrong in the end.

My pride couldn't admit defeat. Not now, not after all the sacrifices I'd made to get here. So while Josh might be right about my bank account, he didn't know the fire that burned within me every day.

My earlier sentiment to be a typical college student rang through my head, and Zel drew me in, making me want to claim it. I needed to spend more time with her and be in her presence. Smirking at Josh, I placed some money on the table for my beer and sauntered over to the guard. He assessed me for a moment as I stared back before asking a question.

"State your business."

"I'd like to spend some time with Zel."

"What do you plan to do with her?"

"Whatever she wants. I just feel as if I need to be around her, get to know her, and figure out what it is about her that calls to me."

I surprised myself at the forwardness, but something about the guy made me feel like he'd appreciate it more and would undoubtedly know if it was only bravado. It must've been the right thing because a moment later, he moved aside and allowed me to pass down the hallway where only two had gone before. I was too nervous to ask, so I kept walking, assuming I would know it when I saw it. I was almost to the end of the hallway and wondered if I had it all wrong.

What if the people who got past him were taken out to be shot? Or were thrown out? Why that was the second thing, and not the first option told me I watched too many mobster movies. Shaking my head at myself, I started to turn around when I heard a sound pulling my focus back to the last door.

"Going somewhere?" a sultry voice rang out.

Slowly, I turned, and there in the doorway stood the mermaid dancer and my mystery seductress. Up close, I could make out all the different colors on her skin, the glitter, and even some jewels she had stuck to herself. If you didn't know she was topless, it was hard to tell because her body paint had been done well.

"Uh, hi," I blushed, realizing I'd just stared at her tits. "I was looking for you."

"Well, you found me. Now, what are you going to do?"

I had no idea as I'd only thought the first part through. So when the words left my mouth, I didn't know who was more shocked, her or me.

"Would you want to play Monopoly?"

CHAPTER EIGHT

ZEL

Waking up in Nix's bed hadn't been planned. Of course, being mugged outside The Tower hadn't been on my agenda either. But being with Nix was the first time I'd felt taken care of and safe. It was one of the best nights of sleep I'd had since I was little, and crazy enough, I hadn't wanted to skip out on him the following day.

Granted, he had to go to work, and I had my meeting with Isaac, Mr. Flynn's assistant. When I realized I was in the penthouse, I almost had a coronary. He'd forgotten to mention that part of the puzzle, but either the owner didn't care, or he hadn't known I was there. Nix only grunted and smiled when I confronted him, not bothered in the least. I'd been given the job, and the past week was incredible.

Dancing here was seductive and masterful, and each number I performed felt like part of me woke up. Now, I looked forward to each day of work, and it didn't feel like something I did to survive anymore. I was beginning to recognize something in my eyes when I stared into the mirror now. It was terrifying in a whole new way.

"Perfect as always, princess," Nix growled in my ear as he escorted me to my room. His voice automatically sent shivers through me, and I had to center myself to not give into him.

In a surprising twist, he hadn't tried to claim me, save me, or make me quit my job. Quite the opposite, in fact. Nix was my biggest supporter and had assigned himself to my shifts to monitor my room. I hadn't minded it at all, actually. I got to see him and know he'd only let back the people he felt wouldn't cross the line.

Now that I was in a safe and well-paid environment, I could stop with the break room blow jobs and other nefarious activities I tended to find myself in. It was actually one of the rules the assistant had told me during my meeting.

"Now that you're here, Zel, things will be different. Mr. Flynn wants to ensure his dancers and staff are well taken care of. You will be provided a place to stay if you need it, meals, and an allowance for costumes and accessories. You'll be given a fair wage with tips. If that's not enough, then we can negotiate. Mr. Flynn wants to keep his dancers safe, and that means no back room blowjobs. While you perform and create a sensual picture for the audience, you're not a sex worker here."

"Then what goes on in the private rooms?"

"Ah, I'm glad you asked. In the rooms, you will find various things. Some rooms are private for members, and the others are the dancers' rooms. You can arrange your room to be whatever you would like it to be. Most have their dressing room in their private suite, a bedroom, and an en suite. They also tend to have an entertaining room where they can provide individual dances, talk with the customer, or even teach their guests some moves. What I'm saying is, whatever you do in your room is your own. We do not monitor these other than screening who is permitted into them. However, if you decide to engage in any type of sexual behavior with a guest, then that is your choice, but it cannot be a monetary exchange of means. Mr. Flynn is not your pimp. Do you understand?"

It turned out his fair wage, tips, allowance, and the accommodations provided to me were well above anything I'd made before. It was as if I could breathe for the first time in years. The clientele were classy, and so far, I hadn't felt threatened or pressured to do anything I hadn't wanted. Most of them wished for a sexy dance and then someone to listen to them. It was easier than break room blowies any day, not to mention much easier on my knees.

Nix left and sent through the first guest. Perhaps it sounded classier to be entertaining guests instead of lap dances, but whatever floated the owner's boat. I was here for it.

Two dances down and a surprise lesson on the art of cunnilingus with one guy; I was surprised when the next person walked through the door. It was my gaming partner, Mr. Pop Tart himself, Nolan. I wasn't sure if he recognized me, so I played my role as the sexy mermaid and gave him my best come hither voice.

Color me surprised when he asked to play Monopoly. Blinking, I stared at him for a minute, trying to figure out if he was serious. His earnest smile made me believe him, and I shook my head, hating to disappoint him.

"Um, sorry. I don't have the pockets to carry Monopoly. What about a game of cards, or I could see if someone has it?"

Nolan blushed, doing that cute shy guy shuffle —ruffling his hair, hand in a pocket, and two-stepping in place.

"Yeah, that sounds great. Sorry, I don't know why I blurted that out. I haven't played the game in years. I think I was mesmerized—"

"By my boobs? Don't worry," I laughed, "it happens to all guys."

"Actually, I was going to say beauty."

"Oh."

Now, it was my turn to blush as I took in his compliment. With him, it wasn't a ploy to get into my pants either. I believed Nolan, and it made his words even more meaningful. Walking over to the wall, I pushed the button on the phone that connected to Nix. I didn't have a phone yet since I'd been informed this was just a temporary room for me. I'd gotten to design it yesterday, and it was being remodeled as we spoke. It would be ready next week. So, in the meantime, I was in an empty guest room members rented if they didn't have a permanent one. I'd been learning so much about this place since I started working here, and it was all fascinating.

"Princess?"

"Hey, Nix. I was wondering, is there a game of Monopoly anywhere?"

"Monopoly?"

"Yep."

His deep chuckle had my clit throbbing as I recalled how it felt to have that beard between my thighs. My thoughts almost had me missing his response.

"Have to give the kid credit. That's original."

"Yeah, I think so too."

I found myself blushing and smiling as I talked with Nix on the phone about Nolan. He was standing in the room and trying not to eavesdrop on my conversation as he took it in. I noticed his ears tint a little red at my statement, and I found it gave me the flutters.

"I'll see what I can do."

"Thank you."

"Anytime, princess."

I didn't know who I was at the moment. I was

flirting with one guy while entertaining another one. And while that was an oddity in itself, the most curious thing was I felt happy. Hanging the phone back up, I walked back over to Nolan. I felt like an awkward teen and not the seductress I'd been a few moments ago in his presence.

"Nix's going to look. In the meantime, would you mind if I took a shower and changed out of this make-up?"

"Oh, no, not at all. Of course, you'd want to put something else on. How rude of me."

Placing my hand on his forearm, I tried to calm some of the nervous energy rolling off him. "It's not rude of you. It's actually generous for you to allow me to do that. So, thank you."

"Allow you? I mean… I don't own you."

"I'm glad to hear that. Not everyone has the same beliefs, though. You can sit on the bed and talk through the crack in the door if you want."

I didn't think it was possible, but his cheeks tinted even more, and I found it adorable. Nolan reminded me of childhood innocence and hope, and I wanted to hold onto that for a moment to remember what it felt like.

"Oh, uh sure, if you're cool with that."

"Tell me, Nolan, are you this nervous with girls in general, or am I just the lucky one?"

"So you do remember me," he said with a grin, a little cockiness leaking through.

I stopped walking and realized my mistake. He

hadn't said his name yet, and I'd opened the door for him. Either I was getting sloppy, or he disarmed me so much, I'd dropped my shields. I didn't know which outcome I preferred it to be.

"Listen, I'm sorry if I'm not supposed to call you by name or something. I won't get you in trouble or tell. I'll keep it to myself. I'm sorry. I didn't mean to sound so smug."

Turning, I watched his face as he sputtered out the world's most awkward apology.

"Okay, here's the thing, Nolan. There's something about you that's familiar and safe, and I don't have a lot of that in my life. So what if we drop all the games, and we can be two people hanging out? There wouldn't be rules then. But you *should* be smug, Nolan," I cooed, turning back to the bathroom. "I never remember names."

Shutting the door behind me, I leaned back against it, my heart thumping loudly in my chest. It was okay. He only knew Zel. He didn't know my full name. I could do this. I could. Tossing the few clothing items I still had on, I unpinned my wig and shook out my golden hair.

Rubbing my temples and neck, I eased some of the pain the pins created. It was the only way to ensure my identity stayed entirely hidden. Everyone knew the golden-haired girl, and she couldn't exist here. Hoping he'd remain on the bed, I opened the door a smidge and placed the red wig on the counter as I stepped into the steaming water.

A few minutes later, I heard him ask a question through the crack. It was hard to hear over the water, but it worked if I stayed out from under it while he was talking.

"So, what's your favorite color?"

"Hmm, purple. What's yours?"

"Probably blue."

"How long have you worked here?"

"About a week. The day I met you was my interview."

"No way! That's kind of cool. You dance like someone who has done it for a while."

"Well, dance I've done my whole life. It's always been part of me."

"There was a girl at my high school who danced almost like you. She was beautiful, and when she danced, the whole world stopped turning."

Sucking in a breath, I tried to calm my racing heart. No, how was this possible?

"Oh. Where did you go to school?"

"Here. Sinhaven High School."

"Um, wow, small world. Were you friends with this, um, girl?"

"Pfft. No, we were *not* friends. She was popular and high school royalty. Rapunzel was prom queen and way above my social status. We were lab partners once, though. She was nice to me, especially after, um, yeah," he cleared his throat, stopping himself. "I always thought she looked kind of sad, though, lonely."

Tears ran down my face as he spoke of the past. At his mention of lab partners, I immediately placed him. I hadn't known his name; I was even worse with them back then. Mainly because all the secrets and lies tried to spill out of my head at any moment, and there wasn't enough room for it all. I got away with it because I was Queen Bee and people assumed it was just because of that, just another stuck-up popular girl.

Deep down, it bothered me. I didn't like how something else had been taken from me—having real friends and an average high school experience one of them. Finishing up, I didn't ask any more follow-up questions, scared my voice would shake. I dried off quickly and redressed into a comfortable outfit of leggings, an oversized shirt, and fluffy socks. I brushed out my hair and debated what to do with it now.

Blowing dry would take forever, and I didn't want to put it up in a wig when it was wet. Deciding to go old school, I wrapped it up in a bandana, hoping it would keep it secure. Inhaling deep, I slowed my breath to calm the beats of my heart. He didn't know I was Rapunzel, and honestly, I wasn't, not anymore. Only in name.

"Hey, that was quick." He grinned at me, all thoughts of his mystery girl out of his mind.

"Yeah, believe it or not, I'm pretty low maintenance in general. I save all the time-consuming things for when I dance."

"That makes sense."

A knock on the door had me heading toward it. Nix held out a cardboard box and handed it to me.

"You found one!"

"Um-hmm. Wesley had the game in about ten different versions. I grabbed one that was open because I didn't feel like dealing with his complaints otherwise."

"This works perfectly, thank you."

Nix grunted, a crooked smile on his face as I began to shut the door. Puckering a kiss, I winked before closing the door. The growly man was becoming an addiction I didn't want to stop.

Shaking the board, the pieces rattled as Nolan smiled, meeting me at the table. "What piece do you want? And before you say the dog, it's mine." My smile was probably a bit manic, but I didn't care. The dog was the cutest.

"Well, you're in luck. I want the tiny shoe so I can feel like a giant."

"Oh my goodness, you're such a dork," I laughed.

"Yeah, well, it takes one to know one."

"That's the worst retort in the history of retorts. You're putting yourself down in the process!"

Nolan stuck his tongue out, causing me to laugh even more. He offered to be the banker, and I happily accepted since I hated money, real and fake. It'd done nothing in my life but brought pain. I needed it to survive, and that was its only use.

A few hours later, I sulked as Nolan claimed another property piece while I had to mortgage my last one.

"I hate this game," I pouted.

"No, I think you love it. It's the losing part you hate."

"Nope. Definitely hate the game."

"How about we offer a trade then?"

"I'm listening."

"I'll give you all my property for a real date."

Stunned silence met me as I blinked at him, my silence caused him to assume the wrong thing, and he started backpedaling quickly.

"Sorry, I take it back. I thought... you know what? It doesn't matter what I thought, I was—"

Cutting off his ramblings, I cupped his cheek and kissed him gently on the lips.

"I'd love to, Nols."

"Yeah?"

"Yeah."

"Okay, then."

We stayed close for a few minutes, smiling wide at one another before I pulled back.

"And now I win! Give me all your money!" I demanded, laughing the whole time.

"Worth it."

I threw all the money up in a cascade of colorful bills and instantly regretted it when we had to pick them all up. Nolan helped me put the pieces away, and I realized how much fun I'd had this evening with him. Not once had I painted a fantasy for him or pretended to be a version of myself that wasn't real.

With Nolan, I'd been me, the real me, and the only money I took from him that night was the fake kind. It was one of the best nights I'd ever had too.

ZEL

Waking up in a consistent place had become my new favorite thing and a comfort I'd find hard to give up. The beeping alarm was about to get tossed at the wall, though. Shoving off the covers, I walked over to the dresser where the annoying sound lived.

Now that I had my own bed, I found myself needing to actually set the bugger. Bed hopping hadn't leaned to the need for one—when you slept with one eye open, you didn't need an alarm to wake up. Nix had given me this one when I moved in and seen the meager possessions I had. Taking it had been burdensome, I didn't want to owe him, but it was worse to be late to work and screw up this gig when it was the best thing I had going for me.

I've been working here for almost two weeks, and my bedroom was supposed to be ready tonight. I was oddly excited about it. The last time I had my own room... Well, I didn't like to recall that time. Before that, I'd shared a bed with

Gothel. I had a room at Max's, but it wasn't convenient for me to be there, so it was more of a room with a bed in it. Thinking of the last time I'd put care into a room brought all the memories back, and I tried my best to shove them down where they belonged.

Dreams were wishes you got to make when your life was good. When every day depended on surviving, dreams were about as practical as diamond-studded toilet paper—pretty to look at but ultimately useless. When shit got real, you didn't want a diamond up your ass.

A knock on my door startled me, and I stood stunned for a while before making my way over. Cautiously, I opened it to reveal a delicious Nix. Smirking, I leaned against the doorframe as I folded my arms over my chest. He didn't say anything for a minute, stunned as he took me in. At the clearing of my throat, he finally looked up and met my eyes.

"Do you always answer the door looking like *that*?"

"I don't know. Do you always knock on doors looking like *that*?" I purred back.

Nix had become a quick obsession I was trying to quit. It wasn't going so well.

In the past week, we'd fucked like bunnies almost every day, and I had a feeling it wasn't ending anytime soon. Nix exuded masculinity and sex appeal, and I wasn't ashamed to admit I craved it. His growly alpha personality did something for me, and when he took me, he owned me. *Fucking owned me.*

Bracing his arm on top of the door frame, he peered down at me with nothing but devious thoughts on his face. He dressed in an all black suit that fit him perfectly. His fitted black shirt and matching tie did naughty things to me. Nix rode the line between dangerous and refined so well. I couldn't help but imagine the body I knew laid below either.

"Done yet, princess?"

"No, not really. How about you come in and let me have a closer look?"

"Oh, *princess*," he purred, licking his lips as he took me in. I wasn't naked, but I wasn't *exactly* dressed either. "If I had the time, I'd show you just how much I like you answering the door wearing that, but I come bearing a message today… unfortunately."

Pulling my robe closed, I suddenly felt exposed as I opened the door wider for him to enter. When he didn't, I looked back to see what the problem was. The look on his face made me feel even worse—pity.

"I can't come in, princess. There's a private party tonight for some VIP's and the boss wants you there."

"Do I have a choice?"

"You always have a choice, Zel."

Scoffing, because when the fuck did I ever have

a choice in my life. Blanking my face, I looked him squarely in the eyes as I answered. "Tell the *boss* if he wants me somewhere, then he can fucking ask me himself. I'm *busy*."

Slamming the door, I marched over to the wardrobe and began to scoot hangers across the metal rod angrily. The noise annoyed me, but it felt like a justifiable punishment for getting my hopes up and thinking someone cared about me. Men were all the same in the end. They only wanted you for what they could use you for. I'd been taught that early.

"Where's my pretty girl? Are you ready to take some pictures and perform for some of daddy's special friends? They're so excited to meet you, Rapunzel—the lost girl who returned. Sinhaven's pride and joy."

"Of course, Daddy."

Kissing his cheek, I skipped down the hall in my pink tutu. Some days, I found it hard to believe this was my life now. Everyone knew me and my story. At one time in my life, I'd been invisible, inconsequential, but now, I was famous. Just like my father said, I'd become the pride of Sinhaven, lofting my father's mayoral campaign for another term.

The lost girl who returned was right, or at least the lost part.

Discovering I'd been kidnapped when I was a baby was shocking. Learning instead of taking the ransom, the kidnapper kept me, even more so. I'd grown up thinking she was my mother. Mother Gothel had always been kind to me, and I was pretty sure she loved me. It was hard to match the story I was told and the life I lived. We lived in our own little hut away from the town in a secluded clearing. It had been fine when I was little. As I got older, I'd started to wonder about the outside world more, but never enough to risk the ire of my mother. If she hadn't become sick, I might have never known who I really was.

When I was thirteen, I found my mother sick with a fever for days. One morning, I couldn't get her to wake, so I took a chance and left the house. I'd been nervous, but the thought of my mother dying pushed me to venture past the clearing despite her warnings. Discovering a whole new world when I walked into Sinhaven had been mind-blowing.

After getting help, I rode in a shiny carriage with red and blue lights that made noise. We made it to the hospital, and while they were working on Mother, a nurse recognized me or who she assumed me to be. My long blonde hair, green eyes, and unique birthmark were all remarkable enough that she called the mayor to confirm.

When Mr. Kingston and Queenie Sonne arrived, I was scared at first. How could they be my parents? Mother was my parent. Eventually, the whole story came out, and I went to live with my 'real' mom and dad. They lived in a big house, with staff and a hundred rooms. The best part was my own room, and I got to decorate it.

When I'd picked a ballerina theme, Daddy had

asked if I wanted to take lessons. Dancing in the clearing had been one of my favorite pastimes, so to have the chance to learn more, I couldn't believe my luck. I'd been so excited.

The first year had been amazing living with them. I got to attend a real school and make friends. Dance class was my favorite, though, and I spent as much time as possible doing it. Daddy even had me dance for his friends. It made me happy that he was so impressed with me, and I wanted to do whatever I could to make Daddy happy. He indeed was my hero, saving me as he had, even if I didn't understand it. The number of times they mentioned it, though, had me taking notice. There were a lot of things I was still learning about this new world, so when they made a point of mentioning something, I tried my best to emulate it.

Today was going to be amazing. Daddy said one of his friends might be able to help me get into a school for ballet. I hoped I could; it would be amazing to do nothing but dance. It was the only thing I dreamed about now. I had all the pretty clothes I could want, a mom and a dad, and even a best friend at school. Getting to dance all day would be the fairy tale dream of becoming a real ballerina.

Yanking the dress off the hanger, I headed into the bathroom. When I looked in the mirror, I jumped back, gasping as I realized the biggest error in judgment I'd made this morning.

And no, it wasn't opening the door wearing only a thong and silk robe.

It was opening the door without wearing a wig or a disguise. I'd gotten careless in my stability and it might've cost me everything.

My golden hair cascaded around me, and my emerald green eyes sparkled under the light. My natural rosy complexion was glowing, and the heart-shaped birthmark on my cheek was as visible as ever, and I'd just shown it to Nix. Fuck!

Frantically, I tried to recall the way he'd looked at me and if he recognized Rapunzel. Fortunately, the boob distraction had seemed to work on him as well because he hadn't shown any flash of recognition in his eyes that I could recall. Trying to slow my breathing down, I turned on the tap and threw some cold water on my face.

Comfort had made me lax, and I'd almost blown my cover and ruined everything. I couldn't afford to let myself get comfortable again. No dick was worth my pride.

After a few splashes of the cool water, I felt calm enough to finish getting ready. After a quick shower, I put on the dress I'd picked out and zipped up the back. It was a basic navy chenille dress that hit me at the knees with a high neck. It was classic and conservative, meaning my mother would approve with the added benefit of keeping my father's handsy friends from undressing me with their eyes.

Applying my make-up, I highlighted my eyes

and put on a nude palette. *Nothing too flashy for the mayor's daughter now, or people might talk!* The scandal that would be!

Finally, I brushed my hair and pulled it back in a fishtail braid. Grabbing the shoes I would need, I slipped them on as I took myself in the mirror. I looked like the picture of innocence and the perfect elite daughter.

Grabbing a trench coat and scarf, I wrapped the fabric over my head, hiding my hair. I absconded some huge glasses to cover my birthmark and wrapped myself entirely in the jacket. In a designer bag, I placed a spare set of clothes and a wig for later. Sneaking out in the morning like this would be easier than trying to return, and I only had time for one outfit change.

Checking the time, I hurriedly made my way out the door, making sure to check no one else was around. It was 8 am on Sunday, so I figured it wouldn't be as occupied yet. Our floor didn't even open until noon today, so it was easy avoiding the other employees.

Sneaking into the stairs, I quietly made my way down to the ground floor. After my last debacle on exiting, I'd scoped it out and now knew all the best and easiest ways to leave this fortress. I'd also found a flashlight left one day, and I had a sneaky feeling it was Nix. I even had a ladder in case scaling the wall was my only option. I would never find myself trapped—not again.

The morning air still had that dewy smell to it as I breathed it in, the sun starting to rise in the distance. Birds chirped their morning song, and for a moment, I could imagine I wasn't in Sinhaven, but an actual fairy tale where birds did my hair.

Though, if this was a fairy tale, I wanted a refund. Where was my cute animal sidekick? Where was my fairy godmother? Unless roaches and druggies counted, mine had missed orientation. Figured —fuck my life.

Once I'd crossed over into Tiara Heights, my tension rose even higher. This part of town pretended to be the best of the city, but they just hid it better. Deceit and betrayal were heavy on the walls of these million-dollar homes—you just had to look closer to see it.

When I made it to the corner of Charming and Diamond, the car was waiting for me like it always was. I guess on the fairy tale front, my carriage was intact, even if it was driven by a fifty-year-old man and not a cute mouse. As they saw me approach, the door opened, and my father's butler stepped out and offered me the door. Exhaling, I prepared myself for the next couple of hours.

Brunch was worse than finding out the pole hadn't been cleaned as you started your spin rotation, or dancing in five-inch heels and break room blowies altogether.

"Darling, you look beautiful as always," cooed Queenie as she kissed me on the cheeks.

"Thanks, Mom. You did pick out the dress after all, and you have excellent taste," I praised. "How are your lilies doing?"

Just as I expected, my mom went on a long spiel about her orange lilies, the pride of her garden. She went on to update me on which ones produced the best with certain fertilizers, yada yada. I could give a flying fuck about lilies, I actually despised them and their smell, but it was the easiest way to not engage with her or have her ask questions I didn't want to answer.

We walked arm in arm into the study, where my father sat behind his desk. Every time I was in this room, I had to visibly hold in my emotions, or I'd snap. The last time that happened, the consequences hadn't been good. I didn't know if I could handle another stay at the State Mental Hospital. It was a place even nightmares feared.

"There are my pretty girls. How are you, sweetheart? I hope *school* is treating you well. You barely even stop by anymore," Kingston greeted as we walked in.

He said it with such ease and grace you'd almost believe he cared. The corners of his eyes, the tightness in his hands, and the stiff posture of his shoulders told a different story. My father knew I wasn't in school. He also knew why I didn't stop by to visit.

This was his way of taking digs at me to get Mom going. Sure enough, she picked up the thread like the obedient lap dog she was and ran with it.

"Oh yes, Rapunzel, you should stop by more often. This sneaking in the middle of the night stuff is not good behavior for a young lady. I know you're 23 now, but people talk, you know. Can you imagine what they would say if they knew? Heavens, I can't even think about it!" She fanned herself, her hysterics a show for no one. "Come, dear, Gertrude has the brunch ready."

Father leveled me a pointed look before he took Mom's arm and strode out of the room. Exhaling for the first time since I arrived, I slumped down onto the desk for a moment to calm myself. Every ounce of me hated being back in this house, but until I could prove what my father was doing, I had to endure it. For Gothel, I would. She needed me.

"Rapunzel!"

You'd think someone so refined wouldn't shout for their daughter through the house. It was in times like these I wish I could wear a costume as well. When I was someone else, I was braver. I didn't have to be *this* version of myself. I hated this version.

Rapunzel was weak, naive, and, most of all, a *coward*.

"Just turn a little for me, dear. Oh yes, like that. Perfect. Okay, can I get you to drop the strap over your shoulder for me?"

"Like this?" I asked, pushing down the strap holding up my leotard. It was a weird request, puzzling me, but he was a photographer and a good friend of Daddy's. So if he wanted this, then it must be for a good reason.

"No, let me show you," he sighed, and I felt terrible for wasting his time, hoping he didn't complain to Daddy.

Giovani walked over and started to "fix" my pose. His hands caressed slowly over my shoulders, and I tensed, not liking how it felt. His palms were rough, and he did it in a way that made me feel weird. He stood behind me closely, pressing himself into me as he positioned me into an assemblé. Something, maybe in his pocket, brushed against my butt. It felt strange, but I ignored it.

His breath was hot as it fanned across my neck, and it smelled of onions. I didn't like this but was too nervous to ask him to step back. I knew how much this was costing Daddy, the favors he got for me to do this. I didn't want to let him down. I would be brave and just breathe through it. I could do anything if I just breathed, I believed.

"Like this," he breathed, running his calloused hand up my front, between my breasts, and over my shoulder. It felt odd for him to go that direction, but again, I didn't want to question him for fear he'd stop the shoot. I felt the

hard thing again at my back as he pushed himself into me more.

"Thank you," I started, hoping it would make him go.

"Anytime, precious."

He moved his hand down over the other side of me, and this time, he lingered on my small breast, and I became uncomfortable. His breath was stale, and he pulled me to him more, making the hardness I felt rub against me. I'd tried to hold it in, but a whimper escaped me, and I wanted to do more than run from the room and never return.

"Now, be a good girl and give me what Daddy promised. You don't want to make him mad."

Squeezing my eyes shut tight, I focused on the dance piece I'd been working on this afternoon. I blocked out the photographer and his touches that I didn't like. I blocked out the way it made me feel. Mostly, I blocked out how he'd said my dad had promised him something from me.

Gathering my courage, I walked out of my father's office and headed to the dining room. It was time for the world's fakest brunch to commence—at least there were scones.

"**R**apunzel, dear, how is school?"

Swallowing the juice in front of me, I quickly wiped my mouth with my napkin. It never failed. Queenie would always ask me questions when I had something in my mouth. I guess it was a good thing she didn't know what I did for a living, or she'd surely pop her head into the break room mid-blowie and cause me to gag on a dick and die.

I could see it now. *"Here lies Rapunzel. Even mid gag, she didn't use her teeth."*

Yeah, I didn't really want to be known for that.

"School is school," I mumbled, the crushing sense of all my mistakes weighed on me in this room. The smells, the noises, and the familiar decor did nothing for my PTSD. Every moment I was back in this house, my body and mind waged war over flight and freeze. There was no fight when it came to Kingston Sonne.

My father's unrelenting gaze fell on me, and I swallowed again—this time out of fear. Picking up my fork, I fiddled with it to avoid his eyes. We had an agreement. I got to pretend to go to school for Mom's sake, but I could never speak of the horrors I've witnessed. At the time I'd made the deal, it had been the freedom I wanted, but now, it was the ever-tightening noose around my neck and weight pressing down on my shoulders that made me question if it was even worth it anymore.

"That's good, dear. How is the ballet coming along? Will you be cast in any upcoming productions?" Queenie asked before placing the world's smallest bite in her mouth.

Stirring the food on my plate in a circle, I distractedly answered, "I'm not sure."

"Oh, Kingston, this won't do! You need to speak with that director and make sure Rapunzel is getting her chance! How he doesn't see her potential is criminal! This will not do," she started to mutter, shaking her head. "I think it's time you enrolled at a new school if he isn't ever going to give you a chance."

Fear bubbled up my throat, and I quickly searched my brain for a way to dissolve this. I couldn't have Mom calling the school and demanding to speak to fake people! Before I even knew what I was saying, I'd popped my head up, and the lies spilled from my lips.

"Oh, no, Mom, that won't be necessary. I didn't want to say anything, but I think I will be the next principal dancer, and it's going to be Swan Lake. I just, you know, I'm nervous and felt if I said anything, it would jinx it. So, please, please, keep it to yourself, and don't interfere, or it might get taken away."

I'd spoken so fast, unaware of what I'd said until it was out there in the room. Mom looked pleased and mimed zipping her lips, but my father had a calculating look on his face, and I didn't want to question it. Nothing good ever came from *that* look.

Thankfully, Mom turned the conversation over to lilies and which family in Tiara Heights was doing better than other families. Naturally, the Sonne's were at the top. Being Mayor did have its privileges. *It was the unspoken ones you had to be wary of.*

I swallowed more juice, unable to touch my food as I debated how I would get out of this mess. Perhaps, I could tell her I didn't get it? Or maybe I'd fake an injury? I had to minimize the chance she'd look into this, or the blowback would be unmanageable. When Mom had taken her requisite ten tiny bites of food, and Father was satiated, he motioned for the dishes to be taken away—damn if anyone else was ready.

My mandatory once a month brunch was almost finished, allowing me to return back to my sanctuary. The thought lifted a smile to my face for the first time in a while. Despite being angry with Nix and fearful of ruining my secret, I felt the safest at The Tower than I had in a long time. Safety was a luxury. Safety was a privilege. Safety was the difference between life and death.

My shoulders relaxed as my plate was taken, and I looked longingly at the food. Typically, I couldn't get enough of the gourmet meals the chef made and would scarf it down despite the unease I felt in the room. Today's leftovers confirmed my anxiety, but also the availability of frequent meals. The Tower was changing my life in ways I hadn't considered when I applied there.

"Dear, it was lovely to see you. I don't like only getting to see you once a month," Queenie pouted. It was hard for me to take her words at face value. She sounded sincere about missing me, a skill I was certain she perfected over the years living with my father. But the blankness in her eyes, the slight tremor in her hand, reminded me I wasn't the only one under his control.

Mom drowned herself in Chardonnay and pills making her oblivious to the goings on in this house. She was about due for her dose of mind-numbing bliss if the shake was any indication of her withdrawal. I used to feel sorry for her, but once I understood her own compliance in things, that emotion had evaporated.

Queenie Sonne wasn't dumb. She knew the true monster sleeping next to her in bed, and yet, she chose to turn her head and allow it. The life of living as the Mayor's wife was more important to her than her daughter's wellbeing. Diamonds and pearls were an easy distraction from the abuse perpetrated here, especially if she never asked where they came from.

Queenie liked the lifestyle and therefore had become just as guilty in my book. There was no world where I could forgive her for allowing the things that happened to me to occur. So, why did I ingratiate myself in this charade once a month? Mother Gothel.

I'd been led to believe a lie, but the woman who'd kidnapped me had been a better parent than the fucking Mayor of Sinhaven. I'd tried to run back to her once, but I'd been caught. It had been a stupid, impulsive decision and had tipped my hand to Kingston Sonne to what I truly cared about. He used it along with dance to get me to bend to his will, and it worked.

"Yeah, I know, Mom. But you know how college is, and if I want to be a principal dancer, I have to focus. No time for outside distractions."

"You're going to be a star," she proclaimed, patting my cheek. Pulling away from her clammy hand, I started to make my way toward the door in an attempt to escape. If I could just get out of here, then I'd avoid—

"Sweetheart, I'd like to see you in my office before you leave. I've also left some things for you in your room. You should get them before heading out."

His words were basic, but the fear they instilled

in me was intense. Nodding, I headed to the stairs instead and made my way to my bedroom. My whole body shook by the time I reached it, and I had to pause against the wall to stop myself from passing out. I hated this house and the girl I'd become here. Mostly, I hated feeling this way.

Slowly, I crept along until I reached my door and turned the knob. My room looked the same as usual, with various shades of pink taffeta thrown about. When I'd been rescued, I'd been so excited to have my own space. I couldn't wait to make it a ballerina one. Now, I thought it looked more like the insides of a cotton candy machine than the ideal room for a girl. It fitted that the decor resembled Pepto Bismol because it made me want to hurl every time I stepped foot into it.

Laying on my bed was a large white box with a red ribbon. Most girls would be excited to receive pretty things. Most girls didn't have to lose their dignity just to survive. The man this gift was from, he never wanted simple things. No, he wanted everything from me.

With trembling fingers, I unwrapped the bow and lifted the lid off the box. Inside was a beautiful gown of blue silk. I ran my fingers over the fabric, and for a moment, I imagined being a princess and wearing this dress. I imagined the ball or dinner I'd wear this to and the gentlemen callers I'd have. Music played in my head and I swayed to it. For a brief second... I could almost picture *that* girl.

A noise in the distance pulled me from my brief daydream, and reality crashed into me. *I would never be that girl.*

"Rapunzel, darling, how did your photoshoot go?"

My father leaned against the door as he studied me, a crease in his brow. I could see him in the reflection of the mirror I was sitting in front of as I brushed my hair. I'd lost count of how long I'd been doing it. It was something Mother had done, and I'd always found it soothing.

Placing the hairbrush onto the vanity, I slowly turned on the bench seat. My eyes were downcast as I gathered my words.

"Sweetheart, what is it? What's troubling you?"

The concern in his voice filled me with hope, and I caved to his questions. Blinking back the tears that had gathered in my eyes, I looked up to my father, hoping he would save me. I didn't know if I should say anything. I didn't want to cause problems, but at his tone, I felt safe and that he would protect me.

"Daddy, the man… he wasn't very nice. He, um, he, um," I choked back the sob that threatened to come up my throat. If I said the words, they became real.

My father sat on the corner of the bed, a look of concern on his face. "Oh, sweetheart, what is it? What happened? Did he not take the pictures like he was supposed to?"

"He did… it's just, um… well, when he, um, he kind of, um, you know," I mumbled. I dropped my head

again and began to fiddle with the hem of my nightgown as I twisted it in my hands.

"Rapunzel, sweetheart, look at me." His tone was firm but caring, so I found the courage to look up.

"Yes, Daddy?"

"Did this man touch… you?" He struggled to get out the words, and I felt safe finally, to tell the truth.

"Yes, Daddy. He touched me."

"Oh, sweetheart. I'm so sorry. Come here."

My father pulled me into his arms and rubbed my back as I cried. His soothing sounds comforted me, and a few minutes later, when I'd finished crying, he handed me a handkerchief to blow my nose.

"I'll take care of it, sweetheart."

At that time, I thought my father was my hero, and I fell asleep feeling protected and cared for. I had no clue the biggest snake in the garden was the one I'd invited into it.

Knocking on his door, I shuffled my feet as I waited for my father to tell me to enter. My hope to leave after brunch had been dashed, and I knew this would be a visit where a request was demanded of me. I hated these requests, and lately, they were more and more.

"Enter."

I braced myself as I twisted the knob of my father's study. Kingston Sonne was sitting behind his enormous cherry desk, a proper king on his throne. The Mayor's name plate sat forefront for all to see in case anyone forgot who they were meeting with.

"Rapunzel, please, take a seat."

He motioned to the leather chair in front of him, and I walked over with my head low. Each minute I was in his presence felt like a part of my soul was being sucked out. Sitting down, I crossed my legs at the ankle and placed my hands delicately in my lap. Keeping my head bowed, I waited until he called on me.

I'd like to say it was by choice, but I, unfortunately, had been conditioned at this point. I heard a sigh and the placement of his tumbler as he sat it down on the coaster. The crystal glass clinked against one another, creating a sharp but all too familiar sound.

"You're slipping. *You* choose to leave and live your life however the hell you do. And I agreed as long as you kept up your end. We made a bargain, a *deal*. But your mom, she's starting to not buy your lies anymore." He leaned forward on his desk, bracing his hands together. "You remember what happened last time? Do you want to go back down that path? I can call up the doctors and have a room ready for you. I'm not sure your mom would survive it this time. I'm afraid her dosage seems to be increasing with each week she doesn't see you. Queenie, well, she's a fragile creature, and there's no telling what might send her over that cliff."

The threat was clear as he laid into me. My head was still lowered, but I could feel the intensity of his eyes on me. My fingernails pressed into my legs as I tried to calm my racing heart. After a quiet moment, he continued.

"Now, I could always share with her what her daughter is really doing, but she's still useful to me at this point, so I'd prefer not to have to go through the trouble. But hear me when I say this, Rapunzel, if you don't hold up your end of our agreement, then I'll have to find new ways to incentivize you."

I sucked in a breath at the statement because, at this point, what else was there to take? Lifting my head, I stared into the eyes of a man I'd once believed cared about me. Now, I saw the darkness that lurked in his depths. The true man that operated beyond the shadows.

"I-I-I-I—"

"Jesus Christ, Rapunzel! Fucking spit it out! Your simpering nonsense is a waste of my time."

"Yes, Father," I dropped my eyes to his desk, unable to hold his glare for long periods. "I'll make Mom understand. I'll do better. You don't need to incentivize me," I pleaded.

"I'll decide that, daughter. Now, did you get the dress that was picked out for you?"

Nodding, I cringed when I realized my mistake. A fist slammed down on the desk, and I jumped, knowing it was my fault. Father didn't like it when I nodded. He wanted, no, *demanded* words.

"Sorry, Daddy. Yes, I saw the dress."

"You know what to do. I expect you to meet the client's expectations. He's becoming impatient and won't let you dismiss him much longer." The sneer he leveled me with could cut glass, it was so sharp. Father didn't understand my avoidance of his *friend* and only allowed me to refuse if I did other things. It looked like that option had finally run out.

"No more mishaps or the freedom you so love will be taken, and the druggie mothers you protect will meet their ends. I can lock you back up, and no one would be able to find you this time. Hell, no one would even miss you, would they?" A twisted smile played on his lips as he pierced me with his words. "Do we have an understanding?"

"Yes, Daddy."

"Good. Now, make sure you bid a farewell to your mom on your way out. I'll be waiting to hear from you."

With that, I jumped out of the chair and ran to the door as I bolted for the front. When I was sixteen, I thought I made a bold choice when I ran away. I'd finally gotten up the nerve to leave. Not only had that set his sights on Gothel, filling her with drugs and addictions, but it landed me in a psychiatric ward for a month when I tried to tell the cops what my father was doing.

At eighteen, I was desperate and struck a bargain with the devil. I'd jumped at it, thinking it was the way out. Yet, with each passing day, his ownership of me tightened, and the one thing I'd held onto for myself slipped away—my pride.

I thought for once, I could choose for myself, and perhaps, it wouldn't hurt as much if it was mine. I prided myself on being strong and independent, on being good at something I could make a living from.

But what was the point of pride when you learned it was all a facade?

CHAPTER ELEVEN

WESLEY

Tonight would be the first time I would come face to face with the illustrious Zel. I'd started to feel like a major stalker with the amount of creeping I was doing from the shadows. I'd even watched her meeting with Isaac, my assistant, on video from the room next door, memorizing her movements.

Each night she danced, I found myself in the shadows as well, not trusting myself to sit at a table for fear I wouldn't be able to stop myself from inter-acting with her. There was no doubt she was beauti-ful, but there was something kindred about her that drew me in. Her dancing alone held me captive, and my brain hadn't stopped choreographing numbers for us together in my head.

The inspiration I was feeling from her was off the charts. That alone had made me obsessed. When I added all the other hauntingly beautiful things about her, I found myself utterly captivated by her. Every time he caught me watching, Nix smiled at me, but he hadn't said anything to my face. *Yet.*

I knew he had a thing for her, and if the sounds coming from his room this week were anything to go by, he had succeeded in his pursuit of her. Part of me felt terrible for obsessing over her when I knew his feelings, but it wouldn't be the first time we liked the same girl. Only, it had never been serious before, just a passing fancy, and it seemed his feelings for Zel were more than that.

My watch buzzed, and I shut my brain down, knowing my pondering time was over and I had work to do. Walking into Consumption's kitchen, the noises of pans and dishes echoed off the walls as I searched for the new chef featured this week. Spotting her petite frame bent over a plate, I beelined to her.

"Gloria!"

At the sound of her name, the motherly woman peeked her head up and gave me a huge smile. "Wesley, how good to see you, boy."

Her use of boy didn't offend me since I'd known her all my life. Gloria Cortez was the closest thing to a grandmother I've ever known. She owned a restaurant in the town I grew up in, and it had become a second home for me. My mother and I would dine there at least once a week, and Gloria had taken me under her wing after her death. When I was home on breaks, she would teach me a new skill and cultivated my enjoyment of good food. I'd been trying to get her to come to The Tower since we opened, and she'd finally agreed.

"What are you working on?"

"Ah, this is my newest creation. It's a banana chocolate peanut butter cake."

"Mmm, that sounds delicious." I inhaled the chocolatey fragrance before looking at her closely as I tried to assess her. "How do you like your room? The kitchen staff treating you well?"

She finished up her piping and turned to me. Patting me on the cheek, she set off in a different direction. This was classic Gloria. She was a firecracker and constantly on the move. Following her, I watched as she checked dishes, grabbed spices, and stirred pots as she walked by. The woman could operate a kitchen unlike anyone I'd ever met before.

Once she'd crossed the entire length of the kitchen, she headed into the little office and motioned for me to follow. I dismissed her ordering me around and the fact I was technically her boss. Gloria Cortez did what Gloria Cortez wanted, and there was nothing I could say that would sway her. I learned long ago to go with it.

Sitting down in the chair, I waited until she had herself sorted, figuring she wanted to tell me something if we were in the office.

"The room is lovely, Wesley, and this kitchen is a masterpiece. You've done well."

Her words had me beaming with pride,

meaning the world to me. "Thank you, Gloria. I'm glad to have you here. It's the culmination of all my hard work coming full circle."

"How are *you* settling in, dear?"

Her words took me by surprise causing me to scrunch my face in confusion. "I don't understand."

"I know things haven't been easy with your father. People in town gossip, dear, and it's known he sent you away to deal with Sinhaven to get you out of his way," she paused, checking how I took her words. "But despite him casting you aside, you've turned this place into something amazing and made this a home. I know you intended only to stay a year, but what if you didn't leave?"

"I… I don't know how to answer that. Come in, make it worth something, and leave has always been the plan. I've done it numerous times now. Why change?"

"Well, it seems this place is different. You've put more of you into this one than ever before. I see your touches all over the place, and I think you could be happy here. From what I gather from all the people who work for you, you're a good boss and treat them well. This place is a success because you make it a success."

Sitting back, I weighed her words in my mind. I didn't know how I felt about setting down roots. Since Nix had come on board with me, we'd traveled from place to place, and it worked for us. But was she right? Could I stay here? It was my favorite of all the places I'd taken over. It was the first one I'd included dance, so maybe she had a point. Regardless, I couldn't think about that now.

"It doesn't matter right now. But thank you for coming. I'm glad to have finally enticed the amazing Gloria Cortez to my establishment."

"Well, it seemed the right time." She grinned, letting me drop the subject I didn't want to talk about at the moment.

We delved into a casual conversation and caught up on things back home. After a few minutes, I brought up the dinner tonight, and we finalized the menu. Maybe this dinner was an opportunity to test the waters about staying. Typically, I met with buyers to sell to once we vacated the premises, but what if, instead of buyers, I bought it? I could be free from my father and his control once and for all.

Excitement bubbled in me, but I pushed it down. I couldn't afford to get too excited about it when nothing solid was established. I still needed this investment dinner to go well. I was hoping that it would be an evening no one forgot with the entertainment I had lined up. With Gloria's food and the dancers' skills, it was bound to be spectacular.

Hugging Gloria tight, I left the kitchen, nodding at a few workers as I did. The restaurant wasn't open yet since it was Sunday, but I could already see the line outside the doors. It would be filled to the brim in an hour, and my mind whirled with the thought of having all of this as *mine*.

Freedom would come at a high price, and I didn't know what I might have to sacrifice to obtain it, but the pride I had in this place might be worth it.

I was adjusting my tie when Nix knocked on my door. Peering at him in the mirror over my shoulder, I took in his expression, and unease filled me.

"What is it? Did you give Zel my message?" His grimace deepened at the sound of her name.

"Yeah, though she wasn't pleased about it," he mumbled, casting his eyes down.

Finishing with my tie, I turned to take in my best friend. "What aren't you telling me?" I folded my arms as I leaned back against the dresser. Nix wasn't one to keep things from me, so this reaction was odd.

Sighing, he looked up at me, anxiety coating his features. "I just have a weird feeling. Something is going on with Zel, and it felt like she closed herself off from me when I left this morning. I haven't been able to find her since."

Nix's words raced through my head. I couldn't lose her yet; I just found her. Ignoring the thought, I began to formulate a plan and weigh the options. "Have you checked the cameras?"

"Not yet. I was hoping she would show up before I had to resort to it, wanting to give her space."

I pretended to understand his response, and I wasn't sure if my first jump to invade her privacy meant I was more of a stalker than I wanted to admit. Walking over to the desk in my bedroom, I flipped the laptop open and tapped on the camera icon to bring all the security feeds up.

"What time did you talk to her?"

"Early, around 8 or 9 this morning."

Scrolling, I started at 8 am and slowed until I found Nix at her door. I watched her facial expression as he talked to her go from fun and inviting to closed off and guarded. He hadn't been wrong about his perception, despite not wanting to admit it.

"What exactly did you say to her?" I asked while scrolling through more to find when she left her room. About thirty minutes later, she left, covered up and took the stairs.

"I honestly don't know. We were flirting, and she invited me in, but I admitted I couldn't because I was delivering your message."

I watched her progression down the stairs and out the back door as I turned over his words. "What did you say exactly was my message? Did you say it as my *guest* or as a dancer?"

Peering up, I watched as Nix's face bunched up, and he scratched the shaved side of his head in thought. Glancing back down at the laptop, I noted the time she exited The Tower. She took off from there on foot, and I could only track her for a few minutes after. Once she was free of the building, I couldn't determine the direction. It looked like she was on her own, but it didn't mean she wasn't meeting up with anyone.

Scolding myself, I pushed away the thought of her meeting up with someone and the surge of possession that reared up. I hadn't even talked to this woman, and yet I was quickly becoming obsessed with her to the point of envy.

"I think I asked her to be there. She said something about needing you to ask her yourself if you wanted her there. Then the door was slammed in my face, and I've spent the last five hours worrying over that damn girl," he admitted. Nix's whole body deflated, and he sank into a chair across from my desk.

"You care for her?"

"Yeah, I do."

"How do you feel… about me asking her then?" I managed to stumble out.

Nix lifted his eyes at my question, and he looked at me as my friend. There wasn't jealousy or anger anywhere in his expression. "Wes, the fact you're asking me tells me everything I need to know."

"How do you mean?"

"When you figure that out, you'll know. Did you find her?" he asked, switching the conversation.

"It shows her leaving not long after, but I don't think she's returned yet. Tell the guards to radio as soon as someone spots her, and I'll figure something out about this evening."

"On it," he said, his confidence returning now that there was a plan in place.

"Nix… what would you think about staying here? Putting down roots for once?"

He paused at the door, looking at me over his shoulder, a smile on his face. "I'd say it's the best idea you've ever had, you know, outside of befriending me, of course."

Settling back, I grinned at his words and thought more about what it would be like to stay. I didn't hate the idea. In fact, I think it was becoming a reality. I pulled out my ledger, and I made some notes on figures I would need to secure this place from my father. The total was less than I'd imagined. It would be tight for a few months, but it was doable if The Tower continued to perform as it was.

Putting everything away, I headed down to the Desire. It was closed tonight to the members and open only for my invited guests. We were dining in a room that had been converted to mimic a small banquet hall with an elegant table and a smaller stage area. There was a separate bar and kitchen that had a dum waiter to pass things back and forth.

It would be the first time we'd used it, but for our guests tonight, I'd wanted the all-star treatment.

The room was decked out in maroon and gold accents and had a very opulent feel about it. It always gave me the vibe of an old jazz club or speakeasy. Waiters and waitresses passed me as I checked on the table and preparations. Now that I had other intentions for this place, this dinner meant even more. Everything could change tonight, and excitement filled me at the prospect.

An hour later, I spotted Nix at the doorway, and I left the event planner to see if he had news of Zel.

"Have you found her?"

"Yes, I just received notice that she was spotted entering the building and should be on her way to her room now. Do you want me to talk to her again?"

I could see the eagerness on his face, and knowing how things had ended between them last time, I should have let him, but something about her words struck me, and I wanted to do this myself.

"I'll do it."

Nix didn't reply but nodded and took his post by the door. Inhaling, I took a deep calming breath as I walked to the other side of the third floor. I didn't know why I was so nervous, but something about her made me feel off-kilter. Pausing outside her temporary room, I listened to see if I could hear anything inside. It was quiet, but that didn't mean much. Raising my fist, I was about to knock when a voice halted me from the left.

"Can I help you?"

As I turned my head, I took in the woman and knew it was Zel in a new costume. However, she had gone to the extreme this time with her makeup giving herself extravagant cat eyes and lipstick, causing me almost not to recognize her. I realized I'd been staring for an obscene amount of time when she cleared her throat.

Everything about her was off. She was harsher than expected in her stance and outfit. Her eyes were more guarded, and she looked like she wanted to stab me with her stiletto. Clearing my throat, I braced myself for the backlash of my secret. Suddenly, it had felt like a truly horrible idea to keep my identity anonymous.

"Miss Tress, we haven't had the pleasure of meeting officially yet. I'm Wesley Flynn, the owner of The Tower."

Her face dropped for a moment before she put the hardness back in place. "Funny, you don't look like the man I met at my interview."

She moved in front of me and unlocked her door with a keycard, and held it open after she entered for me. Straightening my jacket, I tugged at my cuffs as I entered her space.

"You'll have to excuse the ruse. I've just found it's easier to get a true sense of people if they don't know who I am at first. The man you did your interview with, my decoy, works for me in the casino, an aspiring actor."

"Hmm. I find it very disconcerting you go to these extremes to deceive others of who you really are. What type of person am I working for? Do you have something you're hiding?"

I was confused by her line of questions, and it took me a few seconds to reply, probably making me look guilty. "Of course not, Miss Tress. I pride myself on having the best, and that goes beyond their ability to perform their job. I want the people who work for me to be good people as well and hold my standards. That's all, nothing untoward or scandalous here."

"And what did you find out about *me*?"

Something flipped in her, and she moved closer to me, trailing her hands up my chest. I could smell her perfume of roses this close, and it was intoxicating, making my senses misfire with her touch. "That not only are you an exceptional dancer but that you're nice to guests and staff."

"Is that all?" she purred into my ear, and I had to stop myself from grabbing her and fucking her right there on the table. I'd never been so close to losing control nor so tempted to start anything with my staff. Zel pushed me out of my comfort zone in many ways, and I didn't know how to handle it. My hand fumbled for my wrist, and once I made contact, I snapped my rubber band hard, effectively pulling me out of the downward spiral I was headed.

Stepping out of her pathway, I straightened myself as I addressed her. "I believe everything else I need to know is up to you. Nix conveyed that when he extended my invitation to dine with me tonight, you declined unless I asked myself. So, I'm here to inquire if you would be my guest to a VIP dinner I'm hosting."

She watched me curiously, and I wasn't confident what her answer would be. I hadn't felt this unsure about women since I was a teenager, but I kept my face stoic, not letting myself show any weakness.

"As your *date*? Not as the entertainment?"

"Date in a sense, yes. What you decide regarding entertainment is up to you as I would never tell you what you're allowed to do. But no, in an official capacity, I'm not asking you to dance for them, just to accompany me. I'd like to get to know you more and thought this was a perfect opportunity."

She studied me before answering, and it was the longest few seconds in the history of time.

"Then I accept," she nodded. "Thank you for asking. What is the dress code?"

"It's formal. I had something picked out for you if you're interested?" My words caused her face to pale, and I didn't understand what I'd said.

"No, I have something. What time should I be ready?"

"Well, it's in an hour. Is that enough time?"

"I'll be ready."

She ushered me out the door, and I stood there for a second, wondering what the hell had happened. My control was utterly gone. Zel Tress was a tornado in high heels, and she'd effectively twisted up my insides into a raging vortex. I wasn't sure if I would survive or if I even wanted to— she'd be the sweetest chaos.

CHAPTER TWELVE

NIX

When Wesley returned to the ballroom, I couldn't make any emotion out on his face on how his encounter with Zel had gone. I'd been panicking since I left her room this morning, kicking myself for turning her down. My PTSD had roared to life, and I'd been beating myself up all afternoon. It'd been like the flip of a switch, and I watched the girl I was falling for completely shut me out, returning to the zombie version of herself I'd first met.

I didn't know if I could go back to that. Not after holding her in my arms or feeling my cock swell in her. Not after I knew how she tasted on my tongue and the sounds she made. No, I had to fix this. I had to find a way to break through to her. I wouldn't let whatever we have end like this. I couldn't let another person down. It hit too close to home to my failures as a soldier and reminded me why I didn't open up to people. But Zel was different and worth pushing through my bullshit.

I wasn't used to feeling this passionate about something or someone. From my first sexual experience until now, they'd all been a transactional exchange, a way to pass the time and blow off steam. I enjoyed sex as much as the next person, but I'd never done the relationship thing. Wes and I had tried once, but it had been an utter failure, strengthening my resolve to keep things casual.

Zel, in her dynamic way, captured something new in me. At first, I was captivated by the dancer and the passion she wove. Then I'd become intrigued by the person she was and the life she lived. Zel didn't make sense to me, and the puzzle kept me watching her until I realized I watched for more than just that reason alone.

I'd become entranced by her, trapped in her thrall, but I didn't want to be released. It only made me want her more. Now that I'd cracked some of her exterior, I was more sunk than ever. I didn't care that Wes seemed just as obsessed as me either. If anything, I understood it. He was my best friend, and sharing things with him was natural with us. We'd been sharing our lives longer than we hadn't. If Zel could make him happy as well, I'd be even more content.

That was if she didn't ice me out.

Something was bothering me about this morning, and I couldn't put my finger on what it was. Unfortunately, my time to explore it was over, and I had to focus. The investors would be showing up

soon, and I needed to review things with my security. Heading to the main office, I nodded to the guy
at the door, communicating to keep things stable
until I returned.

We had extra people coming in for this dinner
to ensure the best coverage throughout The Tower.
These dinners were always stressful as Wes weaved
them a story and made them want our operation
more than the next guy. I had a feeling tonight
might go a little differently, if he genuinely wanted
to stay this time.

I hadn't ever wanted to stay before. We'd done
this song and dance many times, and this was the
first one where it felt more than just a stopping
place. The business here was different, as well as the
employees, and overall, this town felt welcoming.
For the first time, it seemed possible to have an
actual home. Maybe it was the water here because I
wanted to stay.

I wanted Zel in my life, and I wanted to put
down roots.

Stepping into the command center, I found the
four guards I'd picked for tonight: Sara, Rick, Cole,
and Roy sitting around a small table. They lifted
their heads when I entered, straightening up as I
walked over.

"Boss," the kissass, Rick, greeted. I nodded, not
wanting to encourage him. He was my least
favorite, but all in all, still a good guard if I could
dislodge him from my ass.

"Thank you all for coming in for this dinner. I'll be brief but wanted to go over the importance."

They nodded, and I watched as Roy tried to soak in everything. When I told him about this place and offered him a job, I thought he would kiss me with happiness. Getting out of The Pan and Dante's Circle had been a life-changing event for him. I liked him, but I didn't want the hero worship he seemed to have for me recently. *I wasn't a hero, not even close.*

"We'll be in a smaller room, making it easier to guard. There shouldn't be any weapons entering, but be on the lookout. These are businessmen, but they may have their own security. Between the food, the booze, and the girls, the evening should be an easy one. But don't let your guard down because that's when people get killed."

At that, they all swallowed. I was trying to scare them a little, but maybe I'd gone too far. *Nah.* They needed to understand the environment they were walking into. These men and women might be decked out in thousand-dollar clothes, but it didn't mean they were good people. If Wesley's dad was anything to go by, they were worse.

Reviewing their positions and times, I left them to finish up before heading to the floor. Deciding to attempt resolving whatever weirdness was between Zel and me, I headed to her room, a small token in my pocket. I'd gotten it the other day on a whim, but I didn't know when to give it to her. It wasn't like there was an app for hopeless men like me on when to bring up sentimental shit.

Exhaling, I braced myself for her hostility. I wasn't letting her dismiss me this time. Knocking on her door, I was surprised when she opened it quickly. Her smile dropped when she saw me, and I realized she must've thought I was Wes. Shoving away the envy, I focused on my girl.

Leaning my arm on the top of the doorframe, I gave my best smoldering look. "*Princess*, I think we need to talk."

"I have nothing to say to you."

"That's where I disagree."

"Nix—"

"I like it when you say my name," I growled, stepping into her space. Her breath hitched, and I took my chance, hoping it meant I still affected her. Grabbing her face with my hands, I walked her backward as I crashed my lips onto hers.

She met them greedily and didn't push me away, and I felt my world explode into fireworks. *Zel still wanted me.* The back of her legs hit the table, making the legs wobble as she braced herself. I kept devouring her mouth, wanting to possess her as much as she'd allow. When a gasp left her, I started to trail kisses down her neck.

Part of me wanted to leave my mark, but I knew it wouldn't be good for her if I did. Instead, I traveled further to the top of her dress. I hadn't taken time to appreciate her before, but pulling back a little now, I saw how breathtaking she looked.

Zel whimpered a little when I stopped, but I couldn't help it—she stopped my heart in this dress. It was black, my favorite, and played the line she loved so much between class and seduction. Lace covered her body from her breasts to her ankles with short sleeves on the side. Trailing my hands down her back, I found that it was open, and I groaned out at the thought.

Her skin peeked through the lace holes in the places the slip didn't cover. It was sexy as fuck, and I wanted to rip it right off her. She'd regained her composure in the time it took me to drool over her and put a hand on my chest when it looked like I might rip it off.

"Nope. Gonna stop you right there, big guy. I can't have you destroying all this. Besides, I haven't decided if I'm still upset with you or not."

"Ah, I knew it. Zel, I wasn't trying to reject you or turn you away. You're all I've thought about all day, months if I'm honest. You have to know how much I like you?"

It was the most vulnerable I'd ever been with a woman, and I prayed she wouldn't metaphorically kick me in the balls for it. I saw her soften a little, and I felt like it was now or never. Reaching into my pocket, I pulled out the small antique mirror I'd found the other day. It was an odd thing to give a girl, but something about it made me think of her, and so I bought it.

"I got you something," I mumbled, suddenly finding the floor fascinating.

"You got me something?"

The shock was evident in her voice, and it knocked all my own insecurity away. Zel sounded as if she'd never been given something before. Surely that couldn't be, right? Slowly, I opened my palm and placed it in her hand.

"I know it's an odd thing to give you. But I was in some shop the other day and saw it, and I don't know, it just drew me to it and reminded me of you. I felt like I had to get it for you. Do you like it?"

I watched as she delicately opened the clasp of the mirror and looked inside. One side of the glass was cracked, but the other was still in good shape. She closed it back and traced the design on the outside of the compact. It was cream with gold entwined throughout. There was even a little tiara with a heart on it in the middle.

"I love it."

Zel's words were soft, but they traveled all the way to my heart. Lifting her chin, I wiped a tear that sat on her cheek.

"I'm glad. Can I see you later, princess?"

I held my breath as I waited for her answer. She seemed to search my eyes for something before coming to a resolution. Slowly, she nodded, a tiny smile coming to her lips. Leaning down again, I placed a soft kiss, relishing in the feel of her. When she wasn't fighting me, I got to be gentle and sweet with her. I was starting to believe she needed both.

"I um, have that dinner with Mr. Flynn."

"I know, princess."

"You're not upset?"

"No, princess. I promise to tell you more later. How much longer until he arrives?"

She glanced behind me at the clock on the wall before answering. "I'd say no more than ten minutes. Why?"

"Perfect. I have time to do this."

I mischievously grinned, picking her up before she could ask what, and laid her back on the table. Pushing her dress up her legs, I watched as she caught on, her breasts moving with each excited inhale.

"Won't he hear?"

"Even better."

Dropping to the ground, I rested her knee on my shoulder and started to suck the fabric of her panties. They were, of course, lace as well and barely anything. Licking up her front, I teased her pussy with my tongue as she began to buck up into my mouth. Pushing them to the side, I quickly licked up some of her sweet juices and flicked my tongue against her clit.

I wanted to worship her, but I knew I didn't have time for that now. Instead, I'd make do with having her orgasm on my tongue and leave her wanting more for later. Without warning, I pushed a thick finger into her tight pussy and sucked her clit. Her moans filled the room, and I knew if Wesley were close, he'd be able to hear.

The thought of him listening at the door spurred me on, and I wanted everyone to know how much I pleased her. Quicker now, I plunged my finger in, coating myself with her. Tilting my finger up, I twisted it as I kept rotating it in and out. She was dripping her wetness all over me, and I wished it was my cock as I watched my finger slide out.

"Oh, yes, fuck, Nix," Zel moaned, making me feel like a million bucks.

For once, she was the one getting pleasure instead of giving it to others. The realization that I wanted to provide her with everything hit me as I felt her start to tighten around me as I plunged deeper.

Licking up her wetness in one long trail, I flicked my tongue around her clit before sucking it into my mouth. Like I knew it would, the minute I'd wrapped my lips around her magic button, she detonated around me. I felt her muscles tensing as I slowly pulled out my fingers.

Leaning back, I sucked the digits into my mouth as she panted on the table in a complete mess. As her last moan died in the room, a knock sounded on the door in almost perfect timing. Before she could protest, I pulled the lace thong off her and shoved it in my pocket. I helped her straighten her dress and steady herself as she stood. Zel was smiling at me, and I felt I'd at least helped her relax before she had to endure the boring dinner ahead of her.

"Grab your shoes and whatever. I'll get the door."

I pushed her in the direction of her bed and bathroom, and she easily walked. Zel was still boneless and too blissed out to argue, making her agreeable to my demand. Heading to the door, I straightened my clothes as well despite having no doubt Wes knew what had been going down in here.

Pulling it open, I found a smug Wes waiting. "Marking your territory?"

"Why would I do something like that? Besides, there's no territory to mark when I'm the only one playing," I goaded before continuing. "But no, it was more like making amends. She's grabbing her shoes and will be out in a minute."

Turning toward her room, I shouted, "Princess, I'll see you in a bit. Be nice to Wes. He's *delicate*." I chuckled at my words and jumped back to miss him swatting at me.

"Fuck you, asshole," he laughed.

"I can't make it easy on you. What's the fun in that?"

Shaking his head at me, I left him to take care of our girl. Pulling my hardass mask back on, I thought about how that sounded. *Ours*. It didn't scare me like I thought it would. On top of my earlier realization and the fact that Zel had sealed herself to my heart before she even spoke to me, I knew I had to face the facts.

The problem was, as much as I knew I wanted her, as much as I knew I craved her, and as much as I knew I was stupidly falling in love with her... Could I risk it all?

I wanted to. For the first time in my life, it felt worth it. I just had to risk my pride to open myself up for love, battle wounds, and all. What could be so hard about that?

CHAPTER THIRTEEN

ZEL

Swiftly, I ducked into the bathroom and cleaned myself from the orgasmic present Nix had given me. Fixing a few of the hairs that had been ruffled in the back, I smoothed down the short black wig. The black lace dress was still snug on my frame, accentuating all my best parts. It was sexy without being overly revealing and one of my favorites. Popping on some lipstick, I headed back out into the central part of my room.

Wesley was waiting for me when I entered. His head snapped up, and I observed the first honest expression he'd made since knocking on my door. I wanted to be angry with him for deceiving me, but I understood it on a level no one else would. It stung, and I realized how my own behavior would be perceived. Before, it had always been about surviving, which was the only thing I took into consideration. Now, it made me hate part of myself for doing it to others, *especially Nix*. I was starting to believe I could reveal myself to him.

Pushing that away for another time, I took in the man before me. Wesley's eyes glimmered with a sureness I wasn't used to finding in men. He had a type of confidence that was rare in most people I'd met. Wesley had earned his, and the pride radiated off him at his achievements. Based on the success of The Tower and how it was managed, it was well deserved.

His black tuxedo was sharp, and as I prowled closer to him, his eyes followed my every move. Trailing a finger over his shoulder, I walked around him as I pretended to inspect the cut. Stopping in front, I straightened his tie, grazing my fingers over his throat lightly as I did. The gulp he took sent zingers coursing through me at the small gesture. Wesley's eyes zeroed in on me, and I liked how enamored he seemed to be.

"You're the man who watches me from the shadows, aren't you?"

Nodding, he kept watching me, and I basked in the fullness of his attention. Wesley was successful, sophisticated, and refined. Having his attention meant something. Of that, I was positive. I didn't think he was this attentive to all of his employees despite what he said earlier.

"Why do you watch me, *Wesley*?"

"Because when you dance, I feel like I'm dancing too."

There was some pain in his voice, and it wasn't the answer I'd expected. The honesty and vulnerability behind it threw me off, and I found *myself* swallowing this time. Letting go of his tie, I sauntered over to the door, making sure to sway my hips as I went. I needed to regain some control around him. Perhaps doing this on the eve of a family brunch hadn't been my wisest decision.

Locking the thoughts away in a high tower in my mind, I focused on the dinner before me. This date was already in motion, and there was no getting out of it without it costing me something— vulnerability, safety, or worse, pride.

Turning the door handle, I swung it open and peeked over my shoulder. Wesley still stood where he'd been, observing me. I guess my ass gave a good show.

"Coming?" I purred intentionally. Sex was my weapon now, and I wielded it with exact precision. I learned long ago the best way to have power was to take the pain, the fear, and twist it until it no longer hurt you. If you could overcome the part that made you the weakest, nothing else could touch you. Weaving seduction like a long sword, I'd learned this dance the hard way, on the front lines. It would never defeat me again. That was a promise I prided myself on keeping at all costs.

Wesley blinked before regaining his footing. I watched in appreciation as he locked down his emotions and walked toward me. He had a nice walk and filled out his suit well. Wesley wasn't built like Nix, but he was fit, and it showed in each step he took as I watched the fabric shift. He almost looked like he had the body of a dancer and the grace to match it. My mind blanked for a minute as I contemplated that fact.

"Ready, Miss Tress?"

Now it was me who was taken aback as he presented his elbow for me to link mine with. Nodding, I placed my arm in his, and we stepped out of my room. The hallway was empty, as well as the floor. I hadn't noticed the quiet when I was in my room, but everything was eerily silent as we walked.

"I had the floor rented out for the night to host this dinner. We're in a different room, but I wanted everyone to be off if they wanted. Some of the other girls have offered to dance, hence why I didn't mean for you to be a dancer. However, you're a talent above the rest, and I would never stop you from gracing us with your magic."

He smiled, and I was once again off-kilter from the sincerity in his words. In my experience, powerful men were dangerous. They took what they wanted and didn't care how they got it, as long as they did—collateral damage be damned. The worst part was how it was never enough. Once they had one thing, they always wanted more—gluttons for their own success. The danger lay within the greed and envy that knew no bounds. They'd never stop because it would never be enough.

Wesley didn't appear to be that way, bucking

against the stereotype I used to define people. In actuality, he might be the most dangerous of all. I would need to be wary around him until I figured out what his game was—for nothing in power came without some level of sins.

"What is this dinner for?" I asked, attempting to regain my control.

"Originally, it was to set up some buyers for this place."

"And now?" I asked, hearing the hesitancy in his voice.

"Well, now," he turned to look at my face, "Nix and I are thinking of staying. What would you think of that?"

"I think if it's what you want to do, then you should do it." I kept it simple, afraid I'd give away the thrill that went through me at Nix being here long term.

"So if we go that route, then this meeting is about potential investors. Some of Sinhaven's wealthiest people will be in this room."

Cold fear washed over me at the announcement. "Oh? Like who? I've been here my whole life. I can give you some insider information," I hedged, trying to regulate my emotions and grab hold of the panic.

"I don't remember all of their names, my assistant, you know the one who you met. Well, he reached out. This is one of two I have this week."

"Ah, well, perhaps we could have a code word or gesture for me to indicate if someone is shady or of good standing. I'm assuming you'd want to go into business with someone decent, or *maybe* you don't care."

Stopping, he pulled me into a room off to the side, and the darkness descended around us as he braced me up against the wall. His body was close, his smell of bergamot and birch giving him a smoky confidence. He barely pressed into me, but it was enough for my mind to run wild. Wesley's face was so near his hot minty breath fanned around me.

"I do like how you think, Miss Tress, but I find it *curious*, is all. Why would you want to help me?"

"Well, despite your deceiving me, you're the best boss I've worked for, so I want to keep you here," I deflected.

He stared at me hard, not responding. This wasn't something I'd divulge to him, though. It hit too close to the chest, and any tugging would unravel the carefully crafted security I had to protect me from the monsters of the world.

"So, you *like* working for me, Zel?"

Something in his voice changed, a huskiness to it, and I noticed his drop of Miss. If I'd been wearing panties, they'd be destroyed. Arousal was an emotion I could deal with. Leaning in, my breasts grazed his chest, and I watched as he inhaled. Trailing my fingers up, I brushed across his pecs, feeling them under his thin shirt. I brought one hand back to my face, and I watched as he followed it with his eyes.

"How about this," I asked, tugging on my ear, "as my sign that they're not good business partners?" Dropping my hand down my neck, I moved it around to my front, carefully caressing the skin that peeked out. "Or would this be better?" I suggested, moving my hand across my chest.

"I think no matter what you do, Zel, every man in the room will wish he was with you tonight. You're *captivating*."

Again with his voice, I paused, not used to hearing honesty with the lust. Turning, I grabbed his tie with my other hand and pulled him by it over my shoulder. Walking out into the hallway, I dropped it and allowed him to escort me again. This dynamic we had shifting between us was exhilarating. And yet, I found myself more unsure than I'd ever been.

Wesley Flynn unsettled me with his honesty and control, leaving me questioning where to plant my next step. We were in a tango and kept fighting to lead. I needed to change the dance because it wasn't one I was solid in. The greatest advantage of any power move was playing to your strengths, which always led me back to seduction. It once was used to belittle and control me, and now I was its master, choreographing the steps into a fluid dance no one ever saw coming.

Nix was waiting outside the door, and I smiled and winked at the sexy man. A smirk lifted on the edges of his mouth before falling back into the mask he wore so well.

"Mr. Flynn, all but one of your guests have arrived and are being attended to. Should I announce you and your guest to the room?"

"No, thank you, Mr. Nixon."

I didn't know why that struck me as odd, but it did. I hadn't expected Nixon to be his last name because it suited him so well. I highly doubted his name was Nix Nixon. Though now thinking about it, there was a kid at school whose name was Duffy Dufferson, so really, anything was possible. The thrill of finding out his actual first name sent a devilish thrill through me, and a mischievous smile spread across my face. Nix took one look at me, and before I could say anything, he cut me off.

"Nope."

What he didn't know was it only made me want to find it out even more now. Hiding my determined smile, I batted my eyelashes in an attempt to distract with my cluelessness. He softened and opened the door for us. Chuckling to myself once I was through, I'd forgotten for a second that Wesley was there. That was the power of Nix—he consumed your body, mind, and soul. But oh, was it worth it to be consumed by that man.

"He's never going to tell you," Wesley laughed as he took in my face.

"Oh, I can be very *persuasive*."

"I'm sure you can, but his first name is a secret I've sworn to take to the grave."

"You both clearly don't understand women and how that only makes me want to know more." I grinned devilishly.

Wesley was relaxed and jovial, and I found I liked him like this. Except, as soon as we rounded the corner, it was eerie how quickly that shifted. If I hadn't been looking at his face when it happened, I would've thought he'd been body-snatched. It reminded me so closely of myself that it stunned me. Looking forward, I gathered my own persona's confidence.

I hadn't tapped into it since I started working here. A fact I now realized as Zel and Rapunzel merged. This place had magically become a haven for me, allowing me to be confident in who I was. However, in this room, with powerful men of Sinhaven, I knew I would need to borrow some swagger. Zel was strong and separate from anything tragic. Zel could do whatever she wanted without any consequences. Sometimes, it was nice to be her, but I was starting to blur the line where Zel and Rapunzel met.

Wesley led me over to a table and pulled the chair out for me. Several men and women had already gathered, and no one stopped their conversation while we situated ourselves. It was odd, and I realized how little respect these distinguished guests had given him. Something about that irked me, and I felt my protective instincts perk up.

Wesley might be young, but he'd earned his business and deserved the admiration of those in the industry. Straightening my back, I decided to take matters into my own hands. He said I could do whatever I wanted here, so I'd take his word for it.

Slipping out of my chair, I walked over to the sound system and found the song I wanted. "*Fever*" by Peggy Lee started, and I immediately started to cock my hip to the beat, my hands in the air as I snapped my fingers to the music, rolling my wrist. Keeping my back to the crowd, I built anticipation as I waited for the words to start. When they did, I turned, dropping my hand down my front between my breasts, trailing it slowly.

Casually, I walked and danced as I made my way to the table. Everyone was watching me now, hypnotized by my performance. As I twirled and snapped in simple sensual moves, I enticed them into the story I was building. Out of the corner of my eye, I found Nix along the wall, heat searing me from his eyes.

Making my way around the table, I trailed my hand over the men's shoulders, daring them to look away from me. One gentleman, I cupped his face as I got close and then dropped it as I moved on, weaving in and out of them, striking a pose on the beat. This song's dynamic tempo choreographed itself in seductive steps. As I ruched up my skirt some, I watched as their eyes dropped to the garters on my leg.

I kept everything tasteful but bordering that line as I continued to dance around the room, touching every man at the table. The music had me in its thrall as well, and I relaxed into what was natural to me. When the last verse started, I made my way to Wesley, appreciation shining in his eyes as I did. Grazing my fingers over the back of his chair, I pushed my hands down his front, my head near his as I lightly nipped his ear.

Moving around the front, I dipped and twisted on my heels in tempo, and as it closed on the last line, I spun and dropped myself into his lap, crossing my leg over the other as I did, and wrapped my arm around his neck. I was breathing heavily by the end, but I no longer knew if it was from the dance or the man in front of me. Wesley and I stared into one another's eyes, captivated by one another, and something shifted as we did.

I would've fallen into his espresso eyes right then if the table hadn't started clapping as the song concluded. Gathering myself before I turned around, I searched his eyes, looking for something, and it was like our souls attached in that moment, connecting us.

Pasting a smile, I stood up and bowed for the men, the women leveling me with jealous eyes.

They were all looking at Wesley now, a hint of appreciation in their gaze. It might've been in wonder about me, but my ploy had gotten them to at least look in his direction. Kissing his cheek, I took my seat to his left as the waiters began to bring out drinks and appetizers.

Wesley began to woo them as he discussed his plans for The Tower and how he'd created it into the prime spot in Sinhaven. Wesley was in the zone, and even the talk of budgets and projections didn't bore me because I enjoyed listening to him. As we ate, I took in the men seated around the table. Some of them I'd heard of through my father and knew they couldn't be good news. I took note of them so I could share the info with Wesley later.

The first man I noticed was Julian King, the owner of All That Glitters. He looked like a typical charming businessman on the outside, but icy blue eyes made my skin crawl with the way he continued to leer at me with them. His dark suit gave off an air of wealth, but I was familiar with his kind and wanted nothing to do with him. Especially if what I heard about his gallery was true.

The second man was Marvin Kingsley, the blonde crooked police captain who was so slick, he was like Teflon. He'd gotten my father off more times than I could count, but if the way his eyes glinted were anything to go by, he liked his cruelty a little too much. I always avoided him when he was around the house, scared to find out what was hidden beneath his depths.

The third man was Jeremy Carrillo, a well known loan shark and rumored gang leader. He sat back with his drink, a carefully crafted smile on his face. He was the type of man that presented as one thing, but if you looked close enough, you could see the cracks in the fissure waiting to spill all of his lies and pain. I'd never liked him, always getting the creeps when he was around and knew to stay clear. There'd been rumors at The Pan of how he treated women, and I wanted nothing to do with it. He was one Wesley would need to be careful of as I didn't think he'd take no for an answer if he wanted something bad enough.

The rest I either hadn't met or heard of, indicating to me their relative innocence of the crimes of Sinhaven. Taking a bite of my cheesecake, my fork froze in my mouth when a voice from behind spoke.

"Sorry, I'm late, boys, but million-dollar deals and pussy don't care about dinner plans," he chuckled, mirth in his voice.

He wanted us to all be impressed with him. It was a carefully crafted narrative to portray his image. *But I knew*. I knew the vile things that went on behind closed doors. After all, I'd been his favorite toy.

"Rapunzel, you'll never attract anyone if you don't smile, precious. Come on. It's not that bad. I promise."

He moved the barely-there piece of silk he'd draped over me. My body was cold, and goosebumps dotted my skin. Each time I came to this room, he pushed me to go a little further. Bile coated my stomach, but anytime I brought it up, Daddy got angry with me, and then Mommy would disappear for a few days in a sleepy haze.

It was better if I was silent.

Going into my safe place, I wrapped Mother Gothel's arms around me as she cradled me when I'd been small. At one time, I'd thought she was the villain of my story —the woman who'd stolen me away.

But now, I knew who the real bad guy was. He wore evil like a cloak and sin like a second skin.

His rough hands traveled over my body, touching me wherever he pleased. A whimper escaped, and I scolded myself for showing him my discomfort. He liked it more when I was scared.

Falling deeper into my safe place, I imagined a day when I could dance with my prince, and everything would be beautiful. There would be a million floating lanterns in the sky to celebrate. Nothing would be scary, and everyone would laugh and smile. It would be a safe home, a haven for the misfits of the world.

As I danced away in my mind with my imaginary prince, I escaped the horrors of that room and prolonged my pain for another day. I knew it wasn't over. He would be back, and he'd want more. I just didn't know how much more I had to give. I was slipping away into obscurity, and soon, I'd be nothing but a story... until that too was soon forgotten.

I'd once been the girl who'd returned, but now I was just lost.

CHAPTER FOURTEEN

ZEL

My body locked up, and I had to actively focus on breathing, or I'd pass out. *He was here.* I'd evaded his notice for five years now. Since I left home, I'd been able to get out of his "dates" and avoid him. My father didn't press me, but I knew he was holding back and waiting to strike. When I started to feel strong, that was when he would attack. I'd once thought my father was a snake in the grass, but I'd come to realize how wrong I'd been. He wasn't a snake. He was a scorpion—you never saw the tail coming until he'd already struck.

Trying to regulate my breathing, I pulled in big lungfuls of air and held them. Dancing had allowed me to master breathing techniques, but the fear was too intense today for them to be successful. Panic was edging closer to the front of my mind, and soon I was afraid I'd fall into the abyss. A hand on my knee had me jumping and pulling back, knocking my knee under the table in the process.

Wesley withdrew his hand, keeping them in

sight as he peered at me. I couldn't decide as he watched me if it was with understanding or *pity*. My brain was too far gone at the moment to evaluate him honestly. Though, the pain of my knee had helped ground me, and I focused on that—the pain. Rubbing the area, I could finally slow my breath down.

"Zel, everything ok?" Wesley whispered.

As minutely as possible, I shook my head no and nodded in the direction of the newcomer. Wesley seemed to gather enough information from that little display of communication. He squeezed the hand I'd placed on the table and got up.

"Gentlemen, it's time we take our gathering to the cigar room. Ladies, you're welcome to make your way to the cocktail bar. Shall we?"

Wesley directed everyone out of the other exit, leaving only the staff and me at the table. The girls smiled at me but didn't stay to talk. They all headed back to their rooms. I assumed to change for when the men returned.

Once the room was vacated, my body relaxed, and I felt the room come back into focus. I wanted to be mad at Wesley for noticing my panic, but he'd effortlessly made it go away. I wanted to believe he did it out of goodness, but my past had me feeling otherwise. *My pride couldn't owe him anything.* As I thought through this, I realized that I could justify us being equal now. *Technically*, I'd saved his dinner with my dance by getting all the men to take notice.

It felt wrong, though.

I'd done it because I'd wanted to, not expecting anything in return, only wanting the men to give him the attention he'd earned. As I focused on this dilemma I found myself in; I felt a presence come up behind me and sit.

Nix's body took up the whole chair, and it made me giggle. A story Gothel had told me growing up about Goldilocks and the three bears came to mind. Nix looked like he was in the "too small" chair.

"I like seeing your smile, princess. But what's going on? Why did the boss move everyone after the Judge entered?"

Just hearing his name had me visibly reacting. Shaking my head, I got up from the table and started for the door muttering "no, no, no," as I went, needing to get as far from him as possible.

Nix caught me before I got too far. It hadn't been hard on his part as my freeze reaction had made my muscles stiff. Along with my dress and heels, I was a walking accident waiting to happen. While I could dance in the damn things all night long, *running* was not in my repertoire.

"Princess, stop. I didn't mean to upset you. Just talk to me, okay?"

I didn't turn around, but I kept shaking my head, unable to see out of the tunnel I'd fallen into.

"I need you to trust me, okay?"

Before I could respond, he lifted me bridal-style into his arms and carried me out of the room. Closing my eyes, I willed it all away. Going back to my safe place, I danced with my prince in a world where no one could hurt me.

I awoke in a strange bed but based on the decor, I had a good idea of whose room it was. *Wesley's*. It was minimalist but with exquisite and expensive furnishings. The room was done in grays, silvers, and blacks. The walls were black, the carpet silvery gray, and the furniture black as well. The accents around the room alternated between gray and silver, adding a touch of depth to the darkness.

It was as hauntingly beautiful as the man himself.

The room was very organized, nothing out of place, and had been the biggest clue to whom the room belonged. Swinging my feet over the side of the massive bed, they touched down into the softest and plushest carpet I'd ever felt. Squishing my toes in them for a moment, I relaxed into the comfort they provided. Soft things always brought me peace.

Tiptoeing, I found a bathroom and stood frozen in astonishment for a minute. It was black marble with a massive glass walk-in shower. It also had a black clawfoot tub, making the whole room breathtaking. I never thought I'd like black decor, but it had something about it I found myself drawn to. Maybe it was the man it reminded me of, but I'd deny that if anyone asked.

Using the restroom, I washed my hands and tiptoed back out, hoping they hadn't heard the water. Trying another door, it opened to a closet full of suits. The amount of them hanging in their garment bags was endless. The shiny shoes on their individual shelves, the ties of every color folded neatly in a little cubby on the wall, had my brain stuttering. It was the most meticulous and incredible closet I'd ever seen, and I wanted it. Filled with dresses and heels, of course, but I found myself gaping in envy of this closet.

Maybe I could just live in it? It was large enough. I doubt he'd even notice for at least a week. By then, I was sure some type of occupancy would be met, and he'd have to let me stay. It was something to look into. Just as I was about to turn and try the last door, I heard voices. Being wired to hide, I slipped back into the closet and made myself as small as possible behind some suits. The door was still open a crack, their voices drifting in through.

"She's gone. How is she gone? We've been sitting out there on the couch for the past hour."

"Hmm. She's Houdini on the dance floor, but I don't think she is in real life. Think, Wes. She didn't magically slip out the door, so she's here, *somewhere*."

Damn Nix and his logic. Pulling my legs in, I

slowed my breathing, hoping to keep myself hidden if I wanted it hard enough. Again, I didn't know why I was hiding from them. It had felt natural, and I'd gone with my instincts. I heard a few doors open and close, and then footsteps retreated. I relaxed a smidge, hoping they were looking elsewhere.

The suits were pushed apart two seconds later, and Nix's face appeared in front of me. The man was one sneaky sleuth.

"Princess, are we playing hide and seek?" he teased.

Shaking my head, I seemed to have lost my words, something he noticed instantly. Offering me a hand, his face softened as he regarded me.

"How about I make you a hot chocolate, and we can watch whatever you want on TV?"

Hesitantly, I placed my hand in his, and Nix gently pulled me up, sweeping me up into his arms. I found myself easily smiling as I watched him. If this was how a princess got treated, I might not hate the word so much. Nix kissed my forehead and walked out of the room with me. I hadn't even realized I was no longer in my dress.

Instead, I was in an oversize shirt that had to be his and a pair of boxer shorts. Everything was baggy on me, but it was comfortable, and I didn't even mind he'd changed me. The thoughtfulness of the gesture was there, and I sank more into his arms, laying my head on his chest.

I was going to have to be careful around Nix.

He was the type of man that snuck in and stole your heart without you even being aware. You couldn't help it. Call it his *sleuthingness* at knowing what you needed before you did or his power of magnetism, either way, his gentle caring nature was hooking me in what I hadn't thought existed outside of fairy tales. Nix was like the beast-type prince. His roar kept most people away, but his bravery and selflessness drew others in who took time to see past the beast.

I wondered if he even knew that about himself.

Sitting me down on the counter, I was handed a warm cup by Wesley as soon as my hands were free. He smiled briefly at me, concern edging the corners of his mouth. It wasn't a look I'd expected from him. I sipped the warm liquid, the whipped cream tickled my nose as I drank it down. Wesley observed me, cataloging every detail.

"Nix won't like this," he started, a growl reverberating from the man in question. Placing my mug down, I put my hand on his muscled arm to stop the rumble. Wesley cleared his throat to restart, continuing as I focused on him, "Can you tell me what happened tonight?"

I had to admire the fact he was straight to the point even if I hated the question. It made me edgy, but I couldn't fault his technique. Fiddling with the extra material in my hands, I took a few minutes to gather the courage to speak. I didn't think I was ready to tell them everything. I doubted my pride would let me just yet, but I could tell them *this*. If anything, I didn't want it to affect this place. The Tower was the one place separate from my father's reach. But to open up meant I had to share something dark.

"There were a few men tonight that I've heard things about," I said, looking up to meet his eyes. "Marvin Kingsley, Julian King, and Jere Carrillo are all men I know to have their hands dirty. They are the three I was going to warn you about. The rest I didn't know or hadn't heard anything about."

"There's something else, though, isn't there?"

Nodding, I picked up my mug and took a sip, hoping the warm liquid would fill me with courage or at least counteract the chill I'd experienced recounting this.

"The last guest, Judge Giovanni Baron, I-I-I, um." I stopped, clearing my throat. I noticed my hands shaking, threatening to spill the contents onto my lap, and sat my mug down. Trying again, I focused on a tile in the kitchen; the shiny marble speck was all I could manage.

"H-H-H-He's not a good man," was all I managed before my body locked up.

"Can you tell me more?"

I shook my head slightly, unable to look up at him. I could hear the frustration and disappointment, and I didn't want Wesley to be upset with me.

"Zel, I need a little more. His background is

impeccable and would be a good asset to have as an investor. I'm sorry, but if you're upset with him because he gave you a harsh ruling or something, I can't dismiss going into business for that reason. You *have to* understand. There's a lot of money on the line here."

His words hit me square in the chest, piercing me with a fire that replaced the ice I'd been feeling earlier. *This was what I needed.* I could handle anger and rage. Hopping off the counter, I walked forward until I was standing in front of him. Eyes hard, I locked down all my emotions except for my anger as I stared at Wesley. I'd thought he was *different*, that I could trust him, but he was just another rich snob only looking out for the bottom line. Squaring my shoulders, I tilted my chin up and faced down one more man who'd let me down.

"You asked, and I told you. If you don't want to accept my answer, well, that's on you. He's *not* a good person, and fuck you for assuming because I'm a stripper, I've been arrested. You asked me to trust you, to get to know you. Fine, everything I learned in the past five minutes tells me all I need to know about you. You can go to *Hell*. I don't care that you're my boss. If you want to fire me for saying this, *fucking do it*. You'd be doing me a favor by not having to look at your conniving face anymore."

He looked shocked, not expecting me to say as much or perhaps with as much emotion. I wasn't sure which, but I also didn't care to find out. Passing by him, I bumped his shoulder when he didn't get out of my way, not daring to remain here one minute longer. Leaving my dress and shoes since they were replaceable, the only thing on my mind was getting the hell out of this apartment. As soon as I was past the kitchen, I sped up, my bare feet slapping against the hardwood floors as I ran.

I barreled through the front door and took the stairs, not worried if anyone saw me. I didn't stop on my floor. I didn't even know what floor I was on, honestly. It was hard to see through the tears running down my face. Hearing footsteps following me, I took the next door out, hoping to lose whoever it was. I didn't even know if I could face Nix at the moment. I was in full-blown flight mode, my focus solely on escape.

As I entered the crowd, I found myself on the casino floor. Zigzagging through people, I kept heading for a way out of the building when I ran into a hard chest. Their hands grasped me, and I started to fight against their hold, assuming it was Nix or one of his goons.

"Zel? Is everything okay?"

Nolan's voice stopped me, and I looked up, able to barely make out his features in my tear-stained view.

"Hey, hey, it's okay. Can I help? What do you need?"

His kindness was the drug I needed right then.

Clinging to him, I ignored my pride that I could do this on my own, that I didn't need anyone to save me. I was exhausted from the emotional train wreck this day had been from my parental brunch to that dinner—meals were not my forte today. Instead, I wanted to tell my pride to go fuck herself because Nolan was warm and safe. I needed safety more than I needed pride right then.

"Can you get me out of here?" I finally found the words to ask.

He smoothed my hair away and wiped my tears before replying.

"Come on."

He handed me his jacket and helped me cover up some when he took in my appearance. Nolan noticed my no shoe dilemma and directed me to a section I'd never seen before—lost and found. Nolan rummaged through the pile and pulled out a pair of Chucks and socks. I cringed internally at wearing someone else's dirty socks, but walking barefoot would be worse, so I sucked it up and put them on.

Grabbing his offered hand, I fled into the night —my sweet prince had saved me.

CHAPTER FIFTEEN

NOLAN

I'd decided to go to The Tower after not hearing from Zel, but I had no way to get up to Desire without Josh's dad's membership. So, I'd been loitering around Wager, hoping she'd randomly show up. I was about to give up my lame excuse when she barreled into me. Her tears alarmed me, and her body shook with either fear or adrenaline.

When she'd asked me to get her out of here, everything inside me surged into action. I'd waited my whole life for someone to see me as worthy, and Zel trusted me to take care of her, to rescue her. I wanted to prove to her I could. Spotting the intimidating bodyguard guy careening after her through the casino gave me a little fright, worried I'd have to try to fight him or something, but when he saw I had Zel, he stopped.

I didn't know if it was acceptance or relief that flitted quickly across his face, but he nodded before turning around. It was akin to him passing over the reins in a way. Pride puffed out my chest, and I used it to bolster me as I maneuvered out of Wager. We'd found some shoes for her to wear, and my jacket would hopefully cover her enough to make it to my apartment. I'd parked my old truck a few streets down, so it wouldn't be an unbearable hike, at least.

The chill of the night air hit us as we exited the loud club, the difference immediately noticeable when you left it. When you were in The Tower, everything else faded into the background, and nothing but The Tower existed.

When you stepped foot out of it, though, it was like stepping back through the looking glass. Nothing seemed as bright, as colorful, or as imaginative as it had inside. The Tower had a magic unlike anywhere else. I could see how easily it could become a trap of your own making if you weren't careful.

"My truck is just up here." Zel nodded, staying tucked under my arm.

"Are you hungry? Do you want to stop for food or anything?"

"No, I just want to be somewhere far from here."

She sounded so distant from the vibrant girl I'd met. In fact, she was starting to remind me of the girl I caught sneaking out of Josh's room a week ago. Now that I thought about it, things began to click and why she'd seemed familiar.

"Were you the girl I offered a Pop Tart to?"

I felt her stiffen and berated myself for bringing it up. I could clearly see she was in distress, and now wasn't the time to remind her of my roommate.

"Yeah. I didn't think you recognized me."

"I didn't at first. It wasn't until I thought about it now that it matched in my head. Your disguises are really good."

"Thanks."

"Is there a reason you wear them?" Seriously, Nolan! Could you find a less invasive topic?

I felt her shoulder shrug up, and I knew it would be the only response I'd get. It was all I deserved anyway for trying to pry. My truck came into view, and relief spread through me. Maybe I could pull my foot out of my mouth in a different location.

It was unlikely, but I could hope.

Opening the door for her, I helped her climb up into the cab. Once she was secure, I jogged around to my side. Surprise filled me when I got there to find she'd unlocked my door. A smile lit up my face, but I made sure to wipe it before I hopped into the cab myself.

My mother had once told me a true character test wasn't if a guy opened a door for a girl but if the girl unlocked his door while he walked around. My truck was an old hand-me-down Dodge Ram that had seen better days. It didn't have automatic locks, or anything for that matter, and it was something I often complained about. Except right now, I was happy to have the manual locks because it'd given me the confidence boost I needed with her.

Starting the ignition, I placed my arm on the back of her seat to back up. I was tempted to leave it there, the feel of her neck against my skin enticing me, but I moved it once I was clear. The sound of my acceleration was the only noise as I drove in silence to my apartment complex, the truck rumbling under us as we went.

"This truck is—"

"Ancient, I know."

"No, I was going to say a classic," she laughed. "I happen to find beauty in things that have been discarded by society."

There was something lovely about her comment, but I also caught an edge to her words as well. I didn't want to make assumptions, but it seemed Zel felt she'd been tossed aside in the same way. I didn't think I was anyone special, but I hoped I could be someone to show her how wrong she was. I wanted her to know how beautiful I at least thought she was. We pulled up to my apartment complex a few minutes later, and I watched her tense. Worry seeped into me at the thought she was regretting her decision.

"Is, um, your roommate going to be here?"

"Oh, um, maybe. He's out a lot, so it could be hit or miss. But he's kind of a player," I cringed, hoping she didn't have feelings for him or take offense, "so I doubt he'll recognize you. Plus, you look different than you did last time."

Zel's hands clenched in her lap for a brief second before relaxing, and I saw her leave fingernail slits in her palms.

"I wasn't worried about him noticing, not until you did."

She turned, looking at me with mild anxiety. Brushing her hair off her face, I tucked it behind her ear, rubbing my thumb over the area.

"Yeah, but I see *you*, Zel. It doesn't matter what color your hair is or what outfit you're wearing. When I look into your eyes, I know it's *you*," I swallowed. "You're not just any girl to me."

"Someone else said something similar to me, but I didn't believe them," she admitted, biting her lip. In a small voice, she asked, "What *am I* then?"

It felt as if my future hinged on this moment. Gathering my courage, I leaned forward and placed a kiss gently on her lips. It was soft and sweet, and despite wanting to press for more, I held back. This wasn't about that. I wanted this to be more. Pulling back, I watched as she licked her lips, the heat evident in her eyes.

"You're the girl who refused a Pop Tart because it might mean owing someone. You're the girl who's ruthless in Monopoly but generous with her kindness. You're the girl who dances like she has to, or her heart might break. You're the girl that's so strong she doesn't know how to ask for help, or even if she can. You're the girl who played video games with a stranger and laughed the whole time while doing it. You're the girl I can't stop thinking about. You're the girl who I aimlessly waited for on a second-floor casino on the off chance I might see you. You're the girl who needs no one, but who I hope will give me a chance. *I really want a chance.*"

Her eyes never left mine as I spoke, peering into them the whole time. One tear built on the edge of her eyelid, but it didn't dare fall. I watched as she assessed everything I said and if it had any value for her. I could tell Zel wasn't one to make decisions lightly. She'd been hurt and knew the cost of recklessness, and each choice she made had to be weighed and judged for fear of the consequences.

My life hadn't been easy, and I regretted a lot of things, choices I'd made that led me down paths better left uncovered. While I knew pain was relative, I understood and wouldn't rush her. I hadn't lived her life or carried her burdens, but I could give her this—space to decide without fear of the repercussions.

"What kind of chance do you want?" she finally asked, biting her lip. It was the least confident I'd ever seen her, and whether she knew it or not, it meant she'd started to trust me by showing her vulnerability.

"To get to know you and share in your life. I only want what you can give. I'll never pressure you for anything more. But hear me when I say this. I want to *pursue* you. I want to *date* you. Zel, I fucking want to *romance* you. Mostly, I want you to feel you can say no at any time. If all you want to be is friends, then I'll be the best friend you'll ever have. I think we'd be great together, but I don't want you ever to feel *obligated*."

"I *don't*."

"I'm glad. That makes me happy to hear."

"I think," she paused, clearing her throat, "I think I'd like to get to know you too. If you can promise never to push me to give more than I can, then I'd like to explore whatever this is."

"Yeah?" A wide smile covered my face, surprised she liked me enough to give me a chance.

"Yeah," her smile started to match mine. "I'll be honest, though. I'm a bit of a mess. I don't know why you'd want to date me other than sex. But I like you, Nolan. You make me laugh and smile and make me feel good about myself. I believe you when you say you don't care what outfit I'm wearing, but every time I'm with you, I feel like I'm the most beautiful girl in the room, even if I'm in another man's boxers and shirt."

Zel blushed, and it was one of the most beautiful things I'd ever seen. This vulnerability she was revealing was sexier than anything she could wear. A bit of pride filled me at being the one to make her feel that way. I was a nobody in the grand scheme of things, yet Zel proclaimed *I* made her feel sexy. Me! It was a nice stroke to my ego.

"You're the most beautiful girl, Zel."

"If you keep saying sweet things, I'm going to jump you in this truck."

I had to will the hardness expanding in my pants away, because the lustful side of me wanted to jump all over that idea, but I wanted Zel to know she was valued for more than her body. It seemed important. Taking her hand, I kissed the palm.

"As much as I want to do that, I have a strange proposition for you."

"Go on. I'm all ears."

"What if we got to know one another in the traditional sense of things before we crossed that boundary?"

"Oh, what does that mean? I, uh, haven't really ever had a *steady* relationship."

"Then I think this is an even better idea. Let's have a boring normal relationship," I teased.

"Will you be my teacher?" she purred, starting my dick back up. Swallowing, I nodded, losing myself for a moment.

"Yeah," I swallowed again, my voice cracking a little at the end. "Which means no sex until the third date… at least."

"So what do people do then if they're not banging?"

I wanted to laugh, but I could tell she was serious, so instead, I pulled out the keys and opened my door.

"Stay right there." I pointed at her. "Don't move."

She nodded but looked at me oddly. Crossing over in front of the cab, I opened her door and extended my hand. "My lady."

Zel placed hers in my palm, a smile of pure happiness lighting her face. "Kind sir."

A buzz shot through me at her words, and a sense of familiarity outside of the pop tart incident prickled. I was having one of those deja vu moments where I felt like I'd either witnessed this before or something very similar. As she hopped down, nothing came to mind. Letting it go, I wanted to focus on the girl in front of me instead of ghosts.

Hooking her hand in my elbow, I led her up the stairs to the apartment I shared with Josh. It was quiet when we entered, and I prayed it meant he was out. It would be easier if he wasn't here, even if he didn't recognize her. Flipping on the lights, I took the jacket off her shoulders, hung it up, and realized she was still in the oversized shirt, boxers, and dirty socks.

"Would you like something different to wear? I can grab you some sweats and a sweatshirt. They'd probably fit you better too."

"Oh yes, please. The thought of these socks has been grossing me out. Could I take a shower? Would that be weird? I just, yeah, I need to wash the night off."

"Absolutely. It wouldn't be weird at all."

Pulling her hand, I showed her to my room and sat her on the bed. I was glad I'd made it today and didn't have any dirty underwear lying around. My room wasn't messy, it was pretty clean, but some days it did get out of hand from pure laziness.

"I like your room. It suits you."

"Thanks," I said, turning back to look at her. She was looking around the space, taking in all my movie and comic book posters. As I started to rummage through my clothes, I watched as she browsed my room more, looking at the pictures I had.

"This your family?"

"Yeah, that's my dad, mom, and brother in front of the store my parents own."

"Ryder & Sons Hardware. Is that the place next to the bakery with the good cupcakes?"

"Hunter's bakery is the best. You familiar with that side of town? "

"Oh, you know, I'm kind of familiar with all of Sinhaven from Dante's Circle to Crown Lakes to Tiara Heights," she shrugged. It was a vague answer, and I took it to mean she didn't want to answer, so I honored my promise earlier and dropped it.

"Here, these should fit better, and I'll show you the shower."

Leading her into the bathroom, I turned on the tap, knowing it was tricky. When I stepped back, we were suddenly very close in the small area as the steam started to billow out around us. My mind started to play out fantasies, and I needed to get out, pronto.

"I'll just be out there. I'm gonna find something to eat, and then maybe we could watch a movie?"

She nodded, a smile on her face. "Thanks, Nols."

I didn't want to admit how sexy it sounded when she shortened my name, but my cock had other ideas. Turning away quickly, I exited the bathroom and made a quick dash to the kitchen to give myself a breather. I was committed to the three-date rule, but it might be torture in the process. It would be worth it, though. Zel deserved to feel like the princess she was to me.

Scouring the pantry, I found a bag of popcorn, a box of Reese's Pieces, and some marshmallow drizzle. It sounded odd, but I had a feeling it would be delicious together. It vaguely reminded me of my sister and all our crazy concoctions as kids. Except, I wasn't supposed to be thinking of Natalie. Especially not tonight when the girl of my dreams was here.

Focusing on making my crazy snack, I searched for some drinks and carried it all to the bedroom. I hoped it didn't appear like I was trying to make a move, but the better TV was in here. Plus, this way, if Josh came home, we'd be tucked away out of sight.

Fluffing the pillows, I grabbed a blanket and made a picnic area on the bed on top of the covers hoping to prove my intentions. Queuing up Netflix, I flipped through some things looking at what might be a good show or movie to watch. As I searched, the bathroom opened, and she exited. Her hair was up in a towel, and I saw her hesitate.

"I, uh, I have this thing about my natural hair."

"Okay, you don't have to show me anything you don't want to, remember?"

She nodded hesitantly, almost like she didn't believe me. I patted the side of the bed, inviting her to join me, and she eventually sat down. Zel looked at the bowl of popcorn, a curious look on her face.

"Um, what is that?"

"Okay, so you have to close your eyes and try it. Here, let me."

I grabbed a piece that had all three on it and waited for her to close her eyes. Once she did, I brushed it against her lips to tempt her to open it. Zel shyly stuck out her tongue to taste the salty, peanut butter, gooey goodness.

"Mmm, that's not so bad."

"Told you, now open."

She complied, and I placed it on her tongue and watched as she chewed, a smile gracing her lips.

"Okay," she said, opening her eyes, "that's delicious. What is it?"

"It's Zels Balls," I grinned.

"You made that up!" She shoved me, laughing.

"Maybe, but it made you laugh. Plus, I made the dessert, so I can name it whatever I want. Them's the rules."

"Oh, is that how that works?" She nodded thoughtfully. "Well, if that's the rules, then here, have some Zels Balls."

Laughing, I grabbed a handful and shoved it in my mouth, letting some spill out the sides. "Oh my God, Zel. Your balls are so good," I moaned, only making her laugh more.

"You're such a dork, Nols. I like it."

"Well, I'm glad because I'm afraid I can't change that. Believe me, my parents tried. They even had me tested!"

"What? No way, that's just cruel. You're perfect just as you are."

"Well, it makes me happy to hear you say that because you're perfect just the way you are, Zel."

We sat grinning at one another, popcorn-filled mouths, and it felt like the best first date in eternity. Not wanting to get too caught up in things, I turned back to the TV and scrolled through the options.

"Okay, we have horror, comedy, or drama. What's your flavor?"

"Mmm, no romance?"

"Nah. I don't need to watch a romance movie when I'm living one."

Her mouth gaped open like a fish, her face heating even more than before, and I wondered if I'd gone too far. It was hard to know how much cheese was too much cheese when my motto was 'there was never too much cheese'. Surprisingly enough, that was also my favorite type of pizza.

"How about a comedy then?" she finally said, recovering from my comment, her face still heated.

"Comedy it is."

Hitting play, I settled back against the pillows and pulled the bowl of Zels Balls with me, so it was in between us. I felt the sexual tension building between us throughout the movie, but I kept my promise not to press for more. Each little hand brush in the popcorn, each slight caress of her fingers, had me shifting my hard as steel cock.

At first, I think it started innocently, but midway, I caught her little smirk and knew she'd caught on to the effect she was having on me. Now, she was doing it intentionally. Stealing the bowl, we wrestled for it and ended up mainly spilling kernels all over the bed in our fit of laughter.

It was the perfect night, or early morning since it was 2 am by the time the movie credits rolled. We were both still awake, having laughed throughout the entire flick. The part I dreaded was coming, and I hoped she would take my offer sincerely.

"I'd like for you to stay, if that's okay? I know it's not traditional, and I'll sleep on the couch if you want, but it would be nice just to sleep next to you. I promise, nothing else."

Zel watched my eyes, and I relaxed when she

didn't demand that I drive her back or run out of the room screaming.

"That would be nice. I just, can you turn off the lights? It's just my hair."

"Of course. Here, let's get the bed ready, and then I'll show off with my skills."

Giggles sounded, and I felt happy every time I heard one. As we picked up the loose kernels and pulled the covers back, I kicked off my jeans and slipped on a pair of shorts, not wanting to scare her with only boxers. To be fair, it was to help me conceal my dick too. Despite my intentions to wait, he hadn't gotten the memo. She'd pulled off her pants, and I tried not to focus on the fact she just had on a long shirt.

When she nodded, I got in bed and said the magic words, "Alexa, turn off the lights."

Darkness surrounded us for a minute, and then the stars lit up on the ceiling. I heard her gasp, and I held back my smug smile at surprising her.

"Those are beautiful."

Turning to my side, I took in her profile. She'd tossed the towel on the ground, and I could make out hair surrounding her on the pillow, but nothing else.

"They remind me of someone. I'll tell you about her someday. She's my hard thing to talk about." I managed to get out before my voice croaked with emotion. She turned too, and we laid facing one another. Slowly, I reached out and linked my pinky with hers.

"I'd like that." I saw her smile lift. "Thank you, Nolan, for the best first date I've ever had."

"You're welcome, Zel. It was the best one for me too."

Slowly, we drifted off to sleep, staring at one another as we did. The only part of our bodies touching were our pinkies. And yet, that felt more significant than anything else. In that little pinky finger, Zel had placed her trust in me, and that was everything.

CHAPTER SIXTEEN

ZEL

When the light woke me the following day, I stretched, feeling rested, and a smile immediately covered my face. *Nolan Ryder wanted to romance me.* It was hard to place the geeky shy boy he'd been. Part of me wanted to slap my former self for not noticing him then and wondering what life would be like now if I had. Except it hadn't been my pride or arrogance that kept him out of my purview.

No, it'd been just good old fashion trauma.

The reminder of why I hid now sent a jolt of fear through me when I realized the other side of the bed was empty. My hands went to my head, confirming what I already knew but was in denial over—no wig. Shit, shit, shit, shit, shit. Immediately, I jumped out of bed and ran around the room, imitating a chicken with its head cut off.

I knocked into a dresser, a desk chair, and stumbled over a pair of shoes before I came to grips with reality. Nolan was already out of the room. I couldn't erase time; believe me, I'd tried. When things got really dark, I'd pretend my life had been different, more of that fairy tale I joked about.

I was a princess, loved by her parents and cherished by the kingdom. I'd dance in beautiful gowns and even had a cute pet sidekick. I had friends I laughed with, and we would throw plays for the entire village to enjoy. The best part was the magical power I had. The golden locks on my head weren't only my identifying marker as a royal; they also healed people. Through my song and dance, I spread literal sunshine making people happy and curing them with a lock of my hair.

It seemed silly now when I thought of it, a Disney version of my life that would never exist. And yet, it had once been the only thing that kept me sane. I think I wanted, or even needed, my hair to represent something positive and pure instead of the sinful debauchery it had become. When every man told you how beautiful something was and then used it to justify their pleasure at your expense, it became the one thing you despised.

My hair represented how vanity and pride didn't care about consent or safety. To me, my hair was nothing more than a tangible mass keeping me trapped in a perpetual cycle of abuse. My hair had become a deadweight and the darkest parts of me. When anyone commented on it now, I viscerally shuddered, the bile climbing my throat.

All that aside, it was also the most recognizable

part of Rapunzel. My eyes were a unique green, but by themselves wouldn't raise flags. I often wore different colored contacts to avoid it, but I wasn't concerned about them in situations like now. The birthmark on my cheek was the second most noticeable thing linking me back to my parents and easily covered and dismissed by itself.

Long golden hair, with silvery strands throughout that fell to my waist, inevitably pointed to only one person—Rapunzel. Wesley and Nix weren't from here, so the likelihood they'd known me was slim and why I didn't freak out after revealing myself to Nix. But Nolan? We were in the same graduating class! He already said my dancing reminded him of Rapunzel. I was only one more connection away before he figured me out.

I needed to get out of here.

Sadness and disappointment clawed at my gut, and I sank to the floor. I didn't want to leave. I liked who I was around Nolan. He made me feel carefree and happy. Nolan was showing me all the parts of myself I thought had been lost. He unknowingly showed me I could hope again. It was scary, and my insides were warring not to step over the line, to stay over here in the darkness where the monsters couldn't touch me.

Hiding only got you so far, though. Nix had shown me that.

At the thought of him, I recalled the events leading me here, to begin with. Anger at Wesley surged in me at his insistence I tell him my reasoning. I wanted to trust he hadn't meant the things he said, but the past had made it hard for me to believe the best in men. Nix was an innocent bystander, though, and no matter what issues Wesley and I had, I couldn't group him in with them.

I had a feeling he knew where I was and had allowed it, knowing once again what I'd needed last night—distance and comfort. The need to know his first name overwhelmed me, and I laughed at the brazen idea I had to uncover it. Taking into account my current situation, I knew I needed to face facts.

While it wasn't the first time I'd been on my own or stranded somewhere, I had absolutely nothing with me—no clothes, no costumes, no money, no phone. I didn't even have a pair of underwear and socks! Running off to hide from Nolan wasn't an option. Even if I had things, I didn't think I could leave him now anyway.

There was a part of my bruised heart that yearned for what he so effortlessly gave, and for once, my pride agreed.

Picking myself off the floor, I twisted my hair up as best I could and borrowed a baseball cap I found sitting on his desk. It wasn't ideal, but it would suffice until we could go to one of my hideaways. An idea popped into my head of how I could take care of two things at once to get clothes and answers. *Maximus.*

Craning my head out the door, the eerie sense

of doing this exact same thing a few weeks ago flooded me. Though, this time I wasn't sneaking out. I only hoped to avoid the lumberjack who'd been average at best in bed. Clanking sounds came from the direction I remember the kitchen being, and I made my way there. Watching from the doorway, Nolan flipped a pancake into the air before picking it up and placing it on a plate.

He was standing at the stove in only a pair of plaid pajama pants. They hung low on his hips, and I realized it was the first time I'd seen him topless. Taking my chance to ogle the goods, I mapped out the curves and lines of his muscles as they flexed with every move he made.

I'd never really looked at guys' backs before, but *damn*. Nolan had me drooling for something more than pancakes. Slowly, I crept into the kitchen, using my years of pointe to glide me across the floor. I debated if I wanted to create more sexual tension or have fun with him on my attack. However, I didn't end up needing to decide as he flipped around, surprising me instead.

"Eek!" I screamed, throwing my hands up. The momentum caused me to lose my balance and fall back. Spinning my arms, I attempted to catch myself or throw my weight in a different direction.

He easily reached out with his long arms and hooked me around the waist, pulling me to him. We stared at one another, our breaths heavy from the effort. His crooked smile appeared, and I found myself swimming in his eyes. *Damn, this boy had me believing in true love's kiss and happy endings.*

"Nice try, twinkle toes, but I heard you the moment you left the bedroom. I was trying to give you the chance to leave if you were."

Some of his smile dropped, and I realized he wasn't teasing as much as he meant to. There was valid fear in his statement. With his arms holding me securely, I lifted up on my toes and kissed him. Everything with Nolan had been sweet and soft, and this kiss wasn't anything different. I was discovering how hot sweet could be, though.

His lips brushed mine in a gentle caress as my body begged me to push for more, knowing how good it felt to lose oneself in the sensual pleasures. His words hung in the air between us, though, and I wanted to give "normal" a try. So despite my desire riding me hard, I pulled back before deepening the kiss.

"Your kisses remind me of cotton candy," he breathed.

Cocking my head, I didn't know what he meant by that. "How so?"

"Light, airy, and always leaves me wanting more. Your sweetness lingering on my lips long after."

A blush spread across my cheeks. No one had ever said that before. It was erotic in how sweet and wholesome it was. I needed to change the subject, or I'd throw my resolution to try normal out the window.

"Are you making me breakfast?"

"Maybe. What would you think of it if I was?" he grinned.

"I'd think it counted as a second date. Wouldn't you?"

"Oh, I can definitely get behind the idea. Where would you like to eat? I don't think anyone else is here."

"Hmm, maybe a table since syrup is involved. It takes forever to get out of a comforter."

Laughing, he threw his head back. "I'll take your word for it. Is it bad that I kind of want to test it, though?"

"No." I shook my head. "It's that exploring spirit I find so attractive."

"Oh, you find me attractive? Do tell me more."

Giggling, I took the plate he handed me and walked around to the bar before hopping up on the stool.

"Well, you're kind of the sweetest person I've ever met. You make me laugh and feel at ease, and I never worry about having to be perfect around you. Nolan, you have this boyish charm that lights up your whole face, and I want to spend hours just staring into your eyes waiting for the next crazy thing you'll do." When I realized everything I said, I shoved a big bite of pancakes into my mouth to stop any more from escaping.

"Wow." He cleared his throat, and I didn't feel embarrassed anymore. Nolan was sporting the cutest blush, and I was glad I'd been the one to put it there. Pride for doing something for someone else flowed through me. I was starting to feel and live more emotions, and as I experienced new ones, it was like my eyes were being opened to a world of possibilities I'd never known existed.

We finished the pancakes, and I helped him put the dishes away. Even doing chores with him was fun as he sprayed me with the water hose. I realized why I liked being near him. His energy was pure, and he displayed light like I once had. It was addicting, and I hoped I wasn't using him like I'd been used.

My frown deepened, becoming evident when I felt him smooth the crease between my brow. "What's with the frowny face, Zel?

"I was thinking how I liked to be around you because you have this light about you I like. It makes me not feel so alone, but then I worried I was using you for it as I'd once been."

I realized again how much I'd disclosed, but it was already too late. Words couldn't be unheard anymore than time could be erased.

"Hey, I don't feel used, so I think that's the difference. I enjoy spending time with you, and I want to. The fact I make you feel that way makes me feel pretty smug and thrilled."

He pulled me into a hug, wrapping his arms

around my whole body. My face pressed against his bare chest, and I realized how smooth it was. Nolan rubbed my back, and I relaxed more in his arms. I guess he was right. He had a choice in this too, and if he didn't feel that way, then I couldn't make it about that. Just like when I chose to be sexual now, it was my choice, not theirs. Guilt left me, and I returned the hug with vigor pulling him tight.

"Now," he started, leaning back so he could see into my eyes, "as much as I like seeing you in my clothes, you're probably wanting some clean ones. I don't have class today, so I'd also like to take you to the bakery and on a picnic. And while this isn't the best date activity, my family is having dinner tonight. My brother got engaged and is announcing it to the family. Would you maybe want to come as my date?"

My head was nodding yes before I thought about it. But if we went by Maximus' place, I could get all the things I needed, and there would be no way anyone would recognize me.

"I think I should call The Tower first, but if you take me to a friend's, I can get everything else I need there. I store my stuff all over the city."

"That's *resourceful*."

"You're being polite. It's weird but necessary."

"Well, either way, it works to our advantage today. Here, use my phone. I'll finish getting dressed, and then we can go wherever."

He kissed my cheek before walking off. I

googled the mainline for The Tower and dialed. It rang several times before someone picked up.

"Thank you for calling The Tower. What dreams do you want to come true today?"

Well, that was a new one.

"Hi, yes, I would like to speak to Mr. Nixon."

"Hold, please."

Huh, that was easier than I expected. A few bars into the standard muzak song, it clicked over. "Zel? Is that you, princess?"

"How did you know it was me?"

"Do you need to ask?" rolling my eyes, I let it go. He either had me trailed, had Nolan's phone bugged, or the easy answer, caller ID.

"I wanted to let you know I was safe. I'm going to spend the day with Nolan, but I'll be back tonight."

"Okay."

"*Okay*? That's it?"

"Princess, you're not a prisoner here, and I know you are well versed in taking care of yourself. It doesn't mean I don't have a guy on standby, but I'm trusting in your capabilities as well."

"I can hear your smirk through the phone line, you know."

"Oh, I can hear a lot more than just that, princess," he purred, his voice having the husky seduction I loved.

"You're not mad I'm spending the day with another man?"

"Well, *man* is stretching it, princess. But the kid is alright in my book. He treats you well, and I see how happy you are. And before you go and think I'm watching you, I just meant the night he played Monopoly with you. I stayed outside your door for a few minutes to make sure you were okay, and I heard you laugh. It was this whimsical sound I'd never heard before, and I realized as much as I didn't want to like the kid, you need him."

"I'm kind of shocked right now."

"Just because I growl and grunt to get most of my meanings across doesn't mean I don't have feelings or know how to use my words, princess."

"I'm sorry. I didn't mean it like that." Taking a deep breath, I gave him some vulnerability. "I've never had people care before, not without strings. So to hear you say you're good with me being with Nolan and you, it's not what I'm used to. Men have used me as property and belongings most of my life."

"Princess, the only strings here are the g-strings I want to remove from your body."

"Careful, Nix. It almost sounds like you're smitten."

"Smitten, bitten, and a whole lot of gettin', I hope. Obviously, I'm not a comedian or poet."

Laughing, I found myself grinning wide. "I don't know. I kind of like that. Thanks, Nix. For making me feel worthy."

"You're all that on your own, princess. But I'll take whatever thanks you're giving."

"Your secret is going to get out, you know?" I teased.

"What secret?" His joking tone was gone, and I worried I crossed a line.

"That you're really a cinnamon roll."

"Say what now? You lost me, princess. Is this some hip lingo I'm not up on?"

"It means you're gooey on the inside. Like a cinnamon roll."

"Hmm. Well, I don't know about that, just that I'd do almost anything for you. So if that makes me a cinnamon roll, then icing me up, princess. I'm all yours."

"Wow, that's both sweet and cringey."

"I warned you I wasn't a poet, so you can't blame me."

"You're right. Thanks, Nix, for letting me go last night. You always know what I need before I do."

"Only because I see you clearer than you see yourself, but I think you're getting there."

"I think so too."

"Can I ask one thing?"

"Of course," I responded, despite the fear he'd ask about last night again.

"Would you," he cleared his throat, "would you want to accompany me to dinner later this week?"

"Why, Nix, are you asking me on a date?"

"I'm trying to, yes. So, is that an answer?"

"I would love to go wherever you want to take me, Mr. 'I'm going to figure out your first name' Nixon."

The biggest boom of laughter filled the tiny speaker, and I had to pull it away to save my eardrum. "Good luck with that, princess. You'll never find it."

"Oh, I have my ways."

"So, do I, princess. So do I. Now, there should be a delivery to the door in about thirty seconds. Have fun, and don't be too hard on Wesley when you return. He doesn't always know when he's an ass."

"Hmph. It's going to take a lot for me to forgive him, much less look at him."

"I'll let him know. Bye!"

"Wait!"

Ugh, before I could correct his assumption I was willing to give Mr. Flynn a chance, he'd hung up, the clever asshole. The knock at the door stopped me from dialing back, and I carefully tiptoed over. Nolan answered it and took the package from whoever, and then shut the door. I relaxed once it was locked again. He saw me when he turned, a smile gracing his lips. The very same ones I wanted to feel all over me.

"Looks like you have a fairy godmother," he teased.

"More like a fairy Nix," I joked.

Chuckling, I took it from him and found a pair

of jeans, clean socks, underwear, a bra, and my phone and wallet. There was a note attached as well.

Miss Tress,

Please forgive me for being a royal ass. I don't think before I speak sometimes, and my upbringing isn't the best example of how not to push people. I'm sorry for not considering your feelings. You don't owe me anything. You were right. I do hope you'll choose to return, but just in case, I had your shift covered tonight, so you could have some time off. Please, know I only want the best for you.

Sincerely,
Wesley Flynn

"That your boss?" Nolan asked.

"Yeah." Some of the fun left me with Wesley being the thoughtful one.

"Hmm. Seems like he likes you."

"No. It's not like that." I shook my head, not wanting to think about Wesley as I headed to his room. Before shutting the door, I shouted over my shoulder, "just give me a few minutes."

I changed into the clean clothes and instantly felt better. Keeping the hat and sweatshirt on Nolan let me borrow, I walked out of the apartment with Nolan's hand in mine. I was starting to like this whole normal thing. It was nice when you were with someone like him. I gave him directions to Max's place, and I giggled in delight at the thought of uncovering Nix's name.

I needed to talk to Nolan about Nix, but I would wait until later. Right now, I wanted to pretend I was a girl on a third date with a boy she liked.

CHAPTER SEVENTEEN

ZEL

Nolan followed my directions as I led him out into the middle of nowhere. It was one of the reasons I didn't visit this location often because the trek here was long and torturous on foot. I met Maximus the first night I left the house. I was so naive back then and thought I could count on the kindness of strangers.

My first time alone, I had no plans or knowledge of how to survive. The vital part had been getting out of the house and away from my father. I'd focused on that part, thinking everything else would be easier, or at least not as scary once I was free. It rained that night, and I found myself huddled, soaking wet under a bridge in an attempt to stay warm. When an older woman approached me, I thought luck was on my side, and someone would finally help me. *I'd been so wrong.*

Left beaten and bruised, robbed of the few possessions I had, I laid in the mud and cried for a quick death. If the outside world was as scary as the world within, where did that leave me? Where could I go to be safe? That word had become as unbelievable as hope. What was there left to hope for when you'd seen the true darkness of the world?

Laying in the cold, I blinked the rain from my eyes in a helpless gesture. When a light kept being reflected into them, I was surprised. Raising my hand, I tried to block out the annoying glare. Typical—I couldn't even be left to die without someone annoying me to death. Eventually, the light flickered to a level of annoyance I couldn't ignore any longer.

Pulling myself up as much as I could muster, I crawled toward the shiny light in hopes of stopping it or thinking maybe it was "the light" I needed to reach to end my torture. It probably took me hours to crawl across the road, but I eventually made it, panting as I laid in the filth. A spark of strength began to kindle in me at the effort it had taken to make it across.

"Lookey there, pipsqueak, you made it. Surely, if you have the strength to crawl through Dante's Circles finest shit, you can scourge up enough to pick yourself up out of the rain."

Pushing the dirty, drenched hair out of my face, I tried to make out the guy above me. He was skinny, covered in freckles, and had mousy brown hair that was up in spikes. Despite his punk exterior, I found kindness in his eyes and a genuine smile. Reaching down, he offered me a hand. I stared at it, unsure what it meant, but I figured I had two options.

Take it and risk the price.

Ignore it and stay in the mud.

My current state didn't leave me much further to fall, and when I thought about the price I might have to pay, it couldn't be much worse than where I was currently. Placing my hand in his, I was surprised by the strength his small frame contained.

"There ya go, pipsqueak. Now, how about I get you something to eat and some dry clothes?"

"Why do you keep calling me that?" I frowned.

"Because you're as quiet as a mouse, and you gotta be a rat to survive on the streets."

"I don't want to be either of those things."

"You're either the prey or the predator, babe. Choose your side. The only thing that will keep you warm here is your pride. What's it worth to ya?"

His words made sense as much as I didn't want to believe them. He was also the first person to treat me like I could do something on my own. That I was strong, or strong enough, to survive this.

"So what will food and clothes cost me then?" I asked, tilting my head up, arms crossed as I took in the boy. We were almost the same height standing, him being only a couple of inches taller than me.

"What if I said the first night is free, but starting tomorrow, I teach you the ropes to survive in the trenches of Dante's Circle?"

"Why?"

He regarded me for a time, and I didn't think I would get an answer. "Because you remind me of someone, and I couldn't help them. With you, I have the chance I never did back then. Call it sentimental bullshit or this feeling I have that we could help one another. I just am, okay, pipsqueak?"

Searching his features, I wanted to trust my gut he was telling the truth, that perhaps there was a good guy out there. So far, I'd only met the monsters who dressed in fancy suits and spoke pretty words but had cruel features when no one was looking and even darker desires.

"Okay. But I don't want to depend on you. I want to learn. I want to have pride in myself, like you said."

"I think we're going to get along great, pip. I'm Maximus, but don't call me that unless you want me to ignore you. Call me Max."

"Sure thing, Maximus." Grinning wide, I was surprised to find it on my face as he chased me for my indiscretion. I ran off shrieking in laughter, realizing I'd met someone worthwhile.

I made my first friend in the cold, damp, shit-filled streets of the poorest part of town. Max became my family and helped me learn to survive on pride.

I watched Nolan as he parked and took in the trailer. It looked rickety and like it might fall apart if a wind came by. There were all kinds of odds and ends laying in the yard, cluttering it as well. Max had become a bit of a collector over the years. He liked to build things and invent new ways to do something, but mostly, it was a crafty facade meant to dissuade any trespassers.

Max had helped me learn to stay off the grid and housed a lot of the things I'd collected over the years here. I had a room, but with the schedule I kept, the distance, and checking in on Gothel, I didn't stay here often. The thought of Gothel had me making a note to see her soon. She'd been quiet, a little too quiet, which never boded well for me.

Max liked his privacy and living far from civilization. It reminded me too much of the clearing, some of my PTSD keeping me from ever making this a permanent home. I also needed to be around people as much as I hated to admit it. They were both the bane and necessity of my existence.

Hopping out of the truck, I shut the door and skipped up the porch. I could see the hesitancy on Nolan's face, and I hid my grin. Punching in my code on the door, I opened it and waited for Nolan to brave the disarray.

"And you're sure it's safe?"

"Yep! Come on."

Finally, he braved it and followed me in. His eyes adjusted to the darkness inside, and he gave me a look. The outside appeared like a hoarder's wet dream, but the inside was a different story. Something we learned during our time living on the streets was all about impressions. It was where the idea of my costumes had developed too. It helped me move past the person I'd been and learn to love dance again.

Inside was solid and built to withstand almost any disaster. It had two bedrooms, a full bath, kitchen, and living room on the main floor, but it was the bunker we needed to head to. I didn't waste time explaining to Nolan and instead, had him follow me down the stairs. It was more fun letting him experience the land of Max first hand instead of trying to explain it anyway.

"Um, what is this place?" Nolan grinned, full of wonder as he took in the space. The main area was a nerd's paradise. Every game console known to man was set up with a wall of games. Max had the originals too, Atari, Gamecube, PS2, and even an old Game Boy.

When I met Nolan, I'd had one of those weird thoughts that he would like Max's place before I got to know him. From the instant he offered a stranger Pop Tarts, I think I began to trust him. It was out of character for me, but I'd found it was in the moments where it didn't seem to matter where things felt more significant.

Cheesing myself, I pulled his hand to follow. When I came to a steel door, I knocked in the pattern we'd made as our secret code—four fast knocks, three slow knocks, one knock, and then two quickly at the end. When it sounded back to me, I started hopping on my toes for the door to unlock.

A hiss of the seal sounded, and the door opened outward, revealing a smiling Maximus.

"Maxi Pad!"

Jumping, I wrapped my arms around his neck and hugged him tightly. I always forgot how much I missed him until I saw him again. He'd grown over the years and bulked up from the first time I met him and now stood over six feet tall.

"I told you to stop calling me that, pipsqueak."

He held me tightly back, breathing me in, and for a few seconds, we just held one another. Max was the best friend and brother I'd always wanted. We'd saved each other on the streets and become family. We tried to be more than friends once. It seemed to make sense at the time, but there was nothing there. You really can't force chemistry, and we left our awful kiss in the column of things we didn't discuss.

He didn't like me dancing or sleeping with guys for money, and it had become a point of friction between us over the years, and I think subconsciously it was why I didn't visit as much either. I kept a lot of the things my father made me do to myself, and he never understood the responsibility I felt for Gothel. I couldn't explain it to him on a level he grasped since he wanted nothing to do with his family.

Max had shared he was part of the Battaglia family one night. I didn't know much about them, but I knew he refused to do whatever was requested of him. Someone in the family showed him mercy and let him escape but told him he'd be dead if they ever found him. Yeah, it was *that* Battaglia family.

"To what do I owe this exuberant meeting, pip?" He sat me back down, and that was when he spotted Nolan. "And apparently, we have *guests*. Breaking rules already, are we, pip?"

"This is Nolan, my, um, *boyfriend*?" I didn't know why I was asking or the reason I felt so awkward all of a sudden, but as I grabbed Nolan's hand to introduce him, a sudden wave of uncertainty had hit me.

Nolan beamed at my word and took it in stride. "Nice to meet a friend of Zel's, and I'm envious of your setup down here. There are some classic games out there. Have you ever entered one of The Tower's gaming contests?"

Max crossed his arms, lifting his brow as he assessed Nolan. "Favorite classic video game?"

"Pff, man, it's a toss-up between Final Fantasy VII and Legend of Zelda: Ocarina of Time."

They were nerd speaking now and had lost me, so I stood back and watched what a geek showdown looked like.

"Tetris or Dr. Mario?"

"Tetris."

"Space Invaders or Galaga?"

"Space Invaders."

"Street Fighter or Mortal Kombat?"

"Street Fighter."

"Donkey Kong or Kirby?"

"Donkey Kong."

"Are you guys done measuring your dicks the nerd way yet?"

They'd been staring one another down as they battled out their super weird nerd video game knowledge. I was starting to regret bringing Nolan here. Fortunately, my question knocked them out of their trance, and they both looked sheepishly at me.

"Hmph, well, if Pip thinks you're okay, then I'll give you a chance. Only one, though. I don't know how much I can trust someone who doesn't enjoy Kirby."

"Seriously, Max?" I rolled my eyes. "Your video game challenge doesn't solve every problem."

"I beg to differ. Outside of you, I can judge people based on what games they like. Now, what's with the visit and guest? Are you in *trouble*?"

"Always," I teased, finally walking the rest of the way into the room. It was filled with computers on one wall, a massive bed, a kitchen area, and my favorite, the deluxe spa. He'd put it in just for me. His family background, I guess, was in something similar, but it worked when I needed to reinvent myself. I had my own wall of wigs, salon, hot tub, and revolving wall of outfits.

Max had designed it himself, and it was the most badass thing ever. I could punch in keywords, and it would spit out some costume ideas. With a click of a button, it would be delivered in a few days. I kept most of my best dresses and shoes here and only exchanged things out about once a month when I did inventory.

I hadn't meant to spend so much money on clothes and shoes, but it was a hard habit to break once I started. Now that I had a place to lay my head at night in The Tower, I could probably transfer some of these items there. Maybe I could get a closet similar to the one Wesley had. The thought had snuck its way up into my head unencumbered, and before I knew it, a pang of longing hit me square in the chest. I didn't want to like Wesley.

He was controlling and demanding and *prideful*. He reminded me of some of the worst people I knew. I couldn't deny that. And yet, I saw the vulnerability, the passion for dance, and his desire to be known. Wesley wasn't like them in the parts that counted, and if I was honest with myself, I did like him. He'd hurt me and would need to own up to that, but if he did, wouldn't I be just as bad if I didn't allow him to prove it? Being aware of my feelings sucked when I had to own up to my own.

"This place is fucking amazing!"

"I'm glad you like it. Make yourself at home and don't kill one another. I'm gonna have him look something up for me and then shower and change. I'll pack a bag, and then we can head out on our date."

I tipped up on my toes and kissed him. I meant it to be a quick one, but Nolan wrapped his hand around my neck and pulled me into him, and I succumbed to the desire. I didn't think I could ever get tired of kissing this boy. Max cleared his throat behind me, and I felt a blush rise to my cheeks. Pulling back, I walked over to where Max was waiting and tried not to skip the whole way there. It was harder than it should've been.

"I don't think I've ever seen you smile that way in all the years I've known you, pip."

"I don't think I've ever felt this carefree before."

"I'm happy for you, Ra—"

Putting my finger over his lips, I stopped him before he could say my full name. "It's just Zel."

He nodded, understanding, and I dropped my fingers.

"So, what did you come out here for? I'm not leaving, so you can have a booty call."

"Ha, ha, you're a freaking riot, Maximus. Why did you never become a comedian? Hmm?"

Max laughed and rolled his eyes, and I sat down next to him at his massive computer island.

"I need you," I started, Max raising an eyebrow at my words. "Ew, weirdo, not like that. I need your help to find a name for me. I'm kind of also seeing the bouncer at The Tower, and he won't tell me his first name, and I have a feeling it will provide me with great teasing material."

"Of course, your favor is about teasing someone," he laughed before sobering. "But when did you start at The Tower? I feel like I'm out of the loop."

"Oh, boy. Let me fill you in."

I felt bad I'd been neglecting our friendship and made a vow to be better. I needed to get him out of this place sometime too. I think a trip to The Tower could be what he needed. I would need to ask Nolan about those competitions and see if I could persuade Max out for it.

Kissing his cheek, I told him as much info I knew about Nix and then headed to the shower. Nolan was busy playing a game out in the other room and seemed happy in his own little world.

Flipping through my outfits, I chose a few to take back with me and pulled down their garment bags. When I spotted the flirty yellow dress, I knew it was the one for today. Grabbing it and a pair of brown wedge sandals, I headed to the shower to refresh myself.

Twenty minutes later, I emerged fresh and clean. Drying my hair in one of the hairdryers Max had made, it was dry in sixty seconds. It was a massive feat for me to have it dried in that amount of time. I kept bugging him to make more, but he was worried his family would find him if he ever did.

Slipping on the outfit I chose, I selected an above-the-shoulder brown wig with curly pieces. Clipping everything in, I spun in the mirror, feeling happy with my appearance. Make-up and color-changing contacts later, and I was back to being the confident Zel I wanted to be.

Grabbing the bags I wanted, I headed back out. I expected to find Max still at his computer island, but instead, it was empty. Hearing their laughter from the front, I paused when I heard them talking.

"Zel's special, you know. I might not be as buff as you, but I know people, and if you or that other clown hurt her, *I will destroy you.* She's my little sister, and I'm responsible for protecting her."

Nolan stopped and turned to look at Max. "I think that's where you're wrong. Zel doesn't need protecting. She's strong and a fighter. And I have no plans to hurt her. I really like her. I know I'm batting above my league. She's this Goddess on stage, and I'm just happy to be allowed to get to know her."

"Ah *shit.*"

"What? Did I say something wrong?" Nolan started to look worried.

"No. Quite the opposite. You said everything perfectly. I was testing you. I do know people who can kill you, though. So that part is true. But Zel and I protect one another. She's strong and proved it to me the first night we met by not giving up. Even when some annoying guy bothered her," Max chuckled at the memory. "She's a fighter even when she feels like she's already lost." He stopped and thought about his next words. "I like you, man. Not that it matters, but I approve. Love her hard because she needs it."

"I like you too, Max, and if she lets me, that's the plan."

Feeling a little guilty, or perhaps a little misty-eyed at their bro connection, I decided to make myself known. Knocking my bag into the door, I made a big show of carrying everything. Nolan jumped up to help, and Max used it to his advantage to beat him in whatever game they were playing, and I stood there, stunned.

Nolan had put down his controller for me. He didn't even pause the game. He just put it down.

I glanced at Max, whose mouth was hanging open too as he glanced back and forth from the controller to me. Finally, he nodded and gave me a big thumbs up. I had to agree.

Anyone willing to die for you, imaginary or not, had to be a keeper.

"Here, let me help."

"Thanks, sunshine."

"Did you just give me a nickname, babe?"

"Mmm, hmm. Do you like it?"

"Of course, it's from you. And wow, you look amazing. I have the perfect place in mind for our date. We ready to go?"

"Yeah, let me say goodbye to Max. I'll meet you in the car."

"Sure thing, twinkle toes."

He grinned as he headed up the stairs, calling out a bye to Max. Walking over, Max paused his game, a smirk on his lips. "I love you, pip, but only a pause amount."

"Give me a hug, you dork."

Hugging him, I laughed at his statement. I was glad to have a friend like Max. "I've got my search criteria working. He's removed himself fairly well, as it didn't come up in my typical first searches. I'll find something, though, and then get the message to you."

"Thanks, Max. Take care, and I dunno, maybe step outside once in a while."

"What for? Everything I could want is right here."

"You never know what might surprise you."

He gave me a weird look, but I stood by my statement. A few weeks ago, I had hit another low, wondering what the point was to the day in and day out of my life. There was no joy, love, or laughter. I had my pride in doing it on my own, making my own choices, and looking good while I did it. But what if pride wasn't enough? What if love, hope, and faith were just as powerful?

I once thought pride was my power, but what if it had become my weakness?

CHAPTER EIGHTEEN

NOLAN

Pulling up to my parents' house, I parked the truck in front of the small yellow cottage. It wasn't much, but it had been our home my whole life. My parents were practical people and hard workers. My dad had put his entire life into the hardware store and expected us to follow. Gavin had disappointed them time after time, leaving the weight to fulfill his dreams solely on me, regardless of how I felt. Some days, it felt like I'd never get out from under the weight of his plan.

Zel squeezed my hand, bringing me back to the present. The day had been incredible, and I'd never had so much fun with anyone, but especially a girl. We enjoyed cupcakes from the bakery, tossed pennies into the fountain, and walked among the street vendors in Once Upon A Time town square. Just holding hands and laughing the whole day made it the perfect date.

"You sure about this? My family can be intense."

"If I'm with you, I am."

"You might change your mind after meeting my family. Come on, let's get this over with so we can get to the fun part of our date."

"I don't know, Nols. It's been pretty amazing so far."

Lifting her down from the truck, I kept a hold of her waist. "Yeah, it has." Dropping a kiss to her lips, I couldn't resist pressing her up against the side of the truck. I regretted it a few minutes later when it was pure torture to pull away. The fear of my parents catching us had me stopping. No matter how old you were, the thought of your parents finding you in that state seemed to curb any desire, or at least it did with my parents.

Zel's lips were swollen, her face flushed, and I puffed up my chest at the sight. I hadn't forgotten Max's mention of the bouncer dude earlier, but I was waiting to hear from her what was going on there before I assumed. Besides, I didn't want to ruin my day with her thinking of another guy. Linking my fingers, I pulled her along, the yellow dress fluttering around her legs as she walked.

She looked like a ray of sunshine in that dress. It was comical to me she thought I was the sunshine one when she radiated the sun herself. Stopping at the front door, the weather-beaten wreath with our family names on it hit me with a wave of sadness I hadn't expected. How many times have I seen it there and never once flinched? But today, it *hurt* as I thought of what it represented. Clearing my throat, I hoped she wouldn't ask who all the names were. It was getting shoved over to the column of things to talk about later.

Ringing the doorbell, we waited for someone to answer. I could've opened it myself, but it felt weird not living here anymore just to walk in. A few seconds later, my mother opened the door, her pumpkin and apple smell wrapping around me like a warm hug.

"Toots!" She pulled me into her arms. Peeking around the head of fluffy curls, I gave a sheepish expression to Zel. She had her hand over her mouth, trying not to laugh. I wasn't sure if it was the name or the fact my 5 ft mother had me in a bear hug, her hair almost as big as her.

"It's so good to see you, toots! It's been too long. Come in and introduce me to this pretty girl. Seems like it's a dinner of all kinds of surprises tonight."

She grinned warmly at Zel, and I offered my hand to her. Zel took it, and I pulled her toward me.

"Hello, Mrs. Ryder. It's a pleasure to meet you."

"Oh, this one has manners. I like her, toots!" Before Zel could say anything, my mom engulfed her in a hug. Around the fuzzy hair, I could make out Zel's face, and I was surprised to find a look of sadness there. She quickly changed it before my mom pulled back.

"It's Darla, dear. No need for any of that Mrs.

nonsense. Now, come and tell me how you met my toots."

"Toots?" I heard her ask, and my face flamed. I'd hoped she would've dropped the ridiculous nickname when she saw I had a guest. Apparently, mother embarrassment didn't care.

"Oh yes. He was a rotten tootin' little baby. Give him beans, and you'd be fumigating your house for a week! We started calling him toots, and then never stopped. I like how embarrassed he gets, if I'm honest." Darla Ryder grinned mischievously at my girl.

"Well, now I see where he gets his mischief from," Zel laughed, causing my mom to bend over in one of her own.

"That he does. He's my good boy, though, always kind to everyone."

"Yeah, that he is."

Zel smiled at me, a blush to her cheeks, and I decided to let it go, their banter endearing—especially if I got to see that look. I knew I should be careful. I knew my heart was at risk of being hurt. I knew it probably wouldn't last. I knew all of this, and yet each time she smiled, flicked her eyes to me, or softly touched me, I fell head over heels. I could deny it all I wanted, but it was a foregone conclusion. Zel had stolen my heart, and I didn't want it back.

Entering the house, I tried to imagine what she'd think of our small home. It was cozy and well lived in, the decor dated with flowers and in various shades of country blue and mauve. Pictures hung all around the walls from various stages of our lives. School portraits, family picnics, camping trips, and even some holidays could be found. If you looked closely, though, you would notice a very specific thing. We all stopped aging around six years ago.

Well, one of us had. This wasn't Tuck Everlasting; we didn't have a fountain of youth. Nope, we just had a dead kid story, or sister in my case. Life had changed after Natalie's murder. We didn't talk about it, it was too hard most days, and I hoped my family kept it that way. Mom had moments where she forgot and would say something before realizing it. She'd slip into a depressive state afterward that would last a few weeks before she pretended it wasn't real again. Nat's ghost was alive and well in our house.

Dad grieved by focusing on the store even more, using it to cover his emotions. It didn't help that they'd spent their savings trying to find who had killed her. In the end, it didn't matter. He was too good, too clever to get caught. It had been during my senior year of high school, and I hadn't handled it the best. Life at home was a mess, and I let Gavin talk me into petty crime. A couple of B&E's, and I convinced myself I was helping.

It made sense to my grief-stricken mind to help save my family by providing them with the money they needed. When Gav started selling drugs, that was when I got off his dysfunctional train. He was two years older, but after her death, it felt like I was the oldest. Time after time, I rescued him from alleyways covered in his own vomit. Sometimes beaten, other times mugged, he was never able to stay away from the temptation.

I stayed home and worked at the store, helping to keep the family together. Until one day, l realized I was living my life for everyone else. Talking my father into letting me attend Shire University had been a huge step for me. Under the guise of improving my future for the store, I hoped getting separation from it would allow me to find the courage to admit what I wanted for my life.

Zel's giggles broke my stare off with a picture of three of us, and I blinked, attempting to clear the memory haze from my mind. There was a reason I didn't think of it. *It was too hard.* Natalie hadn't just been my sister. She was my best friend and twin. Every good thing in my life had been shared with her. It felt weird now to experience good things without having her with me.

Walking further into the house, I found my mom and Zel at the counter making cookies. The domestic scene was unnerving, and I didn't want to admit how much I liked seeing her belonging in my family home. Leaning against the door jamb, I watched as my mom showed her the Ryder family secret to good cookies—double the chips. Granted, it wasn't a CIA classified type thing, but it was still our family recipe, and it held meaning my mom was sharing it.

She caught me staring and smiled, mouthing "I like her" before returning back to the cookies. The sliding door opened, and my father came in carrying a pan of burgers and hot dogs. I never understood why he carried them in on one pan, and then out later on a plate. It seemed like excessive dishes to me, but maybe it was because I didn't like washing them.

"Hey, son, good to see you. Can you go and make sure your brother doesn't let the corn burn?"

He nodded to the backyard, and I realized Gav was already here. I hadn't noticed his car, but that wasn't surprising. He was often without one, and I wouldn't recognize his girlfriend's ride since I'd never met her before. Checking with Zel, I didn't want to leave her alone if she would be uncomfortable. At her soft smile and head nod, I went in search of my brother.

He was standing by the grill, talking to a girl with long dark hair. At the sound of the door, he turned and looked at me. Gav had a beer in one hand and the other on her waist, a tiny baby bump visible. The strangeness of the sight struck me, and I found it weird to think about Gavin getting married and becoming a dad.

"Nolan! Come and meet my fiancé."

The girl turned more, bringing her profile into

view. She had sharp features but a kind smile. Walking over, I offered my hand out to shake hers.

"I'm Nolan. It's nice to meet you..." I realized he'd never said her name before, though something about her was familiar.

"It's Blair, Blair Cassidy. I think we went to high school together? At least, that's what your brother tells me." She smiled. Her name sounded familiar, but with Nat's death, the last years had been a blur of grief and attempting to keep everything together.

"Well, it's nice to meet you again after all these years. How did you two meet?"

"Oh well, Gavin was meeting with my father for a job interview and asked me out after. I said no, but he kept coming by every day." Blair grinned at my brother, love shining in her eyes. I'd been skeptical when he told me about his romance, but looking at them, I wanted to believe the best. Maybe this time, he'd actually turned his life around for good.

A few minutes later, the door opened again, and my father, mother, and Zel exited, carrying items to place on the patio table to the left. Mom had a jug of lemonade, dad had plates and napkins, and it looked like Zel was carrying cups. Their activity reminded me why I'd come out here. Looking at the grill, I checked the corn because dad was right, Gavin hadn't focused on it. He was too busy making out with Blair. Turning the corn skewers, I grabbed the pan and moved them off the heat.

"Gav, dinner."

Shaking my head, I found myself laughing at him. It was an odd emotion to share with my brother. The past six years had mainly been tragedy, despair, and apathy. Hopefully, Blair would be good for him, and he wouldn't screw up his life with whatever shit he was in. Because I knew he had to be, no matter how nice he made it sound, Gavin was always looking for his next scheme. I hoped it wouldn't get him killed. Walking over, I placed the corn on the table before I pulled Zel into my arms, loving the feel of her there.

"Corn's done."

My dad glanced up, a nod of appreciation at rescuing the corn from Gav. "Well, Darla should be bringing the rest of the food out, ah, there she is."

My dad smiled as Mom walked over, the tray of buns and condiments in her arms. Walking over, I took some from her and placed them on the table next to the meat my dad had set down after plating it. Perhaps, my mom's presentation rules had sunk into him over the years, and it was a habit. Pulling out a chair for Zel, she turned a look of surprise on her face at the gesture.

Tilting my head, I motioned for her to sit. Once she was situated, I took the seat next to her. It was nice sitting out here and enjoying a meal. The evening was cool, the sun starting to set behind us, giving us the perfect ambiance.

"It's such a nice surprise to meet you both. I can't remember the last time we all sat down for a meal together," my mom said, a hint of sadness evident. My dad cleared his throat, trying to dispel some of the somberness.

"So, Gavin, what's this news you had to share with us?"

Gavin looked up, surprised at being asked a question right as he took a bite of food. Zel had frozen next to me once they'd sat down, and I realized we hadn't introduced her. Since Gavin was still chewing his food, I jumped in.

"Oh, um, apologies, bad manners," I grimaced, "Gavin, Blair, and Dad, this is my girlfriend, Zel." I turned to her, smiling, and hoped she would relax. Her expression was still tight, though, as she smiled at everyone.

"I met the lovely girl inside and told her to call me Tom," my dad replied, grinning wide before taking a bite out of his burger. Gavin finally swallowed the world's largest bite and started to clear his throat to share his news. He stood, and I leaned down to Zel to see if I could figure out what was wrong during the distraction.

"Everything okay? Grab whatever you want to eat."

Her eyes peered up at me before slowly nodding. When she didn't move, I grabbed a bun and burger and sat it on her plate, worried she felt odd reaching for it or something. Lifting the corn, I asked with my eyes if she wanted any. She nodded, a slight smile emerging. Picking up the other bowls of food, from pasta salad to tomatoes and cucumbers, I picked each one up and served her when she nodded.

I hadn't realized everyone had stopped and watched me until I sat the last thing down and wondered why it'd gotten so quiet. Zel had a cute blush again, and I shrugged when everyone stared, their mouths agape. My mom and dad smiled at me, a look of pride on their faces for my apparent affection and attention to Zel. Gavin looked a little pissed for taking the spotlight for a second, but once we were all turned to him again, his face lit back up.

"Okay, now that we witnessed how pussy whipped Nolan is," he started.

"Gavin Franklin! Language at the table!" my mother hissed. Gavin rolled his eyes, and I saw the brother I knew return.

"Anyway, like I was saying," he tried again. "I gathered you all here tonight to not only introduce you to Blair, but to announce we're getting married."

Whatever response Gav had been hoping for, he didn't get it. When no one said anything, Zel piped in, "Congratulations," and seemed to dislodge my parents from their shock.

Despite already knowing, I joined in and responded back in a low celebratory tone, "Congrats, Gav."

"Seriously! I tell you I'm getting married, and only Nolan's booty call seems happy for me!" I started to defend Zel, but she placed her hand on my arm, shaking her head. It didn't feel right to let him disrespect her, but I decided to let it go since she wanted me to.

"It's not that, Gav. Blair, you're a lovely girl," my mother started, attempting to salvage the dinner.

"Oh, what is it then, *Mother*? Hmm? Please, enlighten us all?" Gav became irritated now, his movements sporadic and frantic.

"It just took us by surprise, is all. It's the first time meeting Blair, and then you tell us you're getting married. It was shocking. Promise, honey, we're happy for you."

"Well, you should be because you're gonna be grandparents too," Gavin added, a smug look on his face. Now he'd shocked my parents as they looked at Blair sitting on the end. Slowly, she stood, reaching for Gavin's hand.

"It's true, and I hate that we're meeting this way. I am looking forward to getting to know you all and to call you family."

It was all it took for my mother to break into hysterics. Standing, she wrapped the girl in her arms, tears falling down her face as she rocked her back and forth. "Oh sweetie, this is excellent news. I'm so happy for you."

"Finally," I heard Gavin mutter as he took his seat, resuming stuffing his face with his burger. My dad watched him, an odd look on his face.

"What's your plans, son? Hmm? Last I checked, you didn't have a job you could keep longer than a day. Now, you're telling me you're getting married and having a baby. How do you plan to support not one person but two people?"

My dad threw his napkin down onto the table and began to rise out of his chair. This had been a point of contention between them for years, and I immediately regretted bringing Zel to this. Reaching down, I grabbed her hand and squeezed, hoping to convey my apologies. She pressed back, and some of my anxiety fled. It was always up to me to be the comedian or peacemaker. I kept everyone else in check when everything fell apart. Before I could stand and try to salvage the evening, the girl next to me did.

"Did you know that a duck has a corkscrew penis? I kid you not."

Everyone turned and looked at Zel, who now ate like she just hadn't said penis at the table.

"Oh, and echidnas have a four-headed penis, though only two are used at a time, and the flat-worm engages in penis fights."

When she finished her bite, she looked up,

shrugged, and continued, not bothered. "I like nature documentaries."

Something about the way she said it casually, with no apologies, had everyone roaring in laughter, and the tension officially broke. I didn't think penis had ever been said that many times at our dinner table, only Zel could get away with it. The rest of the meal went smoothly, my father choosing to wait until guests weren't around to interrogate Gav. My mother kept giving me secret smiles across the table, her approval of Zel shining through.

When dinner finished, I was relieved and ready to go. Zel hugged my mother, promising to visit soon, laden down with a container of the cookies she made. Blair and Gavin were ahead of us as we walked out and waited for us at the end of the drive. I felt Zel stiffen, and I wasn't sure why.

"We should do a double date or something, Nolan. That way, our girls can get to know one another better."

"Uh yeah, sure," I hedged, not knowing how I felt about it. "I'll text you."

"I feel like I know you," Blair blurted, looking at Zel quizzically. "Are you sure we've never met? Do you go to Shire?"

"Nope. I guess I just have one of those faces. Well, it was nice meeting you. Bye."

Zel dragged me away quickly, and I let her, not wanting to hang out any longer than necessary either. It always amazed me how fast she could walk in her high-heeled shoes, but I guess walking was a breeze when she did pirouettes in them. Lifting her into the truck, I kissed her quickly before shutting the door. Jumping in my side, I turned, a question on my face and a new feeling of hunger taking over.

"I'm not ready for the night to be over, but I don't want to keep you out longer than you intended. Do you want to stay another night or head back to yours?"

She took me in, assessing me as she thought over the question. "Take me to The Tower."

Disappointment sank in my stomach at her answer, but I hid it as I pulled away from the curb to head there. The drive was quiet, and I assumed we were both lost in our own thoughts. I was trying to figure out where I went wrong to make her want to return home.

When we pulled up, Zel directed me to the private parking lot. I sat awkwardly in my seat, trying to gauge what move to make. "Listen, Zel, I had a great time, and I'd like to see you again."

"Nolan, if you're not up in my room in sixty seconds and naked, then I'm telling your mother that you failed to be a gentleman. Because all girls know, gentlemen make sure their ladies come first. Are you up for the challenge?"

She'd leaned over, her breasts rubbing against my arms as she spoke, her hand grazing my rock solid cock in my pants. Yet, when I blinked, she was gone, and I realized the count had started. Barreling out of my truck, I didn't even care if it was locked as I raced toward her and tossed her over my shoulder as I did.

Her squeals of glee as I swung her around into my arms was music I wanted to dance to. The only sound I thought would be better was the moan I'd pull from her very soon. The guard at the door opened it as we got closer, and I realized it was the growly one. He nodded a look of appreciation on his face for returning her.

"Don't be rude, Nix!" Zel chuckled, causing the man in question to turn to her.

"How am I being rude, *Princess*?"

We'd stopped inside a dark hallway, and I wasn't sure which direction to head in as I waited for them to have their conversation. I saw an exit sign up ahead and was about to head there when I heard Zel's response.

"I know you were waiting there for me, and you didn't offer us use of the private elevator. So, are you going to show me to my new room, or am I going to have to beg?"

He smirked, and I wasn't sure what was going on. Did she want me to come back with her, or did she want *him*?

He took off in a different direction, and I followed, unsure what else to do. Zel's hands were in my hair, her soft kisses on my neck, and I soon forgot all about my worries. Nix stopped up ahead, inserting a keycard into a slot, and the wall disappeared into an elevator. He held it open for us and hit a button before stepping back. Before it closed, he looked at the beautiful girl in my arms, no hint of jealousy she was with me apparent, only adoration for her.

"Breakfast tomorrow, princess. Clothing *optional.*"

The door started to close, but he stopped it when only his head could be seen through the space. "And you know I like it when you beg."

Before she could respond, he let go, the elevator closing all the way. Sitting her down on her feet, I took her hands, knowing I needed to ask before things went any further.

"Where do I stand, Zel? What am I to you? What is he?"

She leaned close, her hands running up my chest, and I tried to focus and not get lost in the lust.

"You're my Nolan, and I'm your Zel. Does it need to be anything else? I've lived a long time not having anyone in my life, and for some reason, coming here, I've met people I do connect with. I don't want to have to choose between you. I need you all. I'm not trying to use you or make you feel unworthy or not enough. It's not that."

The elevator stopped, and the door opened into a room beyond it. She stepped backward, her hand falling from my grasp as she did slowly.

"I want you, Nolan, and I think we could be great together. But I understand if you can't be in a relationship like that."

She stood on one side of the elevator and me on the other, and I knew I had a choice to make. Step over into a new reality with Zel, where I felt more emotions than I had in years. Or stay back in my comfort zone, living each day exactly the same and wondering if there was more to life.

Natalie's voice came to me, and I heard her as clearly as if she was right there with me. *"Nothing good ever comes from comfort zones, Nols. You're meant to live life."*

So as the elevator doors started to shut, I took a step forward into a future I'd never imagined for myself, but one I knew I'd never leave. Because as I looked down at the smiling girl before me, I understood. I was her Nolan, and she was my Zel, and it was all that mattered.

CHAPTER NINETEEN

ZEL

My breath caught in my throat as I waited for him to decide. This was it, the moment I would know if what I felt meant anything. When the elevator doors began to close, my heart dropped until I saw him take a step. In a move only Hollywood could script, Nolan braced his hands on the door, stopping them from closing as he peered down at me with hunger. He stepped in front of me, and the smile I felt inside was unable to be contained any longer, breaking free as he drank me in.

Holding my arms up, he lifted me by the waist, and I wrapped myself around him. Crashing our lips together, I felt all his promises in that kiss. His walls were gone, his heart open, and I risked it, shedding mine along with him. This boy, no, *this man*, had captured me in a way I hadn't known was still possible. Nolan was giving me something I'd thought stolen—young love.

Dating in high school hadn't been an option,

mostly because I wasn't allowed. Why would Daddy want me to give it away for free? He had friends paying millions in cash and favors for a touch, a tease, and a picture of me. I was too valuable a commodity to allow a teenage boy near. It was how my persona of being untouchable merged, of being the Queen bee in school. It was a facade carefully crafted. I'd been too conditioned and naive to identify it at the time. The biggest joke, I had no friends and thought less of myself than anyone else. I wasn't popular or stuck-up. No, I was lost and depressed, wading in a sea of uncertainty.

No dating meant I didn't experience high school dances or movie dates, and no meeting the parents had ever occurred. When I started dancing for money, I figured it never would. Who takes home a stripper to meet Mom and Dad? It hadn't seemed like a scenario I'd ever find myself in.

And yet today, I got to be a twenty-something girl out with a boy she liked. I got to hold hands, feed food from street vendors to one another, and meet someone's mom. I'd never met a mom like Darla. She was kind and warm, and you wanted to make her like you. She was the kind of mom I'd hoped Queenie would've been.

Seeing Blair outside had thrown me, and I'd freaked out when I thought she'd be able to see right through my disguise. Blair had been a part of my life I didn't want to remember. She wasn't a bad person; in fact, she'd always been nice to me during ballet classes. Her father was a different story, and I could only guess what Gavin was getting himself into. I'd talk with Nolan about it later. Right now, all I could think about was him. I shoved all the annoying thoughts away and focused on my sweet boyfriend.

His tongue wrestled with mine, creating millions of flutters to erupt in my heart. Trying to imagine Nolan as the quiet chem partner I had in school made my brain hurt. Nolan took charge, was confident, and knew what he was doing in bed. It was more than I could say for his lumberjack roommate. My back hit the mattress, and I wrapped my legs tighter around him. I hadn't even had time to look at my new room yet, but it didn't matter. I only wanted one thing right now.

Pulling my mouth back, I gulped in air, the heat of the moment crescendoing with each hip thrust. The yellow material of my dress had fallen to the sides, giving Nolan perfect access to all of me. Slowly, I untied the last few bows when he pulled back, amazement on his face as he watched it come undone.

Lifting up, I pushed the dress off my shoulders and knelt before him. My lingerie was white lace, and I had stockings and garters on. I'd gone through the extra trouble today, hoping it would lead me here with him. Reverently, he brushed across my skin, his fingertips grazing me.

"You're the most breathtaking woman I've ever seen, Zel."

Taking his shirt in my hands, I pushed it up, and he helped me get it over his head. Ab muscles and indentions met me as I tried not to drool all over him this close. Reciprocating the same torture, I ran my fingers up his chest lightly, being sure to circle his nipples as I did. His breath hitched in spurts, urging me to continue. Inching forward, I wrapped my arms around his neck, pulling us close.

"Nolan, I love that we've taken it slowish and gotten to know one another better, not rushing the physical aspect. By your standards," I teased, "this was our third date, correct?"

"Hmm, I do believe it was."

"So, I guess," I shrugged coolly, "we get to see each other naked?."

Laughing, I tried to play it off, though inside, I was burning with passion. Other than Nix, I'd never felt this fire before. Once I'd conquered sex, it had been enjoyable, and I chased that release each day and night. It felt powerful to overcome the thing that had hindered me, weakening me in my father's eyes. Each night, my self-confidence increased with the knowledge I'd turned the tables. Not only had I survived by using sex, but I'd also found a way to enjoy it.

It had taken time, not every partner was great, but once I had some that were, I understood the draw and the power sex held. And yet now, I learned a very crucial difference as well. Lust was temporary and faded. It felt good for the moment and fueled the fantasy. Passion and desire came from an entirely different place.

These two burned brighter and longer and stemmed from an emotion I hadn't been familiar with. Nolan's eyes swirled with hunger, but I saw it for the longing it was. Nolan didn't hunger for a naked woman to bend over. No, he yearned for *me*. He wanted to explore my body and devour it. The heat was all-consuming, and I found myself diving in headfirst.

Twisting my body, I pressed my back to his front and used him like a pole as I dipped and dropped myself slowly on him. His moan of pleasure vibrated through me, and I caught myself gasping at the sound.

"I need you to touch me, Nols. Please," I begged, no longer able to push the limits, needing it in return.

He didn't hesitate as he grasped my hips to him, and I could feel his cock against my ass. Slowly, at a torturous pace, he grazed the layer of my panties. Nolan's touch sent shivers down my body, the feeling intoxicating. The simplistic caress was agonizingly erotic as he brushed against me, his fingers telling a story my body wanted to hear.

When his lips grazed my collarbone, my skin felt electric. Each place he skimmed kept an imprint of the touch, sealing it away for my memory to replay later. His breath skittered across me, and I was done.

My body tensed, locking its muscles as I soared into the unknown. Nolan Ryder had set me off with his intensity, passion, and tender care. It was a sensation, unlike anything I'd ever felt before, and had me falling headfirst into a place I hadn't known existed—trust.

When his fingers breached the opening of my panties, I was so ready for him to own my cunt. We were riving bodies of moans and gasps of air as he plunged his fingers into me. My knees couldn't hold me anymore, and I found myself falling forward onto the bed. Flipping me around, Nolan towered over me, his hair hanging down as I pushed it back. He didn't stop touching me. If anything, the new position gave him more reach as he peppered kisses over my front.

Open mouth, hot caresses were left like a trail to find his way. His nimble fingers managed to unhook my bra, keeping me focused on where he was headed. Nolan's attention to detail as he consumed me was unparalleled. Only one other man had ever made me the sole focus before. When he dragged my panties down my legs in an achingly slow crawl, I was two seconds away from pouncing. Foreplay had never felt so amazing before, but I wanted more—needed more.

"Nols, I-I-"

I didn't get anything else out as he hauled my

hips up to his face and ate me out as if I were his favorite dessert. Long licks with the flat side of his tongue traveled up my core until he rolled and thrust it into me. The flexibility and maneuvering he accomplished at the feat boggled my mind, but the sensations felt too wonderful to think about it long.

"Mmm, Zel."

Squeezing my legs around his face, I didn't want him to stop. His chuckle reverberated against my clit, sending zings up my body, throbbing in tandem with my clit. Half my body was suspended in the air as he feasted, and the blood rushing to my head added to the ecstasy. Like a trick on the pole, my body was in two different directions, and my breathing oriented to the effect, heightening my pleasure.

My muscles tensed, and I found myself heading toward the cliff again when the tingles paused, my body floating back to the bed from the cloud I'd been on. I heard rustling and the familiar sound of a condom wrapper when sound returned to me. I was dazed and in a plane where things felt surreal. Touching his face as he returned, I caressed the smooth skin I could reach. How did this guy make me feel so *undone*?

Wrapping my arms around his neck, I pulled him in for a kiss as a need surging in me took over. As I twisted my tongue with his, I felt my heart leaving my body. His chest rubbed against mine, and I found us entwined on our sides, my leg hitched over his hip. This was intimate, this was real, and there was no turning back from here. Locking eyes, palpable energy charged between us as he gripped my leg, sliding into me.

I hadn't gotten a good look at his cock, the orgasmic haze having clouded my view. With each inch he plunged into me, I was surprised at the length he was rocking. When he finally stopped fully seated in me, I gasped for air, never having felt so full before. I didn't know if it was the position, the intimacy, or his apparent elephant dick, but sex had never been this connected.

"You ready, Zel-bel?"

The cutesy nickname belied the intensity of the emotions coursing through me, but I couldn't help but smile at him. Nolan's presence demanded nothing less than carefree joy. Nodding, I smiled as he grabbed my ass cheeks, pulling me forward a centimeter more. Rolling my hips, we found a rhythm together, keeping us sealed tightly as hands laced in hair, wrapped up in one another. I almost expected to be conjoined to him after this.

When his finger slipped into my second hole, a look of surprise lit my eyes. A gasp left me as I felt him time it with his thrust. Falling over the edge, he followed me as I clenched around him, our sounds of orgasm ringing out as we both let go.

Panting in one another's arms, he brushed my hair back, the tender gesture making me want to attach to him like glue. Wrapping my arms, I pulled him close and held him to me, burying my head in his neck. I breathed him in a few times before I felt the wetness on my cheek. Not wanting him to know, I kept a hold of him, but the dam had been opened, and they rolled out, my body shaking with the force.

"Ssh, let it out," he encouraged. "I'm hoping this isn't about me, so I'm ignoring the voice in my head. I don't know what's made you cry, Zel, but I'm here. I'm not going anywhere. I mean, I will have to get up soon and take the condom off, but then I'll be straight back, I promise."

Laughing through the tears, I pulled back to see his face. He smiled at me, and everything felt right.

"I'm going to take care of that now, so I don't have to worry about it. One sec, babe."

He kissed my nose, pulling out slowly. It had felt so good with him in me, and now I felt a sense of longing and unfulfillment. Bringing my legs to my chest, I wrapped my arms around them as I laid on my side, staring at the room I'd been too busy to take in. The side I could see held an armoire, full-length mirror, and makeup vanity. The furniture was dark wood, perhaps a dark cherry or espresso finish. Curious, I sat up to take in the rest of the room.

Nolan walked back, a soft look on his face making me blush. He picked up his shirt, sliding on his boxers before climbing onto the bed. He dropped his shirt over my head, and the thoughtful gesture surprised me. Poking my arms through, I inhaled his clean and warm scent as it fell over my body.

"Thanks." I grinned, smelling the fabric as I did. Mmm, sweet boy smell. He smiled and pretended not to notice my weird behavior. He handed me a Kleenex as well, and I took it, a curious look on my face at the item.

"In case you needed it to clean yourself or for your tears. I didn't know where things were to grab anything else, and invading your privacy felt wrong."

His blush was too cute, and I lifted up, wrapping my arms around his neck again. "Can I keep you?" I hadn't meant to ask it, but it was out there for him to hear now, my vulnerability on display. He pushed me back some, taking in my face.

"*Zel, I'm already yours.*"

His words brought tears back to my eyes, and I found myself crying in his arms again. He pulled me back to his chest, leaning against the headboard, cradling me there. Nolan didn't rush me or make me feel weird for crying after sex. When I finally got myself centered. I blew my nose on the Kleenex he'd given me.

Sitting back, I had an idea what was happening, why I suddenly seemed to be malfunctioning from my eyes. "I think that was the most beautiful sex I've ever had, Nolan. Something about it broke the dam in me, but I think it also healed something I hadn't realized was broken."

"Do you want to tell me about it?"

"No, not particularly," I admitted.

"Then don't. I'll be here when you do."

"That's just it. It's not going to be easy, but I want to tell you."

"I'm not going anywhere, Zel."

Taking a deep inhale in, I let it out slowly as I prepared to share my real identity. It was time to stop hiding.

CHAPTER TWENTY

ZEL

Goosebumps spread across my skin, my fear a living breathing emotion as I contemplated what it would mean. Something bigger than my fear blanketed me though, and I knew this moment with Nolan was right. Somewhere in my blissed-out haze, floating between planes, I realized I'd never fully feel anything until I dropped all my shields. I'd been naked before him earlier, but I hadn't been entirely bare. In order to do that, I needed to shed the armor I'd worn for so long it'd become confused with my safety and freedom.

Because it wasn't freedom—not really. To be truly free, I needed to step into the light and stop hiding. I had to be naked on all accounts.

"Can you close your eyes?"

Nolan nodded, shutting them as he laid back against the pillows. Slipping off the high bed, I found the bathroom and quickly washed my face, exposing my birthmark. Disposing the contacts, I took the pins out of the brown wig and let my hair down. The relief was instantaneous as I laid each pin on the counter. I'd gotten so used to it, I forgot how they felt, but each time I took them out, it was like shedding a weight I hadn't known I was carrying. They'd started as a safety blanket, providing assurance and comfort, but I never realized the trappings they'd become until now.

Shaking out my blonde strands, I gripped the counter as my body began to tremble. On shaky legs, I walked back to the bed, my hands twisting as I went. Nolan still laid there, golden smooth skin on display. He had one arm behind his head, a knee bent, his body on perfect display. The sight had me forgetting my nerves for a second as I drank in my sunshine boy.

My inner thoughts sounded like a broken record as I reflected back five years ago. Had he been this hot in high school? Was I so lost in my own grief I hadn't noticed all that next to me? Why weren't girls lined up to date him? Nolan Ryder was the real deal. He was the type of boy romance books were written about—sweet, caring, and fun with devilishly good looks. He was a warm blanket on a cold day.

"If you wanted to perv on me, Zel-bel, you didn't have to make me close my eyes."

His lips tilted up, and I felt the last shred of fear leave me. I could do this. I wanted to. Tiptoeing closer, I climbed up on the tall bed and positioned myself on his lap. His smile widened to a full one, his hands grabbing my hips as I settled.

"Open your eyes."

Nolan blinked, his eyes focusing on me in front of him. I didn't say anything, staying silent to see if he would know. His eyes glittered with happiness, my heart fluttering in my chest as I waited.

"You're letting me see your hair. I thought you said you hated it?"

"It's not that I hate it, Nols. I hate who I am without my disguise, and what my hair represents. Do you," I swallowed, "do you recognize me?"

I wanted to drop my eyes. I wanted to hide, but I forced myself to be brave and stay in the moment. He kept staring, tracing my face, hair, everything with his eyes. I saw the moment it clicked in his eyes, and waited for the anger, disgust, or even pity to appear. When he kissed me, my eyes had remained open, surprised by the move. He pulled back just as quickly, roaming me now with more urgency.

"It's you. You're her. I-I."

He kissed me again, and this time, I kissed him back. Both of his hands held my face between them, not wanting to let go. Nolan pulled back again, and the amount of awe on his face floored me.

"I don't understand."

Covering his hands with my own, I tried to press the warmth of them into my skin. I hated how scared I was the minute I was me. Put me in a wig and a dress, spinning around a pole, and the strong sex goddess was unleashed. But having to be me, be Rapunzel, crippled me in agonizing doubt and fear.

"I'm going to tell you a story. It's not pretty, nor does it have a happy ending like the paper wants you to believe."

His expression changed, a seriousness taking over as his eyes narrowed. Nolan never let go of me, though, and it was the anchor I needed.

"What do you remember hearing about me?"

He blew out a breath, his eyes skirting to the side as he retrieved the memory. "You were thirteen? Fourteen? When did they find you?"

"Thirteen. And they didn't find me. I found *them*."

"I remember hearing about the mayor's daughter being found. I thought it was something out of a fairy tale. After all these years, to have been taken and then reunited with your family. I was so excited to learn everything about you, me and Natalie, shit, uh. I guess there's something I need to tell you too," he stuttered at the mention of Natalie. I wanted to probe him, but knew it would only derail me more.

"It's okay. You can tell me later, when you're ready."

He nodded, gratitude on his features before continuing. "We were hoping to meet you at school.

I remember the first time I saw you in the hallway. You seemed to float as you walked by, your hair flowing behind you as you did, almost like it had its own airstream. Girls and boys surrounded you, everyone wanting to be your friend. I didn't have any classes with you until Junior year. But I," he blushed, ducking his eyes, "I watched you. When you danced, I always felt like something magical had occurred. I never knew why you stopped, just that one day you seemed not to shine as bright."

Nodding, I reached up to wipe the tears falling, but he beat me to it, swiping them off my cheeks.

"The woman who took me, Gothel, she'd gotten sick one night. When she wouldn't wake, I panicked and left the clearing where we lived. It feels dumb now, but then I didn't know a world beyond our area existed. I'd been allowed only to explore within the confines of the clearing. I played with the animals, I read and sang to them, and mostly I danced—the butterflies and squirrels were my only audience. I'd dreamed of a bigger world where I got to go on adventures and meet people, but I didn't want to upset my mother by asking. She told me people would want me and take advantage of me. I chose to risk it that night to save her, not knowing it would set everything else in motion."

I cleared my throat, needing a minute for the rest. Nolan didn't rush me, patiently waiting for me to be ready.

"A nurse recognized my birthmark and hair, my

green eyes being the last clue. She reported me to the police, and they flooded the hospital like it was a terrorist in the bed. My 'parents' were with them. In one night, I became the lost girl who'd returned, and my whole damn world changed. Sadness enveloped me at the thought of leaving Gothel, she was all I'd known, but they locked her up and I had no choice. I hated the part of me that was so happy for the chance to explore more of the world. I'd already encountered so many things just coming to the hospital. I thought my life was beginning. It all seemed so perfect in the beginning."

Nolan shifted us, laying us on our sides, pulling me closer into his arms. In a way, it was easier not to have direct contact, but I missed the honey brown of his eyes reassuring me. I hugged him for a second before pulling back. He seemed to understand and let me. When I thought about it, I sat up, dragging my knees to me and crossing my arms over them. I couldn't touch him during this. I needed my armor to protect me and distance him from the horrors of my past.

"I started school for the first time, and everyone was so nice to me. My parents' status and the somewhat celebrity role I'd gained made me instantly popular. I didn't know they didn't care about me. My friends had been animals up to this point, and I was excited to make some. It was about a year when things turned dark for me. My, um, father saw my love for dancing and exploited it. He promised me lessons, shoes, and tutus, and when he delivered, they had strings—a price I couldn't pay."

My body shook, but I couldn't stop my story now. The tap had been turned, and it flowed out whether I wanted it to or not.

"The first time his *friend* touched me," I sneered, unable to contain my vitriol, "I convinced myself I'd misunderstood. I was young and naive and didn't know of those things. I just knew it felt wrong. I told my mom the second time, and she ignored me, telling me I'd been mistaken. She started popping pills left and right, and I figured out anything she didn't like, she'd take more pills to ignore. It made her zone out for days. I began to realize she wanted the attention, the fame at having a missing daughter. She'd liked it and when I returned, and she had to mother me, she found she didn't enjoy that aspect as much. She shoved me off to the staff and my father to deal with."

Nolan's hand landed on my foot, and I found I didn't hate it, so I allowed it to stay, still focusing on my hands, I continued.

"The third time, I told my dad, he acted concerned and said he'd take care of it. I believed him. When it didn't stop, I tried again, thinking he hadn't got around to it yet. This time, he twisted it. Made me feel at fault and even said I owed it to him for all the things he'd given me. All the time and grief spent over the years searching for me, and I was living in a field, not in danger. He blamed me for being kidnapped as a baby! A baby!"

Nolan scooted up, holding both my ankles, rubbing circles onto them. My breathing was erratic, my tears and snot covering my face, but I found his circles soothing.

"I discovered much later how far his deceit went and knew I'd never escape the life he had planned for me. As I got older, the requests became greater. It went from posing scandalously for pictures to casual grazes to full-on gropes. By the time I was a woman, I was being molested every week by my father's 'friends'. They were men, associates of his, and he brokered deals with my body as currency. That was the day I realized I wasn't a person to him, just a commodity."

"How did you get out?"

"I discovered his secret, and I made my own deal. Well, I tried to escape first, and he caught me. The second time, I brokered a deal—my pride in exchange for silence. He tossed me out on my own the second the ink was dry. I'd been so desperate to get out, I hadn't read everything. That was the night I met Maximus. If he hadn't found me, I doubt I would've made it. I was close to giving up."

"I'm glad you found each other."

I didn't realize he had me in his arms, cradled across his lap. When he'd done it, I didn't know, but the simple fact I hadn't batted an eye told me everything about Nolan.

"You don't care about the rest?"

"I only care about you." Pure honesty and genuine care dripped from each of his words. I could hear his heart as I laid against his chest, the steady beat a soothing rhythm.

"Is that why you wear a disguise? To hide from your father?"

"It's part of it. At first, I was too ashamed to be seen. Everyone knew my face, and when they saw me in Dante's Circle, it raised too many questions. Maximus came up with the idea, and I found it easier to navigate the city. Soon, I was a connoisseur of different ones, and I found my confidence returning. Covering up Rapunzel meant I could be someone new and forget all the horrors of her life. It was survival in the beginning. When I needed to make money, I turned to the one thing I was good at—dance. It helped me regain myself even more. It had become tainted with my father's sins, but now I could use it to survive. My pride grew, and I became determined to make it on my own. The problem was, my father never expected me to last long on the streets. So when I didn't return home, he sent men to find me. When he couldn't, he threatened the one person I cared about. *Gothel.*"

His look of confusion was clear, and I knew why. It was hard to picture the woman who had kidnapped me as the angel in this story.

"Gothel was the scapegoat, the villain my father needed for his cause. My parents never wanted a child, but the pressure to have one, to be a family man in order to run for office made it necessary. Until he decided to use it to guarantee a win. My kidnapping bought him the election, basically. Gothel worked for my parents. She'd been hired as my nanny and overheard my father making a deal with someone. When she realized what he had planned, she made a choice. Taking enough things to sustain her, she fled with me one night. We lived out there undetected for years. She would go into the town once a month to sell things we grew or made and gather supplies. If she hadn't fallen ill, I probably would still be out there."

"So she wasn't the bad guy?"

"No, the bad guy was hiding in sheep's clothing, lying in wait at home to strike. When I discovered her innocence, I threatened to go to the police. My father laughed, of course, having most in his pocket, including the Captain. Fate was on my side, though, and she was released on a technicality and overcrowding. Kingston threatened her life if I didn't fall in line. He allowed me to live on my own in the guise we told my mother I was at college and would attend brunch once a month. The part I didn't read, the part I hadn't known, was that for Gothel to keep her life, I had to *pay* him."

"And I'm guessing he didn't want money," Nolan gritted out, the anger evident in his features.

"Nope. I had to continue to meet with his

friends once a month to ensure Gothel's life. I could pick and choose who, but I had to choose one."

"How long has this been going on?"

"Five years," I admitted, shame thick in my throat.

"So, for five years, you've continued to be used over 60 times!"

The anger he directed at me shocked me. Pushing back from his hold, I found the fire within like I had with Wesley.

"Screw you, Nolan! You think it's been easy? You think I don't hate myself a little more each day? You think I don't wish I was dead at times? You think for one second I could risk her life for mine? She protected me when I couldn't. She provided for me and loved me. I'm not going to abandon her just because the cost is high. That's not who I am!"

"I'm sorry, Zel. I didn't mean to yell at you. I'm not mad at you. I promise," he pleaded, reaching out for me. "I'm angry at how trapped you must feel. How lonely your life has been. I'm mad that your father continues to use you to stay on top. I'm angry at a lot of things, but not you, gorgeous. *Never you.*"

I wanted to hit and slap him, to make him pay for the sins of my father. I could hear the emotion thick in his throat, his eyes shining, and I knew he wasn't lying. Sitting back down, I barely stopped myself from falling into his arms. I needed to say the last thing without any comfort.

"There was one man who was worse than all the others. The first one. I've been able to avoid him since I left, always dismissing his invitations. The night I ran into you, it was the first time I'd seen him in five years. I once thought avoiding him was the way to survive. I believed as long as it was on my terms, I could take pride in that. I thought I was okay with the arrangement."

"What are you saying, Zel?"

"I'm trying to say," I began, panic clogging my throat until I cleared it. "I'm tired of being scared to be who I am and only surviving. I don't want to live in constant fear of being discovered, of making one wrong move. I made sex my weapon and pride my shield wielding them to stand on my own." I paused, the next part the hardest to admit.

Peering deep into his comforting eyes, I spoke the truth I'd always been too afraid to admit. "I was wrong. I never had a choice, it wasn't consent but coercion. This whole time I believed I was in control, but I haven't been. It's why inevitably I became covered in shame." The weight of the shame had consumed me, beating me down into the shell of the person I wanted to be. I hated Rapunzel because I was ashamed of who I let her become.

"Your anger shifted something in me. I felt a spark of the girl I'd set out to be, the Rapunzel I wanted to be. I thought my disguises kept me safe and gave me confidence, but they've only been covering my secret, my shame. I think… I'm ready to face the monster. Would you help me?"

"Zel, I'll give you the world if you let me."

Nolan Ryder melted my non-existent panties and heart in one swoony motion.

"But," he hedged, and I sucked in a breath, dreading what would be next. "I think you were wrong about one thing."

"Oh?"

"Did you know there are two types of pride?"

Shaking my head, I furrowed my brow, not sure where he was going with this. It hadn't been what I expected, and the relief he wasn't dismissing me was instant.

"One form is said to be the root of all evil, the deadliest sin of all. The corrupt selfishness that puts personal wants above the needs of others. It's vanity and self-absorption that steals away the joy of others. How I see it, almost every important person in your life falls into this category, and doing so, has made you doubt your own worth in the process."

Nolan peered so intently into my eyes, begging me to believe him.

"So, what's the second type?"

"The second form is a healthy belief in self. To have pride in the home you've worked hard for, to have pride in your grades you studied for, to have *pride in providing for yourself all on your own*," he emphasized for my benefit. "This kind of pride is healthy and builds strength and character. It doesn't take from others. It only shines the strength within. Zel, you are the embodiment of this, even if you don't believe so."

"How do you see me clearer than I see myself?"

"Because you're not the only one who struggles with this. I think we both need each other to remind us who we can be."

"I'd like that."

Snuggling back into his embrace, I found myself sleeping unbidden of fear, of shame, and free. Before I fell asleep, the words escaped my lips in a mumble, "*I don't need the world when I have you.*"

Chapter Twenty-One

WESLEY

Throwing my cards down on the table, I resigned myself to not winning tonight. It'd been an impulsive decision to try to distract myself with the game. I should've listened to my own rule —never gamble with love, time, or cards. It was a recipe for disaster, and not even Chef Gloria Cortez could save this one.

The dealer picked up his deck and nodded as he left. Everyone else at the blackjack table had gone hours ago. There were only a few stragglers now around tables and slots in Wager. It was 2 am, and most people were home in their beds. Only the truly dedicated or addicted, depending on who you asked, remained. Nix sat down beside me, a frown marring his face.

He was angry with me, but I struggled to know why. I'd pushed Zel, but was that it? I didn't understand why she wouldn't tell me. If it affected my future and income, I needed to know, *deserved* to. Nix stared at me, wanting me to grovel. The only problem was I didn't know how to fix this. I'd apologized, sent her things, and rescheduled her shift, but I hadn't heard from her. Usually, if I bought a woman something, all was forgiven. Zel had me twisted up inside, spinning me out of control, and I didn't like it. Snapping the rubber band, I exhaled before addressing my friend.

"I know you want something from me, but the problem, Nix," I pleaded, "other than upsetting her, I have no clue what I did. She offered to help and then when I asked, she refused to give me the information I needed! I apologized. Sent her clothes. What else must I do?"

He didn't answer, staring at me with his unwavering gaze. Softening my tone, I tried one more time before I threw in the towel. "I'm asking for once. I need your help."

"The problem Wes," he gritted, "was you weren't listening to what she was saying to you. You focused only on the words, so fixated on your end goal you missed what her body was screaming at you."

Blinking, I felt attacked by his statement. I didn't like to think I had flaws or to admit them. My focus and drive were what had always worked for me. I prided myself on getting the job done, whatever it took. I tried to be a good person and give back as much as I profited by helping the community prosper. I didn't want to only think of myself and become my father. I hadn't thought I did that, but had I?

"I hadn't meant to, I-I-I…" Panic filled me, and I snapped my rubber bands more. I couldn't become like him. Had I lost my sense of self in pursuit of proving I could do this on my own? Had I let myself be clouded by ambition to the point all I could see were greed and pride? My thoughts spiraled, and I found myself falling into a panic attack.

Hard pressure met my hands, the pain stopping my spiral. Looking down, I found Nix's hands bracing my wrists. He gripped them tight enough to break me out of the fog, pushing on the pressure points. Shame at failing coated me, combined with the realization I was in the middle of Wager, all my staff around me to witness my greatest weakness.

"No one saw. There's barely anyone here. If anything, it looks like I'm holding your hand."

A chuckle slipped past my lips, and his grip lessened at the sound. Nodding, he let go completely, and the pins and needles sensation took over. Flexing my hands, I attempted to get blood flowing to them to lessen the sensation. Guess it had been harder than I thought.

"Thanks, Nix."

"You don't have to thank me, but you do need to apologize to Zel. Listen with your eyes instead of only your ears to what she's saying. There's more going on than what you're hearing." He waited for me to acknowledge the command before continuing.

"I think we could have a future with her, Wes. I know I want one. And I believe she'd be good for you too. Based on how she was with the kid when they returned, I think he'll be a permanent fixture as well. Something to consider going in, but I think it could work. If you ever had a grand gesture in you, now would be the time to pull it out."

In typical Nix fashion, he stood, leaving me with my thoughts. Glancing around, I noticed he was right. It was deserted, and no one paid any attention to me. Relaxing, I sank back into the chair, deciding it was as good as any place to think. Recalling the incident, I tried to remember how Zel looked, how she responded. Like a movie playing before me, the memory ran across my mind with all the facts I'd collected.

Zel's body tensed when the Judge walked in.
Nix told me she fainted before he could get her upstairs.
When he undressed her, she hadn't budged.
Searching for her, she'd hidden away after waking up in a strange place.

All of it together should've clued me in to the simple fact there was more going on. Her body language, tone, and refusal to say more had me wanting to slap myself. I'd seen it so clearly before staring back at me in my own mirror.

I wasn't certain, but I could wager a guess. Zel

had been abused, and it looked like this Judge character had a part in it.

When the realization sank in, a fire raged war within me. The audacity he had to hurt someone as pure-hearted as Zel made my fists clench. Nix was right, she'd been screaming for me to listen, and I'd ignored it in pursuit of my own pride. *I didn't deserve her, but I wanted to.*

Slapping my hand on the table in a decision, I made a waitress jump who'd been coming to collect the glasses. Apologizing, I made my way out of Wager and headed up to the penthouse. The memory I'd been trying to ignore filtered through my mind as the elevator climbed.

"Wesley! What is the meaning of these grades? I send you to that school so you'll have the best opportunities, dance is extracurricular. I didn't send you there to bring home B's. If you don't fix this by the next grading period, there's no amount of bargaining that will save you. You'll be shipping off to the military school. Maybe then you'll become a man instead of this pussy whipped freak your mother made you. I can't even look at you in that, that thing!"

Storming away, my father slammed the door to leave the dance hall. My classmates tittered behind me, enjoying my humiliation. The teacher stood upfront, aghast at the intrusion of my father. Fitzherbert Flynn didn't care. He stormed into the middle of rehearsal to berate me. He didn't care. He'd basically embarrassed me in front of my entire class, ensuring to ruin my reputation. He didn't care if the ballet teacher now looked upon me with pity. He didn't care.

False. He only cared about the things which affected him. My 'dismal' school grades being one of them. The fact a B was a bad grade to my father screamed the insane expectations he had for a thirteen-year-old. He'd gotten worse over the past year, ever since my mother had died. She'd been the one advocating for me to attend the school for the gifted so I could focus on dancing. She's been the one to believe in me and nourish my love of ballet.

She'd been the one, and now, she was gone.

Swallowing back my tears, I stared ahead, focusing on counting in my head. One, two, three, four, five, six, seven, eight. Exhaling, I nodded to the teacher to start the music. Getting into fifth position, I focused on the moves I knew by heart. Starting with a petit battement, I kicked from one side to the other as the piece started. A brisé and a cabriolé later, I found myself relaxing into the moves. My partner and I moved into our hold, and finished with sissonne side by side.

When the music stopped, I'd expended all the negative energy from myself and basked in the joy dance brought me. My soul was made to dance, and without it, I didn't know how to breathe. No matter how hard things were at home, no matter how much I missed my mother, no matter how much pressure he put on me, I could dance it out and leave it on the floor. The hardwood floor took *my abuse, my pain, and accepted the offering I laid before it in this room.*

Everything made sense in an eight count.

"Wesley, good job today. Your dancing continues to astound me. You're going to do great tomorrow night at the spring exhibit. If you don't have multiple offers at the end, I'll be shocked."

"Thank you, Mrs. Morrison. And I'm sorry about before; about my father. I didn't know."

"It's okay, Wesley." She patted my shoulder, the pity returning. "No one blames you for his behavior. Keep your head up, okay? Your mother would be so proud."

The mention of my mother had me shutting down. The sentiment had been nice, but I didn't like being reminded when I wasn't ready to accept she was gone. The horrors of that night still plagued me, the sounds of the glass shattering returned as I flashback to the crash.

I never got to know how many offers I would've gotten from the showcase. My father apparently hadn't wanted to take the risk and decided for me. Walking out to my driver, I'd been jumped by some hired thugs and left beaten to a bloody pulp. Both of my legs had been shattered by baseball bats, never able to dance again—not without pain. The physical therapy had been torturous, but I'd been determined.

It didn't matter, though.

As soon as I was healed enough to walk. I was shipped off to military school. I hadn't trained since, the pain still present, and a constant reminder of what had been stolen from me. The longer I went without, the harder it became to start. The anxiety and fear mixed with my mother's crash and I froze any time I had to step onto a stage. The only good thing to come from the experience had been Nixon and the vow we made.

"In the pursuit of our goals, we never take it for granted. Brothers above all."

I needed to remind myself what was important and the people I cared about. Zel was someone I wanted to know. I'd never craved attention from a woman until I tasted hers. Now, it was my turn to make it impossible for her to ignore what I was saying.

I t was 8 am, and I'd only had about two hours of sleep, but I was antsy as I waited for it to be an appropriate time to approach Zel. When I returned to the penthouse, I knew what I needed to do. The grand gesture Nix had spoken of. I had to be as vulnerable as she'd been with me, and I only knew one way to do that.

Bracing myself, I knocked on her new room. I'd taken great care in picking out the details and hoped she liked it. My obsession should've been obvious to me, the level of care and attention to detail I'd done for everything involving her, but somehow, I'd ignored it. The fear of admitting it was almost as great as the rejection that could accompany those feelings.

Nothing could be done, though. Nix was right. Zel called to me in a way no one had before. Her pain was beautifully written in every dance step she took. I was an idiot for not recognizing it. I was drawn to her because our souls were the same—entwined in beauty and pain. It felt like forever before the door opened, but the Goddess that awaited me stole my breath.

Zel was in her natural state, and I had to stop myself from lifting my hand to touch her. She shimmered, her hair a golden beacon of light as it spilled out behind her.

"Wesley," she greeted formally.

"Zel, I was hoping I could borrow you for the morning. I have some things I need to say and something I'd like to share with you, if you'd let me."

She regarded me for a moment before nodding. "Sure thing, *boss*."

It stung, but I deserved it. Nodding, I took in her state and decided to have her meet me there. "Meet me at the end of the hall in thirty minutes. It's room number 310. Wear something you can dance in."

I didn't wait to see her response, not able to bear the rejection or indifference. This would be better anyway. I could warm up and get myself ready. Opening the door, I took in the one room I'd designed but had never been able to bring myself to use—the ballet studio.

The hardwood floors gleamed under the lights. The wax was still fresh, having never been used. The barre against the mirror had no scuffs, the mirror no fingerprints. It was as pristine as the day it was built. Running my hand over the barre, the familiar sensation of positions flitted through my head. The muscle memory wanted to take over from touch alone. The anxiety was there, but it wasn't overwhelming. I think I was ready.

Pulling in a deep breath, I sank down into my warm-up, going through the positions, my knees cracking with each movement. Rising, I stretched my leg up to the barre, bending forward until I felt the pull. I'd come to believe dancers were sadists at heart. Almost everything involved with dance, ballet especially, hurt to some degree. Between the muscle aches, the toenail damage, and the injuries, ballet was brutal. Yet, somehow, the more delicious the burn, the better it felt. For all the beauty the body performed in graceful measures, the toll it took often seemed unmerited. In my opinion, it was the dancers who wanted it the most who pushed through it.

If it didn't hurt, you weren't doing it right. My muscles screamed, but I accepted my punishment as I fell into the familiar routine of stretching and warming myself up. Ten minutes later, I had more fluid motions and already felt better having done that. Maybe I'd been wrong all these years to avoid it. The memories had constantly bombarded me. The snap of the bat as it cracked against my knee and the pull to dance would vanish.

It seemed I found something worth dancing for —Zel.

Starting slow, I turned on some music, falling into the rhythm naturally. Starting with a coupé so one foot lifted and landed before the other, I transitioned into a pas de chat. I leapt, my knees bent and toes lifted toward the center of my body. Doing a few pas de bourrée, a three step lateral movement, I danced on my toes before ending in a ciseaux. They were a favorite of mine, a split leap with one leg in the front of the body and one in the back. It all came back to me and I found my heart soaring with each step.

Finishing the leap, I bent over, my breaths coming fast as I panted, my knees groaning at the effort. Fucking hell, my endurance was shit. Wiping the sweat, I was surprised when I met green eyes in the mirror. Spinning, I found Zel staring at me like she wasn't sure of who I was or what she'd witnessed.

"I see you found the room okay."

"Yep."

"I, uh, I wanted to apologize for the other night. I was out of line and had no right to push you for something you didn't want to share. I needed to trust you were telling me what you could. Instead, I only cared about my own selfishness and getting the info I wanted. You didn't deserve that, Zel. I hope you can forgive me."

She regarded me, walking closer. Her hand met my chest, and I sucked in a breath. Every touch felt electric. "I'll accept your apology on one condition."

"Anything."

"Dance with me."

"What?"

"Dance with me."

"No, that wasn't why I asked you here. I wanted to show you who I was by sharing dance with you and the story of why I love it."

"Okay, that sounds great, and all, and I look forward to hearing it. But right now, Wesley," she stepped forward, bringing her close enough for me to feel her breath on my skin, "I want you to dance with me. Are you brave enough?"

Her taunt sparked the courage I needed. My body already throbbed, my muscles screaming, but it yearned to dance with her more. I'd already begun leaning toward her, ready to share the space to create a story with our movements. Pulling her to me, I held her close, enjoying that I took her by surprise. Her gasp of breath had my cock hardening, and I knew I was going to have to figure out how to dance with one.

Jekyll and Hide started playing, and I moved. We

stared at one another, our focus unwavering as we let our bodies do the talking. It was easy falling into the movements with her. As I expected, our souls seemed to merge, and an outpouring of energy and passion flooded out of us onto the floor. Inexplicably, in what could only be the magic of dance, we began to anticipate and feel the movements of the other as we weaved a contemporary dance full of passion and fire as we worked out our emotions together.

Spinning her, I dipped her down low, grinding into her more than I should as a dance partner. My cock grazed her as I did and the inhale and gasp she gave didn't go unnoticed. I found myself wanting to do it more and more, but managed to stop myself. Lifting her, I caressed her side as I dipped down with her in my grasp. Spinning her around, I realized the level of trust she'd placed in me. We spun, hands grasped, lifting in circles, as we twirled, our heartbreak evident in our steps. Wrapping her around me, her legs naturally fit as I dipped her, slowly moving her from one position to the next. It was the most captivating and natural dance I'd ever performed.

When the song ended, and another one started, something shifted. No longer were we pouring out our hearts, but following our desires. In what could only be called dirty dancing, every move became sexual in nature. Teasing and pushing one another to the limit, we grazed and roamed with our hands, leaving Zel and me breathless as we stared at one another.

I decided to quit being scared and listen to her with my eyes. Closing them, I leaned forward and met her lips with mine. It was wrong on so many levels, I was her boss and older, but as our lips met in a fiery passion that matched the dance we did with our bodies, I knew to my core it was right. Lifting her, she wrapped her legs around me, and I tried not to hobble as I walked to the barre. My legs screamed in agony, but never in a lifetime would I regret the dance I'd done.

Any amount of pain was worth it to dance with her.

It should've been clearer to me, the obvious answer to demonstrate to her how I felt would've been this way. Dance had been pushed to the back of my mind for so long; I hadn't seen it for the solution it was. Words were good, and I needed to be held responsible for the ones I said, but they weren't the only way to communicate.

Our bodies wrote our story in this ballet studio. They spoke of our pain and heartbreak, of seduction and need, but mostly, hope.

Sitting her on the barre, I found relief for my knees and had her at the perfect height. Moving back from the kiss, we stared at one another, waiting for the other to break the silence. Shifting her again, I slid to the floor, my back to the mirror, and shared the story of how I once danced and it had been my everything. It was hard, the memory painful, but therapeutic as I shared it with her.

"So this was the first time you've danced? And with a partner?"

Nodding, I watched closely as she digested my words.

"Wesley, I think you need to keep pushing yourself. When I came upon you dancing, it was the freest I'd ever seen you. You were a different person as you moved, and I felt connected to you in a whole new way. It was then I started to understand. To you, dance became the pain, and for me, it was the only thing that kept it away. For a few hours a night, I get to be free. Free of the restraints that grow tighter every day, free from the pressure placed on me by everyone else, free from the disappointment, I'll never be enough. Dancing has saved me countless times. It's the only time I'm safe."

"It used to be that way for me until he turned it into something I feared. I didn't know if I could bear both the physical pain and the emotional pain if dancing failed me again."

"What do you think now?"

"I think I wasted too many years being scared of the one thing I needed the most. Thank you for giving me back my soul."

"Oh, Wesley, as much as I'd like to take credit for that. If only for the mere fact of rubbing it in your face would be priceless, I can't. All I did was remind you."

"The fact you don't understand how monumental that is," I shook my head, "let me remind you."

Kissing her again, I lost myself in her taste, her touch, and the way she felt. It was a different kind of dance, and I never wanted to stop. I'd come to share my story with her, and ended up gaining my heart.

CHAPTER TWENTY-TWO

ZEL

L ife started to fall into a routine over the week as I danced, hung out with the guys, and had copious amounts of fantastic sex. I wasn't complaining, but I found myself unsure how to navigate this new reality. Stability hadn't been a part of my vocabulary in almost ten years. I didn't know how to trust it. Regardless of my feelings, reliability seemed to blanket my life at The Tower. I hadn't told Nix or Wes yet about who I was, the moment not right yet, but I found myself skirting the edges of danger more and more with my disguises.

When I was in their presence, I rarely wore it anymore, finding freedom in my anonymity with them. I knew it needed to happen soon. I could see the questions building in their eyes. It was only a matter of time before they discovered the truth, and I wanted to do it on my terms. Nolan visited a few nights a week when he didn't have to work or school. Some nights he would sit in the crowd and watch me, a salacious smile on his cute face.

He'd changed me so much already. *They all had.* I was no longer doing private room activities outside lap dances. It didn't feel right to engage in anything else when I'd started to catch feelings for them. They were all surprisingly supportive of my job and life, never pressuring me to quit or getting jealous when I had to attend to a customer. It was odd for me to have people who trusted me implicitly, but I liked it.

With the wage I was making now, combined with my tips, I could support Gothel and still have enough leftover. Life for me was changing, and I started seeing a future for myself, past making it to the next day. It could be due to the fact that Nolan never shut up about me returning to school.

"I'm just saying. You'd be really cute in a school-girl outfit."

"Nolan, if you want to live out some teacher-student fantasy, you don't have to get me to enroll in college for it."

Laughing, I counted out my spaces and placed my man on the board. We were playing Sorry, and I had yet to beat him. Nolan had started bringing a different board game each week, and we would spend time playing. Nolan brought fun into my life, shining his sunlight into all my dark crevices. It was hard not to fall into his good moods and nourish that part of my soul.

"Oh, twinkle toes, you don't know what door you just opened. I'll be back with a plaid skirt quicker than you can say, *fuck me, Nolan.*"

"Fuck me, Nolan."

He stared at me, blinking. "Well *damn*, I didn't expect that to work."

Quicker than I could blink back, he pushed the game off the bed, pieces flying everywhere as he stalked toward me like a jungle cat. My breath hitched, the playful fire turning to heat as he neared me. Just as he was about to pounce, a knock at the door interrupted his prowl. Dropping his head to my shoulder, he sighed and chuckled.

"I knew it was too good to be true."

Flopping down next to me, he stretched out his legs as he posed nonchalantly. With his head leaning on his hands, you'd almost believe the pose if his massive dick wasn't tenting his pants. I couldn't contain my giggle, and he took the opportunity to shout for the guest to enter.

"Enter, Sexy Nexy."

His assumption and name had me laughing even more, and I bent over at the waist, clutching it as I lost myself into the fit of giggles. Nix walked in, a smirk on his face as he took us both in. Nolan was bound and determined to get Nix to laugh. Their relationship was interesting to watch, and it made me happy they were trying to be friends. Wes and I still only hung out just the two of us, but I could feel his resolve lowering. His fear of being caught with an employee wavering with each kiss we snuck.

"Cheeseball, isn't it past your bedtime?"

Nolan laughed, throwing his head back onto the bed. "Good one, Jolly Green Giant! But it's only 2 pm on a Saturday, so I'm afraid you're out of luck there!"

"Hmm, we'll see about that *nuisance*."

"What brings you to my quarters, *Filbert*."

Maximus still hadn't found his first name, so I'd started playing my own game by calling him the weirdest ones I could think of every time. So far, I hadn't been successful, or at least Nix hadn't confirmed I had.

"Good try, princess, but no. One, I wanted to remind you about our date tonight. I'll be by to pick you up at 6 pm. The second thing is you have a visitor. Do you want to see them?"

Scrunching up my brow, I didn't know who it could be. Maximus wouldn't leave the bunker without messaging me, and the other two people I knew were in this room. "It's a woman. She said she was your mother?"

My face drained of all color at what this could mean. Was it my mother, Queenie herself, or was it Gothel? Neither boded well for me. Nodding, I slipped off the bed and approached him. The mood had shifted in the room; a tense quiet had fallen on all of us. Nix reached out and grabbed my hand as I passed.

"Hey, I can send them away."

Shaking my head, I swallowed a few times to clear my throat. I needed to see for myself. At the thought of the implications, panic crawled up my throat, and I found myself panicking. Nix's strong arms wrapped around me, pulling me into his embrace. His comforting strokes down my back had me slowing my air to a manageable level.

"I set them up in the dining room. There's a camera there that I can pull up on my phone. Would it help to see who it is before you walk in there?"

Peering up, I nodded. Nix always understood my fear in a way only someone who'd experienced it himself could. He hadn't told me yet, but based on the few comments he'd made, I'd wager it had something to do with his time in the military.

Nix pulled out his phone and pulled up the feed. Once he had it, he turned the phone to me. Nolan's arms wrapped around me from behind, and I hadn't realized he'd moved. Sinking into him, I found the courage to look. Sitting at the table, hands jittery as they looked back and forth from the door, was Gothel. Instantly I relaxed until a different type of panic climbed my throat. Taking off, I was at the door when I heard the guys calling out.

"Zel, you might want to put more clothes on for your mother."

Glancing down, I saw I was in a tank top and

booty shorts. Yeah, I guess I better cover up some. Turning, I found Nolan holding out a sweatshirt and leggings, a smile on his face. Throwing them on, I left the hood up to help hide my hair while in the hall. I started to leave again when Nix cleared his throat this time. Quirking an eyebrow, I was about two seconds from going postal on him when he held out a pair of slippers. Ah, yeah, those.

Blushing, I took the shoes and slipped them on, finally dressed to leave my room. Grabbing the handle, I paused for a brief second to check nobody else had something to say. When neither stopped me this time, I wrenched it the rest of the way and flew down the hall. I knew they'd follow, and I didn't care. I think I even wanted them too. Having people in my corner was taking time to adjust to, but each opportunity was helping me see I could.

Walking into the dining room, I took a closer look at Gothel. Her legs bounced, and she picked her nails as her gaze skirted the room. When she saw me, she jumped up and ran, her tiny frame clinging to me.

"Sweetie, I've been so worried. It's been ages since you stopped by, and I was fearful he got you. I haven't gotten any food, and they're threatening to turn off the water."

Something about her words didn't track. Pushing her back, I braced her biceps to hold her in place. She fidgeted under my glare, avoiding my eye contact. Her body continued to tremble, and I could make out the faint sign of a bruise on her temple. Anger rose in me, and I knew what this was about.

"Did you not get the money I sent?"

She shook her head, denial heavy with each tilt. Fucking hell, she was high as a kite and withdrawing from something else.

"Mother, you know I pay the bills separately and have groceries sent each week. I also sent money for you to use. What happened to it?"

"I don't know. They must've stolen it."

"What did he give you this time? What are you on, Mother?"

Her shaking increased as she tried to form the lie in her head. "Nothing, nothing, dear. I promise. I just need a little more. Be a good girl, will you?"

It was at this moment I realized the damage I was doing to her. I'd always thought I was helping, making a difference. My pride had been assuaged by the motions I performed to drown my guilt. All along, I'd thought it was enough if I provided for her—a place to live, food to eat, and money to entertain herself with. Everything I'd done had been to *keep her alive*. But what type of life was she living?

Deep down, the seed Nolan had planted, the anger he'd first directed at me, surfaced. I was angry with *her*. I was *so fucking angry*. I hated it. I hated myself for it. But it was there.

Resentment bubbled up, and I knew I had to let

go of her arms, or I'd be leaving bruises too. Dropping them, I took a step back and then another. My head was heavy as I shook the denial off now, not wanting to admit the truth.

I'd allowed myself to believe I was good, that I was helping. I told myself to take pride in the fact I provided for me and her on my own, that I didn't care how, just that I did.

But that was a lie. I did care. *I fucking cared a lot.*

Sixty times, I let men touch me without permission to protect her. Sixty times, I went on those stupid dinners and smiled while dying on the inside. Sixty times, I hated myself a little more each time. Sixty times, I wished she'd died that day, stopping me from being found. Sixty times, I lied to myself, believing I was in control but knowing I wasn't.

My father still had control over me. He was using me and manipulating me to further his end goals—and this time, *I'd* allowed it.

If I cared about her, I would've done more, tried harder, made her stop. Just something! I was an enabler, and I wasn't any better than my father.

Falling to my knees, the pain didn't register as I thought about my crimes. Tears flowed freely as I came face to face with my own failings. How could these men care about me when I didn't even know how to care?

Long ago, I thought I was better than my abusers, priding myself on the knowledge I had a secret. Under their noses, I masked myself, disguising my identity and parading around in my vanity. I wanted to believe Nolan that I had the good pride in myself for overcoming the odds stacked against me, but it was false. His words had unknowingly uprooted all my carefully planted lies, and I was seeing clearly for the first time.

I'd been a victim trapped in a cycle of abuse with no clear direction of how to get out. I made excuses for my own behavior, not taking responsibility for the half-assed effort I'd done at protecting someone. Gothel had fallen into my father's snares many times, the drugs he supplied her with, a knife to my heart, and I never did anything to stop it.

I could be angry at myself. I could be disappointed in myself. I could even be disgusted with myself. But none of those things were productive. They were a by-product of surviving. I did the best I could with what I had at the time, but I could do better now. I wanted to live a life that was more than surviving, and it started with change.

Rising to my feet, I strolled to the woman shaking in the middle of the room, confusion on her face at my reaction. She perked up when she saw me walking toward her expecting to get what she came for.

"Come, Mother, let's get you some food."

Directing her by the elbow, I caught Nix's eyes as I left. I knew he was close, his protectiveness never straying far, and I took comfort in that. He was showing me what it meant to be strong by supporting me. Nix made it easy to ask for help but gave me space first to try, never doubting my ability to handle it.

"Can you ask Wesley if we could have some food sent up to my old room? I'm assuming it's still empty?"

Nix regarded me thoughtfully before nodding. "It is, princess. I'll have the chef send you something there."

"Thank you, *Sexy Nexy*. You know, I kind of like that one. Nolan might've just found you a nickname."

He rolled his eyes, but I caught the blush as he went to do as I requested. I wasn't surprised to find Nolan outside either. He took in my tears, concern on his face, but when I smiled, he relaxed.

"Nols, this is my mother, Gothel."

Ever the sweet man he was, he smiled, taking her into his arms. "Well, hello, Gothel. It's a pleasure to meet you. Please, allow me to escort you the rest of the way."

Even high and strung out, my mother giggled like a schoolgirl at Nolan Ryder's attention. Stepping in front, I led our strange trio to the other side of the building and entered my combo for the room. Walking in, I was surprised to find Wesley already waiting. I couldn't help the blush that rose every time I saw him now.

Our time dancing together had shifted something, and I felt like a girl with her first crush. He was so put together, so proper, I often felt out of his league, but he never made me feel that way. A little fear developed at the thought all three guys would be in the same room together in a matter of minutes. While they all knew of one another, outside Nix, they hadn't interacted.

This should be interesting.

To my surprise, Wes greeted both Nolan and Gothel like they were distinguished guests.

"Hello, and welcome. I'm Wesley Flynn, owner of this establishment. Please, let me know if there is anything you need. It's nice to meet you."

He nodded before approaching me. "Could I speak with you for a moment, Zel?"

I glanced at Nolan to see if he would be okay, and he smiled, telling me to go ahead. He sat down with Gothel at the table and laughed over some story he was telling her. Nix walked in with food as we exited, giving them something else to focus on.

"Everything okay, Zel? I was worried."

"Yeah, well, I dunno. I was wondering if I could ask a favor, though. I need to get her real help. Do you know a place that would be good?"

"I do, actually. I'll make some phone calls and get her in as soon as possible. Until then, she can stay here, and we can have someone watch the room when you leave for your date."

Hugging him, I surprised us both with the gesture out in the open, but I didn't care. He was doing more than I deserved, but I'd take it.

"Thank you, Wes. This means everything to me."

"Don't you get it, baby girl? You mean *everything* to me. If your family needs help, then I'm there."

Leaning down, he kissed me softly before pulling away and heading back to whatever he did during the hours I wasn't with him. I watched him go, his suit fitting him snuggly as he sauntered away, and a sigh left me. I couldn't help it. Wesley was so yummy, and I couldn't wait to be with him.

"How you'd snag such a whale?"

The voice behind me was irritating, and I immediately tensed as I realized she'd seen our kiss. Not everyone knew his real identity, and I hoped it was that way with whoever was behind me. Turning, I smiled before walking back into my room. Nix had waited there for me and pulled me into his arms as soon as the door shut.

"We can reschedule, Zel. It's not important."

Peeking up at him, I shook my head no. "It's important. Didn't you say it was a reunion or something with some of your old military buds?"

"Yes, but—"

"No buts. Wes is helping me find a place. She might be gone before it's even time. I promise I'm good. I really want to go with you. I even bought a new outfit, just for the occasion." I winked.

"Well, in that case, I'll shut up. I'm suddenly looking forward to tonight."

He sealed his lips over mine in a searing kiss

that had me cursing my mother being here, but I reminded myself I was trying to be there for her more. Slapping his ass as he turned to leave, the cutest little sound escaped his mouth. Laughing, I went to save Nolan before Gothel tried to throw herself at him or something. I could already see her scheming as she twirled her hair.

Mothers.

CHAPTER TWENTY-THREE

NIX

There was a part of me dreading this dinner with my former squadron. When my Sergeant had messaged me stating he was getting together with some old unit members, I'd been excited about the chance to see him. I hadn't seen him since my term ended, and only gone on a few outings with a few of my comrades in arms. Each time I met up with them, the nightmares seemed to increase, and I eventually quit answering their calls. It felt easier to push it out of my mind, to forget the things I'd seen and done during my service—the things that still haunted me.

I'd asked Zel to go with me in the hope it would force me not to cancel at the last minute. I also felt it would be more enjoyable with her there. At the few things I'd attended, I'd gotten to meet the other guys' wives and families, and I'd been envious of it. Now, I had someone to share, and I wouldn't hate showing off my hot girlfriend to the others. Nah, I'd love it. Rubbing their faces in the fact I'd met someone would feel good.

Since I wasn't getting out of this, I dressed in my best jeans, black boots, and a button-down black shirt. Rolling up the cuffs, I observed myself in the mirror. It was odd for me to care what I looked like. My reflection usually consisted of solid black attire with my work dress code. Seeing something other than a black shirt, black cargo pants, or, on rare occasions, a black suit was disorienting.

Granted, the only new color was blue, but the jeans stood out to me, and my forearm tattoos were now displayed as I continued to turn in the mirror. A chuckle broke my stare down, and I caught Wesley laughing at me, arms folded as he leaned against the doorjamb.

"I don't think I've ever seen you check yourself out before. You tend to fall into the wrath category more than pride when it comes to sins. You'd beat someone's head in over vanity any day."

My face flamed at his statement, knowing it was accurate. "Well, things are different now."

"Mm-hm. Zel sees you in all black all the time. Adding some jeans isn't going to break her mind. You have nothing to worry about."

"I," swallowing, "you're right. I just, I don't know."

"You like her. It's understandable, but I don't think you have to be nervous."

"I was going to share my past with her tonight."

"Ah, well, that makes sense. I still don't think you have cause to worry."

"No?"

"That's not who Zel is. She isn't going to judge you. If anything, she'll understand you better than most."

Exhaling, I nodded to him in the mirror. "You're right. And before you say you're always right, don't forget the big pile of shit you recently found your-self in." He grumbled but didn't retort back. "Were you able to figure out something for Gothel?"

"Yeah, someone is coming in the morning to talk about placement. Nolan said he'd stay with her tonight. I'll check in as well. You both won't need to worry."

"You just want brownie points."

"Maybe, but I also want to do whatever is neces-sary to help Zel."

"Ah, papa, he's a real boy! Finally!"

"You know I can fire you, right?"

"Nah, you'd be miserable and lost without me."

He rolled his eyes, but I caught the slight smile on his lips. "Get out of here. *Go*, enjoy your date."

Laughing, I took one final look before I turned and stalked out of the bathroom to get my girl. Wesley's chuckles followed me out of the apart-ment, giving me the boost I needed. It had been easier being vulnerable with him through the mirror. Not that I had anything to hide from him, but talking about it hadn't felt as weird. His response was the confirmation I needed to know where he stood. Whether or not he realized it, things were headed in the direction of forever with Zel, and I couldn't be happier about that.

Jogging down the stairs, I found myself smiling at seeing her. There wasn't a day I didn't have my breath stolen by her. The way she walked, moved, or said my name had me falling headfirst into a lovey swoon. It was a good thing I'd perfected the jackass stare years ago, or I would've been laughed at for hearts coming out of my eyes like some cartoon character. Besides, it was obvious I was the Yosemite Sam of the cartoon world. I wasn't meant to get the girl, but here I was, living my best life and proving them all wrong.

I stuffed the edge of fear down that threatened to pop up in my head of how I could lose it all so easily. The slamming of the stairwell door, however, took me by surprise, the sound so eerily similar to gunshots, and I found myself falling headfirst into a flashback without notice.

Crack. Crack. Crack.

Boom!

"Nixon, get down!"

Bombs were exploding all around me as I dived for the nearest cover. When the humvee exploded above, I army crawled as far as I could as bullets rained down around me. Looking left and right, I couldn't see anything but bodies. I was left exposed in a field of my dead comrades. Body parts spread across the grass, blood and gore oozing in every direction. I tried to dismiss them, to not focus on Johnny's arm right in front of me or the head that laid next to me staring blankly. The smell of burnt flesh stung my nose with each inhale, and I wondered if I'd ever be able to get it out. My ears rang from the explosion, and ash fell from the sky, clogging my throat.

Desperate and with limited options, my survival instinct took over. Thinking the unthinkable, I rolled myself under the bodies of my unit and hid. Lying in the field of dead soldiers, the weight of them crushing, but I didn't move. I didn't budge. For twenty-four hours, I laid under the corpses of my friends and brothers covered in blood and grime as I waited. I was a coward. I was no hero.

"Nix? Mr. Growly? Hey, you there?"

"Princess?"

"Yeah, stud. It's me."

Blinking, her face swam in front of me as I came back to the present. *Fuck.* I hadn't slipped into a memory in years. The impending dinner, stress of The Tower, and fear I could lose Zel had been the perfect combination to ease passed my walls. Her worried face came into clear focus, the worry for me a balm to my pride for appearing weak.

"You okay?"

"Yeah," I licked my lips, "yeah."

She didn't appear to believe me but nodded and

stood. Apparently, I'd fallen back against the wall. I ignored all the curious onlookers as I stood, focusing on shaking off the feeling of the dead bodies that lingered. Taking my hand, she pulled me back in the direction I'd come, and we headed down the back stairs together. It was cute watching her take charge and comfort me. It only made me fall in love with her more. Months ago, she'd sealed herself onto my heart, enveloping me in a connection I couldn't ignore. Now, it seemed she'd penetrated my heart wrapping me in her arms tight, promising never to let go.

It was a nice place to be, and I had no qualms of ever leaving.

Pulling her to a stop, I barricaded her against the wall. Her breath caught as I took her in. She had on a grey sweater that sat off her shoulders, displaying her delicious skin to me. Dropping a kiss to one, I had to forcibly hold myself back from licking up her collarbone.

Below her sweater, she had on a black leather skirt. It had some weird bow contraption on the side, but it was short and sexy—the perfect Zel combination. Her heels were high, making her the perfect height for me to stare down into her eyes. They swam with emotion, more alive than I'd ever seen them. Her breath caught again at my look as the heat in my eyes rose.

Bending down, I met her mouth, sealing our fate in a kiss that could burn down towns with the heat. Grabbing her thigh, I lifted it to my waist, holding it there as I consumed her lips. Slowly, my hand began to trail down the back of her thigh, feeling her skin respond in goosebumps. Grabbing her ass, momentarily stunned, and I stopped my movement as I worked out the puzzle before me—nothing but bare flesh met me.

Zel's lingerie selection was extensive, and she constantly surprised me. As my large palm encompassed her cheek, my fingers grazed two strings. Following them with my finger, I found them attached to the barest of material in the front. My fingertip brushed against her pussy lips on my search, her moan of approval echoing down the hall. Pressing her more against the wall, I rubbed the steel rod encased in my pants against her.

"Princess, I have half a mind to fuck you against this wall."

"Yes, please."

"Mmm, sounds like someone is feeling needy tonight. Maybe I should drag it out? Just a little tease now."

My voice was thick with need, rasping against her ear as I circled my hips into her. Zel's hands clung to me, one tight in the back of my hair, keeping my face close. My mind screamed to take her, to ease the stress by sinking into her hot center and forgetting earlier. My body agreed wholeheartedly, my cock practically threatening to break the zipper it pressed against.

My heart, however, said to wait, to cherish the woman, to show her how much more than a quick fuck in the hall to erase my fear she was. I never wanted to use her, and that was what halted me.

Listening to the only organ thinking clearly, I sank my fingers into her, pumping them quickly as I felt her wetness around me. Stroking her clit, I plunged deep before I pulled out, leaving her on edge, her arousal slick between her legs. Gasping, Zel's eyes popped open as she watched me suck my fingers into my mouth.

"I want to be mad at you for stopping, but I plan to tease you mercilessly all night now."

She straightened her skirt and walked off only as Zel could, with seduction and fire, leaving me leaning over the wall. Chuckling, I shook my head and ran to grab her. Spinning her, I locked eyes with her, my earlier mood disappearing completely by being around her.

"How about we make a wager?"

"Oh, now you're talking."

"Whoever *sustains* the longest wins."

"Mmm… no. I counter with whoever gets the other to fold first wins. If I manage to get you to fuck me before we return to your bed or mine, then I win. If you manage to hold out until then, you win."

"Hmm, I could possibly agree to those terms. What's the prize?"

"Well, besides the orgasm?"

"Yes, princess," I smirked, "besides the orgasm."

"Fine. Let's see." She brought her finger to her lip, tapping it as she thought. "If I win, then you have to join Nolan and me for a sexy trio." She smirked, thinking she had me, not knowing Wes and I's history. "And if you win," she leaned in close, biting my ear as she did, "you can have access to my back door."

Stunned, this time when she walked away, I watched and tried not to give in to her taunting right then. Damn, she was good. If sex was her weapon, she was one hell of a negotiator and sharpshooter. I'd follow her into battle any day.

Finally, coming out of my stupor, I jogged to catch up with my spunky princess. When I thought of the exuberant woman she was now, it amazed me how different she'd been back at The Pan. I'd do whatever it took to protect her light, the sunshine in her now. She radiated with it, shining it on all of those around her. Zel tended to stay to herself, but I noticed how the other girls watched her, transfixed by her as well.

The staff and clients could tell something was different about her and flocked to be in her presence as much as possible. She didn't know the number of people I turned away now for her time or how Wes had added extra staff during her shifts. Zel was clueless about her power, and that made her even more beautiful. Her humility was rare, her love pure, and it made me believe in fairy tales and happily ever afters.

She waited for me at the door, and when I got close, I held out my hand for her. Grinning, she took it, and we walked hand in hand to Hunter's Lodge. Callum was a buddy of mine from my military days and had settled in Sinhaven after his service. He owned the bar, and it had become a watering hole for those of us in the service. Before Zel, I had found myself here most nights.

"Oh, I've been to this place before. The bartender kind of reminds me of you, actually," she laughed.

"How so?"

"Growly and gruff."

Her laughter rang out into the night, and all I could do was gruff at her, confirming her point. Walking in, I spotted a few of the guys in the back by the pool table and directed her there. Callum was tending the bar and nodded when he saw me enter, an unusual smile lifting his lips as he took in the girl beside me. Staring him down, I made him laugh out loud as we made our way to the back. Shaking my head, I'd have to talk with him later.

The lighting was low, the split-level cocktail bar providing a fun and elegant environment. Blues music played, and I settled into the space as I took in all the exits. Despite being here several times, it was a habit, and I made sure to clock anyone I felt was a threat. When we entered the room, uproarious hello's greeted us, and Zel beamed up at me, the prettiest smile on her face. Zander made his way over to me, but instead of greeting me, the flirt grabbed Zel and swung her around. A growl slipped out of between my lips, making the man in question grin even wider.

"Well, it looks like 'mean old' Nixon has found himself a leading lady!"

"And here I thought he was only mean to me," Zel flirted back.

I didn't mind her banter, knowing she had no interest in these loons, but as Zander's eyes filled with lust at her sass, I barely held back another growl and the anger I wanted to rain down on him. Clenching and unclenching my fists, I counted to ten in my head. Wes had been right earlier. Wrath was more my speed than pride.

Pulling it back, I raised an eyebrow at the cocky fucker until he finally let my girl go. Wrapping a possessive arm around her waist this time, I pulled her tight to me. None of these other assholes would be touching her.

"It's good to see you, Nixon." Zander slapped my shoulder, showing he'd been messing with me earlier over Zel. I didn't care. *Zel was mine.*

"I don't know if I'd say the same, *Zander.* Is that how you greet everyone?"

Zel slapped my stomach, a nudge to turn down the dramatics. "Zander, is it? I'm Zel."

"It's a pleasure to meet you, Zel. I'd kiss your

hand in the honor you deserve, but I'm afraid this one might bite mine off if I did. So, I shall bow and escort you both to our section."

Zel laughed at his comment, but Zander hadn't been far from the truth. I was feeling very territorial with her. He led us over to an area, and everyone went around introducing themselves. They were all interested in meeting Zel, and I kept a tight grip on her as they shared stories. We ate food, and everyone had a few beers, enjoying the company of one another. Zel fit right in, and it was nice to see her in my world outside The Tower.

She kept her promise to drive me wild, though, and not even halfway through the date, I was rock hard. We'd started playing a round of pool, and I didn't miss how she kept bending over to flip me her skirt, reminding me how little she had on under it. I also didn't miss the way she brushed up against me each time she went to chalk up her stick, and I especially didn't miss how she flashed me her tits when she leaned in the other direction.

The only thing holding me back was my stubborn pride and the desire to take her ass.

I was losing badly to her at pool when her phone rang, and she motioned to step away to answer it. I watched her go, my eyes following her movements like the hawk-eye I was. Zander moved over, leaning on his stick, and regarded me.

"You know, at first, I thought she was some side

piece you brought to mess with us all. It's why I gave you a hard time."

"Mess with you? Why would I mess with you, Zander?" I looked at him in confusion, not understanding his statement.

"Because you always seemed unflappable, so above it all. You didn't need anyone or anything. You had your job and were happy with that. The rest of us, man," he exhaled, a sadness etching into his voice. "Every single one of us has struggled since the day we returned. Divorces, addictions, gambling problems, you name it, we've all struggled with the things we saw there. But not you, Nix. You work your job and come to these things, but you never struggle."

His words were like a bucket of cold water as they rushed over me. They thought I didn't struggle. How? The reality of my numbness, of closing off my emotions, hit me like a ton of bricks.

"That's not it at all," I choked out.

"Then how is it?"

"Fuck man, I had a flashback just on my way here. I grapple with the memories every day. I'm not better than any of you, nor have I ever meant to make you feel like I thought I was. I shoved it all down to get through to the next day."

Zander's face softened at my confession, a look of understanding passing between us, brothers in arms. "I can tell she means something to you. That's how I knew. You were either a sociopath with no feelings, or she helped you face them. Watching the two of you, I wagered it was the second. You're not alone in this, Nix. I'm here if you ever need to talk to someone who was there."

He gripped my shoulder this time, emotion heavy in his words, and I nodded. It was the most honest conversation I'd ever had with him. I realized how valid his words were. *Zel had helped me.* Unlocking emotions I hadn't known and showing me it was okay to be vulnerable with others. I was about to go search out Zel when another hand landed on the opposite shoulder.

"Sarge!"

"Nixon, I'm so glad you could make it. Come and fill me in. I hear there's a girl who willingly came with you tonight?" he chuckled.

Clasping the man who'd been a father figure to me, I walked with him over to the table, filling him in on my life as I went.

"So Wesley is thinking of staying here this time?"

"Yeah, I think so. We've seemed to have found a home here in Sinhaven."

"Well, I'm happy for you, son. You deserve some stability and happiness. What are your plans if you do stay? And where is this girl I've heard so much about?"

The realization that Zel had been gone far too long smacked me across the chest. Setting down my beer, I moved without saying anything to my sergeant. I slinked out of the room and headed to the hallway I'd last seen her in. When I found it empty, I tried to ignore my racing heart and all the cold sweat that swept over me as I headed toward the back entrance. If anything happened to Zel, I'd never forgive myself. It would be the thing that finally broke me.

CHAPTER
TWENTY-FOUR

ZEL

"Did you find his name?" I grinned. "Please, Max, tell me you did!"

I was giddy as I waited for him to answer. I could see him lounging back on his bed, his hair all over the place on the video call. His chuckle had me dancing a little jig as I waited to hear what Nixon's first name was.

"Oh pip, how you doubt me."

"I never doubted you, my friend! Is it something embarrassing like Nixy? Or I know, Seamus? Oh, oh, what about Burt?"

"Seriously, pip, if you'd stop talking for half a second, I could tell you."

I mimed zipping my lips and bounced on my heels as I waited for the information. Once I was quiet, Max grinned wide.

"It's *Eugene*."

My mouth dropped open, and I peeked over the phone back to the room to see if Nix was watching me. I was surprised when I found him talking with Zander instead. Looking back to Max, I laughed at finally having some ammo.

"You're brilliant, Maximus! Absolutely the best hacker in all of Sinhaven!"

"Don't be shouting that too loudly? Where are you anyway?"

"Um, some bar. Hunters Lodge is the name. You know it?"

"Oh yeah." His eyes went wide at the name. "Shit, I gotta go, but you owe me."

"Yeah, yeah. Drop by The Tower, and I'll set you up."

Puckering up for a kiss, I laughed when Max made an 'ew' face and pretended to gag before hanging up. I turned to check if Nix was still occupied and found him talking to an older gentleman now. Taking the chance, I popped into the ladies' room and used the bathroom quickly.

Deciding to play dirty, I slipped the barely-there undies and placed them in my clutch. I had an evil plan of slipping them into his pocket the next time he pulled me close. I was hornier than ever after the buildup, and I was determined to get my dicking before we got home. If I played my cards right, I could have two tonight. Either from Nix, or maybe I could persuade Nolan for some joint fun.

Gothel popped into my head at the mention of Nolan, souring my mood a little. I was hopeful

Wesley's connection would be able to help her tomorrow. I wanted to do right by her and not continue to enable her bad choices. She'd done the right thing but was punished while the guilty party lived in his mansion, parading his misdeeds in front of everyone and getting sympathy for his misfortunes.

It was sickening, and I no longer wanted to contribute to the problem. I could do better, and I would.

Thoughts of Gothel had me focused, and I missed the shadow looming in the dark hallway. My brunette wig was yanked, the long curls giving them plenty of leverage. The pins dug into my head with the pull, and I instantly tried to protect the strands, placing my hands on them.

"Ow! Ow!"

Pulled back into a body, I froze when his smoky scent of cigars and rain aftershave hit me. My body locked down, tremors raging through me as he held me firmly in his grip.

"You've been a bad girl, Rapunzel. I've watched you all night flaunt my *property* to every male in the place. When you avoided me these past years, I believed your father when he said you were away or perhaps had fallen ill. Why else would you ignore me? I've always been *so good to you*."

He ran his hand down my arm before he forcibly squeezed my breast, causing a whimper to escape as he did. Licking my neck, he nipped me before he started to talk again. Internally, I screamed at myself to fight back, to head butt him, to do something! But I could only stand frozen in fear as he groped me.

"Your little friend hid you well. It's taken me *years* to find you. But the other night, I thought you looked familiar, but I couldn't place it. I came back this week, waiting in the back to see if I could figure it out. When you danced, it clicked. You've been clever. I'll give you that, using disguises. But you can't fake how your beauty shines in your dance. It would've been better never to dance again if you wanted to escape, *precious*."

His breathing was heavy, and his hands roamed me without pause now, and I blocked it out of my head. Giovani's breath skirted my neck when he spoke again. "I think you wanted me to find you, that this whole time you've been playing hard to get. Well, you don't have to play anymore, precious." He squeezed again, pushing his hand further south, and I locked my legs as I ignored the bulge behind me.

"That asshole bouncer wouldn't let me see you, though, so I had to get creative. Did you like the gift I sent today? Being reunited with your mother? You didn't fall into the trap as I planned, but thankfully, you still left. All I had to do was wait. It was only a matter of time before I could get you. I've been *patient*, Rapunzel, but that ends *tonight*."

My heart raced, thoughts whizzing quickly in

my head as I tried to find a solution, a way out of this mess.

"If not, I'll have to take drastic measures and punish the men who've so freely taken what didn't belong to them. Starting with that little friend of yours, Maximus, and then your sweet little blond lover. I'll have his family destroyed before you say good morning, if you don't play along."

It was the mentioning of the people I loved that broke me out of my freeze state. Hardening myself, I pulled all the confidence and sex appeal I've gained over the years and my resolve to be strong. Locking and loading my weapon, I found my inner diva and let it ooze out of me. I stood straight, no longer trembling as I prepared for battle. Trailing my fingers up his arms, the gesture had him pausing, allowing me to use the distraction for what it was.

Grabbing his arm, I pivoted and faced the man who'd been my tormentor, my abuser, and my greatest shame. Remembering Nolan's words, I pushed the guilt outward and channeled pride in myself for overcoming my odds, for finding a way to beat back the demons and reclaim what was mine. It wouldn't be advice any therapist would give you, but it was my salvation and redemption. *It was mine.*

"Oh, Giovani, how I've missed you," I purred, his eyes widening as he took me in now. I'd always been the simpering pet for him, scared of my own shadow. He used his intimidation and position to con me into giving him what he wanted for years. It wouldn't work now.

I was older and a hell of a lot more wiser. The biggest difference? I wasn't alone.

"I, uh, Rapunzel, you have?"

"Of course, silly. But there's one thing I don't understand," I pouted, playing with his collar. My body pressed up against his, his domination no longer present as I took the lead.

"What's that, Rapunzel?"

It was fascinating to watch him panic as he struggled to know what role to play. I didn't for one second think I had this in the bag, knowing it could flip as easily, but I focused and pushed forward, hoping to continue to disorient *him* for the time being.

"You said you've been reaching out to me over the past five years?"

"Yes, I have." He nodded. "I sent a request, like always, to your father."

"Oh?" Cocking my head, I dug a little deeper. "But didn't you know it changed? Were you not part of the upgrade?" I faked shock as I placed the seed of doubt into his mind.

He scrunched his brow, never having considered this part. "But," he shook his head, disbelief written all over his face, "I sent the money to PO Box 762 every 10th of the month. I sent messages to the chat with your codename, golden child. I, I, I… I don't understand. You haven't gotten any of my gifts?"

"You got me gifts?" My eyes lit up with excitement despite internally wanting to vomit.

"Yeah." He nodded slowly, trying to work it out. "Dresses of all colors, purses, and shoes. I even got you a few tiaras to wear. You didn't get *any* of them?"

His brow furrowed; I couldn't help the surge of power I felt at dismantling the man who'd been the villain of so many nightmares.

"Uh oh, I think you've been had, Gio. Did you do something to get on the Mayor's shit list?"

"No, no," he pleaded, shaking his head vigorously. And then he stopped, something clicking in his eyes.

I swallowed, nervous he figured out my ploy.

"What can I do, Rapunzel? Why were you at The Tower? Is your father trying to win the bid? He told me he wasn't interested, and I could have free reign with whatever I wanted to do there. I want to expand the operation, you know, I want to have my own little studio haven for young girls and boys. You could be their teacher. Think of all the pictures and moments we could make together, all the stunning imagery."

The amount of glee he got from this ludicrous idea was sickening. Expanding his child pornography business couldn't be allowed to happen. I never thought about the fact he could be doing this to others. The more he rambled, the clearer the picture became.

It hadn't just been me. I was one girl in a whole network of child molesters and pedophiles. Swallowing the bile, I pushed forward, encouraging myself to hold out for just a few more minutes. My constant mantra returned, reminding me I could do this.

"I could talk to the owner for you," I purred, brushing my hand over his neck. "I'll set something up. If I were you, though, I'd check in with the Mayor. It sounds like he's been keeping you out of the loop. I don't want to think about what it could be about. Isn't there an election coming up?" I blinked innocently.

With concern on my face, I hoped to plant the seed of doubt deeper in his head so he'd focus on my father instead of me. It seemed to work as his face went white. Kissing his cheek, I patted his chest and stepped back.

"I'll be in touch."

Walking backward, I kept him in my view, but it didn't matter. Once I was out of his range, he straightened and fled out the back door. As soon as the door shut, my body relaxed, the adrenaline leaving me. I started to fold inward at the waist, the strength to survive the encounter fleeing me as the danger disappeared. Before I could hit the ground, thick arms wrapped around me and caught me, the smell of cinnamon hitting my nostrils. Cradling me, he breathed me in, his nose in the crook of my neck as he held me to him for a minute.

I could hear his heart hammering in his chest, and I wondered how long he'd stood there listening. Shame wanted to coat me again at the realization, but I swatted it away. I'd owned that and had taken control, flipping the scene on him. There was nothing for me to be ashamed of except for keeping it to myself. When I thought about it, I was impressed, and thankful Nix had stayed back and allowed me to handle it.

That warm sense of self blossomed, and I leaned up and kissed his cheek, cradling his face in my hands.

"Princess, I think it's time you tell me what's going on."

Nodding, I didn't argue, knowing it was. An idea had started to form, a plan I'd toyed with for five years but never felt strong enough to enact.

"Thank you for letting me handle it. I think I needed to."

He held my eyes, the fear close to the surface as he let me see his wounds. "It was one of the hardest things I've ever done. I found you when he still had his hand in your hair, and I was two seconds away from punching him into next week. But then I saw it, the flip in your eyes. I knew you needed to prove to yourself you could do this, so I waited. But if he had tried to leave with you, there would've been a dead body to contend with."

"Why is it kind of hot you were willing to kill for me?"

He smirked but didn't answer, his fear was still too close as he held me.

"You know what I realized?"

"That I'm amazing, and you can never leave me? Also, that I am *so* winning the bet."

"No." I smiled, loving this side of my protector. "That fairy tales have it all wrong."

"How so?"

"Who needs a prince to bring her crown jewels when I have a soldier threatening to kill the bad guy for me? I think it's the most romantic thing you've ever said to me, *Eugene*." I smiled, his eyes going wide at my use of his name.

"I take it back, *princess*."

My smile dropped, his voice deep, and I started to panic, thinking I'd messed up.

"What?" I swallowed.

"You're gonna win the bet after all."

Barreling into the bathroom, he managed to lock the door and prop my ass on the counter in under three seconds before he had his zipper lowered and his cock poised in front of me. When he didn't plunge into me, I looked up.

"I just wanted to make sure you were okay with this, you know, after what happened in the hall."

Grasping his face, I pulled his lips to mine, kissing him deeply. "The only thing that kept me from losing my shit was thinking of you, Nols, and Wes. I'll share everything with you, but please, for the love of pizza, fuck me so hard I can't walk straight."

Nix's growl reverberated in his chest, sending tingles down my spine, and apparently had a straight shot to my clit. I understood his hesitancy, but every touch Nix gave me replaced the horrible one from earlier. Every kiss, every caress, every deep thrust showed me the person I was and not the girl I'd been. Grabbing my hips, he plunged deep into me, filling me up as I grasped his head to my chest. Like a man possessed, he rutted into me hard, barely giving either of us time to breathe as he fucked me into oblivion.

Bracing my hand on the mirror, we moaned together loudly as he surged up. My legs were tight around his waist, my heels digging into his ass. His hands gripped mine, fingerprints blooming on my cheeks. My pussy wrapped around him tightly, moving easily with each pump of his cock in me. He took my words seriously and fucked me hard. All the buildup from the night had me flying over the edge within seconds, and I felt him follow me as he held me, tremors wracking his body as he came.

"Is your first name really Eugene?" I whispered. Nix's head was cradled on my chest, laying on my breast. At my question, he lifted his eyes to me, pulling back some.

"Yes. It was my grandfather's name. He was a great man, and I idolized him. When my parents died, I wanted to live with him, but he was too old, so I was sent to a military school instead. Kids weren't kind and made fun of the name. I stopped using it because I couldn't bear the thought anyone would sully the man I loved and admired. After a while, everyone forgot or moved, and I just became Nixon or Nix."

"So when I said it out there, that was the first time since a child you'd been called it?"

Nodding, he studied my eyes. "Hearing it from your lips made me realize how much I missed him and how sexy it sounded coming from you. I knew I needed to be in you right then, to remind myself you were mine and okay," he paused, hesitant. "I'm sorry if I was too aggressive. I never want you to feel like you don't have control."

"You never have to worry about that because you don't make me feel that way. You never take control from me."

"I have all of these strong feelings for you, Zel. I hope you know that."

"Good, because I have them for you too, Eugene."

"*Fuck*, why is that so hot when you say it? Shit, we better go before I decide to give you round two right *now*."

His chest rumbled with a deep possession, and I was about to hold him to me. Smirking, he pulled out slowly, lowering my legs to the counter as he did. It was then I realized I didn't know if we were in the men's or women's restroom, not paying attention at the time. A voice piped up from the stall, mortifying me in the process as I got my answer.

"Wow! You need to marry him, girl, before I do. I don't even care that I have a husband. I'll take two! But is it okay to come out now? That was really hot and all, and I didn't want to embarrass you, so I stayed hidden, but my foot is starting to cramp from the weird position I've been standing in."

Laughing, I hopped down off the counter and fixed my skirt. "All clear," I yelled, deciding to embrace our bathroom rendezvous. Nix grunted, turning to wash his hands, but I think it was more out of embarrassment at being overhead, his cheeks tinting a little pink beneath his beard.

A petite girl around my age stepped out, her brown hair pulled back as she took us in. She winked and walked over to the sinks herself, giving Nix a once over as she took him in fully. I stood back, quietly laughing at how uncomfortable he was as he waited for her to be done.

"Well, thanks for the free porn show. My husband will be grateful when I go and jump him. See you around, hopefully though, not in the bathroom. Leah, out!" She laughed, grinning wide before she walked out the door, throwing her hands up in the air like she'd just mic dropped.

Grabbing Nix's hand, we left the bathroom, and I enjoyed Nix's blush as it rose more when we said our goodbyes to his friend. Walking back, I sent a

text to Max and prepared myself to share my
history with the two other guys who'd become part
of my world.

> **Me:** Max, it's no longer safe. The big bad
> wolf found me. Come to The Tower. It's
> time I let my hair down.

CHAPTER TWENTY-FIVE

WESLEY

While Nixon and Zel were on their date, I prepared a romantic gesture. I wanted to put in the effort with Zel. Not just because she deserved it, but I wanted her to see how I viewed her. She wasn't just an employee to me. She wasn't even just a convenient hole to fuck. No, Zel was someone I could be honest with.

Each time I kissed her, I could see the arousal growing in her eyes and the frustration of waiting. In my defense, I'd gone a little overboard in my attempts to distinguish her from the rest. As much as I'd wanted to take her against the ballet barre last week, I hadn't earned the right yet. Partially to punish myself, my self-inflicted wounds were always the deepest, and somewhat to prove I could.

Tonight, I'd gone all out and had roses covering the bed: Chocolates, strawberries, and champagne to dine on, and soft music playing. I'd spoken with Nixon earlier, and he knew my plans. I didn't care if he joined, as long as I could make it memorable. I wasn't someone who needed our first time together to be only us; the gesture was the important aspect. By now, my *proclivities* weren't a secret to Nixon and hopefully, wouldn't be an issue for Zel.

I didn't like to think of my needs as different because they were part of who I was, but I knew from previous lovers not everyone appreciated them.

I had what most would say fell on the obsessive-compulsive spectrum. I was obsessive about how I liked things, which sometimes led to compulsive behavior. But to me, it was how I wanted to live. Things had a place, a purpose, and when they were organized, life made sense—*I made sense*. In intimate relationships, this translated into exploring senses and exquisite things.

This club might appear to be designed by a team, but every detail that went into The Tower came from me. I'd been obsessive over it. I knew it, but I was good at the details, and the extra level of care set me apart from the competitors. In business, my obsession was classified as passion. It separated the successes from the failures. If my father had taught me anything, it was how to be a success.

In the bedroom, that trickled into setting the mood and using textures. I loved silk ribbons, petals, and even food play. My need for the luxurious skirted the line of obsession, and I found myself wanting to take my partner to a level of pleasure which exceeded the physical. I could have sex without it. Hell, just thinking of Zel often brought me to the point of coming in my pants, but when you could have the best, why not *have* the best.

Placing the last of the petals, I stepped back and took in my handiwork. My cock started to harden at the thought of Zel splayed out with them around her. The elevator dinged, and I adjusted myself, shutting the bedroom door as I went to meet them. I instantly knew something was different when I took them in.

Zel had a confidence about her that was new, something shining outwardly as well as internally. They held hands, and the intimacy between them had me envious for a second. Knocking it away, I reminded myself of what awaited in the bedroom. Despite my need driving me, an air of trepidation met me.

"How was the Lodge? Did you enjoy your time?"

Crossing my arms, I didn't mean to be standoffish, but the uncertainty I could feel had me pulling out my defenses. What if Nix had told her? What if she wasn't into it? What if she thought I was a freak?

The what-if merry-go-round started, and I couldn't get off.

"It was good, but listen, Wes, we need to talk."

Disappointment, followed by shame, settled in my stomach. I knew it was too good to be true. My downward spiral had me missing the rest of what they said. When Zel's hand met my cheek, I jumped, not expecting her to be there, much less touch me.

"Wes, are you okay? What's wrong?"

Worry dotted her brow, and it confused me. Why was she worried about me? *She thought I was a freak.*

"I don't think you're a freak. Wes, what's going on?"

Her furrow deepened as she took me in, her thumb casually caressing me. I hadn't realized I said it out loud until Nix gave me a look. Assessing me, he rolled his eyes, immediately understanding the situation.

"Wes, it's not about you. It's about Zel. I'm getting someone to cover Gothel so Nolan can join us. Talk to her about all that," he motioned," before you snap your wrist raw."

"What does he mean, Wes? What do you need to tell me?"

Zoning in on Zel, I took a calming breath and blew out air slowly. "It's better if I show you. I wanted it to be special, to mean something."

Pulling her along, I opened the door to my bedroom and flicked on the light. Soft fairy lights lit the space, a few electronic candles shimmering in the shadows. It was the numerous rose petals she focused on, taking them in as she turned. Her hands covered her mouth, and I couldn't decide if it was from disgust or surprise. When she turned back with tears in her eyes, I started to backtrack, thinking I'd fucked up.

"I'm sorry, Zel. It was stupid. I just—"

"Shut up, you stupid man. It's perfect. *You're perfect.*"

She kissed me, her words bouncing around in my head. *You're perfect.* No one had ever said those things to me. I'd always been found with fault, always lacking, never enough no matter how hard I tried. From my father to ballet teachers, even the military, I'd always been found out.

"I'm not, but I like that you think I am. I've searched far and wide for someone to make me feel the way you do. I don't think you understand the effect you have on me, baby girl."

I hadn't meant to call her that earlier in her room, but it had slipped out. Once it had, and I saw the way her eyes heated at the words, I knew I'd never take them back. Falling back into a kiss, the heat was increasing when Nixon entered.

"As much as I like where this is headed, I'll be all for it in about thirty minutes." He paused, looking at the girl in my arms. "Princess, it's *time.*"

Her head dropped to my chest, a large breath in and out before she stepped back and nodded to him. Pulling me with her this time, she led us back out to the main sitting area. When we sat down, I was surprised to find she climbed into my lap. It was an odd occurrence, but I wrapped my arms around her, hoping never to let go.

"Oh, I texted Max too. He's headed here. Do you have a place he can stay? Or actually, I could stay with you, and he could take my room, if that's okay?"

"Who's Max?"

"Oh, right." Zel facepalmed, and I couldn't stop the chuckle.

"Zel, did you just facepalm in real life? Do people do that?"

"Well," she turned, rolling her eyes playfully at me, "I just did, so yeah, I guess so."

Her smile was infectious, and I leaned in for another kiss when the elevator dinged. Nix laughed, shaking his head as he waited for Nolan. "I never thought I would see the day Wesley Flynn was all lovey-dovey."

"Like you have room to talk, *Eugene*."

"No shit, you uncovered Sexy Nexy's real name?" piped in Nolan.

Zel grinned wide, a proud smile on her face at discovering his hidden identity. "Yep."

"Princess," he growled, "I told you what happens when you say my name like that." I was surprised to find he wasn't mad but instead incredibly turned on.

"Oh yeah," she swallowed. "Okay, I gotta stand, or I'll take my clothes off to avoid this, and it needs to happen."

She stood, all of us blinking at the vision she'd

just implanted in our minds. When Zel started to pace in front of the fireplace, I focused on her.

"Okay, so first, my real name is Rapunzel Sonne." Zel paused, waiting for us to say something. When neither of us did, she glanced at Nolan, who encouraged her with a nod to continue.

"Okay, well, my dad is Mayor Kingston Sonne. The short version of my life, my dad planned to sell me as a baby, claiming I'd been kidnapped to get him elected. When my nanny overheard, she took me instead and hid me away in the woods for thirteen years. She got sick one night, and I left our home to find help. Stepping out the clearing, a whole world was opened to me. At the hospital, a nurse recognized me by my heart birthmark. Oh yeah, one second."

Turning, she flipped her head up and undid some pins loosening the brunette waves and handing them off to Nolan. Taking off the cap, she ran her fingers through her hair until the golden locks fell to her waist. It shimmered in the light, and I wondered why she didn't show it more. It had a beautiful, almost ethereal quality about it.

"I was returned that night to my biological parents, and Gothel, who you met, was imprisoned. And I lived happily ever after, right?"

Nix and I looked at one another, not sure what to make of this story.

"Ehnt. Wrong. Turns out, Daddy dearest was a pedophile and child molester. He used me and either started his child pornography ring or advanced it like a king to gain favors from men in positions of power. The worst offender?" She paused, and I had a feeling I was going to hate myself with the answer. "Judge Giovani Baron."

Hanging my head, shame-filled me at pushing her about him. Nix had been right. I should've listened to all the things she wasn't saying. Small fingers lifted my chin, and her green eyes peered back. I'd never seen them before, and they took me by surprise at how pure and magical they were.

"I'm not saying this to shame you. I'm telling you this because he attacked me tonight, and I want to take him down. To take them all down. But I need your help."

I stared, running everything she'd said through my head. There had been one goal since my mom had died. Prove I was worth it. I'd always assumed the path to the goal was making my father proud through success. It was the language my father understood, and, in my child's mind, it was the greatest love I could gain. Looking into her pools of emerald green, hope and promise swirled within, I knew. I knew I'd been wrong.

Zel was asking *me* for help. She believed in me enough to trust me with her secret and to assist in her revenge. She saw me as someone worthy. It was the promise in her eyes that told me all I ever wanted to know—worth. My brain took off in a stampede, running away with ideas and formulating plans when the perfect idea struck me.

"We throw a ball. A masquerade ball. We draw them all out and to one place. I know someone we can trust at the police station that might be able to help. Is that what you want?"

Nodding, she smiled. "Yeah, I think that would be perfect." She kissed me, and I found myself drowning in her taste. My hand skimmed her skirt, feeling the bare skin as I did. A throat clearing had us pulling apart, Zel turning in my arms. I didn't know what her face looked like, but mine was tinted red as I took in the cheeky grin from Nix. Though, Nolan had been the one to draw our attention.

"Um, sorry," he laughed. "Max texted he's here, and I should get back to Gothel. I'll, um, leave you guys to it. I'll fill Max in too."

He stood and walked over to Zel. She didn't move from my arms but held her hand out for him to take. Once he linked with her, she pulled him in and kissed him. It was odd being this close to another person who wasn't Nix, one I didn't know as well yet either, but it wasn't awful. I guess Nix was right; I'd have to get used to it.

They pulled apart, and Zel rubbed against my groin as she did. "Thanks, Nols."

He smiled and walked out, taking the stairs down this time. She spun back around, a mischievous look on her face. "How about you tell me more about the stuff in the bedroom?"

"Are you sure? I don't want you to feel you have to, especially after what happened tonight."

"Even more reason to. They don't get to control my body anymore, and I want to see what's under Wesley Flynn's suit," she purred, licking her lips. Trailing fingers up my chest, she pulled the tie, bringing me closer to her face. "Besides, I already fucked Nix's brains out on a bathroom sink, and I'm ready for round two."

She ran her hand down my tie, letting it fall from her grip as she got off my lap and backed up. Pivoting, she sauntered away, hips swinging with each step and flipping her skirt to show her bare ass. When she got to Nix, her hands trailed up his chest, pulling him down into a kiss. When she pulled back, she peered over her shoulder. "Did I forget to mention I'm not wearing any panties?" Winking, she kept strolling toward the bedroom.

Stunned at her brazenness, I watched her drop her sweater as she pulled it off, followed by her skirt on her trek to the bed. Her naked body from behind was perfect, and I knew I'd found a new obsession—tracing every inch of her. When she made it to the bed, she turned, sitting on the edge before bracing her arms behind her and crossing her legs.

The petals laid all around her, and I didn't think I'd ever seen anything as erotic or sensual before. She crooked a finger, pulling me even more. "What are you waiting for, boys?"

It was the starting gun, and Nix and I charged for the bedroom. His clothes came off as he cozied up next to her, beating me to the bed. Nix wasted no time kissing her neck as he massaged her breasts. I watched in fascination as I unlinked my cuffs, slowly unbuttoning the crisp white shirt.

Zel was the embodiment of sexuality as she gave into her body and all it craved. Her hair fell down her back, pools of gold as she fell backward on the bed. Nix traveled with her, his hands roaming as he went, never stopping from touching her. Untucking my shirt, I popped the button on my pants, letting them drop to the ground. With each item I removed, I devoured the show before me. Discarding the rest of my clothes, I strolled toward the bed, my eyes never leaving them.

Grabbing the thick ribbon on the nightstand, I slid it through my fingers, the silky texture setting my nerves on fire. Kneeling, I leaned over Zel and whispered, "baby girl, just trust me." My voice had become velvety smooth, causing her breath to hitch.

Zel opened her eyes, nodding as she peered back at me. Lowering the ribbon, I tied her wrists together, lacing them up like ballet slippers. Putting them above her head, I picked up a petal and lightly trailed it over her skin.

"Oh, God. That feels so good. Mmmm."

Nixon moved down and began to pleasure her core as I took over the top. Tracing every inch of her, I watched as goosebumps broke out on her skin in my wake. Stroking over her nipple, I devoured the sight before me as it pebbled, the dusky pink hue darkening with the touch of the petal. Zel continued to moan, the pleasure from Nix and I overwhelming her.

Placing the petals down, I grabbed the chocolate strawberries and drizzled them over her, tracing them around her mounds and stomach. The chill the chocolate brought had her gasping. Zel lifted her body, moans escaping as she tried to chase her pleasure. I saw her hands try to move, but I stopped my ministrations as she started to raise them. Knowing what I was doing, Nix followed, and without even having to say anything, she placed her arms back, knowing we wouldn't continue until she did.

"Good job, baby girl," I purred, reinforcing her choice. Her gasp and almost exhale of relief when we started again had my cock rock hard. Licking up her torso, I followed where the chocolate was, sucking her nipple into my mouth. Swirling my tongue around, I blew air on it before nipping the tip with my teeth.

"Oh, Gods. I can't take much more. *Please*."

Her begging was the sound I needed to hear. Placing the strawberry on her lips, I traced them and pushed it in, waiting for her to bite. She moaned around the fruit, the flavor bursting on her tongue. As she did, I plunged my finger into her, coating it with her liquid heat. Nix had moved, standing to the side of the bed as he fisted his cock, and waited for me to direct the next part.

"Zel, I need you to rise to your knees."

She lifted up, following my command as she waited for me to tell her more. Taking the ribbon off her wrists, I tied it around her eyes now. Pushing on her back to bend her at the waist, Zel's free hands went to the bed in support. Nix moved closer, and I watched as he traced her lips in the same fashion I had with the strawberry, but this time with the head of his cock.

Zel licked them and started to suck him down. Moving behind her, I smoothed my hands over the globes of her ass, massaging the skin. Retracing my finger down the middle of her core, I drawled the wetness back to her entrance. Doing this a few times, I had her heightened as I readied her. Grasping her ass tighter, I pulled her cheeks apart and speared her pussy on my cock.

The sudden force took her by surprise, thrusting her forward and swallowing Nix's dick, deep throating him as she did. Waiting for her to adjust, I began to move once she'd recovered. Back and forth, we teetered her on the edge, a rhythm perfectly developing between us.

"Fuck, Zel. Gods, baby girl, you feel so good wrapped around my cock."

Keeping a tight grip on her ass, I pounded into her as my balls slapped her clit. The movement set

Nix off, and he came deep down Zel's throat. Grabbing the back of the ribbon, I wrapped it around my wrist and nodded to Nix as he slowly pulled out. When he was clear, I pulled Zel to me in a swift movement, changing the position. Never stopping the speed, I held her tight to me as I nuzzled her neck. She was a limp noodle by this point, my strength keeping her up as I brought us both closer.

I felt her tightening and knew I wouldn't last long. Holding her to me snuggly, I grazed my teeth against her collarbone as I came, pinching her clit simultaneously. Zel's mouth opened wide in a moan as her body spasmed around me from her orgasm. She started to collapse, but I caught her and carried her into the bathroom. The water had grown cold at this point, so I detoured to the shower. Sitting her on the bench, I removed the ribbon and knelt down to her.

"Are you okay, Zel? Was that good for you?"

She grasped my cheeks, her eyes lighting up as she took me in. "It was everything."

Kissing her, I stepped back and rinsed us both before drying us in big cotton robes. Nix stepped in as we exited, a smirk on his lips at my softness for her. Shaking my head at him, I ignored his good natured jab and took Zel to bed. Once she was settled, I brought the rest of the food and drinks I'd gotten together and made a small picnic in the bed.

"This is wonderful, Wes. No one's ever done anything like this before. I've never really experimented with either." She took a bite of the strawberry, the juice trailing down her chin.

"It wasn't too weird?"

Leaning into me, she kissed me, transferring some of the juice to me as she did. "It was with you and Nix. I *more* than liked it."

Relief lifted, and I realized how worried I'd been. Settling back, Zel recapped how it was meeting Nix's friends as we dined on strawberries and champagne. Nix joined, taking up the foot of the bed as he laid across it, listening to her.

It was nice, and I knew I could do this for the rest of my life and be happy. It was an odd concept to me, not worrying about work and basking in happiness, but I wanted it. I wanted it with these people, even Nolan.

Pride had always felt like an insurmountable thing, something I would know and feel when I achieved it. Sitting on the bed in a robe, I realized it wasn't the big overwhelming thing I'd assumed, but the small quiet heartbeats, the laughter, and even later, the snores as I fell asleep.

Pride was in the way I loved and was loved back, and that was the insurmountable thing —love.

CHAPTER TWENTY-SIX

ZEL

The cocking of the gun pulled me from my chocolate-dipped dream, and I tried to reorient myself to my surroundings. The bed shifted, the feel of the sheet rustling over my skin as I heard Nix growl.

"Unless you have a death wish, I'd rethink your next steps."

Blinking my eyes open, I tried to figure out what was going on. The room was pitch black, the walls and decor cutting any light that managed to enter. How Nix even knew someone was there astounded me.

"Uh, it's just me. We have a *problem*."

Nolan's words had me bounding out of bed, the body next to me moving as well. My brain was muddled with the time, but I could hear the fear and anxiety in his voice, and I needed to get to him. The robe slipped off my shoulder at the jostle, and I remembered I fell asleep wearing it. Tightening the belt, I made my way in the direction I assumed

Nolan was. Nix turned on the light a few seconds later, and I blinked against the brightness, everything finally coming into focus. Nolan stood in the doorway, his hands raised with a look of worry on his handsome face. Going to him, I wrapped him in my arms, trying to offer him some comfort.

"What is it, Nols? What's wrong?"

"I'm so sorry, Zel, but Gothel? She's gone."

Pulling back, I tried to make sense of what he was saying. "Gone? But how?"

"I checked on her after I left here, and she was fine, getting ready for bed. The guard was still posted at the door, so I went to meet Max. I was updating him on the situation, and then we, um, " Nolan scratched the back of his head, a blush rising to his cheeks, "got into a Street Fighter match, so I didn't return to the room to check on her until now."

His face was stricken, and I could see the guilt he carried. I squeezed him again. It wasn't his fault, nor the first time she'd done this. Gothel had always been a flight risk and a seasoned addict. It would take her wanting to get help before she'd accept it, but it didn't mean I'd stop trying.

"It's not your fault, Nolan. I'll call around and see if I can find her at any of her normal haunts."

Nix approached, and I realized he and Wes had run off to do things while I'd comforted Nolan. Looking at him, he lowered the phone, an unreadable expression on his face. I realized then he was only in a pair of boxers, and my mind started to run away with ideas as I took in his abs and tattoos —fucking beautiful man.

"I'm afraid it's worse than that, princess. The camera shows she was lured out to meet someone. I'm not sure how she got around the guard at the door, but I'll be questioning him now. When she stepped out of The Tower, a man was waiting for her. They argued, and he knocked her over the head before carrying her away. He stayed in the shadows and was wearing all black. I think if you get Max up here, he might be able to pull the partial plate the camera caught."

In the span of his update, I'd gone from holding Nolan to ending with *him* comforting *me*. He pulled me over to the couch, where we sat down together. Shock raced through me, twisted with fear. There could be several people who'd take her, but I had a suspicion it was only one of them—my father.

Wes placed a warm mug in my hand, and I distractedly brought it up to my lips. The whipped cream tickled my nose, causing me to focus and look at the cup as I drank it. Hot cocoa warmed my throat as it slid down, the richness giving me a feeling of solace. Licking my lips, I sat it down, strangely feeling better. Wes smirked, the sight odd from him, and it provided me with confidence.

I wasn't alone—no more hiding in the shadows.

Life hadn't given me my happily ever after, so I would make my own, and it started with destroying the men who'd hurt me. I needed to regain my identity, and part of that meant facing the demons within.

"I need to go to brunch."

"Brunch?"

"Yep, brunch." I nodded, firm in my statement. "It's time I stood up to my father."

"Do you think he had something to do with this?" Wes asked.

"I'd wager yes, it's him or the Judge, but considering how I left the Judge last night, I doubt he'd retaliate. Either option leads me to start with my father. I need to face him and show him I'm not the scared teenager he manipulated. I-I-I." Swallowing, I squashed the fear of facing him down that had tried to choke me. "Would someone come with me?"

It was the first time I'd asked them for anything outside the bedroom. I knew I'd need their strength to stay firm in the den of the lion. Nolan squeezed my hand, jumping in quickly. "Whatever you need."

"Princess, I'd slay dragons for you, but the kid might be the better choice in this instance. I'm likely to punch your father, and that wouldn't accomplish anything. If you take Wes, they'll either get big eyes thinking of all the ways to exploit it or become suspicious. Better to keep that under wraps."

"As much as it grieves me to admit, he's not wrong," Wes huffed, a smile playing on his lips.

Turning to Nolan, I grinned. "Looks like you get to meet the mayor."

"Stop fidgeting. You'll be fine."

Nolan pulled the cuff of his shirt down and straightened his tie for the millionth time. Since he'd been at The Tower, Wesley had lent him some clothes to wear. Nolan was a little broader in the shoulders, so it pulled slightly, but otherwise, it was almost a perfect fit. The navy tie suited him and brought out his honey eyes. It was funny to me how nervous he was and it helped to quell my own nerves.

Nolan reminded me of the woman I'd become and not the scared girl who'd lived in this house, scared of her own shadow. Taking a fortifying breath, I knocked on the front door. Since it wasn't my regular brunch date, they wouldn't be expecting me. The element of surprise would hopefully be in my favor.

The butler opened the door, a quick flash of surprise on his usually stoic face. "Miss Sonne, we weren't expecting you," he started before seeing Nolan, "and you have a guest. Please, come in. Your father is in the foyer. Should I announce your arrival?"

"I think we have it handled, thanks."

He nodded, a tilt to his lips indicating he

approved of my decision. Nolan squeezed my hand as we walked down the marble floor. The ostentatiousness of it all made me sick. Wes had shown me you could have nice things, *exquisite things*, without being gaudy. The Tower was designed beautifully with care going into every detail, and I had a suspicion Wes was behind it all. But no part of it was done to draw attention to status.

My father had zoomed past pride right into smugville, and his whole purpose was to develop greed and envy simultaneously. I'd once thought having all these nice things meant I was special, *privileged*. The only thing this lifestyle had done for me was to create discord, loneliness, and shame, trapping me in a prison made of lies.

Despite the hardships of living on the street, life had been free.

"You ready?"

Nodding, I took a step forward into the room. I hadn't expected to see my parents meeting with anyone, so catching Captain Kingsley's wicked glare as he spotted me took me off guard. I stopped, unable to move as the man disarmed me with his predatory glare. I'd never liked him, and the number of dirty deals he'd helped my father cover up disgusted me.

Nolan squeezed my hand three times, and it gave me the courage I needed. Three squeezes, three hearts I adored, and three men I would fight for.

"Rapunzel! Oh, dear, we weren't expecting you," Queenie started, pausing when she spotted the tall man beside me. Instantly, she began to fluff herself, wanting to present the best picture. "And you brought a young gentleman."

Internally, I rolled my eyes so hard, they had to be stuck, but outwardly, I smiled and fell into my perfect daughter roll. "Mom, this is my boyfriend, Nolan."

"It's nice to meet you, Mrs. Sonne. If Rapunzel hadn't introduced you, I would've thought you were her sister."

A chuckle slipped out, and I covered it by clearing my throat. "Um, sorry. And this is my father, Kingston."

Nolan tensed as my father regarded him. He'd yet to acknowledge me, not happy with my inter-ruption and unplanned visit. Kingston tightened his jaw, rising slowly. He didn't take any steps forward, but Nolan didn't let it phase him. Walking, he stuck out his hand, offering my father a shake. Kingston couldn't ignore it then because that would be rude, but he didn't make it easy.

"I'd say it's nice to meet you, son, but that would be a lie since I had no clue you'd be here."

Ignoring his jab, I sat down and crossed my legs as I smoothed the soft tulle skirt. It was very balle-rina-esque with the tutu material, hitting at my shins. It was a pale grey with flowers embroidered on it. I'd picked my outfit to be soft and feminine, a visual reminder to the daughter they wanted me to be. The flats I had on even had ballet ties up my calves. The best part, though, in my opinion, was the top.

Taking a slight risk, I showed some skin. It was pink and cropped. It had long ribbons that tied around my midriff, again giving the illusion of ballet. My hair was braided in a bun and pulled back. It had taken effort to look this demure, a confirmation I'd grown into myself as a woman.

The way the ribbon rubbed against me, another example of my growth as it created sinful desires. Flashes of last night flitted through my head, and I wondered what else Wes would do with the ribbon. Each brush against my skin had me growing slick between the legs, but this wasn't the place for daydreams. Focusing back on the role I had to play, I placed my hand delicately on my knees as I waited for my father to address me.

"Rapunzel, you remember my good friend, Captain Marvin Kingsley?"

"Yes, Father. Hello, Captain Kingsley. You look well. Been to any good places lately?"

I'd turned, giving him direct eye contact as I spoke. He'd been arrogant when I'd entered, sitting back with his chest puffed out, thinking he was the predator. He didn't know I'd seen him at The Tower. Blinking innocently at him, I challenged him, throwing him off-kilter. I'd never looked men like him directly in the eyes before, much less confronted them. They preferred me weak and unsure, trapping me under their thumb.

I was no longer weak. I knew that now. No matter what I wore, the color of my hair, or the name I went by, I was me to my core. I just had to believe it.

I swung around poles, danced in mega heels, and dealt with handsy men every night. The disguises gave me freedom, but it was still me. I'd trapped myself in a prison of my own making, limiting myself to thinking I was only capable of a few things. Once I'd acknowledged myself last night, I'd lit a particle so hot, all of my fear had burned up, and I no longer needed to hide.

This was absolute freedom.

"I, uh, I was just talking with your father about a place."

"Oh, what is it?"

"The Tower, I was telling him about it."

Smiling wide, my face probably appeared manic at the moment, but I couldn't have planned it better than if I'd tried.

"What a surprise! I heard about a who's who masquerade ball taking place in a month. It sounds decadent and exclusive. Word is only the best of Sinhaven will get an invite. It's going to be the talk of the town and an honor to get invited. Do you think you'll get one?"

I leaned over the side of the couch, resting my chin on my hand as I peered at him in earnest. He appeared flustered by my question, not expecting me to ask him anything. Nolan chimed in, helping push my story.

"I even heard there's going to be some secret club invitation or something, and if you don't get a code word, then you're on your way out of Sinhaven. Wesley Flynn is set to enter into business with one person, making them rich beyond their wildest dreams. He's some business prodigy guru or something. I know my father wants me to set something up with him."

"Your father?" Kingston interrupted, throwing Nolan for a second as he turned back to him.

"Ah yes, Tom Ryder, he owns the hardware store on the square."

"Hmm, I seem to remember something about your family in the news a few years back."

This caught me off guard. I turned to Nolan in surprise, wanting to comfort him. This wasn't part of the plan. I didn't want my father to turn his sights on Nolan to get to me. Kingston knew what he was doing, and he'd gone after what he felt was my weakness to attack. My father was wrong, though, so wrong.

Nolan wasn't anywhere near a weakness. Squeezing his hand this time, I gave him my support. Whatever my father was about to use, it wouldn't be good, and I knew Nolan would've wanted to tell me on his terms and not like this.

"Um, yes, sir. There was a death in the family."

"Oh dear, you poor thing," my mother chimed in, her hand to her chest in sympathy.

I hadn't expected Nolan to say that, especially after meeting his family. I tried to recollect my memory from school, but everything from then was a blur, only tiny things sticking out.

"Hmm, yes, I recall this now. Your sister, if I'm correct? They found her body brutally attacked, most appearing self-inflicted."

Nolan swallowed, nodding. Both of his hands squeezed mine, sweat lining his brow, and I searched my brain for a way to stop this line of questioning. Kingston didn't get to have the upper hand here. This was our play, our game. Something came to me, and I turned to shut him down when he delivered his last blow.

"She was part of that child pornography ring. You remember that, don't you, Marvin?"

The question hung in the air, a threat to me at the implication. My air clogged my throat, and I focused on breathing, on remembering my purpose, my plan. The pain in my hand pulled me back, and I focused on Nolan. This wasn't only about me anymore. No, this was about all the girls they'd done this to. It was clear I wasn't the only one.

I'd always wondered but naively hoped it had been only me. Giovanni had let it slip last night, disclosing an entire network of men taking advantage of underage girls. Who knew if they were in similar situations as me, being sold by a parent, or by their own desperate choice, but none of us deserved it or wanted it. Even if they consented to promises of a better life, it was coercion and child pornography.

With the fire raging in me, I wanted to strike him at the knees, hoping to weaken him.

"Interesting, you should bring that up, Father. It seems the bargain you and I struck years back, well, you didn't keep up your end of it. You took something from me last night, and I expect it back. So, I'm afraid that does make our contract null and void."

Standing, I pulled the shell-shocked Nolan up with me.

"Mother, I dropped out of college three years ago. I'm sorry I didn't tell you. Father paid me to stay away, and I thought it was the only way at the time."

Before yesterday, I'd wanted to hurt her for all the times she'd let me down, but my cruelty wouldn't do anything but keep her trapped in this life. If I was going to try to be better for Gothel, I could try for her as well. It was up to Queenie if she wanted to open her eyes to what was going on here or stay numb to it.

Turning, I faced the men in the room. "Father, I won't be attending any more special dinners, and if you fail to return *her* to me? Well, I have my own ace up my sleeve."

His eyes leveled me with disdain and hatred at

being called out in front of others. He gritted his jaw, his fingers flexing as I stood up to him. Kingston didn't like this, and if I failed in my plan, there would be hell to pay.

I stopped in the doorway when the butler entered with the invitations I'd known would arrive. Wesley and I'd timed it, hoping for a grand exit. I rolled my eyes at the card being delivered on a silver platter. The airs my father attempted to gather were moronic. He acted like he was the king of this town, with all of his subjects needing to bow at his feet. He couldn't even open his own mail.

I watched to make sure he read the card. The thick card stock invitation with his invite and code-word held proudly in his hands as his greedy eyes took in the details. His ego would believe anything because he'd already accepted it as accurate.

I pulled Nolan with me, and we exited. I didn't need to see anything else. I only needed to know they had. My mother hadn't moved, shocked as she pondered the deception. I felt terrible, but I didn't want to pretend anymore. Though, I kind of wanted to be a fly on the wall to see the bolstering that would occur once we were gone, but not enough to stick around. I hoped she gave it to him as well for hiding things from her. I didn't have high hopes she'd stick up for herself, though. She'd never done it before.

Zipping through the hall, Nolan and I practically ran as my skirt flew up around me. Adrenaline coursed through me, along with bile at having stood up to my father. The mention of the photos and the info my father had known clearly connected him to Nolan's sister, causing a cyclone of topsy turvy emotions to churn within me.

Once we were free of the door, I slowed, catching my breath. A tall man leaning against a nice SUV brought a smile to my face as we made our way over to him. I didn't know what I'd done to deserve Nix, but my broody alpha was always there, protecting me. He never stepped in unless I needed it, teaching me I could stand on my own. It was one of the greatest gifts a man had ever given me.

"I thought you two could use a ride."

"Ah, Sexy Nexy, I knew you liked me. Look, Zel, our knight in a shining Mercedes is here."

Laughing, I jumped into the car, not wanting to be on this street for another minute. I looked at Nolan once we were a few miles away, the question burning in my eyes.

"Her name was Natalie, and she wasn't just my sister, but my twin sister."

"Oh, Nolan, I'm so sorry."

Pulling him into a tight squeeze, I caught Nix's eyes from the front. He nodded, understanding something significant had happened.

Nolan moved back, cupping my face as he spoke, "The thing I don't get, Zel, the part about the pictures, that was never in the news or reports.

We kept it *hidden*." He paused, waiting to see if I would understand what he was saying.

"Which means, either my father saw it as part of his job, or he was the one… to do it."

Nolan nodded, not wanting to be the one to say it.

"Nix, I think we need to stop somewhere first," I stated, holding Nolan's eyes. "We've got a ball to shop for. Let's head to August's store. He always has the best stuff. I need something I can kickass in."

I'd intended to destroy my father's career along with the Judge and the men involved in this ring of his. But now, the stakes were higher. If we couldn't get Detective Ardyn to help us, then we'd have to take measures into our own hands. I was done waiting for justice. I'd make my own if necessary.

Kingston Sonne had used me from the moment of my conception to get what he wanted, from respect of the townspeople, political prowess, even sympathy. He thought he had a golden goose, an endless supply of good fortune, by keeping me under his thumb.

But I was no longer a naive, weak girl. I'd transformed into a sexy, strong, and sassy woman, and I was fucking prideful. It was time to show Daddy dearest just how sinful that made me.

CHAPTER TWENTY-SEVEN

ZEL

Planning had consumed almost every free minute I had over the last month as we prepared for the ball. There hadn't been any leads on Gothel that were promising either. Max had been able to track the van she'd been taken in, but it was abandoned and reported stolen when we got there.

I tried to break into the Judge's house to see if he was keeping her in the basement, but that hadn't gone well for me, and if Detective Ardyn hadn't been the one to show up, I'd probably be waiting for court in a jail cell right now. When I thought about it, I realized how stupid and careless it was to hand myself over to them like that, but it had felt necessary in the moment.

Nolan hadn't told his parents what he'd learned yet, afraid of what it might do to them. His plot to convince me to enroll back into school was still going strong, and while I gave him grief over it, it had merit. Wes had offered him a job, so now he was at The Tower almost as much as me. He and Max were running the gaming tournaments and had brought in a lot of new ventures with it. Max had reluctantly agreed to stay here as well, and despite his grumblings, I think he was enjoying it.

"Just one more, Zel."

Nix and I were currently working out at Fairy Godmother's gym. We started coming here a few weeks ago. He knew the owners, and I found it hilarious how many more people in this town he knew than me. Mainly because he mostly grunted at them, but I guess part of his job in the new cities was to scout out the scene and know who the players were. Didn't mean I wasn't going to give him a hard time about being a social butterfly, though.

Nix was teaching me self-defense and helping me build muscle definition. After the situation with the Judge, I didn't want to be unprepared ever again. I never went anywhere alone, even at The Tower, but I didn't want to live my whole life worried. Nix had suggested teaching me how to defend myself and get out of holds as a way to build my confidence, and I was amazed at how well it worked.

Pushing up the bar, I held it before lowering it back down. My arms were jelly, but I'd beaten my personal best, and the warm feeling of satisfaction bolstered me. The exercises had benefited my dancing as well, and I wanted to talk Wes into getting some aerial wraps to try out. His contraption with the pole rising out of the floor had me believing he could make something extraordinary from the ceiling too.

"Good job, princess," he purred, helping me off the bench. "Let's head back and shower."

His eyebrows raised, and I knew exactly what type of *wet* he wanted to get. Winking, I grabbed my stuff after wiping off the sweat, and we headed out together. Nix nodded at the ginger man behind the front desk, and I watched in fascination.

Both guys who owned the gym were muscular and handsome, though they did nothing for me. I could appreciate their athletic forms, though. To be fair, they only had eyes for the petite blonde I saw around, and it was comforting to know I wasn't the only one in this town with a more than one dick appetite.

When we entered the penthouse apartment, a flurry of activity met us. It had become the central location for our party headquarters. Wes converted part of Wager into the ballroom since Desire didn't have a large open area. The rest of The Tower would be shut down to guests, allowing staff who weren't working the ball to attend if they wanted.

Wesley was a great boss and took pride in his company. No one was treated poorly here, and it showed in the love and dedication the staff had for their job. The Tower had become a haven and a place of hope in a town built on sin.

"Oh good, you're back. The costume designer will be here in an hour for your outfit, and hair and makeup are set up in Wesley's room. Shower, and they'll get you taken care of," Isaac, Wesley's assistant, conveyed. He'd been a big help through this whole ordeal with coordinating things, and I'd come to think of him as a friend.

"It's good to see you too, Isaac!" I sang, sticking my tongue out at him as I sashayed into the room. Nix headed to his. Our shower had to wait now that there were people in our place. I caught one last heated glance before he shut his door, and I took a step in his direction, people be damned. A hand fell onto my shoulder, halting me, and I found Isaac smirking at me.

"No time for you to climb that tree today, Zel. Now, get to your own shower, or I'll sic Maggie on you."

"Ah, Isaac! No fair, you know I can't say no to her."

Crossing my arms, I turned and headed back to shower alone. Maggie was the grandma of The Tower. While she was sweet and grandmotherly, she had a ruthless underbelly you didn't want to cross either. She both intrigued and terrified me, and I planned to stay on her good side. The best part, though, she brought me cookies. Anyone who did that was someone to keep happy.

The next few hours were gruesome, and I felt more tortured than I did pampered. I'd been waxed, plucked, tweezed, and just about any type of pulling you could imagine. Since I needed to be in costume first for my dance, they curled my hair before putting on a dark black wig with a colorful headpiece with feathers. By the time they were finished, you couldn't tell who I was.

The makeup they put on me transformed me into a beautiful Goddess, and I kept twisting and turning my head as I took in the details. Instead of a mask, they'd painted jewels around my eyes. My costume was purple, blue, and turquoise, in the old showgirl style with the long feather tail, short front, and extravagant bra piece. I felt like a peacock, but it was beautiful nonetheless.

Tightening the straps on my shoes, I stood and took myself in the mirror. Three hours of hard work, and I was unrecognizable. It was crazy. A knock at the door broke my focus, and I turned to see Wesley entering. He stopped when he saw me, swallowing as he traveled the length of my body.

Over the past month, things have been good with all the guys and me. Wesley had been the hardest to crack, but once he'd opened himself, I'd understood him a lot better. He walked over and held me close as he peered down into my eyes.

"Wow, Zel. You look beautiful."

"Thanks, Wes. You look really handsome too."

"You ready for this?"

"Yeah. It's time."

"Okay, baby girl. We'll be there with you through it all."

"I know."

Kissing his cheek, I smiled as I pulled away and headed out of the room. I was about to perform the show of a lifetime.

Peeking into the main room, I was astounded by the transformation. The room glittered all around with stars and lights. It had been transformed into a starry landscape, and it was magnificent. Navy fabric hung around the room with white gauzy fabric giving the effect of the sky and clouds. Couples danced to the music in ball gowns, tuxedos, and elegant masks.

As the lights shifted on the floor, it gave the illusion of light dancing, and I immediately started to sway to the music. Nolan came up behind me, hands landing on my hips as he rocked with me, humming along to a song only he could hear.

"How are you feeling, twinkle toes?"

"As long as I don't overthink it, I feel good. If I start to think about what I'm doing, I want to throw up. I'm trying to convince myself I'm the strong, sassy girl I pretend to be."

Twirling me, the door shut behind me, shutting off the sound to the main room. We were in the smaller area typically used as a VIP section. It was decorated as well, but it didn't have the same effect in the smaller area without the vaulted ceilings. We were all in position, ready for the secret invitation guests to arrive. A few mingled, drinking cocktails as they eyed one another, wondering what was so special about them. Focusing back to Nolan, he'd waited until I was present and lifted my chin to peer directly at me.

"The answer is easier than you think, Zel. You feel like you're pretending, but you can't be something you're not for very long without people realizing it. I bet the person you're pretending to be is the weak one. When no one is around and watching, how do you feel?"

"I dunno. I guess I'm happy." I shrugged, pondering what he said.

His face lit up in a grin. "Well, I'm glad to hear that, but how do you feel about yourself?"

"Free," I answered without hesitation. Blinking, I tried to determine what that meant.

"Well, there's your answer. When you're free, you're strong, sassy, and a bit badassery," he chuckled. "You don't pretend to be those things. You've convinced yourself it's an act for so long, you forgot what it feels like not to be. Those two have conditioned you to feel weak, and you began to think you were too. But you're not, Zel, not by a long shot. Don't let them make you feel any less wonderful than you are."

"How did you get so smart?"

"Well," he huffed, "I'd like to think it was natural."

"Oh, is that so?"

"Mmm, hmm."

"Nolan?"

"Yes, Zel?"

"I'm so glad I met you. You make my life pretty wonderful."

He stopped our swaying, a serious look coming over his face. "After Nat, I didn't think I'd ever find someone who'd make me feel like I could hope for a future. I didn't know how to think of one without her. And yet, you popped up and wouldn't go away. You intrigued me when you refused my Pop Tarts, enraptured me when I watched you dance, and captured me with Monopoly. In the middle of all that, I fell in love with you, and it wasn't because of your crazy sexiness."

Nolan paused, my heart in my throat, his words circling my head. "I fell in love with the way you touched me without even using your hands. I heard that quote before, and I didn't get it, but one day, we were goofing off, and it hit me. I loved you. Seven billion smiles, Zel. Seven billion and yours is my favorite."

Sucking in a breath, I started to reply when the emcee for the event began to speak to the room.

"Ladies and gentlemen, we are so happy to have you here with us tonight in our VIP section. This masquerade ball is not only a great way to celebrate the success of The Tower and raise money for a good cause, but also to honor some of Sinhaven's leaders right here in this very room. You've all been selected because you're what makes this city what it is."

I held Nolan's eyes, and all I could do was kiss him, my cue to head to the stage already past. I tried to convey everything I felt in the kiss, hoping to be still here later to return his words. Pulling away, he nodded, a lopsided smile on his lips as our fingers clung to one another until the distance was too great.

Turning quickly, I rushed away, knowing the more I delayed it, the harder it would be. I saw my father and the Judge walking to the stage along with the other nominees. The announcer had them all sit in a row in the front of the stage. Heading behind a curtain, I found Nix waiting for me. Handing me my pointe shoes, I quickly slid them on, lacing them around my ankles, a skill I'd done a million times. Wrapping one side and then the other, I tied it twice before tucking it under.

Nix watched me a bit transfixed as I did it, a slight smile tilting up my lips at the cuteness of it. Helping me stand, I went up on pointe and flexed the arches. I'd beaten and smoothed the edges earlier, getting them ready to wear. Nixon and Nolan had looked on in horror as I did it, not understanding how I could beat my shoes into submission. Wes laughed at them, used to the ordeal dancers went through to get their shoes in shape to wear.

Taking a deep breath, I kissed his cheek, at a perfect level now on pointe, and smiled. Dropping back down, I headed onto the stage. The announcer was still speaking, drawing out the time until the music started. Wesley nodded from the other side, and I gathered my courage. I could do this. The music started, and I fell into the routine, the dance portraying my emotions better than I'd ever been able to speak them. Sashaying with the feathers, I embraced the character, pulling my seduction to the forefront. I didn't have to hide it. I didn't have to mute. I just had to be me.

The best way to make my father and the Judge pay was to use their sin against them. I wanted to be wrathful and destroy them beneath my heels as I danced on their bones, but Wes showed me a better way. He showed me how not to lose myself in the pursuit of revenge. The music changed, and a beat started playing, building suspense. I stopped, my back turned to the crowd, and shook my ass, the feathers rumbling as I made them dance. A spotlight shone on me, the rest of the stage in darkness. My heart fluttered as I watched Wes approach me, hidden from the crowd.

"You ready?"

Smiling, I nodded. He unlocked the feather skirt, and it fell to the floor, the music changing to a heart-filled ballad, emotion pouring through each note. Loosening the pins of my wig, he stepped back once I was ready. I moved my arms, turning my head as I stepped over the skirt. In a black leotard and tutu, I extended my leg out in front, my attitude on perfect point as I bent my knee and flexed my foot as I held the pose.

Dipping down, I used the momentum of my hands and legs to fling the black hair completely off and rise with my golden hair flying out behind me. I heard some gasps from the crowd, but I ignored them, focused on what was coming up. Spinning, I pas de chat across the stage until I came to an end, where I turned into the arms of Wesley. The crowd had faded away, the music and Wes all I could see as I fell into the story we'd created.

We moved together, doing what he could to partner me, modifying moves as we went. A white screen lowered, and as I told the story of my abuse, all the evidence I had collected over the years began flashing behind me with my voiceover.

"I thought I was the luckiest girl in the world the day I was found and returned home to my parents."

Pictures of me from the paper flashed up, along with some others from those first few months, me bright-eyed and hopeful. I kept dancing, spinning, and moving with the music as I alternated from glissade and gliding across the floor to an emboité where my right leg was on point while the other was rotated inward. As I flitted back and forth, I focused on dancing and blocked out the pain.

"One day, I was told to be a good girl, to make my daddy's friends happy."

As much as I hated to share this part, the pictures taken of me began to flash up. I'd found them on a drive in my father's study a few years ago, blackmail he kept on the Judge.

A half-naked fourteen-year-old, looking at
the camera seductively, tears in her eyes.
A fifteen-year-old, practically naked, a boa
around her to cover her parts, her lipstick
smeared.
A sixteen-year-old, her hair laying over her
naked body, barely concealing her.
A seventeen-year-old, her straps off her
shoulders, nipples peeking above the barely-
there tank top, sitting in her underwear and
pointe shoes with her legs open.

There were worse ones, but I hadn't wanted to blast those to a room full of strangers. These were bad enough.

*"I tried telling. I tried asking for help. I tried saying no.
Every time, I was told to 'shut up and be a good girl'. I
walked the halls every day, the pain inside hidden from
everyone."*

A few pics of me in high school as the

homecoming queen and surrounded by
peers flashed.

My smile always forced, my eyes heavy and sad,
the pain in them easy to see if you looked.

Max had been able to do a morph part that
flashed the first pic of me and morphed to all the
faces of me and how I looked at eighteen.

The sadness was tangible, a heavy blanket
covering me.

I pirouetted into Wes, and he lifted, our movements synchronized. I drowned out the fear of what
my father was thinking, of the Judge, and only
thought of dance. Doing an arabesque, I held the
pose as I came down into an inward position for the
finale. The lights went out; the silence was eerie as
everyone waited to see where I was going with this.

*"I struck a deal with my father. I could leave and have my
own life, but he wouldn't give me anything. I would have to
survive myself. It was better than living a life that was slowly
killing me. In my desperation, I'd only bargained for two
things, just happy to get out of his control. I asked for safety
for the woman everyone believed was a villain, and I asked
that no other girls had to go through what I did. My father
granted it, but in return, I had to attend family obligations,
his image needing to remain intact, and I had to continue
having 'dinners' with his friends."*

The spotlight turned on, the pole in place as I

stood on pointe, gripping it with my curls down my back. This spotlight was a blacklight and highlighted the words written on my leotard in glow in the dark ink. They were the names and ages of the victims we'd found. The music sped up, and I swung around, spinning and flipping as I climbed my pole. Stopping in position, I froze as the voice-over started again, the pictures of all the other girls, their faces obscured, flashing quickly up there. Max had been able to find them from the info the judge had spilled.

"I thought I was doing something good. As long as I kept my mouth shut, I saved others. I lived on the streets, ate garbage, and continued to be used, thinking I was protecting people. I made some friends but kept myself distant, afraid of caring for anyone else. Using dance, I found something I could love again, a way to survive financially and emotionally. When I danced, I was free. Free from the restraints and pressures, free from the self-hate and free from the fear he'd one day change his mind."

Dancing across the stage, Wesley lifted me into his arms, my dirty dancing dream met. I held it and then fell into his arms. Turning toward the crowd, I spoke myself this time, into the microphone I was wearing.

"I was scared, stuck in the shadows, hiding from the truth being discovered. I lost who I was, trapped behind my own fear, disguising myself just to live.

I'm stepping out from the dark, shedding light on what is going on in our town. I'm no longer willing to stand idly by. I'm no longer willing to ignore the abuse and corruption. I'm no longer willing to sacrifice my happiness for your greed and pride, *Father*."

My father glared daggers at me as I continued to speak and ruin his good name. Once they'd taken a seat, the guards had formed a perimeter around them, cutting off all exits as Detective Ardyn Hunter waited for me to finish. I'd met with him earlier in the week, going over my case and the info I had and what I wanted to do. He hadn't wanted me to blast myself to everyone, caring about protecting me and the trauma I'd endured, but accepted I knew what I was doing. I knew no one would believe me unless I came forward, giving them a reason to listen.

I had to damage the mayor's pride in the eyes of the ones he respected, his peers. Going to the papers or news station wouldn't have done anything. He had people everywhere, and they'd stop my story or spin it to fit their narrative, faster than I could say breaking news. No, the only way to make sure he was done was for him to lose the only thing he valued. **PRIDE**.

Mingling about with the vile men who were part of this network were the wives and daughters of Sinhaven. The ones who ran their own companies supported women's rights and had their own network of connections. They were lawyers, doctors, therapists, nurses, teachers, and politicians. They were women who had their own power and voice. And most importantly, they were *mothers*, and they were pissed.

"It's over, Daddy dearest. You have nothing on me. You're *done*. You can no longer hurt me or any other girls."

"That's where you're wrong, sweetheart. I'm the fucking lion of this kingdom, and I always come out on top of the pride."

His words weighed heavy in the air as he spoke them, a chill running down my spine in foreboding. He lifted a gun right at me, and I knew it was over. I'd overplayed my hand, and evil would win again.

CHAPTER TWENTY-EIGHT

NOLAN

People believed life flashed before your eyes the moment before you died. As I watched the Mayor aim a gun at my heart, I realized they'd been wrong about one thing.

Life flashed before my eyes, but it wasn't mine. It was a person—Zel.

Almost in slow motion, I watched as Nix, Wes, and I moved to try to stop what was about to occur. Wes moved to grab Zel since he was the closest to her, and Nix and I went for the Mayor. Neither of us were within reach, our movement a reflex rather than an actual ability to stop it.

When the gun sounded in the room, screams and shouts rang out, causing everything to ricochet in the small room. Covering my ears briefly, I tried to figure out what was happening. I couldn't see the Mayor or Zel as I searched through the sea of bodies. People were screaming, huddling together, and only a few had moved into action. The guards hovered over a section, so I headed there, assuming it was the best place.

Frantically, I tried to squeeze through the behemoths, but they kept their wall, holding me back. Running around, I ducked down and found a section between their legs I could see through. Blood coated the ground as it spilled, a lifeless hand on the floor a few feet from me. With more strength than I knew I had, I pushed through the legs in front of me.

The guy above me cursed, but I plowed my way to the bodies needing to know if my heart would become unmendable this time. Hair laid strewn on the ground, blood masking the color. The body was unmistakably female as I crawled the rest of the way. Red stained the ends of golden hair, and I felt my air get trapped in my throat.

When she lifted her head, tears streamed down her face, and I didn't understand what I was witnessing. Blinking, my brain processed I wasn't breathing, and I sucked in a lungful of the delicious necessity. Sound returned as the spots cleared, and I could make out the words Zel was stating.

"She saved me, Nols. She knocked into him, and saved me. Now I have to save her."

Her arms were wrapped around a body, but it wasn't the Mayor lying there. It was Gothel. Jumping into rescue mode, I slid off my jacket, bunching it up to apply pressure to the wound. My motion seemed to have dislodged Zel from the panic as she looked around for her father. I pressed down, hoping someone had called an ambulance as she stormed over to the man kneeling, held down by Nix's hand on his shoulder.

"This is all a misunderstanding, sweetheart. We can work this out. Tell the nice man you made it all up."

He was speaking fast, stumbling over his words as the lies spilled from his lips, seeming to forget he'd shot her moments ago. She looked to the Detective before she said anything.

"You might want to close your eyes for this, Detective Ardyn."

Before he could respond, she reared back and punched her father square in the nose. "That's for making me believe I was nothing," she panted. Lifting her knee, she nailed him in the groin as a collective sound of "*oohs*" rang out from the guards watching. "And that's for Natalie. I hope you rot in Hell and never get to see daylight. But knowing you, you'll somehow manage to survive it. But you had one thing wrong, *Dad*," she sneered, tears and blood mixing and marring her perfect makeup. "The lion doesn't have to roar after his kill to announce to the pride he's the biggest and baddest. You're the furthest thing from a king. You're a nonentity, a pleb. *Kingston Sonne, you're nothing but a sheep.*"

Turning, she paused before continuing to me. "You can open your eyes now, Detective."

Wes walked up with a medic, and they began transferring Gothel onto the gurney. They took over the pressure I held as they moved her, and I stepped back to let them work. Zel wrapped her arms around me as we both watched them hook IVs and started what I assumed was prepping her for surgery.

"What are they doing?"

"I have a medical room on the third floor. They're moving her there."

The hardness dropped from Zel's face as she relaxed into me at the news. The Detective nodded as he walked by, the Judge and Mayor in handcuffs. There were a few other men who were restrained, but I only focused on those two. He marched them through the main doors, no hidden back tunnels for them. This was part of the punishment, to besmirch their names and make their sins visible for all to see.

Gasps rang out as they were escorted through the main ballroom, filling me with hope justice would be served. Some of the women Zel had invited walked over a look of respect on their faces. I recognized a professor of mine and smiled at her nod of acknowledgment. She and another woman appeared to be the leaders of the crew as they approached.

"Rapunzel, or do you prefer Zel?"

"Zel is good. Thank you all for coming."

"I feel like we should be thanking you, dear. It's

nice to meet you formally, Zel. I'm Rhiannon. That was quite a show you performed. Not only was the message you conveyed powerful, but the dancing and artistry were magnificent. I have a feeling things are going to be messy moving forward, and we'd like to offer you support."

She handed Zel a card. When I looked, it had an acronym. Flipping it over, it said, "Powerful, Resourceful, Independent Divas Ensemble."

"We started an organization to help women, and we'd like you to join. It would also mean assisting you with the legal case and any other needs you may have. We believe in what you started and want to help you mobilize."

I watched Zel as she digested their offer, her body relaxing at the realization it was over. People believed her. Tears formed again, this time, I suspected, from relief and happiness. "I would love that, actually."

"Good. We'll be in touch, but call us if you need anything before then." They started to walk away, but my professor stopped and turned back. "I'm a professor at Shire University. If you ever think about returning, give me a call. I have a connection with the Ballet Mistress, and I know they'd want to talk to you. Just in case you ever wanted to pursue it more."

Zel nodded, but I think she was too stunned to do anything more. Wesley returned, and I realized Nix had been guarding our backs the entire time as the room had cleared out. Most of the guests headed back into the main area, the guards and cops having left with the pornography ring, leaving some staff cleaning up the blood and spilled items.

"She's stable. Thankfully, the bullet missed her organs when she jumped in front of him. Based on her dehydration and weight, it looks like she's been in captivity for a few weeks, and that's why she passed out. They're going to sew her up, get some fluids in her, and then you can visit. We should head up to the suite and change out of these bloody clothes."

Zel looked down at herself realizing the mess, and cringed. Nodding, we all left happy to have this behind us as relief settled in our bones.

ZEL

After changing into my dark purple dress with tiny stars, the hair and makeup people retouched my hair and pulled it into a braid side pony. They handed me a black lace mask to wear, completing the look. As a group, we stopped and visited Gothel, and, like Wes had reported, she was sleeping soundly. Relief invaded my body, and I finally felt all the fear and shame evaporate from my bones.

Gothel had saved me again. I'd do everything in my power now to make sure she survived.

Heading into the dance, we still had a role to play. This ball was more than an elegant takedown, it was also the setting Wes would become the official owner of The Tower. It felt fitting that as we took down Sinhaven's scum, new growth could emerge. I felt giddy from the adrenaline coursing through me at making it to this point. Wesley went to mingle with the investors he'd finalized on, and Nolan left to greet his family once he spotted them.

Despite being excited to be here, worry and exhaustion weighed heavy on me and I stayed hidden in the shadows with Nix. He was leaning against the wall, and I cozied up into his arms, just enjoying the quiet as everyone around us danced.

The ball looked to be a massive hit, and I was excited for what it meant for Wes. When he'd called his father earlier in the week announcing he'd bought The Tower, his father had been pissed. I could hear the screaming from a room over as the man ranted and screamed at him. Surprisingly, Wes hadn't snapped his rubber band once. He'd finally realized he didn't need his father's approval, just his own. A laugh left me as I watched the brunette from the bathroom dance with her friend.

"What's so funny, princess?"

Tilting my head, I found heat and dirty promises staring back at me. "Remember our time at the Lodge?" He nodded, a smirk lifting the corner of his mouth. "There's the brunette, Leah. I was just thinking how small this town can sometimes be. She's friends with the blonde from the gym, the one who's dating those two hot guys you're friends with."

"The only thing I'm focusing on in that sentence is the part where you and I fucked like our life depended on it."

At the sound of him saying fuck, my nipples pebbled, and a throbbing between my legs began to grow. I was about to rub my ass into him when the two girls in question stumbled into our hideaway. Stepping to greet them, I hadn't meant to step into her path, and we ended up knocking into one another.

"Oh, so sorry," I gasped, grabbing onto her hand to steady myself. I hadn't had as much champagne as they both appeared to, but between the bubbles, the height, and the adrenaline, I wobbled on my heels for the first time in years.

"How do you walk on those things?"

"Oh, I can do more than walk on them." I winked, unable not to have some fun. "But I don't think you need any of those pointers. I saw you earlier with those two delicious-looking guys that own the gym, right?"

Leah didn't appear to recognize Nix or me as she muttered something to the blonde, and I only caught the "Ivy" before she walked away, stumbling into Nix. He righted her, a hidden smile for me when she hadn't remembered us or our bathroom rendezvous. I was locked in his gaze when Ivy spoke again, her speech a little slurred.

"I think I need to get some fresh air. The alcohol and atmosphere have gotten to me a little. Is there anywhere I can sneak out for a few minutes without everyone seeing? I don't want to be followed everywhere I go."

I watched her for a minute, wondering if I'd read things all wrong, but in the end, her words rang true. Plus, I knew what it was like to have multiple men steal all your time. It wasn't a bad thing, but every now and then, I just needed some peace. Looking at Nix, he appeared to trust her words as well, and since he was friends with the guys, I took a chance.

Grabbing her hand, I started to lead her to the back stairwell. "Yeah, actually, here, let me show you. It's a bit tricky. I'm Zel, by the way, and you're Ivy? That's what I heard your friend say, right?"

She hung onto me, and I doubted she would've made it without my assistance, her coordination impaired from the alcohol. Picking up the flashlight I mysteriously found one day, I flicked it on for the rest of our journey. I'd come this way so many times now, I could do it in the dark, but I feared for my arm she was clinging to we wouldn't have made it. Feeling like I needed to say something in the quiet, I started to ramble. I was utter crap at making friends. I doubt she'd remember if I blurted out, "so you like to ride the dick-go-round too?" or "Why choose, am I right?" I had a horrible vision of me trying to wink and lift my eyebrows but instead looking crazy with an eye problem.

"Nix put that there for me after the first time I about tripped to my death in this hallway. It runs along the back of the kitchens, so only staff use it, but it's always pitch-black. Perfect escape, though." I grinned, trying to control the hyperness I felt, wanting to burst free.

Pushing open the door, I heard her exhale at the feel of the night air on her face. It was warm in the ball, and the cool breeze did feel nice. A weird sensation to protect this girl fell over me, and I found myself doubting if this was a good idea. I reminded myself Nix had cameras put up and a guard to patrol this section after my mugging. It was as safe as any part of Sinhaven, which, to be honest, wasn't saying much.

Leaving her with some parting advice, I tried to come across as helpful. "Just be careful. There are some unsavory people back here at times. I'll leave this flashlight by the door for you to use, you know if you decide to return. And I recommend the frying pan there for a weapon. It's my favorite."

I internally laughed at the inside joke Nix and I had, but in honesty, it did work.

"Thanks, Zel." She started to exit but paused, and I hoped maybe she would say something about getting together. I didn't know why I was suddenly so desperate to be her friend, but it was the first time I'd felt connected to a person.

"What about you, though? Those heels in the dark won't be fun."

Her question wasn't what I'd expected. Her concern for me was a good sign we could be friends. I peered back toward the dark shadow I knew was Nix briefly and smiled at my hopeful new friend.

"Nix's never far from me." I winked before leaving her to her peace. Walking toward Nix, naughty thoughts entered my head until I realized how tired I was. Per usual, he knew my needs before I did and scooped me up into his arms. Who needed a flashlight when you had your own personal carriage?

Laying my head on his shoulder, I snuggled close to my gentle giant. He nuzzled my neck, and I felt tears fall on my face, surprising me. Cupping his cheek, I wiped away the wetness as I peered deep into his crystal blue eyes.

"I thought I was going to lose you tonight."

"I'm not going anywhere. I'm too stubborn to die."

Placing his forehead to mine, we stayed in our bubble, holding one another as we dealt with the emotions we'd faced tonight. Kissing me, he made his way to the elevator. When we stopped on Desire, I gave him a weird look, not having spent the night here in almost a month.

"I figured you'd want to check on Gothel first."

Nodding, I smiled at his thoughtfulness and headed in the direction as he returned to the elevator. I found her sleeping, the nurse telling me her stats were improving, and she should be alert by the morning. Taking the chance, I headed upstairs, thinking I could surprise the guys with some new lingerie.

Putting on the black lace bralette and panties, I slipped on the thigh-high socks with ribbons around them. Sitting on the couch, I sent a picture of my legs to them and waited.

Waking the following day, I was surprised when I found myself in bed. The last thing I remembered was sitting on the couch as I waited for them to return. I guess the exhaustion had hit me harder than I thought. Wesley was sleeping in front of me; his arm draped over my hip. He was always the most relaxed in his sleep, his long lashes flat against his cheek. Rolling out from his hold, I found Nolan on the other side.

He was spread eagle, and I held in my laugh as I crawled over the log. Nolan slept like the dead and wouldn't wake for anything. I still had on the lingerie, so I grabbed the dress shirt hanging on the back of the chair. Slipping into the bathroom, I took care of my urgency to pee and fixed my hair.

Walking into the kitchen, I found the menu and

called down to the kitchen to order breakfast for us all. I wasn't the best cook, only knowing the basics, but there was no need to learn when you had gourmet chefs available for all of your dining needs.

Checking Nix's room, I was stunned when it was empty. Looking on the couch, it wasn't filled either. Had Nix not come home last night? I was about to call security to check when the elevator dinged, and Nix exited. In his hands were muffins, donuts, and coffee. It wasn't the breakfast I'd ordered, but it would do.

"Well, I'm not sure what's tastier, the donuts or you."

"Oh, princess, I'm sure I could entice you."

"You wouldn't have to try hard," I laughed.

"Well, if we're talking about hard things, the sight of you like that has me getting there."

He set the items on the counter, the heat burning in his eyes as I prowled around to him. Pushing him with my hand, I directed him to the couch, where I had him sit. Straddling him, my voice drew husky as I leaned forward, the shirt still unbuttoned in the front.

"I think it's time I gave you a lap dance, Eugene. Would you want one?"

Licking up his throat, I felt him swallow before he managed to get the word out.

"Ye-e-s-s-s."

Sucking behind his ear, I pulled his earlobe into

my mouth and nipped before whispering again. "You know the rules, keep your hands to yourself, or my very tough, bouncer boyfriend will beat you up."

His grin lit me on fire, and I found myself undulating my hips as I thrust forward. Turning, I placed my feet on the floor, using his knees to lift my ass in the air. These panties were crotchless, and I couldn't wait for him to discover it. Twerking, I heard the moment he realized, the groan sending chills straight to my clit.

Tilting back, I rubbed my ass against the bulge I felt, my arm going around his neck. His hands tensed on the couch, the need to grab me strong. Rolling up to a standing position, I turned and slid the shirt off my arms, dropping it to the floor. Walking around the ottoman, I turned on some music and bent over again. My pussy had to be glistening now, my own arousal coating me.

The throbbing between my legs was intense, the need strong as I maneuvered myself closer. His jaw ticked, and I watched the hunger grow in his eyes as I traced my nipples and belly. Tiptoeing to him, I bit my lip as I approached. Placing my knees to the side of his thick thighs, I leaned back, rolling my body up and down as I continued to intermittently brush against his hard as steel cock.

Lasting longer than I expected, he grabbed my hips and surprised me when he brought my pussy up to his face instead of my mouth. His tongue licked up my core, and I moaned, tilting my arms back to not fall on the ground. I was in a backward handstand, my legs still bent. Nix must've felt my strain, and with one hand, placed my knee over his shoulder and then the other, giving me more support. My head still hung upside down, but I was no longer attempting to hold myself up as it rested between his thighs on the couch. Bracing my arms around his legs, I gave in to the sensations he had coursing through me.

"Now, this is what I call a Pop Tart because you're so hot, Zel, I want to pop your tarts into my mouth."

"Nols, oh, mmmm," I started before a moan took over. At the sound, Nolan got a cocky smirk on his face as he eyed the tongue god between my thighs.

"You hear that, Sexy Nexy, Zel moaned *my name*."

"Princess, the only name I want to hear is mine, and we both know Nolan isn't ever going to beat me at pleasing you."

"Oh, this is a competition I can get behind." Nolan rubbed his hands together, a look of competitive fire in his eyes. Kneeling, he took my breast into his mouth before I had time to understand what they were doing. But when I was the main course, I didn't care if they were fighting over it.

Nolan's chest was in front of me now, so I began to give him kisses, moving my hands to his ass.

Rubbing the muscles in his back, I slipped them down his shorts to palm his cheeks. He hummed around my tit, wetting the lace as he continued to suck them. Reaching between his legs, I found his balls and started to massage them. He moaned loudly, and it was like I'd snapped his control.

Nolan pulled the cups of my bra over my breasts as he began to massage and flick them. Nix picked up the speed as well as he thrust his tongue and finger simultaneously. I could barely focus; the blood rushed to my head, but I kept fiddling with his balls, my only goal to orgasm.

I started to spasm around Nix's fingers, a loud moan leaving me when Nolan stood, his shorts falling, and he brushed my lips with the tip of his cock. I licked it before taking it in, sucking it as much as possible from my position.

"I have a better idea," said the velvety voice behind the couch. Nolan pulled back, his cock falling from my lips, and I found Wes with a devilish grin on his face. He leaned over Nix and offered me a hand. Grabbing it, I didn't know why it surprised me when he pulled me up, bringing my cunt even more in contact with Nix as I sat up with my legs now wrapped around his head. I squeezed my legs reflexively, thinking I would fall, and then afraid I'd suffocate the poor man.

Surprisingly, he gripped my ass and sucked me harder. Wes chuckled but lifted me up, taking me away from Nix's hoovering of my clit. Wrapping my legs around Wes' bare chest, something about my cum rubbing against his abs was hot to me, and I moaned into his neck, sucking the flesh I found there. When he dropped me onto the ottoman that was as large as a small bed, I groaned from the loss of him.

"Don't worry, baby girl," he soothed in the voice that did things to me. "I have something very special planned for you."

His eyes lifted, and he somehow communicated to the other two to move. Nix landed on one side and Nolan on the other. Being able to touch them all at once definitely had me in better spirits. Rubbing my hands over the two chests, my head fell back as they returned the favor.

Gripping the hard cocks I found, I squeezed and pulled as I gave in to my first group orgy. Hands touched me everywhere, and I had no clue who was doing what, not caring in the moment. When I felt the tip of a cock trace my pussy lips, I lifted my head to find Nolan. He smiled before plunging in, my head rolling back to where it had been.

Once he had a good rhythm, he lifted me by my ass cheeks, bringing me parallel to his body. The nice thing about being a dancer and stripper? Excellent core muscles and flexibility. Grabbing onto his shoulder, I kissed him as he bounced me up and down on his hard dick. Nix had laid back on the ottoman during this time, stroking his cock as he watched us. Nolan moved us over, a predatory look in his eyes as we got closer to Nix.

Nolan pulled me off him, but before I had time to complain, I was thrust onto Nix's cock. Falling forward, I braced my hands on his chest as I started to ride my new cock-cycle. Wesley stood to the side, his dick in his hand, and I opened my mouth for him. Licking the sides, I hollowed my cheeks as I took him down in a long swallow before moving back up. Slowly, I found my rhythm as I fucked them both, forgetting where Nolan went.

When I felt the cold liquid hit my backside, I moaned in anticipation. His finger worked me over as I started to push back on it, hungry for more. When I felt his tip, I stopped as I waited for him to drive in further. The fullness of it was overwhelming. While I'd been with two of them before, I hadn't ever had two of them in me this way, at the same time.

Once I adjusted to the fullness, I found myself moving again on all three cocks. Thankfully, Nix and Nolan orchestrated the lower half, and I focused on Wesley's dick as I grabbed and massaged his balls with my free hand. Feeling naughty, I moved my thumb to his ass and started to play with his tight pucker. He stilled, unsure of my movements, but as I felt myself getting closer to that high again, I pushed through, hoping he'd like it once he felt it.

The slapping of skin as two cocks fucked me

below, and the moans around the cock in my throat could be heard throughout the penthouse in a song of bliss. Wesley gave in to his desires and grabbed my hair, fucking me harder down my throat as he picked up the speed. Pushing my thumb in, I massaged his prostate and felt him detonate down my throat at the action.

Licking my lips, I leaned back against Nolan's chest, a look of satisfaction on my face as Wesley blinked. No time to rest, though as the two dueling cocks continued their competition I'd long forgotten and had me falling over the cliff as an orgasm took me.

"Ahhhh, fuck, yes, oh my God," rang out as everything turned starry.

A few minutes later, I found myself cleaned up and snuggled on the couch as we munched on donuts and muffins, naked, and I realized how perfect this was.

Sex and donuts. Life couldn't get much better than that.

EPILOGUE

ZEL

The bell rang, and I quickly finished filling in the last bubble. Midterms were upon me, and I'd been studying forever, but I felt confident about it. Between Profesor Henn and Nolan, I'd returned to school and slowly caught up on all the things I missed both from high school and college.

When Gothel saved me, she hadn't thought through what all it would mean, and well, she wasn't a teacher. So while I'd taught myself a lot of things, I'd still been behind on rudimentary elements I hadn't learned in high school. The teachers hadn't done me any favors by automatically giving me A's, not wanting me to feel bad after my "ordeal," and to keep my father happy. Even my education had been a lie in the end. With the help of the guys, I'd worked hard to change it.

Life sped up quickly after the prideful fall of the Mayor and Judge. Queenie had been arrested in the end, charged with neglect of a minor. She'd been given community service, which I'd been able to have placed at the new community center we were opening today—*Humility*. In a twist, the masquerade ball had been an actual fundraiser for the center. It felt justified that those pompous men's last deeds had been used for something good.

Thankfully, with the evidence we'd collected, Kingston and Giovani weren't able to get away scot-free. The best had been the treatment they'd received from their fellow inmates. One incident had been so bad, they'd ended up having to shave off all of their hair. It felt justified in the end they should have to lose theirs after they'd obsessed over mine.

Making my way inside the building, my short hair fell into my face, and I tucked it behind my ear. I'd decided in the end to cut it, giving me a new reign on life. No longer having to wear wigs unless I wanted, I embraced who I was—Zel Tress. I'd made it official and everything, shedding the last skin of the trauma I no longer had to carry.

The women's group had been instrumental in helping me navigate everything from the case, the center, and school. My days were filled with my men, classes, dancing both at The Tower and with the ballet, and getting the center ready. I was busy in a whole new way, but I loved it. It felt like I had a purpose now.

While I was happy to be back with the ballet, it

was no longer my dream. Something new had emerged there as well. Now, I wanted to help other girls like me who'd been through similar situations. The first start of that was the center and all the things we'd added there.

Dante's Circle needed something like this, and I wondered if it had been there five years ago if I would've struggled as much. Not that I regretted any of the decisions I'd made or where I'd ended up, but some of those traumas could've been skipped. Nix and I both were stepping out of our comfort zone and starting support groups.

His for vets to have a safe place to talk and readjust to civilian life, and mine was for survivors of sexual abuse. We both knew it would be challenging, but it was something we felt was important enough to try.

"Here's the last of the food," Blair said as she waddled into the kitchen. Rushing over, I took the platter, her tummy protruding far from her body.

"Girl! You know all you had to do was ask!"

"What's the fun in that?" she teased, groaning as she sat down on a stool. "Besides, none of them were paying attention anyway."

I'd come clean to Blair and Nolan's parents, revealing my story and the part my father played in the death of Natalie. I'd been scared they'd blame me, but Darla had hugged me while she cried. Later, she pulled me aside and told me I wasn't my father, and his sins weren't mine. She missed her daughter, but she was happy to have met me. We cried together, and I gained the mother figure I'd always desired. Telling the Ryders about dating three men had been scarier. And while she was still getting used to it, she was happy for Nolan and me and welcomed me into the family. I wasn't the only one who appreciated having a 'mom' figure in our lives.

When she met Nix and Wes, she soon fell under their spell and mothered them just as much. Gavin even came clean about the dirty deeds he'd found himself in. Wes and Nix called some people they knew, and within twenty-four hours, his debt was paid. Wes had made a deal with Gavin, and he could work off his debt by working at The Tower and agreeing to attend AA meetings to stay clean. Gavin had easily agreed and was on his way to living a better life. I was hopeful for him, Blair, and the little girl on the way.

Gavin and Nolan's relationship had also been repaired, and I was happy Nolan had his family connection back. Once Nolan had come clean to his parents about his dreams of designing video games, his dad had apologized for forcing him into something his heart wasn't in. Tom had even started to let up on Gav and accept he was taking responsibility for Blair and the baby.

Shaking my head in solidarity with Blair, I walked around to the swinging door and peeked out. Sure enough, all the men were sitting around a table as they cheered the two playing. Max had found an old Ms. Pacman tabletop game, and ever since they plugged it in, the guys had become glued to it in an intense battle.

Moving back, I returned to the island, where I finished stacking the drink tray. Gothel pushed through, laughing as screams of joy rang out from a few through the door.

"I swear, I think you're going to have competition soon for your boyfriends. That Ms. Pacman is moving in on your men."

Laughing, I ignored her as I counted the last of the cups. She'd recovered from her injury fully and had attended a rehab facility. She'd already been through her withdrawal while she was being held, so she'd been committed to sticking with it. She'd been able to escape the night after hearing my father talk about a plan for me. I had a suspicion the butler was in on it. The door to the basement had *magically* been left open.

Gothel had gotten to The Tower just as she saw the gun, and her mother's instinct took over, throwing herself in front of him. Gothel was getting stronger, and back to the mother I'd known growing up, and I couldn't be more thankful.

"Some days, when they're all farting, burping, and scratching their balls, I'd gladly give them over to her."

"Oh, is that right, *princess*?"

My cheeks heated as Gothel and Blair laughed at me getting caught.

"Well, you guys do have a certain flair," I joked, trying to get out of the trap I'd fallen into.

As Nix began to nuzzle my neck, Blair and Gothel made themselves scarce, having been around all of us enough to know. We had a hard time keeping our hands off one another, but with three sexy boyfriends, it was hard to resist. When I heard the bus pull up out front, I pulled myself away from my growly protector with great effort.

"Princess…" he growled, begging me to come back to his arms.

Peeking over my shoulder, I leveled him with my own dark promise. "Don't worry, Sexy Nexy. I plan to revisit all that later. I'm thinking we play Goldicocks and the three holes and find which one fits the best *where*."

His eyes heated, and if I hadn't gone through the door, I would've been on the table spread eagle with his dick in me already. I almost stepped back through the door until I heard the laughter and sounds of glee of the children out front. Picking up the box of lanterns, I headed out for our ceremony.

Wes caught my eye, smiling as I walked over and started handing out the paper lanterns to all the kids. Nolan followed behind me, and we had them lit and floating up into the sky, a kaleidoscope of colors as they all lifted into the air. Nols placed his arms around me, and Nix sidled up next to us, grabbing my hand, not caring if others saw. Wes joined us a few minutes later, the four of us watching as the guests around us enjoyed the festivities.

"This is all you, baby girl. You did this."

Smiling, I held back the tears that wanted to fall in happiness. Smiling at Wes, I reached out for his hand and felt grounded by my men as I stared in wonder at the scene. The lanterns seemed to infuse everyone in Dante's Circle with hope for the first time in a long time, their lights twinkling in the night sky, carrying wishes on their journey.

When The Tower had called, I'd thought it would be a chance to escape the life I'd become trapped in. Instead, it had been the door to the life I'd always wanted, dreamed of even. It might not be happily ever after, but it was pretty damn close. The only thing missing, my cute animal sidekick, and well, there was always my birthday.

The End

Next in the series is Lust by Alexandra K. Martin, out Aug 1st.

ZEL

I hung the last stocking on the fireplace and stepped back to admire my handiwork. Four stockings hung this year in a row, bringing a smile to my face. If you'd told me I would've ended up here at the beginning of the year, I would've slugged you. Yeah, I hadn't been much for happy endings— unless it was the sexual kind.

Adjusting my stockings, I made sure my naughty elf get-up was secure. It was green lace lingerie set with all of these crazy straps that criss crossed over my breasts. Thank God the panties were crotchless because there was no way I was coming out of this until I had to, and I planned to get busy getting naughty real soon. That was, if my guys ever showed up.

Checking the clock for the twentieth time, it was

official; they were late. Huffing, I stomped over to the fridge and ripped it open. Reaching in, I pulled out the champagne bottle I'd been chilling all day.

"Well, if they're going to be late, then I'll start this party without them," I mumbled to myself.

Popping the cork, I took a swig from the bottle as some of the foam dribbled down my chin. Fuckers. I'd show them. Hopping up on the counter, I now had a perfect view right to the main door. Taking another swig, I placed the bottle down next to me on the counter. The bubbles had gone to my head quickly, and I felt more relaxed, giggly even, and *turned on*.

Champagne was my weakness, especially expensive champagne, and Wesley kept it stocked for this purpose. He was still a fucker, though, for leaving me waiting.

Spreading my legs, I hooked one up on the counter and began to stroke myself through the slit in my panties. I was now a literal naughty elf on the shelf. Leaning back against the cabinets, I circled my clit more with my wetness before stroking along my lips. Inserting one finger, I began to pump in and out of myself. Soft moans escaped me as I gave into the ecstasy I was creating. With my other hand, I brought it up and tweaked my nipple through the lace. Fuck, this outfit was hot. The straps rubbed against me in the best places, and I got even wetter when I imagined all things Wes would do with it.

Picking up speed, I was lost to the sensations

and my impending orgasm. Pinching my nipple one last time, I circled my clit with my thumb as I pumped two fingers inside my wet cunt deeper. Just as my orgasm started to overcome me, I heard the keys at the door. Ha! Served them right for making me wait. Riding out the waves of ecstasy, I locked eyes with Nix when he entered to the sounds of my moans.

Instantly, his eyes heated, and he licked his lips as he took me in. Spread wide on the counter, fingers deep inside me, and my other hand groping my breasts, I imagined I made a sexy sight. Even I was turned on by the picture I presented. Quietly stalking forward, the predatory gleam in his midnight blue eyes promised very naughty things were to come. Bring it, Sexy Nexy!

"What do we have here, princess? Is someone being *naughty*?" Nix's voice rasped out, making my toes curl.

"You know better than that, Nix. I'm *always* naughty."

Somehow, his smirk grew as he closed in on me, bracketing his forearms on the counter.

"That. You. Are." Desire and love swirled in his eyes, and I couldn't wait to feel his hands on me and all the dark things they promised.

"Well, you're late. What's a girl to do when she looks like this?" I motioned to my outfit. "I couldn't let my hotness go to waste. Your punishment is to know I can take care of myself just as well."

"I'm not sure who you're punishing here, *princess*. Walking in and seeing you like this was hot as hell. In fact…" His voice trailed off as he grabbed my fingers still inside me, placing them in his mouth. When he began sucking them, moans poured out of me as he took them deeply, cleaning them free of my juices. Once he'd had his fill, he dropped my hand before clasping me behind the head and bringing our mouths inches apart.

"Now, it's time I remind you why my cock is always better."

Slamming his mouth to mine, Nix devoured me like I was his favorite meal. To be honest, I probably was. The man was insatiable, but I wasn't complaining. Not when he kissed like this. His tongue plunged into me, swirling around and reminding me how dominant he liked to be at times.

The hand at the back of my head tightened as his kisses became more frenzied. As I was about to come up for air, the madman surprised me by thrusting his cock deep into me. Nix always surprised me with his magician ways, getting his pants down and cock out in record time. Moaning deeper, I took a breath as he started to thrust harder. My head fell against the cabinet with a thunk, but the slight pain felt good. Nix's hands grabbed my knees and lifted them under his arms, bringing me forward to penetrate me deeper.

"Fuck, yes."

Nix responded with a grunt moan combo of his

own as he pounded me hard. Bracing one hand behind my head on the cabinet, I stopped my head from reverberating off it with each deep thrust. His mouth was level with my breasts now, and he began to suck on my nipples through the lace, nipping at them.

"Fuck, princess. You're so wet. What were you thinking about before I got here? Don't worry. You'll soon forget about anything but my cock."

Worried? Who, me? Fuck no. Give me all the cocks. I was an unabashed lover of cock. Cock for days, I say. Cock a day kept the prudes away.

His pace was brutal as he pistoned into me on the counter. There was now a noticeable wet spot below me from my cum. Moans, slapping skin, and the thump of the cabinet filled the air bringing our cacophony of sex noises to a crescendo. Nix let one of my legs go and grabbed my neck again, bringing my lips to his in another crushing kiss, this time biting the bottom of my lip.

That was the thing about Nix. He might be an ass at times, he might fuck me rough, but he always kissed me like I was the air he breathed. Opening my eyes, I stared into his midnight blue ones full of emotion as we both orgasmed. Fucking intimacy, man. But secretly, it was my favorite part. His smirk as he pecked my lips one last time before pulling out confirmed he knew it too. Like I said, *fucker*. Nix had a knack for knowing my needs before me. By this point, I accepted it as a foregone conclusion.

When he stepped back, a very naked Nolan was revealed. He stood in the doorway to the kitchen and had on a Santa hat and beard and nothing else. Well, there was a stocking strategically placed on his hard cock at full attention.

"Looks like Santa got here just in time, boss man."

His statement made me realize Nols wasn't alone, and when I looked beside him, I found Wesley. His tie was crooked, his shirt mid unbuttoned, and his dick strained against his trousers. On top of his head was a single red bow. The kind with the peel and stick label. It might not seem like much, but for Wesley, it was basically his version of the penis stocking Nolan was rocking. Which he was now making rock as he thrust his hips up in the air.

I couldn't help but laugh at him. Licking my lips, I took them both in more, and I was ready to unwrap my presents. Nix had turned at their voices and leaned back against the counter, his arms crossed next to me. His dick was still out and wet, but none of them cared about those things anymore. Getting past your first foursome seemed to be the trick to making everyone comfortable. My guys all walked around naked without care and had the occasional sword cross. Unfortunately, it never went further than shared space despite my insistence. Again, fuckers.

"You should ask the princess what she was up to when I got here." Nix's smug face could be felt next to me without even looking. Two could play that game. I wasn't embarrassed. Did he not know me? I stripped for a living. I wasn't shy about my sexuality.

"Oh, you mean when I finger fucked myself, right here on this very counter like the naughty elf on the shelf I am?"

To prove my point even more, I propped my legs back up, spreading them wide. I now had Nix's cum dripping from me in addition to my own. Which he noticed as well, by the covert side eye he gave me. His cock began to harden again as he watched me rub my finger through our combined love juices. His muffled groan confirmed he found it hot. I'd taken my eyes off the other two, so when I was pulled off the counter, a squeal of surprise left me as I met a naked hard torso. Wrapping my legs around Nolan's waist, I peered down into his grinning face.

"Hey, Santa. I think I'm on the naughty list this year. Is there anything I can do to make sure you stuff my stocking full?" I purred. Nolan was my lovable goofball and allowed a brighter side of me to emerge. Hence, my Christmas puns, but when he looked at you as if you hung the moon, they naturally came out!

"Oh, I think I have some things in mind for you."

His devilish smile promised naughty things, and I was on board with this plan. He laid me back on the dining room table and placed a kiss on my lips. Slow and soft, Nolan made me feel like the girl I'd once been and accepted for the girl I was now.

Pulling back, I found Wesley had followed Nolan over. He'd lost his shirt, tie, and pants on the journey and now stood in his boxers and bow. In his left hand, Wesley held the discarded champagne I'd left on the counter. He noticed my stare and lifted an eyebrow in response to the opened bottle.

"Oops. I got bored and thirsty waiting on you."

"Always with that mouth, Zel. You're lucky it's Christmas, or I might have to punish you, more that is."

His silky voice dripped over my skin, his words causing goosebumps to rise to the surface. The promise in his voice set my skin aflame. Suddenly, Nolan was between my legs, licking up the joint cream and causing my eyes to roll back into my head as moans slipped out. Cold liquid hit my belly, followed by a warm tongue licking it up. Why did my eyes keep forgetting to track them?

Wesley was leaning over the table as he poured the champagne onto my body. In my belly button, between my breasts, on my nipples, some in my mouth, and even my pussy. After each spill, he would lick and suck up the champagne, offering me the cold and warm contrast. Squirming on the table, I was officially hot and bothered and wanted more dick.

"Zel, this outfit you have on is hot as hell. But I think it needs to go."

Before I could protest, hands ripped the lace covering my breasts first and then followed down to the lace covering my cunt. A small squeak left me at the sensation, but as I was about to mouth off, a cock was shoved into it instead. Touché. This was my favorite way to be shut up. Nolan grabbed my head and began to fuck me as I sucked and twirled my tongue around his long length. Forgetting my earlier promise to keep my eyes trained on them, I was taken by surprise again when something cold entered my pussy.

"Since you like champagne so much, Zel. I decided to fuck you with it."

Nolan used my gasp to push his cock further down my throat. They soon found a rhythm together and were both pushing me to the edge of another release. The slick glass of the bottle slid into me easily, and the tapered shape offered good tension. It was a decent dildo, and the naughtiness of it all ramped up my desire. My orgasm began to rise, but instead of sending me over the edge, they both stopped. Legit stopped. What. The. Fuck.

Thankfully, before I could tell them off for leaving me hanging, I was picked up, this time by Wesley. His intense steel eyes bore into me as he carried me into the living room. I ran my fingers through his hair, messing it up more. I loved the tousled look on him. Sexy Wes was here to play now.

The bow still sat atop his head, and it made me smile. The simple gesture showed his love for me in more ways than he could ever communicate. Kissing him on the nose, I was lost for a moment in his eyes.

"I know, baby girl. Me too."

When words weren't needed to communicate your love, that was when you knew it was real in my book. Before I could respond, he kissed me deeply as he lowered me down. I'd assumed he would place me on the ottoman in front of the fireplace. But instead, he lowered me down onto Nolan's waiting cock.

Throwing my head back in pleasure as he continued to lift me up and down on Nolan like he was my own dildo. Once he had thoroughly coated Nolan's cock in my wetness, he picked me up higher and started to lower me down onto Nolan again, but this time, his cock entered my ass.

"Fuck. You feel so good, Zel-bel."

Hands grasped my hips as Nolan steadied me onto him. My eyes were locked the whole time with Wes, and I couldn't deny the heat reflected there. Wes loved sharing me and seeing my pleasure increased by the other guys' ministrations. Laying back against Nolan's chest once he was entirely inside me, I wrapped my arm around his neck and kissed his full lips upside down. Tasting Nix and me mixed with the champagne on his tongue caused me to moan even louder.

While I was kissing him, his hands traveled over my body and onto my breasts as he began to rub and caress them in his big hands. Wes entered me, causing us both to moan out, breaking our kiss. My head rolled back onto Nolan's shoulder as they both thrust in and out of me in earnest. Wes had my legs in his arms as he pistoned into me. Thankfully, it allowed me to enjoy it all as my orgasm began to rise again.

Nibbling on my ear, Nolan whispered, "How do you like this stocking stuffer?" Seriously, this guy. Smiling up at him, I nipped the bottom of his chin between my teeth and proceeded to give him a hickey on his neck. I was claiming him, bitches, back away. The boy was mine.

"Princess, I think I have something tastier for you." Nix purred into my ear, causing me to turn my head. Nix was standing butt-ass naked with a strand of blinking lights around his neck. Traveling down his delicious abs, I was face to penis with a whipped cream cockisicle. I tried not to laugh at his smug face because, let's be honest, every movement stuffed with two dicks felt orgasmic, and I didn't want this to end yet.

"Why don't you bring that closer, and I can give it a taste test?"

Fisting the base, he stepped toward me and brought the tip of his cock to my lips as he swirled the whipped cream around them. Chasing him with my tongue, I was momentarily lost in a haze of bliss as Nolan and Wes amped up their thrusts. Not one to wait his turn, Nix grabbed my neck and pushed his dick into my mouth, smearing some of the whipped cream onto my cheek.

So many sensations as I was touched by all three of them in unison. Nix caressed my cheek as he thrust his fat cock between my lips. Nolan pinched my nipples and nibbled on my earlobe as he pushed up into my ass from below. Wes rubbed my clit with his thumb as he pounded me from the front. Feeling all three of my guys had me crashing over the hill I'd been cresting earlier. The orgasm was powerful, and my whole body locked up in spasms, and I teetered on the edge of blacking out.

Setting off a second orgasm, well technically fourth, erupted through me. I felt all the guys cum as well. Nix had pulled out of my mouth at the first signs of my orgasm, probably in fear I might lockdown and bite him. To be fair, a valid concern. So when his warm cum hit my breasts, it took me by surprise.

Nolan's hand absently ran through the cum as he held onto my breasts in a death grip as he jutted up into my ass, filling it with his cum. Wes locked eyes with me as he held my legs to him. I could feel his ass muscles tighten, and I knew he was cumming as well. Something about seeing all of them blissed out because of me set off the fifth orgasm leaving me truly blitzed.

"Merry fucking Christmas. I love you all."

"I think our naughty elf had her stocking stuffed full. We better get her to bed before Santa catches us."

"You're such a nerd, Nolan. I'm always amazed why Zel even likes you," Nix grunted.

"It's because I know how to fill a stocking, man."

Which caused us all to break out into laughter. Fucking, Nolan. He was right, though, he did have the biggest cock, but it wasn't why I loved him. All three of these men gave me something different, and together, we'd found a home.

Merry Christmas and all that jizz.

It's crazy to think this is my fourth published book now! Thank you for taking a moment to read it. This was a lot of firsts for me. My first shared world venture, my first standalone, and my first themed concept. When I was asked to be part of this series, I had to think about it for a couple of days. But then, Rapunzel's story started to change and grow, and the concept of how pride can affect us all in different ways rooted itself.

So, I hope you enjoyed my fairy tale retelling of Rapunzel and how pride can be a strength or a weakness depending on how you use it. Go out there and embrace yourself and show everyone how fierce you can be!

If you liked this book, you might also check out The Council Series. It's a sports contemporary RH revolving around a winter sports school. There is humor, steamy scenes, and a mystery. If you've ever wondered what Pretty Little Liars and The Cutting Edge would be like mashed together, then the Council Series might just be what you need! It's now a completed series. This series does contain MM.

In August, my dark contemporary Mafia romance will be releasing, as well. Lots of fun goodies for you to explore.

ACKNOWLEDGMENTS

Thank you to all my fellow Sinners Fairytale Authors and inviting me to be part of this, especially AJ Blackburn who reached out and said, "Hey, you'd be great at this!"

Thanks to my Alpha readers who went above and beyond to make this book great. Emma, you know I couldn't do this without you. There aren't enough words. Becki, thank you for your insight and love of the characters. Cat, thank you for finding the time to give me feedback and crucify all my would's. None are safe!

Thank you to Erica for reading this on a tight deadline and the feedback you gave as well. For once you didn't have to yell at me!

Thank you to all the ARC readers for your kind words and reviews, and your excitement for this series.

Thank you to my husband who endlessly listens to me even when he doesn't know what I'm talking about. You're the best sounding board, babe.

Thanks to all the readers for picking up this book and reading a retelling of Rapunzel.

ABOUT THE AUTHOR

Kris Butler writes under a pen name to have some separation from her everyday life. Never expecting to write a book, she was surprised when an author friend encouraged her to give it a try and how much she enjoyed it. Having an extensive background in mental health, Kris hopes to normalize mental health issues and the importance of talking about them with her characters and books. Kris is a southern girl at heart but lives with her husband and adorable furbaby somewhere in the Midwest. Kris is an avid fan of Reverse Harem and hopes to add a quirky and new perspective to the emerging genre. If you enjoyed her book, please consider leaving a review. You can contact her the following ways and follow Kris's journey as a new author on social media.

Join the newsletter

Join KB's Mavens of Mayhem

Check out the Sinners Spotify made by the authors of the series

Join Kris on Tiktok

Merch for the Series can be found here

The Council Series (completed series)

Damaged Dreams

Shattered Secrets

Fractured Futures

The Order (Council Spinoff)

Stiletto Sins

Summer 2022

Sinners Fairytales (standalone)

Pride

Dark Confessions

Dangerous Truths

August 27, 2021

SINNERS FAIRYTALES SERIES

Catch up and Pre-order the rest of The Sinners Fairytales

Gluttony by Kira Roman

Out Now

Sloth by AJ Blackburn

Out Now

Wrath by Jay Leigh Brown

Out Now

Greed by J. Kearston

Out Now

Pride by Kris Butler

Out Now

Lust by Alexandra K. Martin

August 1

Envy by Kat Blak

August 15